THE SINFUL WAYS OF JAMIE MACKENZIE

MACKENZIES BOOK 12

JENNIFER ASHLEY

JA / AG PUBLISHING

CHAPTER 1

April 1908

Jamie Mackenzie stood the rail at the Southampton docks and craned his head for a better view of the young woman who strolled down the gangplank of the massive ship moored before him.

The lady was surrounded by chaperones, the tall man and harried-looking woman probably her parents, the other two matronly women likely aunts or a former governess or two.

The liner, the *Baltic*, the largest in the world, blocked any view of the ocean with its vast, dark bulk. A large opening in its hull disgorged passengers onto the open pier, more than two thousand of them, into the blustery late April day.

The young woman stood out, not only because she wore a gown of soft yellow—not the most practical choice for the sooty pier—but because she carried herself with a grace that set her apart. Golden hair peeped from under a white hat— again a questionable choice of attire for the docks, but perhaps her family had instructed her on what to wear

A black-clad man with a large photographic apparatus

bumped past Jamie. "Sorry, guv," he said cheerfully. "Almost missed her."

He set up his tripod, unfolded his camera, pointed his long lens at the young woman, and began snapping away.

"Who is she?" Jamie asked.

Click ... click ... click. "You don't know? Imogen Carmichael, American heiress, richest woman in the world—so I'm told—come to these shores to land herself a titled husband."

"Title, eh?" Aristocratic monikers held glamour and romance for Americans, and not only for them, Jamie reflected. So many, even in this country, were entranced by a *Lord This* or *Marquess of That*.

As the nephew of a duke and cousin to the duke's heirs, Jamie knew the true worth of titled gentlemen.

He leaned on the rail, wind tugging at the Mackenzie plaid kilt around his hips. "She is a beauty."

"She's fair enough." The photographer shrugged. "Whether I like her or not, my instructions are to get as many photographs of the lovely lady so those what put pen to paper can write all sorts of guff about her."

Miss Carmichael turned slightly, and Jamie swore she stared directly at him. He inclined his head, rewarded by a slight flush to the lady's cheeks. Or maybe that was the sudden wind that streaked down the dock, an icy, briny blast from the Channel.

Never mind that Jamie himself wasn't titled. Mackenzie was an old name, a revered one—one spoken with awe and a little shiver. He could convince Miss Carmichael she didn't need a title. Persuade her to let him steal her away, as Old Dan Mackenzie had done with his bride so long ago—

Someone slammed into Jamie's back with the suddenness of a cannon ball, sending him hard against the railing. He slipped on an oily patch and felt his too-tall body begin to pitch over the side, gravity inevitably taking him down to the black water between ship and dock.

The young woman in drab brown who'd run into him dropped her portmanteau and seized handfuls of Jamie's coat, sucking in a lungful of air as she hauled him upright.

"Trying to drench yourself again, are you, Mackenzie?" she demanded breathlessly.

Jamie turned when she released him, meeting blue eyes the color of delphiniums. Those wide eyes had gazed at him another day, long ago, on the banks of the Cam, when she'd pulled him to safety as she'd done just now.

It couldn't be …

She had hair like darkness, cheeks pink from the wind, and was bundled in a practical coat, her hat squashed down over her ears. The brown coat and hat were as dull as their surroundings, but her eyes emerged from them like bright sky after gloom.

Jamie hadn't seen her in half a dozen years, but her wry smile hadn't changed. The blasted woman had always laughed at him.

"Evie McKnight." Jamie took a step back from her, meeting the solid rail. "Trying to push me in again? At least you didn't bring your oar this time." He glanced behind her as though searching for it.

"Is that all you remember about me, Mackenzie?"

"It is burned upon m' memory, McKnight." Jamie's backside even now recalled the sharp *whap* from the oar that had inadvertently landed on it as Evie, on the lady's rowing team at her Cambridge college, had rushed with it to her scull.

"I didn't need it today," Evie said, eyes sparkling. "You were so lost in the famous Miss Carmichael that you could have gone straight into the drink without my help."

"No, lass, I was minding my own business when a lady barreled into me."

Evie flushed — she could never control her blushes. "Ogling

women will be the death of you, Mackenzie. At Cambridge, it was your interest in girls in rowing costumes that was your undoing ..."

"Not ogling," Jamie said with indignation. "I'd come to cheer on the team."

"Not what you said when you were climbing out of the river."

Jamie's language had burned the air. Evie's face had been beet red at her blunder, and her fellow teammates had laughed themselves sick.

Jamie Mackenzie, the arrogant Scotsman, up to his waist in muddy water, had cursed and floundered until Evie had lowered her oar to him and pulled him from the river. The mud had made a sucking sound as it disgorged him, which had thrown her teammates into further glee.

"I did apologize," Evie said.

"I know. Ye did it beautifully."

Evie's face went even more red, and Jamie knew why. His own was heating at the moment.

"Well, I am glad that is cleared up," Evie said briskly. "I recommend you don't fall in here. Far too dangerous."

Evie leaned to retrieve her portmanteau, but Jamie beat her to it and held the bag out to her. Her hand closed on the handle, half an inch from his.

"What are you doing here, anyway?" Jamie asked. "Besides trying to push me in ... *again*."

Evie dithered, her feet shifting as though ready to flee. She glanced at their hands, both still on the bag's handle. Jamie withdrew unhurriedly, but Evie moved the bag to her other side, as though worried he'd try to grasp it again.

"Returning home from a sojourn in New York with my mother and sisters. My sisters are all grown up now, and Clara is ready to marry. Hence the journey to New York, though both Clara and Marjorie have declared they prefer Englishmen." She spoke in a rush, the words pat, as though her thoughts roved far from the docks, the shock of running into Jamie diverting her only momentarily.

"I notice you're not speaking of *yourself* rushing to America to snare a husband," Jamie said. "Or did you? Engaged, are you?"

Evie jumped, returning her full attention to him. "I am, as a matter of fact."

Jamie's brows rose. "To an American magnate? Ready to bathe in goat's milk and honey, or whatever American magnates put into their baths?"

"Hardly." Evie's sunny smile blossomed. "He's a respectable Englishman and a gentleman. Mr. Hayden Atherton. We've been betrothed nearly a year now."

"Oh, yes?" Jamie feigned excitement then shook his head. "Never heard of him."

Evie laughed, her face lighting up and driving everything else from Jamie's thoughts. "No, of course, you haven't. He isn't one of your reprobate university friends. He is kind and genteel. Polite, cultured."

"Sounds a right dull stick." Jamie made a mollifying gesture when she puffed up like an indignant hen. "My apologies, McKnight. You know how to stir up my fractious side. Congratulations on your upcoming nuptials."

Even as he spoke, Jamie had a curiosity to meet this Mr. Atherton. Was he as polished and perfect as she implied? Good enough for the fiery Evie McKnight? Would Mr. Atherton tame her fire, or would she pry him from his boring stupor?

"Thank you." Evie's air of condescension was incongruous with the windblown curls trickling from under her hat. "What are *you* doing here? Besides ogling heiresses, I mean? I saw Miss Carmichael onboard. She's lovely, but a bit vague."

"I was *not* ogling …" Jamie growled. "Never mind. Here to meet my cousins—Danny and his wife and bairns. They were racing cars and risking their necks in America. I told him I'd assist in the unloading."

A gleam of interest lit her eye, but everyone was fascinated by motorcars. "Ah yes, I saw them during the voyage. I wasn't able to meet them—my mother kept us herded together. They seem a warm family. You at least have kind relations, Mackenzie."

"Ha. I wouldn't call any of them *kind*," Jamie retorted. "Some more interesting than others, maybe. Why have ye strayed then, from your herd?"

Evie darted her gaze about, as though debating what to tell him. He wondered very much what she'd been in a hurry to do when she'd nearly knocked him down.

"I saw an unusually tall Scotsman in danger of falling from the pier," she said glibly. "I thought I'd warn him."

Not at all true. She hadn't noticed Jamie until she'd run smack into him.

"Very amusing. Warn me? Or push me over?"

Evie rubbed her chin, leaving a smudge from her sooty glove. "Actually, I hadn't quite decided." She scanned the pier once more but this time, she grinned. "Oh, dear, Mackenzie. Your heiress has gone."

Jamie turned his head to see that, yes, the lovely Miss Carmichael had disappeared into the sea of brown and black coats, likely whisked off by her parents to a train or a posh hotel. Ah, well …

He abruptly realized that as soon as the radiance of Evie McKnight had entered his sphere, the pale beauty of Miss Carmichael had faded to nothing.

"There he is!" a voice floated to them. "There's Jamie!"

A straw boater hat on a young lady bobbed up and down in the morass of disembarking passengers, and a thin arm waved frantically.

"Your family at last," Evie said with a touch of relief. "I must dash. So nice to have caught up with you, Mackenzie. *Do* be careful while leering at young ladies near bodies of water."

She whirled in a flutter of practical wool and dashed down

the pier. Jamie watched her go, in the opposite direction of the ship, white petticoats flashing around dark boots.

Who was she racing to meet? The fiancé? And if so, why had he not been at the foot of the gangway, ready to lift her into his arms? Jamie would have grabbed her the moment he saw her and smothered her in kisses.

But if not the fiancé, then who was she meeting? Jamie gazed after Evie until he lost her in the crowd, his curiosity aroused in a way it hadn't been in a long time.

The journalist, whose camera Jamie realized was now pointed his way, clicked one last frame then began folding up the apparatus.

"What the devil?" Jamie growled at him.

The journalist answered with a grin. "Mackenzies are always good for copy." He shouldered his camera and marched away, unmindful of Jamie's glower.

———

"Who was that delicious man you were speaking to, Evie?" Clara McKnight settled herself into the second-class train compartment amid boxes and bags that the ladies had not wanted to entrust to the porters. The porters, already burdened with the bulk of their baggage, had relinquished the extras with relief.

"Speaking to?" Marjorie repeated in delight. Evie's younger sisters, Marjorie and Clara, were seventeen and nineteen respectively, and held the energy of youth Evie fondly remembered in herself. "Evie was speaking to a man? What would Mr. Atherton say?"

Evie dropped into her seat across from her mother, who regarded her too shrewdly. Mrs. McKnight's soot-black hair was styled in a soft pompadour that suited her slender face, her body poised on her seat. Clara had inherited her looks, Clara who'd turned heads in the hotels and public spaces of New

York. Evie's mother had turned plenty of heads in her day, so said their besotted father, and still did.

"Do tell, Evie," Mrs. McKnight said, her dark blue eyes watchful.

Evie found herself flustered. "He is an old friend. I met him at Cambridge."

"Cambridge?" Marjorie asked with interest. "Where you were locked into your ladies' college down the road and never spoke to the gentlemen?"

"We did see them from time to time." Why was Evie so disconcerted? Her encounter with Jamie today had been a harmless one, old acquaintances chatting about past times. Distracting, though, as she'd not been able to send the telegram to her friend Iris she'd hastened down the docks to do, before her mother and sisters had called her to them. "They came out to cheer our rowing team."

"I'm certain they did." Marjorie collapsed into mirth, sagging into the piled up bags at her side.

"What nonsense." Evie did her best to be haughty while Marjorie went off into gales, and even Clara, more composed than her younger sister, smiled knowingly.

"You haven't told us his name, dear," Mrs. McKnight said gently.

"Jamie Mackenzie." The words came out in a rush. "I mean, *Mr.* Mackenzie. He is nephew to the Duke of Kilmorgan."

"Duke, eh?" Marjorie crowed.

"Hush, darling." Mrs. McKnight could rebuke without raising her voice. Marjorie stifled her giggles, but her eyes danced. "I am certain the young man is perfectly respectable," Mrs. McKnight went on.

"He is," Evie answered with a straight face.

Had Jamie always been so tall? There'd been a hardness about him he'd not had as a youth, his skin bronzed from a sun far from English shores. Evie was suddenly curious about where he'd been and what he'd done. Would he laugh as she'd seen him do, throwing back his head and roaring without abandon when he heard something hilarious?

His handsomeness was altogether different from her fiancé's. Jamie had a slightly crooked nose—from a scrap in his first year at Cambridge, she'd heard—red-brown hair, brilliant blue eyes, and as she'd observed, a hardness that lent him an air of danger.

Hayden Atherton, by contrast, had a chiseled face that any sculptor would wish to capture, a warm smile, golden blond hair, and fine brown eyes. He'd recently grown a trim beard that made him quite distinguished.

Ladies regarded Evie with envy whenever she appeared on Hayden's arm. General opinion was that Evie and Hayden would produce quite beautiful children.

Such statements made Evie contemplate the method for conceiving those children, and there her imagination went hazy. As much as she tried to picture her wedding night with Hayden, something inside her—modesty?—would not allow her to form a clear vision.

Today, however, a memory had thrust itself up into her thoughts, scattering all contemplation about Hayden.

Evie saw an angry Jamie charging at her out of the river, eyes flashing fury. Before Evie could dodge from him, large, wet hands cupped her face in a strong grip. She'd gazed up into steely blue eyes framed by damp red-brown lashes.

Before Evie could apologize or admonish Jamie for touching her—or say anything at all—his mouth had come down on hers, crushing a firm kiss to her parted lips.

Evie had tasted rage in the kiss, but also excitement and a hungry need she'd never before experienced. To her consternation, the same hungry need had stirred in *her*.

Jamie had kissed her thoroughly, his hands holding her steady, his wet coat damp against her rowing costume. He'd kissed her while her mates on the team had watched avidly, while Evie's knees had gone weak, and her breath had deserted her.

He'd kissed her until she'd gasped, then Jamie had released her, brushed a thumb across her now-wet lips, and turned and walked away from her. Even now, the image of his waterlogged kilt clinging to his backside, his bare thighs flashing as he strode from the river, came to her too vividly.

Her teammates, her closest friends in the world, had watched in shock and delight. The teasing Evie had endured since that day had been merciless.

She'd seen Jamie now and again in the next year until he left Cambridge, he talking or laughing with friends, wind blowing back his academic gown to reveal the kilt he insisted on wearing. He'd nodded at her when he'd seen her, sometimes flashing a bone-warming smile, sometimes feigning fear that she might have her oar with her, as he'd done today.

Today, when he'd gazed at the ship, wind tossing his hair, every line of him strong …

The train bumped over a crossing, jerking Evie back to the present. Marjorie was watching her, her youngest sister too perceptive. Evie quickly turned her head and peered out the window at the passing countryside.

Evie was engaged to the handsome and eligible Hayden Atherton. She had no business thinking about Jamie Mackenzie, speculating on what sort of man he'd become. She especially had no business daydreaming about the astonishing kiss he'd given her years ago.

Absolutely no business at all.

CHAPTER 2

$\mathcal{T}$he first class car in the same train swerved as the train took a bend. Fleur, Jamie's seventeen-year-old cousin, twirled with the train's swaying and plopped herself down next to Jamie.

Her father, Daniel Mackenzie, shook his head at her. "You'd think you'd have worked off all that energy on the crossing."

"You'd think," Fleur echoed. "Jamie, there was so much dancing." She pressed both hands to her pink-clad chest. "A different handsome gentleman every night. It was like floating on air. Heaven."

Dougal, her nine-year-old brother, snorted a laugh, Daniel's expression became quietly aggrieved, and Fleur's mother, Violet, smiled indulgently. "The dancing was exquisite, I agree," Violet said.

From Violet's calm reaction, Jamie deduced that Fleur had not been in any danger of falling heedlessly in love with any of these gentlemen. She'd been pleased with the dancing and no more.

Fleur let out a long, happy sigh, then she turned to Jamie and skewered him with a knowing stare. "I'd not pin your hopes on Miss Heiress, Jamie. She's only looking for a title. Our ducal cousins would be good enough for her, perhaps, but not you."

"Eh?" Jamie's thoughts were full of a laughing young woman with very black hair every bit as wild as it had been that faraway day on the Cam. He blinked a few times before he realized who Fleur was talking about. "Oh, you mean the American lady."

"Oh, you mean the American lady," Fleur mocked. "Of course, I do. Every gentleman was vying for her, elbowing each other aside to reach her. It was disgusting."

"Fleur exaggerates," Violet said in her smooth tones. "But yes, Miss Carmichael was the center of much attention."

"Including yours, love." Daniel's smile when he regarded his wife held deep affection. He winked at Jamie. "Violet read her future."

Violet flushed. "I was curious to speak to her, I will admit. I wondered what the fuss was about."

"You should have seen Mum, Jamie," Fleur said. "She was quite the stage fortune teller, with a husky voice and mysterious promises. Miss Carmichael was most entranced."

"It worked rather too well." Violet wrinkled her nose. "The other ladies onboard then wanted *their* fortunes read. I had to plead fatigue—what I saw for Miss Carmichael had worn me out, I claimed. Also the ship's entertainers, one of whom was a fortune-teller himself, were glaring daggers at me."

"And what did you learn about this lady?" Jamie asked to distract himself from his wayward thoughts.

Violet's expression filled with sympathy. "That she is pushed forward and backward by her father and brothers and rather a pawn in their long game, poor thing. She told me she was eager to marry, and wished for a loving man with a fine country home where she could putter in the garden and find some peace. She didn't use those last words, but that's what she meant."

"You are kindness itself, love." Daniel squeezed Violet's hand. "Always searching for the best in others."

Violet rested a gaze on Daniel that revealed her naked love for him, which nearly twenty years of marriage had not dimmed.

Their children, intent on Jamie, did not notice. "Mum isn't telling you what others said about Miss Carmichael," Fleur said. "*Very highly strung*. Like a racehorse. They meant *brat*."

"Not her fault," Violet chided gently. "The stewards and waiters fell all over themselves to bring her anything she wanted, while other passengers signaled to them in vain. Probably the crew were obeying orders. Miss Carmichael seemed more bewildered than demanding."

"Dad is right," Fleur said to her mother. "You are too kind."

"Not necessarily," Violet said briskly. "I have learned to read people, is all, more accurately than others do. And I do not believe in dissecting strangers when they are not here to defend themselves."

Fleur took her reprimand with good grace. "Sorry, Mum. But Jamie seems so interested. Did you see how he was staring at her?"

Jamie shrugged. "I admire a pretty woman."

He let them believe what they wanted. Why he didn't mention Evie or protest that Miss Carmichael didn't intrigue him at all, he wasn't certain. Evie was a private memory, one he hadn't shared with his family. His close-knit, everyone-in-everyone-else's-business, teasing, overly large, nosy family.

Daniel shot Jamie an understanding look. "Let us allow Jamie to tell us what he's been up to while we've been away."

"Yes, let's." Dougal bounced on his seat. "What adventures did you have this time, Jamie? Will you take me with you on the next one?"

Jamie felt suddenly exhausted. "Don't know, lad. Might be time I was settling down."

All occupants of the compartment stared at him in disbelief.
"You?" Dougal demanded. "Never."

"I hurt myself pretty badly in Baghdad." Jamie flexed the
arm that had been broken the year before and taken nearly six
months to completely heal. "It was a daft idea."

"But it worked," Dougal declared. "Your flying machine
worked."

"For a few minutes." The daft idea had been deciding that
the open desert outside of Baghdad would give Jamie the
space he needed to experiment. That had been true, but also
the hidden gullies and treacherous rocks had made for a hard
landing.

"A few minutes is longer than most people have stayed
aloft," Violet pointed out. "You should be proud, Jamie."

"No one saw it but my friend Daoud—well, him and a
camel. Daoud fixed me, but our machine was beyond him.
Difficult for me to help him with a broken wing."

Jamie stretched his fingers again. He remembered lying in
great pain, and Daoud peering down at him in terror. Jamie
had felt glad he'd insisted on flying alone, because if he'd had
to carry Daoud back to his family a battered mess, he'd have
never heard the end of it.

Daoud's mother could blister the hide off a man when she
was displeased. She didn't approve of the British and was not
happy that her son had befriended one from those isles, even a
rebellious Scotsman. Jamie swore he'd seen a glint of satisfaction in her eyes when Daoud had carried Jamie home, though
the woman had made certain Jamie received the best of care.
Still, she'd been relieved when Jamie had made his return to
Scotland.

"What about you?" Jamie decided it was time to change
the subject. "How did things go in America?" He directed the
question to Daniel, who took the hint and removed Jamie from
under the microscope.

"Splendidly," Daniel said in his big voice. "I had some interest in my designs. A few orders."

"More than a hundred," Violet broke in proudly. She squeezed Daniel's arm. "Danny's being modest."

"You helped, love. Twas your tinkering that convinced the buyers we had the best car in the world." Daniel beamed at Jamie. "Violet was in the driver's seat when the car broke its own speed record. She is amazing."

Daniel wrapped a fond arm around an embarrassed but pleased Violet, and their two children regarded them in indulgent exasperation. A happy family, Jamie reflected with a touch of envy.

Not that he wasn't a member of a large and loving, not to mention interfering, family himself. But watching Daniel—or indeed, Jamie's own parents, who were not ashamed to kiss passionately in front of everyone—Jamie wondered if he'd ever find someone to share such a bond with.

The memory of Evie's impact against him on the dock resurfaced. Jamie had felt a crush of soft woman in her wool coat, and her sharp exhale as she'd collided with him. In spite of her joke that she'd hurried to him to keep him from falling, Evie hadn't expected to see him there.

Her wide eyes had hidden something, though she'd quickly pretended she had nowhere to be but on the dock bantering with Jamie.

Jamie fleetingly wondered if she'd been meeting a lover—and he didn't mean the fiancé. The Evie he'd observed at Cambridge would never do such a thing, but people changed—as Jamie had.

How much did Jamie know about Evie, truly? Only how she'd tasted during that one, heated, spectacular kiss when he'd been enraged at her. A kiss he'd never forgotten.

———

THE TRAIN CONTINUED ITS NOISY AND PUFFING WAY TO London, at last pulling into Victoria Station. From there, Daniel, Violet, and children would depart for their home in Hill Street, near Berkeley Square, while Jamie would return to his bachelor digs in Piccadilly.

After disembarking, Jamie and Daniel lingered at the end of the baggage cars to supervise the unloading of Daniel's motorcar. Daniel had hovered over the vehicle's transfer from ship to train like a worried aunt, and now winced as its tires bounced over the ramp that five porters guided it down.

"Jamie," Daniel said once the motorcar was safely on the pavement. "Would it be inconvenient for you to drive this around to my lock-up? I need to see Violet and the children home—they're exhausted, though they'd never admit it."

Inconvenient? Jamie grinned. "Be delighted to?"

Guide a sleek racing car through the streets of London? Of course, he would. Jamie was longing to see how the thing ran —the new motorcar had barely come out of Daniel's workshop before he'd whisked it off to America.

Daniel gave the car a fond glance, then nodded resolutely, as though entrusting a maiden daughter to the care of her first gentleman caller. "Go easy with her, lad."

"She won't have a scratch on her, I promise."

"See that she doesn't," Daniel returned severely.

Violet interposed herself between Jamie and Daniel. "Jamie knows what he's doing with a car, Daniel. You taught him yourself."

True, Jamie had been driving Daniel's cars since he'd been twelve years old. He knew every gear, every lever, and every inner working of every engine Daniel and Violet had built.

The automobile in question was a long, red-bodied touring car, ostensibly made for an outing in the country, but well-tuned for both speed and stamina. It had two seats in front and a large bench seat in back. Daniel always made certain the cars he designed could hold his entire family plus a contingency of dogs.

Jamie hugged his cousins—except Dougal, who preferred a solemn handshake—and waved goodbye as Daniel and family sought their carriage. Jamie tried not to rub his hands in glee as he turned to the motorcar.

He first put the top down, as the day was fine, if windy, folding the leather canopy and its frame out of the way in back.

Leaning over the driver's side door, he set the gear in neutral, turned on the ignition, and closed the choke. Then he removed the hand crank from its compartment and set it in its slot in the front of the car, making sure his thumb was folded out of the way before he cranked.

He yanked the handle upward once, twice. Daniel's engine, finely tuned, fired up almost immediately, and the crank came free. Jamie darted to the driver's side once more and released the choke, feeding the engine and letting it settle.

As he straightened from returning the crank to its compartment, he realized he'd drawn a crowd. Evie McKnight stood not a dozen feet from him in the midst of the fascinated audience. A younger version of Evie, presumably a sister, watched as avidly. Evie's mother and second sister, by contrast, were busy gazing rather frantically up and down Vauxhall Bridge Road.

Jamie lifted his hand to Evie before he leapt into the driver's seat and guided the car carefully through the throng that had gathered about it. Motorcars were no longer as rare in London but were still unique enough to attract attention.

Jamie navigated his way to Evie and her sister, the car purring like a contented cat. "May I assist you ladies?" he called.

"Are you Mr. Mackenzie?" the younger sister gushed, her eyes wide with astonished delight. "Will you take me riding in this motorcar someday?"

"*Marjorie,*" Evie said in mortification.

Jamie winked at Marjorie, who grinned at him. "Have you been deserted?" Jamie asked Evie.

Mrs. McKnight, who approached in time to hear Jamie's question, wore the look of a woman annoyed, frustrated, and worried that she'd have to tramp across London on foot. Or worse, cram herself and her offspring into an insalubrious hansom.

"Our carriage has not arrived," Evie told him. "Mama hired it via telegraph, but apparently they got the time wrong."

"Or wires crossed." Jamie unfolded himself from the driver's seat. "I'd be delighted to convey you to your lodgings."

Marjorie clasped her hands, the handbag that dangled from one wrist swinging wildly. "Oh, yes, please. Mama, just think. Mr. Mackenzie will take us to our hotel in his car."

"Yes, we hear you, Marjorie," Mrs. McKnight said. "But you cannot demand such things of a gentleman. Thank you very much, Mr. Mackenzie, but of course, we could not accept."

"Agreed," Evie said, a bit too quickly. "We should not impose."

Marjorie's face fell, but Jamie would not accept defeat.

"Miss McKnight and I are old friends. I'd be callow to allow you to wait in vain for transport when I have one handy."

Mrs. McKnight darted another hopeful glance down the road, her shoulders drooping as she did not see the longed-for carriage. "I do hate to ask you, Mr. Mackenzie."

"You would be assisting me, madam." Jamie loped around the car and opened the rear passenger door. "I make it a vow to do a good deed every day, and today, this will be it."

At any other time, Jamie suspected, Mrs. McKnight would proudly refuse, but she was harried, tired after the long voyage and train journey, and was telling herself it would do no harm. Marjorie bounced on her toes, and the older sister—Clara,

Evie had called her—gazed with much curiosity at the motorcar.

Mrs. McKnight made a show of reluctantly conceding. "Very well. It isn't far to the hotel. But we have much baggage."

"And I have a large baggage compartment." Jamie opened the boot, which contained only his modest overnight valise for his stay in Southampton while waiting for the ship. "Allow me, madam."

He heaved the bags—most of them devilish heavy—into the boot, managing to cram them all in. While he worked, the ladies arranged themselves in the car. When Jamie returned to the driver's side, Mrs. McKnight and her two younger daughters were in the back, and Evie, for some reason, was in the seat next to Jamie's.

Evie's gaze held defiance as Jamie took his place, as though she expected him to tell her to switch places with her mother. Jamie said nothing, only put the car in gear and gave it some throttle.

Marjorie made a little squeak as the car rolled forward. "It's moving by itself," she shouted. "I mean without anything pulling it."

Her sister's joy softened Evie's expression. "You would think she'd never seen a motorcar before."

"I have," Marjorie retorted. "Lady Maborn has a Silver Cloud. But I like *this* car so much better."

"Excellent," Jamie called to her over the sound of the engine. "I will inform Mr. Rolls and Mr. Royce that my cousin Danny has bested them."

As he slid the motorcar through the crowd toward the street, they passed Miss Carmichael, surrounded by her retinue and family as they waited to board a sumptuous carriage. The young lady paused to gaze at the crowded car, and Jamie thought she looked wistful.

With a gentle bump, he turned onto Grosvenor Street,

which skirted the gardens of Buckingham Palace, shut behind its high walls.

Evie gestured interestedly at the levers Jamie shoved into place. "What do all those do?"

"You shouldn't ask me, lass," Jamie said in warning. "I'm apt to explain it in vast detail."

Evie's defiant spark returned. "Do you think I wouldn't understand?"

Jamie hid a grin. "Of course, you would, love. It's just that I can go on a bit. My cousin Gavina threatens to throw cold water on me."

"I shall keep a bucket standing by," Evie said. "Do tell."

"All right then." Jamie gave her a moment to change her mind, then when she simply waited, he dove in.

Evie listened with every show of attentiveness. She lost her reticence and asked questions as Jamie guided the car along Grosvenor Street to Piccadilly and then to the hotel on Regent's Street where Mrs. McKnight directed him.

By the time Jamie pulled the car over—to the scrutiny of a crowd of small boys and grown men—he'd explained to Evie how pistons fired with their controlled explosions, which turned the driveshaft to move the car forward.

Evie's questions had been apt and astute. Jamie was used to ladies who admired the motorcars, but mostly they wanted an excuse to lean close to him and clutch his arm as he careened around corners.

Jamie knew that all Evie's interest had been directed at the car, not him. She'd never lock her hands around Jamie's elbow and squeal prettily as he sped along the street. He could have been a squawking parrot for all Evie cared.

He adjusted the choke and let the engine idle before he leapt from the car and around to hand the ladies out. Evie superseded him by climbing out of the car herself, already waiting calmly on the pavement by the time he reached her.

Jamie passed her without missing a step and ushered out

Mrs. McKnight, Clara, and Marjorie. Marjorie gave Jamie a mock simper as she took his hand, and Jamie grinned at her. Marjorie returned the grin, released him, and trotted into the hotel after her mother, Clara following. Only Evie lingered.

Two porters descended on the car and the bags began to come out, lifted by Jamie's strong hands and the porters' gloved ones.

"Fine motor, lad," one said in admiration.

"Not mine, alas." Jamie heaved a sigh. "My cousin's. She was kind enough to lend it to me."

The porter blinked at the "she," and Jamie hid his amusement. But the car was technically Violet's, Daniel had insisted, for all the work she had done on it.

Evie stood as though supervising the unloading, but Jamie saw that she continued to study the car, her fascination clear. Maybe once she and her family settled Jamie could jaunt with her into the countryside and find a quiet stretch where he could teach her how to drive.

Something warmed inside him. He pictured his gloved hands on hers as she navigated the stiff gears, her dark brows coming together as she concentrated. Her glossy dark hair would be tucked beneath a driving cap, but tendrils would trickle out, as they were doing now.

Jamie opened his mouth to invite her, then snapped it closed. She was bloody engaged, he made himself remember, to an inconvenient fiancé. By convention, Jamie would have to extend the invitation to both of them, which was not appealing.

He envisioned the fiancé—what had she called him? Oh, right—Atherton. Mr. Atherton would be stiff and upright in striped flannels and a boater hat, sporting a waxed mustache he thought made him appear dapper. Evie would gush all over him, and he'd make stupid jokes about horseless carriages or kilted Scotsmen or both.

Jamie's irritated thoughts scattered when Mrs. McKnight

stormed out of the hotel, followed by her two younger daughters, all smiles gone.

"What is it, Mama?" Evie asked in alarm.

"Dratted hotel. Dratted telegraph offices …" Mrs. McKnight adjusted her hat with a vicious tug. "I don't believe anyone in England received *any* of my messages. Oh, do pardon my language, Mr. Mackenzie."

As most in Jamie's family used language far more foul than a simple *drat*, he shrugged.

Mrs. McKnight began scrabbling in her handbag. "The hotel never received our reservation—or so they say. The clerk told me, in a *most* officious manner, that they had no rooms for us, regardless. The hotel is fully booked. The Olympic games, didn't I know?"

It was true that the world had begun to descend on London for the start of the international games, athletes and spectators alike. It was one reason for the mob pouring out of the *Baltic*.

The two porters, hands full of luggage, began edging back toward the car.

Clara was pale with worry. "They said all the hotels in London are full. Whatever shall we do?"

"Could the clerk not help in any way?" Evie asked.

Where the devil was the inconvenient fiancé? If Jamie's beloved had landed in London with no transportation and no lodgings, he'd have been on hand to supply both. He'd have arranged everything for her and her family in the first place, and been prominent on the docks to meet them.

Observing Evie's thundercloud face, Jamie decided not to ask about the absent Mr. Atherton.

He turned to Mrs. McKnight instead. "Is it far to your home, ma'am? I'm happy to oblige with the car, though I might need to refuel."

Mrs. McKnight shook her head. "Bedfordshire. It is much too far. We do not have a house in Town at the moment …"

"We've never had a house in Town, Mama," Marjorie said in surprise.

No one shushed her, but none of the ladies looked at her either. Jamie pretended not to notice her outburst.

"I suppose we shall have to find another train," Mrs. McKnight began.

"No, indeed," Jamie interrupted her. "You'll be wanting a rest and a good meal after your journey. Happily for you, madam, I know just the place." He opened the passenger door. "All aboard, once again, ladies. I will deliver you to fine accommodations."

CHAPTER 3

*N*o, no, no, Evie could *not* sit in the motorcar again so close to Jamie. Her interest in the car itself had helped, but she'd been most distracted by Jamie's large hands, strong under tight gloves, manipulating the gears and steering wheel, the wind ruffling his hair.

Now he was offering to drive them on, and Evie would be next to him once more. His arm might brush hers as he shifted the gears, or perhaps he'd have to reach across her for some unknown reason. She did not like how easily she imagined it, and the heat that would crackle through her at his touch.

Evie should be relieved that her mother immediately refused. Shouldn't she?

"Mr. Mackenzie, we could not possibly impose ourselves on you," Mrs. McKnight protested. "You've already done too much. We will simply have to find a train."

"Most have gone for the evening, ma'am," a porter put in helpfully.

Mrs. McKnight's shoulders sagged. "Oh, dear."

"Never fear, madam." Jamie swept her an exaggerated bow that would make another man ridiculous, but with Jamie, it was only graceful. "I will simply convey you to another hotel."

Another hotel. Evie felt a hard twinge of disappointment, then admonished herself. What had she expected—that Jamie would rush them to his own home? Where Evie could see where he lived, what sort of things he collected, who he'd become since Cambridge?

But then Jamie likely had lodgings in a building where women weren't allowed. There was his parents' home in Belgravia—Evie had read that was where they lived when they stayed in London—but a family of four descending on them unexpectedly would hardly be civil.

That left a hotel. Logical. Then why her disappointment?

"Hotels are full up," the porter said. "Nary a room to be found." His cheeriness began to grate on Evie's nerves.

"Not this one," Jamie said without concern. "My Uncle Cameron is a permanent guest, but he's not in Town at the moment, so his suite will be empty. He lets me squeeze in friends when he's gone."

"Absolutely not," Evie's mother said firmly.

"Only for one night," Jamie assured her. "Tomorrow you can make arrangements to take yourself back home. It's either the hotel or Uncle Hart's Grosvenor Square house. Aunt Eleanor would welcome you with open arms, but then you'd have to put up with Uncle Hart. Trust me, one needs a good night's sleep and a rousing breakfast before facing him."

Jamie spoke breezily, as though this were a good joke, but Evie had heard things about Hart Mackenzie, the Duke of Kilmorgan. He was a difficult man with a hard temper and a determination that made lesser men quail. King Edward himself was said to have stated he'd never get into an argument with Hart Mackenzie.

Marjorie danced from foot to foot, clearly wanting to take Jamie's offer. Clara too, while she was less impulsive than Marjorie, obviously found the idea of another hotel appealing, though they'd be obligated to a stranger.

No, not a stranger. A man who'd once kissed Evie with such strength on the bank of a river.

"Well." Mrs. McKnight wavered. Evie held her breath, not daring to show what she felt, if she even knew herself. "For one night, I suppose we must." Her mother bent a severe eye on Jamie. "Nothing too extravagant, Mr. Mackenzie. A respectable hostelry is all we require. Though I suppose beggars can't be choosers in this case."

Jamie flashed her a brilliant smile. "You let me worry about that, Mrs. McKnight. Now, let's settle ourselves once more."

The porters had shoved and jammed their bags back into the car. Jamie's one small leather valise appeared neat and efficient next to Evie's family's overstuffed portmanteaus.

The McKnights climbed in, Marjorie and Clara rapidly filling the back seat after Mrs. McKnight had resumed her place there. Why Evie ended up next to Jamie again, she couldn't say. She'd have thought Marjorie would wish to be in front, but Marjorie bounced on the cushioned seat behind her, beaming happily.

Jamie slid in, his large body far too close to Evie's. He competently shoved the gearshift into place, the car gliding smoothly forward.

To cover her nervousness, Evie babbled, "It must be splendid to drive." A cool gust swarmed down the street, and she clutched at her hat.

Jamie sent her an unreadable glance. "It's easy enough when you practice."

He showed no inclination to offer her lessons on the spot, but perhaps one day she could persuade him to teach her.

But no, that could never happen. Jamie would convey them to the hotel and then disappear from Evie's life.

As he should. Jamie Mackenzie was merely an acquaintance from her Cambridge days, even if it was an unnerving acquaintance. He would fade from her world, and Evie would continue as she was.

Why did that thought dismay her?

And when had she become so unsettled? She'd been perfectly contented on the ship, enjoying fine afternoon teas and dancing with polite gentlemen every evening. The weather had been unexpectedly fine, and she'd stood on the deck many a night gazing at the stars.

The solitude of the empty space under the dark sky, coupled with the vastness of the sea, had soothed her. She'd been at peace, serene, for the first time in a long while, old sorrow easing.

Not missing Mr. Atherton at all, a small voice whispered to her.

Nonsense, Evie snapped at herself. Simply enjoying the beauty of the stars. It meant nothing.

Did watching every twitch of Jamie's fingers, every slide of tartan over his thigh mean nothing at all either?

Evie forced her gaze from the plaid folds and pretended to study the road as Jamie guided the car through the abundance of carriages and carts packing the London street. She could not keep her interest away, however, the kilt drawing her eyes.

His coat covered its waistband, so she could not see how it fastened, though a silver pin flashed above the hem on the kilt's right side. The plaid was of a deep blue and green pattern, with a single red and single white band working through the darker colors. The cloth was faded, the colors no longer bright, as though Jamie wore the kilt in the rain, wind, and sunshine.

He'd always favored a kilt at Cambridge, no matter how much his fellow students ragged him about it. The mockers had learned to cease, knowing he'd defend his choice masterfully with his fists.

They rounded Regent Street's crescent, the tall golden-colored buildings rising majestically along its curve. Jamie continued around Regent Circus at Oxford Street, and not

long later, navigated the car into a drive in front of one of the
largest hotels Evie had ever seen. Their usual hotel her mother
had tried to book them into, and even their fine lodgings in
New York, shrank into insignificance beside it.

"Mr. Mackenzie." Mrs. McKnight leaned forward to tap
Jamie's shoulder. "I said nothing too extravagant. This is the
Langham, for goodness sake."

Jamie lifted his hand to a uniformed porter who sped out
to them. "Only place in London with an empty suite today," he
answered Evie's mother, unperturbed.

The hotel reared its way up to the evening sky, seven
stories that Evie could count, plus a square tower that rose
higher still. A profusion of windows peered at her, rectangular
ones on the ground floor, arched windows in the upper floors,
square ones near the top story, and above those, round-
windowed dormers flanked by many chimneys.

A carpet stretched from the car to the front door, which a
doorman held open to reveal the glittering glory of the hotel's
lobby.

"It's beautiful," Clara whispered in awe.

Evie marveled more at the way men and women poured
out of the hotel to greet Jamie and almost beg him to tell them
what he needed. Several youths in red suits with pillbox hats
soon had all the bags pulled out of the car, with trollies rolling
to collect them.

"The suite is ready for madam, of course." The hotel's
majordomo had glided out and now smiled beneficently at
Jamie. "I have sent maids upstairs to make sure all is dusted,
with clean bedding installed."

Evie and her family weren't allowed to touch a bag. As
she, her mother, and sisters strolled, dumbstruck, through the
wide expanse of the lobby, swarming pageboys guided their
many pieces of luggage through a narrow door and out of
sight.

In very little time, Evie found herself in a gilt-doored lift, operated by a stately uniformed man, the box gliding them smoothly upward.

They did not go far—the lift doors opened to let them out two floors above the lobby. A grand staircase, which they could have easily ascended, spilled downward not far from the double-doored suite the majordomo led them to himself.

Evie and family had not received such a welcome even in New York, where they did not have the money or titles to garner much attention. Now Mrs. McKnight and three daughters were ushered into a high-ceilinged and well-furnished sitting room as though they were royalty.

Not for our sakes, Evie realized forcefully, *but because we are Jamie Mackenzie's guests.*

Marjorie, for once, was speechless at the grandeur. Mrs. McKnight stood awkwardly under the splendor, but Evie could see she was grateful. It would have been a long, arduous railway journey northward, if they'd even been able to find a train, with no guarantee that anyone would be on hand to fetch them and their mountain of luggage from the station.

Clara gazed, enraptured, at the sitting room's silk wallpaper and plush chairs then wandered to the open doors of the three bedrooms that surrounded the sitting room. Clara dreamed of marrying a wealthy man who would give her everything she wanted, and perhaps she was deciding that this was the sort of thing she had in mind.

Evie wanted a man who would let her explore the world. One who would let her be herself and arrive at the serenity she sought. She'd found him in Hayden—hadn't she?

She firmly turned from these thoughts. "I understand why your uncle stays here," she said to Jamie, who lounged near the front doors, watching them admire the place. "This hotel must have everything one could need."

Jamie shrugged. "Uncle Cam prefers to be in the country, in the mud with his horses. He tolerates Town only so long." He chuckled. "When I was a lad, I dreamed of being a jockey and riding his beasts in all the races. Steeplechase, flat—didn't matter to me. Too bad I shot up so tall so fast." He smiled down at her from his lofty six foot and a few inches height.

"There is an advantage to being tall," Evie babbled from a foot or so beneath him. "You can reach things on the upper shelves."

Clara gaped in horror at this rudeness, and her mother sent her a frown of disapproval, but Marjorie giggled, and Jamie's deep laughter rang out. "So says my mother when she needs my assistance," Jamie said. "My sisters too take full advantage."

His laughter brushed heat down Evie's spine, no matter how hard she tried to banish it. "I trust your parents are well," she said quickly, for something to say.

"Oh, aye, they usually are." Jamie pushed himself from the doorframe. "Well, I'll leave you to it. Anything you need, you ask, and the staff will be happy to fetch it for you."

Did he sound reluctant to go? Or did Evie only hope that were so? And why on earth should she be pleased that he wished to stay?

Mrs. McKnight stepped in front of Jamie. "The bill shall be sent to me," she said severely.

"Of course." Jamie spoke with compliance but shot Evie a wink. He sketched them all a salute before he grinned and ducked out of the room.

Evie heard him loudly greet someone in the hall, and then a maid shut the double doors, and Jamie was gone. She did not at all like how far her heart sank as Jamie's voice faded into the distance.

———

JAMIE BREEZED OUT THE DOOR OF THE LANGHAM, CALLING good-byes to the staff who returned the farewell as though they were sending off a beloved brother. They enjoyed waiting on Mackenzies, any Mackenzie. Aunt Ainsley had won them over, beginning the day Uncle Cam had brought her here as his wife.

Jamie cranked the waiting car to life once more and slid into the driver's seat, revving the engine. As he did so, his unguarded thoughts slid back to the humid day on the river when he'd kissed Evie McKnight.

Her lips had been parted in consternation as he'd emerged from the water. She'd upended her oar once Jamie had ceased using it as a handhold, planting its end on the ground and clutching it like a spear. Jamie, torn between hilarity and outrage, hadn't suppressed his wild need to kiss her.

He'd cupped Evie's face, which she'd turned up to him without hesitation. Her dark blue eyes had gone soft, a flare of desire filling them. Her first experience of desire, Jamie had realized.

The sensation of Evie's mouth under his, her face wet from the water on his hands, came pouring back to him as Jamie eased the throttle forward to give the engine fuel. He recalled in exact detail the taste of her tongue, the scrape of her teeth, the warm strands of her sable hair that had escaped its bonds and curled around his hands.

Jamie jerked the throttle and almost flooded the engine, which gasped and sputtered. He quickly eased in the lever and patted the wheel.

"Sorry, lass. Distracted."

He'd always been pleased by the gift he'd inherited from his father to remember things with sharp precision, even kissing a lady six years ago. Jamie cursed the gift now, which did not let his memories be pleasantly fuzzy.

He gazed up at the hotel, locating the windows he knew belonged to the suite's sitting room. Did Evie watch him from above, also remembering their kiss? Or had she already turned to unpack for the night, Jamie forgotten?

Jamie waved at the window on the off chance, then made himself put the car in gear and drive away.

Images of Evie would not leave him alone—her thin rowing uniform wet from his dripping body, the flannel clinging to her curves. He'd wanted to slide his hand upward, cupping her breast, as he leaned in for another kiss. One hadn't been enough.

That kiss had seared an awareness through him—of Evie, of a need for her. Jamie's powerful longing had amazed him, and now, six years later, it was surging anew like a beast tired of being suppressed.

Evie's mouth had been hot, her response unfeigned. She'd leaned into Jamie, kissing him back, fingers clutching his sleeve. Not to push him away, but to hold herself up while she kissed him more deeply.

Even now, Jamie wasn't certain who'd first broken from the other. One moment, they were taking each other greedily, the next, they'd been apart and staring, breaths coming fast.

Jamie had forced a nonchalant grin as he'd released her, as though his heart hadn't been pounding uncontrollably. Evie had flushed brick red as her teammates' laughter had rolled to them. It had been all Jamie could do to turn and stroll away, dripping, to change his clothes.

Now as he navigated the traffic on the way to Regent's Park, Jamie's imagination continued to feed him images of Evie, not only at the riverbank, but what might have happened if he'd pursued things further. He pictured himself and Evie in a lavish hotel bedroom, bed hangings shimmering in the candlelight as he slid his hands down her unclothed body, she arching to him as he stroked and kissed her.

A cart swerved past him, the drover snarling about noisy motorcars, snapping Jamie back to his surroundings.

Ridiculous fantasy. Few hotels Jamie stayed in had bed hangings anymore, and most used electric light.

But the vision of Evie under him in the dark, he becoming

reacquainted with her in many enticing ways, would not leave him.

Jamie had been aware of her sensuality today, first as she'd teased him at the dock and then as she'd ridden in the seat next to him, unconsciously leaning to him as he'd explained how the motorcar worked. Her warmth had touched him, making him nearly forget everything about the engines he'd known by heart since he'd been a lad.

His fantasy was also ridiculous because Evie was engaged. Whoever this Mr. Atherton was, he had a treasure, and the man had better understand that.

Jamie ground his teeth all the way to a lane just east of Baker Street, where Daniel rented a lock-up to store the cars he kept in Town.

Leaning against the doorpost of said lock-up was a tall young man with red hair, a fierce countenance, and a well-muscled body hugged by a kilt and a long coat. He would not have been out of place with a sword in his hand, screaming at redcoats as he charged through the heather, nor in the slums of London, relieving passers-by of their purses simply by terrifying them with his glare.

Jamie leapt out of the car, passed the young man without a qualm, and inserted his key into the padlock.

"Now then, Alec," Jamie said cordially.

The young man scowled, his dangerous air intensifying. "Where the hell have *you* been, Jamie? I've been holding up this wall for an hour."

CHAPTER 4

*L*ord Hart Alec Graham Mackenzie, Marquess of Ardmore, was the oldest son of Hart Mackenzie and heir to the dukedom of Kilmorgan. Called Alec by the family, he had the formidable features and mannerisms of his father, his fearsomeness softened only by a glint of humor that came from his mother.

Jamie shoved open the lock-up's door. Alec caught the edge and helped him.

"Rescuing damsels in distress," Jamie said in answer to Alec's question. "Just hold that back, will you? It likes to swing closed."

Without a word, the heir to one of the wealthiest dukedoms in Britain held the gate for Jamie, son of the duke's youngest brother. Jamie leapt back into the car, guided it through the gate, and shut down the engine.

Alec eased the lock-up's door closed then retrieved a cloth from the workbench and began to wipe dust from the motorcar's front fender. Evening sunlight from high windows illuminated the space, motes dancing in the still air.

"What damsels?" Alec asked as he worked, but the inquiry

held only idle curiosity. Three years younger than Jamie, Alec had ladies clamoring for him, both respectable ones and those from the demimonde. Alec never had to worry about lack of female company.

"Old friend from university and her sisters. And her mum." For some reason, Jamie did not want to talk about Evie, not casually. She wasn't a tart from a tavern's back room.

"Ah." Losing interest, Alec busied himself polishing the travel grit from the car.

Jamie procured a bottle of whiskey from the recesses of a cupboard. "Wet your whistle?"

Alec didn't raise his head. "All right."

Jamie poured out two fingers for each of them into tin cups he kept for the purpose and tucked the bottle away. Alec had obviously come to talk to Jamie about something, but he continued to polish the car in silence.

Jamie laid a clean rag on the car's fender and set Alec's cup on it. Alec took it, then the two men clicked vessels together with a clank of metal, and drank.

Jamie leaned against the warm side of the car. "What is it, lad?"

The younger generation of Mackenzies had taken to turning to Jamie for advice. Since he was the oldest cousin — apart from Daniel, who was fifteen years Jamie's senior — and the firstborn son of Ian Mackenzie, they regarded him as their leader. Never mind that Jamie was a long way from the dukedom — thank heaven. Jamie had become a guide to the others, a confidante who helped solve their problems.

Alec didn't speak until he'd set down his cup. "I am considering my future," he announced. "Reconsidering it, you could say."

Jamie regarded him with disquiet, though he remained outwardly calm. With Alec, this declaration could mean any number of things.

"My future as duke, I mean," Alec finished.

Jamie held himself stoically as he waited for Alec to explain, but Alec returned to rubbing at a spot on the car's red paint as though determined to polish the metal bare.

"Are you going to be more specific?" Jamie asked after a time. "Before supper, anyway? I'm getting hungry."

Alec heaved a long sigh and tossed the rag to the fender. "I'm contemplating my future where I'll have to take up Dad's political career. I love Dad—and I respect him—but he hasn't gone out of his way to make himself loved, has he?" He grimaced. "I can't walk anywhere near Whitehall without someone buttonholing me and demanding to know what the Duke of Kilmorgan plans to say about whatever topic is giving them apoplexy this time. Doesn't matter when I explain he's more or less retired. Apparently, I know every scheme in his mind. They expect me to step directly into his boots, be exactly like him."

"Not anytime soon," Jamie said reassuringly. "Unless Uncle Hart is ailing, and I haven't heard?"

"No, no." Alec waved this away. "Dad's in robust health. Obnoxiously robust, as Mum would say. But it's more than people expecting me to be political. It's ..." Alec rubbed one hand through his hair. He'd picked up oil from the car, and a black streak now decorated the bright red. "Don't tell anyone ... but I don't want the title. It's brought Dad nothing but misery, and did the same to Grandad, from what I hear. *He* went completely mad. Not something I enjoy contemplating. I'm thinking of refusing it."

"Are you now?" Jamie kept his voice quiet.

He sipped the whiskey, a smooth, fine malt created by his father. Alec had resumed his scowl, not about to give Jamie any more information. He was stubborn, was Alec, as stubborn as any of the Mackenzies, with an extra dose of it straight from Uncle Hart.

"Let's talk this all the way through, lad," Jamie said. "If

you refuse the title, which you can, after going through legal machinations, many documents, and plenty of solicitors—with newspapers printing every detail—it will pass to Malcolm, your wild little brother."

Alec's eyes flickered. He hadn't thought of that, Jamie saw.

While Alec had Hart's growling strength, his younger brother, Mal, had decided to live up to the reputation of Old Malcolm Mackenzie from the '45 Uprising, which meant being as unrestrained as possible. Mal had recently turned twenty-one, reaching his majority and coming into a large allowance. Uncle Hart rumbled with worry about him, though Aunt Eleanor had more faith in the young man. *Mal has a good heart,* she liked to say. *He'll turn out all right ... Eventually.*

"I haven't spoken to Mal about this," Alec admitted. "But I think he'd do the same. Refuse the title, I mean."

"Entirely his choice." Jamie nodded. "With the same legal documents and disapproval from the world at large, but Mackenzies have never worried much about the opinion of the world at large."

Alec raised his cup, as though relieved Jamie understood.

"Now then," Jamie continued. "If you and Mal both refuse the title, it will pass to Uncle Cameron, as Uncle Hart's next younger brother. I think we all know Uncle Cam's feelings about that."

Alec's certainty began to slip. Uncle Cam was fond of saying in his loud, gravelly voice, that he thanked God every day that Hart had found the brains to marry Eleanor and give her two sons to keep him—Cameron—from the dukedom forever.

"He'd never accept it," Alec said glumly.

"Which brings us to Daniel, *his* oldest son. We know Daniel would take Violet and family and disappear to the ends of the earth if he thought he was in danger of becoming duke." Jamie grinned as Alec's face sunk into even more gloom. "As would Stuart, Uncle Cam's younger son. Thus the title would move to Uncle Mac, who would likewise snatch up his family and race to the Continent, pretending he couldn't sully the dukedom with his paintings and unruly ways. Robbie, as Uncle Mac's only son, has already expressed to me that he is happy he's a long way from the succession."

"That leaves Uncle Ian," Alec said. He pinned Jamie with a hopeful gaze. "And you."

Jamie couldn't prevent his laughter. "Dad would come up with a very complicated argument about why he couldn't take the dukedom. He might not tell you the argument, and simply say, *No,* but if pressed, he'd have his reasons lined up carefully in his head. And you know what *I'm* going to say."

Alec's mouth turned down, and he gave Jamie a formidable frown worthy of his father. "What if I ordered you to take the title?"

Jamie's amusement grew. "Lad, if you don't become duke and head of our branch of the Mackenzies, you can't order me to do anything. As though I'd listen, in any case. And yes, I'm refusing. I plan to do great things in my life, which I can't if I'm sitting on my arse in the House of Lords all day, listening to lugubrious men drone on and on about all sorts."

"You think that's what I want?" Alec burst out. He waved the cup until precious whiskey fell in droplets across the floor. "Dad expects me to carry on the work of prying Scotland loose from England's clutches. If he thinks that is possible in our lifetime, he's a dreamer."

"Uncle Hart is single-minded about that, I grant you," Jamie agreed.

Alec let out another sigh and took a calming sip of whiskey. "I suppose we'll have to search for more distant cousins to take up the burden, then."

"No, we won't. Do you not know how the dukedom of Kilmorgan was set up in days of old?"

Alec scowled. "Can't say that I do. I have better things to occupy my time."

"Well, I live with a father who loves old records, stories, and documents of the past. Dad has been regaling me with these tales all my life." Jamie suppressed his glee as he led up to his point. "When Old Dan was made duke back in the fourteenth century, he demanded a stipulation that female members of the family can inherit the dukedom, with *her* eldest son, if she has sons, becoming duke upon his majority. This is not unprecedented for ducal families—some do not want their power diluted by the title passing to ever more distant cousins. Therefore, if all the immediate male heirs of the Duke of Kilmorgan are deceased, or in this case, if they abdicate, the dukedom can pass to the oldest female in the line."

Jamie paused to sip while Alec watched him in growing understanding. "But that means—"

"Exactly," Jamie said. "The title would pass to Gavina."

Alec's eyes rounded as the full implication of Jamie's words hit him. "Oh."

"Yes. *Oh*."

"I wager she wouldn't refuse it," Alec said slowly.

"No." Jamie let his grin emerge. "She'd embrace it."

"Oh," Alec said again.

They fell silent, regarding the scenario with foreboding.

Not because Gavina, Uncle Cam's daughter, was a woman. Jamie would be happy to see a lady become the head of the Mackenzie family. He'd prefer it, in fact.

No, what made them pause was that Gavina was Gavina.

Beautiful, vivacious, unstoppable, strong-willed, uncompromising Gavina. She'd take up the mantel of power with relish and make everyone tremble before her.

Again Jamie wouldn't mind that so much, but he would mind if he had to go pry her out of prison for whatever daft idea she took it into her head to do. If Gavina were duchess in her own right, she of course, wouldn't go to prison—peers didn't. But she might end up in exile or sentenced to execution, even in this day and age. Gavina Mackenzie was a whirlwind, not a person to be lightly regarded.

Alec took a long gulp of whisky. "Well, you've given me much to contemplate."

"Aye. Contemplate it well, lad."

They drank in silence for a time. Jamie wondered what had prompted Alec's sudden need for Jamie's advice. Perhaps the expectations thrust upon Alec had suddenly made him panic — if Alec could ever be said to panic. He glowered at problems instead of running from them, very much like his father. Well, Jamie would pry it out of him one day.

They finished the whiskey with a tacit agreement to say nothing more about the dukedom, and turned to the car, cleaning and polishing it, Jamie lighting a lamp as darkness fell.

Their conversation centered on Daniel and Violet's apparent success with this motorcar in the United States, but Jamie put only half his attention on the topic.

He realized that the other half was going over every word Evie had uttered since their encounter on the quay, every movement, every smile, every frown.

She is betrothed, Jamie told himself firmly, as Alec speculated on what design Daniel would tackle next. *I should send her a wedding gift and be finished with her.*

But thoughts of Evie lingered, no matter how much he tried to banish them.

When the motorcar gleamed to Jamie's satisfaction, he and Alec put away all their tools and packed up the dirty rags to take to the laundry. Violet had trained them well.

Alec slung the laundry bag over his shoulder, offering to drop it off on his way back to Grosvenor Square, and Jamie did not protest. If a marquess wanted to visit the laundry, Jamie would let him.

They left the lock-up, carefully closing and engaging the padlocks. The wooden door appeared rickety, but in truth, it was solid and well reinforced, protecting Daniel and Violet's precious motorcars.

The evening had darkened as they'd worked, and the street was inky, except for a light at the corner. More than enough darkness for the toughs who abruptly stepped out of the shadows and faced the two Mackenzie men.

CHAPTER 5

*J*amie counted five of them. They were drunk, but just drunk enough to seek trouble instead of stumbling home to sleep it off.

"Evening, gentleman," Jamie said. Alec dropped the laundry bag, folded his arms across his broad chest, and remained silent.

One of the toughs swaggered forward. They always had to swagger, Jamie reflected. The man's thick body was hard with muscle, and the scars on his face attested to many previous fights.

"Gentlemen, eh?" The man glowered at Alec instead of Jamie. Because he thought the younger man an easier target? Fool if he did.

"Fine night for a walk," Jamie went on amiably. "To a nearby pub? I'll stand you a round, if you'd like."

Usually when Jamie offered to buy a belligerent ruffian a pint, said ruffian softened and accepted. Jamie had made many friends this way, all over the world. The drink might be different in Samarkand or Argentina, but the sentiment was the same.

This man remained unmoved, his eyes glittering in the dim

gaslight from the end of the street. "Won't be seen in a pub with a man in a skirt. A *Scotsman*." A sneer pulled at his face. "Go back north, where you came from, why don't you?"

Alec rumbled in his throat, the sound of a growling bear. The tough turned the sneer on him.

"Like an animal, ain't ye? A pig most like. Go suckle your Scottish pig mum's teat."

"Ah," Jamie said, the humor never leaving his voice. "I don't think ye should have said that."

"I don't give a—"

The man managed to grate out those four words before Alec became an inferno. Alec was a big lad, with the energy of generations of Mackenzie men eager to unleash the warrior within. He also was very protective of his mother, and any disparagement of Eleanor, even a generalization, ignited Alec's fires.

Jamie stepped aside to enjoy the show.

The tough feinted back, momentary triumph on his face, as Alec attacked. He and his friends had been spoiling for a fight.

The triumph evaporated as Alec's large fist landed on the tough's jaw, sending him reeling. The other four thugs, seeing their leader in peril, dove in to save him.

Alec spun and punched, kicked, and hammered at his assailants. They seemed to have forgotten about Jamie, who watched, entertained, as Alec pummeled all five men with tornado-like moves.

Alec's father, along with Uncle Mac, used words to smooth their way through life—Ian didn't speak much, but he always managed to make his point. Uncle Cam, on the other hand, relied more on his fists than conversation. Jamie and the Mackenzie cousins had learned well from Hart, Mac, and Ian, but Alec took after Uncle Cam more than the rest of them did.

Jamie saw Uncle Cam's teachings as Alec held his own against the pack, managing to gradually thin them out. Two quit the fight abruptly, one with a hand on his bleeding cheek, the other cradling a wrist.

Alec continued to punish the remaining three ruffians, his golden eyes alight, fists flying, the rebellious Jacobite in him rising to the surface.

Jamie let Alec enjoy himself without interfering until the thug's leader pulled out a long-bladed knife.

Jamie launched himself from the shadows and wrapped a strong arm around the man's throat. "No, you don't, lad."

The thug gasped, swiping at Alec then Jamie with the knife, until Jamie twisted the blade from the man's hand. The tough fought for breath, his thick body relaxing as Jamie's chokehold rendered him unconscious.

The remaining two thugs hovered, debating whether to help their leader or run for it. Alec spun to them, opening his arms.

"Come on, lads," he announced. "I've got more in me. What about you?"

The toughs glanced from confident Alec, poised to attack, to Jamie lowering the first tough's body to the ground and tucking the knife into his own pocket.

They ran. The sound of their thick boots disappeared into the mists, at the same time the whistle of a constable floated their way.

"Time to go, I think." Jamie grabbed the laundry bag and then Alec, who'd been about to charge after the last two, and hauled him away.

Once they'd rounded the corner, blending in with the crowd on Baker Street, Alec jerked himself from Jamie's hold.

"I was doing fine," he growled.

"You were about to get your belly sliced open. You have the Mackenzie berserker in you, true, but that doesn't help ye when your guts are spilling out all over the pavement."

Alec dragged in a long breath. "Suppose. Thanks."

"Oh, such grudging gratitude for saving your life, or at least bits of your skin. Where are you off to now?"

Alec took the laundry bag from him. "As I said, drop this off, then home."

"No, you don't," Jamie said sternly. "Look at yourself. Your eye is puffing up and you're bleeding all over your clothes." Scarlet droplets dotted the fine white shirt and cravat that peeped over the top of Alec's black coat. "Your mum won't be too happy with that."

Alec glanced down at himself and examined his torn and ruined gloves, his scraped knuckles peeping through the fine leather.

He shrugged. "I'll pop into the Langham and clean up in Uncle Cam's rooms. They won't mind—"

"No," Jamie said hurriedly.

Alec blinked at the abrupt answer. "Why not?"

Damnation. If Jamie told Alec about Evie he'd never hear the end of it. Or, Alec would charge around and see Evie for himself, unable to control his curiosity about what lady his cousin was hiding.

"Spring cleaning," Jamie extemporized. "I was around there myself before this. Everything's a mess in Uncle Cam's suite."

Alec's Mackenzie-golden eyes narrowed. "Spring cleaning, my eye. What are you on about?"

"They don't want us there." Jamie started off down the street, shutting off the discussion. "Take my word for it."

Alec laughed suddenly, his sunny countenance driving away his dour expression. The real Alec, when he let himself relax, was more like Aunt Eleanor, finding humor in the direst situations and charming all around him.

"Go soak your head," Alec said good-naturedly. "I'll brave Mum's wrath and go home. I'll tell her this was *your* doing." He waved at his swelling face.

"Oh, thank you. Then Aunt El will light into *me*, and my life won't be worth living."

"The least you can do to repay me for fighting those toughs off you. Think of it as your gratitude for me saving your life."

"Saving my—" Jamie broke off, realizing Alec was baiting him. Usually, Jamie would laugh with him and send him off. What was the matter with him today? "I was talking those lads around into having a drink when you dove into them like a Highlander in a clan war. You can take the blame for your own injuries."

Alec laughed again. "Go home and calm down. I'm too peckish to argue with you now. Love to Aunt Beth and Uncle Ian. And your obnoxious sisters."

Without waiting for an answer, Alec swung the laundry bag over his shoulder and headed back up Baker Street toward the Underground station. Jamie watched until Alec had been swallowed by the stairs that led down to the platform, then he turned his own steps south toward Hyde Park.

He hadn't decided where he'd go this evening until Alec's parting words, but Jamie realized that the comfort of home would be the best thing he could do for himself on the moment. An evening around the dining table with his family would be a balm on his restless soul, if only a temporary one.

Jamie whistled for a cab, leapt aboard one that slowed for him, and directed it to Belgrave Square.

———

GAVINA MACKENZIE STOPPED SHORT AS SHE ENTERED THE parlor of the Chelsea house she shared with three other young women, including her cousin Belle.

Her younger cousin Alec turned to her with a flare of coat, the left side of his face sporting a spectacular set of bruises.

"Good lord," Gavina said sharply. "What the devil happened to you?"

"Jamie happened." Alec's grin pulled at his puffy lower lip. "No, he didn't actually do this. But I want to know what he's up to. Dearest coz, will you do me a favor? A bottle of Dad's best whisky if you do. Besides, you'll know what Jamie's hiding too."

Alec explained, and Gavina brightened, the ennui that had crept over her this dull afternoon evaporating.

"Of course, I'll do it," she said with enthusiasm. "I'll go straightaway."

————

JAMIE ARRIVED AT THE BELGRAVE SQUARE HOUSE JUST AS Baines was about to serve supper. Without turning a hair, the butler, who'd been with his parents for the past decade, ordered a footman into the dining room to set another place for Jamie.

Jamie's mother, Beth Mackenzie, skimmed down the stairs as another footman took Jamie's coat.

"There you are." Beth kissed Jamie's cheek and smiled up at her tall son, her eyes as bright as ever, her dark hair barely threaded with gray. Jamie's first memories were of his mother's smile and brilliant blue eyes.

"Here I am," Jamie responded, returning the kiss. "Were you expecting me?"

"No, but I heard you'd journeyed up from Southampton. Violet sent word. I hoped the prodigal would return to the nest."

Jamie wound his arm through his mother's and escorted her into the dining room. "You are mixing metaphors, and I live a short distance down the road."

"Yes, but you've been wandering the world and don't always stay in London long."

That was true. He'd only been home from his latest journey —this one to the back country of Australia—a few weeks.

Jamie led Beth to her place while the footman hurriedly finished laying the silver at Jamie's customary spot. Except for the three of them and the butler, the room was empty.

"Where is everyone?" he inquired.

"Belle is at home—her home—and your father is … ah, here."

Beth's smile warmed as she beheld Ian Mackenzie, tall and unshakable, his kilt moving as he strode into the dining room. His brow was furrowed as though he pondered the secrets of the universe, and knowing Ian, he likely did.

Ian's scowl dissipated as he leaned to kiss his wife on the lips. The kiss turned lengthy, Beth's hand coming up to rest on Ian's chest. Jamie, used to the constant displays of affection between his parents, studied the ceiling until they were finished.

Ian straightened, his hand lingering on Beth's waist as she took her seat. Ian released her, then briefly met Jamie's gaze and rested a hand on his shoulder.

"Son."

That was all, one word, but in it, Jamie read warmth and a gladness of Jamie's presence.

Jamie had spent his life interpreting the emotion behind his father's perfunctory sentences, learning the great caring and love that lay within Ian Mackenzie.

A rustling of skirts announced Jamie's youngest sister, Megan.

Megan had inherited her mother's beauty without doubt. Her hair was a rich, dark brown, her eyes the deep blue of Beth's. She had Beth's gentleness as well, though Jamie knew that Megan's kindness did not mean she was meek. His sister had a backbone of steel when she needed it.

Megan wore a mauve tea gown that was too subdued for Jamie's taste, she at twenty-three deciding she should no longer wear frills and laces. She wanted to appear a serious composer and teacher of music, not a frivolous girl.

"Evening, Megs." Jamie pulled Megan into a one-armed embrace and kissed her smooth cheek. "Teaching the scales to brats still entertaining you?"

Megan returned the kiss with a reproving look then took her place at the table across from him. She unfolded her napkin before the footman, who strove to be utterly correct, could do it for her.

"I'll have you know I have a new post. At a country house in the Cotswolds. I begin at the end of summer."

Jamie glanced at his father in surprise. "Truly? So far away?" Ian did not like his brood to wander, as he'd told Jamie many a time. Ian had given up trying to make Jamie stay home, but Belle and Megan had been happy to remain close.

"It is quite exciting." Beth tried to sound quite excited, but didn't succeed. She liked her offspring nearby as well.

"Do tell." Jamie took his seat, hitting his chair at the same time Ian did his.

"My employer is Lady Alford," Megan said as the footman brought around the soup under Baines's watchful eye. "She has a daughter who is very gifted, and Lady Alford is looking for the teacher who will bring out her talent. Her exact words." Megan beamed.

"Hmm." Jamie accepted a ladleful of creamy soup. "Very gifted could mean extremely difficult."

"Not at all. I've met the girl. Hortense is as sweet as sugar. I spoke to her away from Lady Alford, so I know she wasn't putting on a show for her mother's sake. An unpretentious child. I can understand how she could be ruined by the wrong teacher."

Jamie politely declined a second ladleful of soup, the footman remembering how heartily he'd eaten when he lived here. "Good for you. She'll learn what a strict taskmaster you are. Be terrified of the forbidding Megan Mackenzie."

Megan made a face at him and began eating her soup.

"Megan is not a taskmaster," Ian said from the head of the table. "She is far more gentle than any of us."

"I know, Dad." During his travels, Jamie had missed his father's literal interpretation of whatever was said. "I was teasing."

"Yes." Ian's nod told Jamie he understood exactly what was going on. "I think you should not."

"Sorry Megan." Jamie gave his sister a nod, which she graciously accepted.

The conversation continued, but Jamie remained evasive to questions about his day, other than to explain how he'd met Violent and Daniel and family in Southampton and then driven the car to the London lock-up before he returned home, and had met Alec there. He said nothing about the fight, though Aunt Eleanor would have the story from Alec and tell Beth soon enough.

His mother's and sister's voices flowed around him—punctuated at intervals by Ian, who would make an astute statement then fall silent again. As Jamie ate the marvelous meal and listened to them, he realized that his heart was here. Home. With people who loved him and accepted him for who he was.

Jamie had always longed to impress his father by accomplishing something brilliant, and he'd set off at an early age to do so. So far, he'd crashed an aeroplane near Baghdad, nearly killed himself in India and again in Egypt, and almost got himself lost forever in the Australian desert. Not the most impressive of careers.

He pushed these thoughts aside and tried to enjoy his supper, their cook being one of the best in London. His thoughts were far from that dining room, however, as he imagined Evie tucking into whatever meal the staff at the Langham brought in, her eyes lighting in delight. Dark blue eyes, like a deep lake under the sunniest skies.

When supper ended, Jamie prepared to follow his mother and sister from dining room to the small sitting room. Unlike in some households, where the men and women would separate after the meal, this family adjourned together to continue whatever conversation they'd begun while dining. After that they might have a game of some kind or listen to Megan play the piano for them, always a treat.

Beth and Megan disappeared into the sitting room, but Ian stepped in front of Jamie.

"A word," he said in his calm voice.

Jamie uneasily curled his fingers into his palms. Ian wouldn't request to see Jamie alone unless it was to discuss something important.

Without waiting for an answer, Ian walked up the stairs to his private study, a chamber filled with books and papers, neatly filed, along with a Ming bowl in a glass case, the lights positioned to bring out its beauty.

As Jamie entered, Ian strolled to a side table to pour out two glasses of whisky from a crystal decanter. Jamie almost dropped his worry about why his father wanted to see him in anticipation of tasting it. Ian stocked this house with only the best from the Mackenzie distillery.

Almost.

Ian was a big man, hard with muscle that hadn't diminished in the nearly twenty-seven years Jamie had been alive. Ian rode, walked all over the Highlands, and strode for miles through London's streets, too impatient to wait for transport.

He did not hurry as he measured out the whisky exactly and carefully returned the decanter to the center of the tray. Only then did he hand a glass to Jamie.

"Slàinte." Ian lifted his goblet.

"Slàinte," Jamie responded. They clicked glasses and drank.

Jamie's anticipation was rewarded. The whisky flowed across his tongue like silk before burning pleasantly down his throat.

Ian lowered his glass and fixed Jamie with an unblinking stare from golden eyes.

"Son." Ian liked to call Jamie *son* rather than by his name, which Jamie did not mind at all. His golden gaze intensified. "Who is the lady?"

CHAPTER 6

$\mathscr{E}$vie had taken a sip of the most marvelous tea she'd tasted in an age, when she heard a woman's brisk voice outside the suite's front door. Evie was alone in the sitting room, her mother and sisters still in their chambers, washing up and changing.

"Never worry, my good man," the woman was saying. "I have my own key. I'll just pop in and see if my mother's embroidery basket is there. It is her favorite, and she's been in a tizzy since she mislaid it. You know how she is about her embroidery."

A key rattled in the lock, and the door swung open to reveal a young woman of extraordinary beauty on the threshold.

"Oh," the apparition said as Evie sprang to her feet. "Good evening."

"Good evening," Evie returned hastily.

The young woman in a splendid dark blue gown with a flowing skirt peered at Evie in avid curiosity. "I beg your pardon—my manners are atrocious. I am Gavina Mackenzie."

"Evie McKnight." Miss Mackenzie must think Evie's manners were even more atrocious. As Miss Mackenzie had been speaking of searching for her mother's embroidery basket, she must be of Lord Cameron's family, whose suite this was. "Mr. Mackenzie—Jamie—suggested we stay here," Evie continued quickly. "Out of kindness, as no other hotel in London could take us."

Evie's face heated as she blurted the explanation. She watched Gavina assess her, trying to place her among Jamie's friends—or conquests, perhaps.

"Yes, that sounds like something Jamie would do," Gavina concluded. "How do you know him?"

Evie had no intention of repeating the whole, sordid story. "From Cambridge. I met him briefly there. I was at Girton."

Gavina's interest grew. Her hair was the gold of a brilliant sunrise, tinted with enough red to glow. She had eyes of clear gray, like the sea under cloud-filled skies.

"Truly? I was at Newnham." She named the other ladies' college at Cambridge. "You knew Jamie only briefly? I'd say you were better friends than that, as he's installed you in our suite."

Evie regarded her in dismay, not liking her implication. But was it not true? She wasn't a friend of Jamie's—she was a woman he'd kissed.

"Did you need the rooms?" Evie couldn't recall when she'd felt so awkward. "Mr. Mackenzie gave us to understand your family was in the country."

"Dad and Mum are, yes. Racing season is upon us. But no, I don't need a place to stay." Gavina strolled inside, and a pageboy in the hall quickly closed the door behind her. "We were curious, is all. Alec and I were, I mean."

Evie frowned, lost. "Who is Alec?"

"Another of our many cousins. Alec deduced that Jamie had placed someone in the Langham he didn't want us to know about. I agreed to pop around here and find out who." Gavina beamed Evie a warm and beautiful smile. "You are not who I expected."

"Gracious, who did you expect?"

"No one respectable, I confess." Gavina's impudence faded. "Forgive me, Miss McKnight. I did not mean to offend you."

Evie's throat tightened. "Do you mean that Mr. Mackenzie slips *un*-respectable ladies into these rooms?" She took a step forward and lowered her voice. "Please do not mention this to my sisters, and certainly not to my mother."

"No, actually. Jamie has never done that *here*."

Elsewhere then. Evie was supposed to laugh or shake her head at the licentiousness of gentlemen, but she did not like the thought of Jamie installing paramours here and there. Remembering his easy laughter and warm eyes today, the idea sent a dart of pain into her heart.

"I'm certain he was only doing a good deed for a friend," Gavina said quickly. "That is Jamie Mackenzie all over. He'll go to great lengths to help others, often nearly killing himself to do it."

"Killing himself?" Evie's unease turned to alarm.

Gavina glided across the room to a seat and waved Evie to resume hers. Though Gavina moved gracefully, Evie sensed an energy about her that was barely contained.

"Have him tell you about all his adventures sometime," Gavina said. "He nearly got stuck in a wadi in Egypt once, trying to rescue someone's goat. When the goat's owner disappeared, leaving Jamie at the bottom of a sheer drop, he thought he'd be there until he died. Fortunately, the man only ran to fetch his brothers and ropes. Jamie was pulled to safety, obviously, along with the goat."

Egypt. In spite of the harrowing tale, Evie felt a restless longing. How splendid to be able to travel to such remote locales. Some women did journey to these places nowadays, but most were wealthy ladies or daughters of peers who'd decided to break away from convention. Alone in a desert night Evie might forget heartache and sadness.

"He also almost fell off the top of a train in India," Gavina went on. "Again, in a daring rescue—this one of a child who was falling between cars. Pulled up the boy and then nearly went over himself, silly thing."

Evie's heart missed a beat at the thought. Jamie had looked whole and healthy, none the worse for wear, but even a hearty person could meet death so easily.

"I assure you, *this* rescue was not dangerous at all," Evie said. "Our reservations went awry, and Mr. Mackenzie was on hand with his motorcar. Or, not his, I understand …"

"Cousin Violet's." Gavina nodded. "She and Danny build the cars together. They will talk your ear off about them if you let them." Her flashing dimples told Evie she found them more amusing than annoying.

"Jamie—I mean, Mr. Mackenzie—said the same thing about himself." Evie remembered Gavina was also the cousin he'd said would threaten to throw cold water on him.

"Yes, Jamie loves the cars. And aeroplanes and any machine he can go very fast in and crack himself up in. His mum is in constant worry, though she insist he's charmed. And perhaps he is. Only thing that explains why he's still alive."

"That is frightening." Evie did not like to imagine the handsome, capable Jamie falling between train cars or perishing in a wadi or crashing to the earth in an aeroplane. Although the adventures did sound exciting. She pictured herself sitting with Jamie, perhaps here by the cozy fireside, listening to his tales with rapt attention.

"A bit," Gavina conceded. "I certainly envy him for it. Girls are supposed to stay home and attend to their husbands. Not that I have one of those, thank heavens."

"I will have one soon," Evie said, then wondered why she sounded glum. "I am to be married in the autumn."

Gavina's eyes widened. "Will you really?" she asked in disbelief. "Your pardon—that sounded rude. I'm just surprised … No, that's rude too." She beamed Evie a smile. "Congratulations. I hope you will be happy."

Her words rang with sincerity, though Gavina continued to peer at Evie as though quite perplexed.

Before Evie could ask why she was so surprised, or think of any reply at all, Mrs. McKnight emerged from her bedchamber, followed by Clara and Marjorie. All halted at the sight of Gavina, who sprang to her feet.

"This is Miss Mackenzie," Evie said, rising as well. "Cousin to Mr. Mackenzie—"

Gavina cut her off. "There are so many Miss and Mr. Mackenzies we'd better be clear. I am Gavina Mackenzie. This is my dad's suite, and Jamie was wise to tuck you here. It's comfortable, and if you need an item, you have only to ring. This hotel is amazing. They will find you anything."

"Anything?" Marjorie repeated with interest.

"I do mean anything. Once my father heard about a new sort of bit that was supposed to be easier on the horses. He asked the concierge if the man could find some literature on it. Not an hour later, a sheaf of papers about the bit, plus the bit itself, was delivered into this very room. My aunt Eleanor read about a fossil the British Museum had recently acquired and merely mentioned it to the maid who does the rooms. The next morning, a chap from the museum was here to show it to her."

"How very delightful," Mrs. McKnight said. "Well, I doubt we'll want anything more than fresh towels and a pot of tea."

"This is my mother," Evie said when she could jump in. "My sisters Clara and Marjorie."

"Very pleased to meet you all," Gavina said with true friendliness. "Any friends of Jamie's ..."

"*Evie* is his friend," Clara said. "We've only just met him."

"So I gathered." Gavina's eyes twinkled. "Well, I shall leave you to it. Do remember, you have only to ask for what you need. So glad to make your acquaintance, Miss McKnight." Gavina sailed to Evie and enclosed her hand in a firm grip. "I hope I can see more of you, and your family."

"We're off to Bedfordshire in the morning," Marjorie

volunteered. "But Evie isn't. She's staying in London, with her *fiancé.*" She emphasized the final *é* sound.

"Oh?" Gavina shot Evie a look of great curiosity.

"With his family," Evie explained hurriedly. "They have a house in Upper Brook Street. Hayden isn't in much. He works with his father, and he often stays the night at his club."

"That sounds splendid." Gavina's wide smile held all kinds of merriment. "Perhaps we can lark about together after all. Plenty to do in London while the gentlemen lock themselves away."

Evie hoped her mother would not quash this idea, though Mrs. McKnight appeared to be taken with Gavina. Like Jamie, Gavina had a way with her.

"It is kind of you to look in on us," Mrs. McKnight said. "We promise to keep the place tidy."

"I have no doubt. Lovely to have met you all. Good evening." Gavina waved as she headed for the door with her animated stride. The door instantly opened for her, a pageboy hovering just outside. With a swirl of skirts, Gavina was gone.

Evie let out her breath as the door closed. Gavina Mackenzie was dizzying.

"She is quite beautiful," Marjorie said with feeling after they heard Gavina's footsteps and voice fade down the stairs. "I hope you can be friends with her, Evie. Then maybe you can ride in Mr. Mackenzie's motorcar again."

"She is an exquisite young lady," Mrs. McKnight said with a frown at Marjorie. "I hear her mother was once lady-in-waiting to Queen Victoria."

Such antecedents did not mean the high-spirited Gavina could not get up to mischief. Evie secretly hoped, as they turned to ordering the meal Mrs. McKnight declared they all needed, that when Gavina next got up to mischief, she'd include Evie in it.

———

JAMIE KNEW BETTER THAN TO ANSWER HIS FATHER'S question with *What lady?*

He sipped his whisky and wandered to an armchair, sinking into its welcoming cushions. "How did you know I was thinking about a woman?"

Ian seated himself on the sofa, his feet in their casual shoes lined up precisely, the kilt, a threadbare one he wore about the house, falling in neat folds over his knees.

"The train you traveled on reached Victoria Station at five thirty-five. You arrived here at half past eight, saying you'd come directly from the lock-up. It is thirty minutes from the station to the lock-up, considering the traffic load, and another thirty here in the hansom I saw you alighting from. That leaves one hour and fifty-five minutes unaccounted for. You could have been cleaning the car and speaking to Alec all that time, but probably not." Ian paused to take a sip of whisky. "Also, you let your sister do most of the talking at supper, and that is unusual."

Jamie heaved an aggrieved sigh. "Save me from a dad good with numbers. Yes, all right. I met a woman today. Her name is Evie McKnight."

"A lover?" Ian asked.

Another son might be startled that his father mentioned such a thing, but Ian was a practical man and believed in plain speaking. Jamie was plenty old enough to have a lover, and had in fact, taken several in the past.

"A friend. There's nothing in it, Dad. She's betrothed to another man."

Ian thoughtfully studied the light glinting from the facets in his glass. "Your mother was betrothed when I met her."

Jamie had heard the tale many times. "I know. You saved her from a blackguard, and she fell in love with you instead."

"I saw that she would be very unhappy with him," Ian stated. "I knew he would not appreciate what a priceless jewel he had in her, and so I told her the truth about him."

Jamie took another sip of the glorious whisky. "Mother says it was wildly romantic."

Ian met Jamie's gaze. "I was not trying to be romantic. I wanted her to be happy. Would have done anything to make her so."

"Including coaxing her to marry you one rainy night in Paris."

Ian shrugged. "It was necessary."

Jamie let out a laugh. "Necessary, he says. Well, I am selfishly glad you talked her into it, or I would not be here."

"That is true." Ian lifted his glass to Jamie. "I am four-fold glad. I have spent my life with my Beth, and you, and Belle, and Megan."

"Happy Families."

"Yes." Ian nodded.

Jamie chuckled. "It's a card game."

"I know."

For a moment, the two men drank in amused silence.

"Are you going to let Evie McKnight marry this other man?" Ian asked abruptly.

"I don't think it's my choice, Dad." Jamie set his glass on the table next to him. "It's not the same thing as you and Mum."

"Is it nae?" Ian asked quietly.

The question, in Ian's rumbling baritone that was much like Jamie's own, made Jamie pause.

Jamie's mother, when Ian had met her, had been Beth Ackerly, the widow of a vicar. She'd had a happy first marriage and had decided to marry a second time because she was lonely. She'd come into a fortune and so hadn't needed to seek a husband to support her. She'd looked for companionship, Beth had told Jamie, but not very wisely.

Likewise, Evie showed no sign of poverty or desperation. Her mother was a practical gentlewoman, disliking extravagance, as she'd made clear, but Evie's family would never have been able to send her to university or to make a trip to New York so her sisters could meet eligible Yanks if they were destitute.

Therefore, she must be marrying either for love or because it was what young women did. Jamie would discover which was the case.

"I don't know," Jamie answered his father. "But I will find out."

Ian nodded. "Good."

They drank in silence for a while, Jamie draining his glass, which Ian refilled.

"Dad," Jamie asked after his father had resumed his seat. "If Mum *had* been happy marrying Lyndon Mather, would you have left it at that? Not interfered, and let her marry him?"

Ian sipped whisky, his face not changing expression, but Jamie knew he was turning the question over in his mind. Or else, he already knew the answer and was simply enjoying the drink before bothering to speak.

A gleam of gold sparked in Ian's half-closed eyes. "No."

Jamie's resolve strengthened. "But what if Mather had been a good bloke, instead of the idiot he is?" He'd met Sir Lyndon Mather several times in his life—the last instance, about a year and a half ago, when Mather had given Jamie the cut direct. Jamie had pretended not to notice.

Ian set aside his glass and gazed at Jamie directly. "I would have taken my Beth from Mather even if the man had been a saint. I saw her, and I knew I had to marry her. No matter what."

"Ah." Jamie hadn't heard this aspect of the story before, but he saw in his father the stone-hard determination that had let him live through all the things people had done to him because they'd believed him mad. "You had no doubts, then?"

"None at all." Ian studied Jamie with a quietness that belied the lightning thoughts that went on inside his head.

"Look at things more closely," he advised. "They aren't always what they seem."

Meaning Evie might be happy marrying the best man in creation, or she might have accepted the engagement for another reason entirely. Jamie needed to find out which.

"Thank you, Dad." Jamie raised his glass to Ian. "Very sound advice."

Ian gave him a nod. They sipped, and then Ian's gaze went to the Ming bowl, the blue in it exactly matching that of Beth Mackenzie's eyes.

CHAPTER 7

$\mathcal{E}$vie took leave of her sisters and mother the next morning with mixed feelings. She would miss them, as they returned to Bedfordshire to soft days in the old brick house, picnics in the garden, lazing in hammocks as the clouds drifted above them.

On the other hand, Evie had much to do in London. Jamie Mackenzie had distracted her, but she'd promised Iris, one of her old rowing teammates, she'd help her, and help she would.

She'd been able to send Iris a telegram at last—running into Jamie had prevented her at Southampton—but the concierge at the Langham had sent it for her, even agreeing to not let her mother know about it. He'd readily conspired with Evie, performing beautifully.

Evie and her family left the suite with reluctance. The bed she'd slept in had been wonderfully comfortable, and Gavina was correct—anything they needed had been eagerly fetched for them. They'd dined and then breakfasted in the suite's sitting room, the hotel staff whisking the table and all its silver cutlery and wonderful food in and out.

"It's like a fairy tale," Marjorie said as she and Evie stood in the suite's doorway, saying farewell to the high-ceilinged sitting room with its lush sofas and chairs. The chandelier hung dark now, but it had blazed with light the night before, its facets glittering like diamonds.

"But now we must return the glass slippers and continue with our real lives," Evie said whimsically. "I will write Mr. Mackenzie and Miss Mackenzie notes of thanks. They have been so kind."

Marjorie regarded Evie with wise eyes. "The prince brought the glass slipper back to Cinderella, and they lived happily ever after. Perhaps your prince will return for you."

Evie could see she meant Jamie, and something hot stirred in her body.

Her sleep hadn't been entirely unbroken. Dreams of Jamie, he in his wet clothes, eyes full of sin as he'd leaned to kiss her, had threaded into her slumber, making her wake, breathless and too warm. She'd also dreamed of riding beside him in the motorcar, watching his broad hands on the steering wheel, he sending her sly smiles that burned her blood. He'd halt the car and gather her to him to sear her lips with another kiss …

"Don't be silly," Evie said, desperately trying to banish the visions. "There is no prince in this story."

"Mmm-hmm."

Marjorie did not much care for Hayden Atherton, though Evie wasn't certain why. The man had done everything he could to befriend Marjorie, but Marjorie remained cold, which was odd for her, because she was usually so friendly.

Marjorie said nothing more, but stuck her nose in the air and wafted out, the black ribbon that hung from her straw boater dancing.

Downstairs on the carpet outside the hotel's entrance, Evie embraced each sister and then her mother, bidding them good-bye. Mrs. McKnight held Evie hard, making Evie's eyes sting and her heart wrench. When she saw them again, she would be getting married.

"Write and tell us everything," Mrs. McKnight whispered before she released Evie.

"There won't be much to tell," Evie said. "Planning for the future, is all. Very responsible and steady plans."

"Mmm-hmm." Marjorie's *mmm-hmms* were playing on Evie's nerves. What did Marjorie believe she knew? Her smirk spoke volumes.

At last Mrs. McKnight, Clara, and Marjorie were bundled into a hansom cab, which rolled them away toward their train station. Marjorie waved and blew kisses to Evie until the cab was lost among the thick traffic heading toward Regent's Park.

Another hansom slid forward, and the hotel's majordomo opened its door for Evie. "Good day, Miss McKnight. I hope we see you again."

He was being polite, doing his job, but Evie returned that she too hoped so, though she knew it was unlikely, which made her sad.

She had a sudden vision of entering the glittering lobby once more, this time with Jamie Mackenzie at her side. Evie would be in a glorious silk gown, her ears and bosom sparkling with jewels, while Jamie waltzed along next to her, a greeting for each of the staff who came out of the woodwork to wait on him.

"Nonsense," Evie said out loud as the cab jerked forward. She must simply be tired. A few good nights' sleep, and Evie would think of Jamie no more.

She had much more important things to occupy her time, didn't she? Such as helping Iris with her troubles. Or rather, her family's troubles.

Iris Georgiou had been a dear friend at Girton and a member of the rowing team. Evie would have felt a loyalty to her for that alone, but Iris was such a sweet young woman, and she and Evie had become fast friends. When Iris had returned to Greece with her family after she'd finished university, Evie had wept. They'd written often, but it hadn't been the same.

When Iris had telegraphed Evie that she and her father were traveling to London, Evie had been ecstatic. She'd received the cable on board the *Baltic* en route to New York, and had been excited for the reunion upon her return. That is until she'd received Iris's letter, delivered to their New York hotel, outlining her problem.

Poor Iris. Her father faced ruin, and possibly worse, and Iris was desperate to help him. The first person Iris had thought of to assist her was Evie.

Now that Evie was back in England, she could put plans in motion. She had many ideas.

But first, she would reunite with Hayden, her fiancé, for the first time in two months.

Hayden's mother, a small woman with flaxen hair, smiled when Evie alighted at the Upper Brook Street house and entered its large foyer.

"How lovely to see you again, dear." Mrs. Atherton hugged Evie with plump arms, her rose-scented perfume wafting. "How was your journey? Cook has just sent up luncheon, and you must be hungry."

Evie could not help thinking, as a footman took her coat, that the majordomo of the Langham hotel had spoken in much the same tones as did Mrs. Atherton. Perfectly polite phrases, but rote and rehearsed.

Evie scolded herself for being uncharitable. Mrs. Atherton had been brought up to be expertly polite, was all. Plus, she had to make up for her husband's gruffness.

Sir Hector Atherton, a gray-haired, bearded man in a well-tailored suit, folded the newspaper he'd carried out of the drawing room and looked Evie up and down with hard blue eyes.

"Well, I can see that gadding about New York hasn't turned you into a frivolous ninny," he growled. "At least not obviously. Thank heavens you still dress sensibly."

Evie had worn a fairly plain blue gown, styles simpler this

year. Bodices draped softly instead of being tightly cinched, and her skirt flowed gently to her high-heeled Oxford shoes.

"Is that a way to greet our returning traveler?" Hayden's good-natured voice floated from the drawing room, and Hayden himself soon followed. "Ignore him, darling. Welcome home."

The handsome man with a shock of golden hair and keen blue eyes, who dressed like his father in a well-fitted dark suit, flashed Evie a wide smile.

Evie waited for the thump-thump of her heart and the warming of her skin that should wash over her. *How lucky I am,* she'd told herself. *He is attractive and charming, and many people like him.*

Nothing happened. Her heart remained unruffled, as usual, her face cool. Perhaps one day, she'd feel that quickening of excitement—like the one she'd experienced when she'd run smack into Jamie Mackenzie yesterday …

She quickly broke off the thought.

Hayden, either not noticing Evie's numbness or deciding to overlook it, took her arm and led her into the dining room, as he'd done every other time she'd visited Hayden's home. It was as though she'd never been gone.

The dining room's curtains were closed, as always, lest any sunlight leak in and mar the perfect decor of the blue and green chamber. A chandelier lit the scene, crystals dancing like those in the Langham suite.

Sir Hector escorted his wife to her chair at the foot of the table at the same time Hayden escorted Evie to one of the long sides. Both men waited until the ladies had been seated before they took their own chairs.

A footman sprang forward and offered Mrs. Atherton soup. She requested a polite ladleful and then the soup came to Evie.

Cream of chicken with lots of potatoes floating in the broth. *Mmm.* Evie, hungry, snatched the ladle before the footman could serve her, as she did at home, filling her bowl partway. She reached in for a second helping, but the footman, supposing she would release the ladle, had already started moving the tureen toward Sir Hector. The ladle slipped, and soup splashed her blue skirt.

"Careful," Sir Hector snarled at the footman, though his glare caught Evie too.

The footman had deftly moved the tureen back to Evie. *Sorry*, she mouthed at him and quickly laid the ladle in the tureen, scrubbing at her skirt with her napkin.

She glanced at Hayden as the beleaguered footman continued to serve. Amusement lit Hayden's eyes, and his small smile held reassurance.

Once the footman retreated, Mrs. Atherton lifted her spoon and very carefully scooped up a dollop of soup—the signal for the others to begin.

Evie shoveled soup into her mouth, knowing that the moment Mrs. Atherton finished, the footmen would rush in and remove all the bowls, regardless of how little the others had consumed. Mrs. Atherton had a birdlike appetite and would only take a few slow mouthfuls. Hayden had become adept at eating as much as possible during his mother's leisurely bites, and had instructed Evie how to empty her plate quickly without seeming to rush.

Evie wished she had mastered Hayden's skill. She fumbled with the spoon and slurped, feeling Sir Hector's eye upon her.

"My dear Miss McKnight," Mrs. Atherton said. *Blast.* Evie would never eat her fill if Mrs. Atherton insisted on conversation. "I am happy to have you grace our table once more. My friend, Lady Featherstone, insists she saw you traveling about London in a *motorcar*, of all things. I told her that was nonsense. You would never ride in a motorcar." She took a hushed sip of her soup.

"Oh." Evie's spoon froze. "I actually did ride in the motorcar, Mrs. Atherton. Mama's carriage never arrived at the train station, and a friend offered to drive us to the hotel."

Mrs. Atherton's perpetual smile faded at this news, and Sir Hector's formidable brows came down.

"Exciting," Hayden interposed. "A few of my chums have motorcars. They go like the wind once you get them outside the city and on a decent road."

"The lot of them should be melted down and the metal used for something sensible," Sir Hector snapped. "Smelly, noisy things clogging up the roads. Not safe to cross the streets these days."

There had been far many more wagons and carts careening dangerously through the streets, Jamie's motorcar barely having a space to squeeze through, but Evie did not say this. She scooped more soup into her mouth, savoring the tasty chowder while she could.

"Father will certainly not approve of *me* buying one," Hayden said, his voice light.

"Waste of money." Sir Hector slurped his soup. "Frivolous machines."

Mrs. Atherton laid down her spoon. Evie gulped one more hasty mouthful before gloved hands slid her half-full bowl from the plate. Hayden, drat him, had managed to finish his.

"Which hotel?" Mrs. Atherton asked in the tone of one calming the waters.

Evie hesitated as the footman began to pass the fish. Mrs. Atherton accepted a minute portion. Evie pointed to a plump, delectable-looking filet, and the footman laid it on her plate along with a good dollop of butter sauce.

Mrs. Atherton did not touch her fork, even after the men had been served their fish, as she awaited Evie's answer.

Evie found it difficult to lie. "The Langham."

"The Langham?" Mrs. Atherton jerked in surprise. "Good heavens. Did your father come into a sudden fortune?"

"A bit rude, Mama," Hayden said jovially. "Perhaps her sister Clara got herself engaged to an American millionaire."

"No, no," Evie said. She snatched up her fork as Mrs. Atherton finally lifted hers. "My sisters decided Englishmen were good enough for them."

"Quite right," Sir Hector mumbled around his fish.

"Then how did you get into the Langham?" Hayden went on, eyes alight. "Do tell, Evie."

The collective interrogation was beginning to wear on Evie's temper. "If you must know, a friend put us up. In a suite."

"Friend?" Hayden persisted. "Someone you met in New York?"

"No, someone I met right here in England. Mama's hotel reservation was mislaid, and we were at our wits' end. My friend's family has a suite permanently reserved at the Langham, they are not there at the moment, and my friend kindly booked us in for the night. It was that or sleep on benches at the train station." Evie stabbed her fork into her fish, hoping the lengthy explanation would satisfy everyone.

"Of course, you could not have done that," Mrs. Atherton said. "It was very good of your friend."

Evie noticed that Mrs. Atherton did not exclaim that Evie and her family could have spent the night in this large house with its eight bedrooms. Mrs. Atherton did not like to have many guests in her house at once—she only just tolerated Evie's presence.

"Who is this most generous friend?" Hayden asked in continuing interest. "Have I met her?"

"Him. His name is Jamie Mackenzie." Evie's face heated. "I also met his cousin Gavina," she added swiftly.

"Mackenzie." Hayden turned the name over as he ate several mouthfuls of fish. "Have you mentioned him before?"

"Probably not. I'd forgotten all about him." Not quite true, but she could hardly explain how she'd met Jamie the first time. "His cousin Gavina was at Newnham. That is another ladies' college at Cambridge," Evie explained as Mrs. Atherton looked mystified. "Mr. Mackenzie comes from a very large family. His uncle—he's the one who takes the Langham suite—races horses. Famous ones, I believe."

"You mean Lord Cameron Mackenzie?" Hayden asked, astonished. "Indeed, his horses are celebrated. What a treat for you, Evie."

"Yes, it was quite grand." Evie snuck in a bit of fish with its wonderfully herby butter sauce.

Sir Hector had been dragging his fork through his sauce, brows lowering. "This Jamie is not the son of *Hart* Mackenzie, is he?" The words held an ominous rumble.

"No, I believe Jamie is the son of Lord Ian." Evie said quickly. "Not the duke."

"Hart Mackenzie is a menace," Sir Hector said through her answer. "He claims to avoid Whitehall to rusticate in idyllic Scotland, but he has plenty of toadies do his dirty work for him."

Evie wasn't certain how she was to respond. Mrs. Atherton continued to nibble at her fish, a blank smile on her face.

"Does he, sir?" Hayden asked dutifully.

"That damned, sneering bastard, Fleming, for one." Sir Hector shoveled in a mouthful of fish and masticated while he spoke. "They want to tear Scotland from the bosom of the Union as though they could chop it off at Hadrian's Wall and set it adrift. What will they do then, eh? Damned Scots fight so much amongst themselves they'll be bashing each other with claymores before we know it."

"I believe there are more sheep in Scotland than claymores these days, Father," Hayden said mildly.

"Don't be flippant, boy. That's another thing. Many Englishmen have estates in Scotland, running sheep for wool. They'd lose fortunes if Scotland became independent. And those blasted Scots would lay waste to the land and run through all that money the English have made for them over the years."

"That is rather a long shot, isn't it?" Hayden pointed out. "I doubt even the Duke of Kilmorgan can make Scottish independence stick."

"But the Mackenzies can make all sorts of trouble about it, can't they?" Sir Hector demanded. "Insisting the Stone of Scone is returned. Never heard such blasted poppycock. Whole family is a nuisance. One's an artist—can you credit it? If I were a duke, I'd die of shame to have a brother as an artist. It's a fine thing to daub in one's garden as a hobby, but to sell the bloody paintings far and wide is quite another."

Hayden's expression remained neutral. "I hear Lord Mac gives his paintings away."

"And that one who runs the horses," Sir Hector went on, ignoring him. "Gambling is a disease in this country, and Mackenzie lures men into it."

"Father lost a pile of money at Newmarket years ago," Hayden confided across the table to Evie.

Sir Hector's color rose. "And the youngest one is mad, quite mad. Why he was ever let out of an asylum, I have no idea. You say his *son* drove you in his motorcar?" His piercing gaze lit on Evie. "Surprised you didn't end up overturned in a ditch and left to bleed to death. Never do it again, girl." He jabbed his fish fork in Evie's direction. "Never again."

Evie drew a breath to respond—she could jolly well ride in any car she wanted, and besides, her own mother had been with her—but Hayden gave her the barest shake of his head. Then he winked.

Evie relaxed slightly. At least Hayden didn't share his father's stances, though she doubted Hayden would ever openly defy Sir Hector. She glanced at Mrs. Atherton to see what she made of her husband's diatribe, but the lady only watched her husband with adoring eyes and quietly ate her fish.

Evie gulped a few more bites of hers. Sure enough, the footmen whisked away Evie's unfinished serving as soon as Mrs. Atherton laid her fork across her plate.

Sir Hector continued his theme of why Scotsmen were terrible for the country, haranguing about the rebellions of two hundred years ago, while Hayden slipped in remarks about the contributions of James Watt, Adam Smith, and Alexander Graham Bell.

Evie concentrated on downing as much capon in white sauce as she could, trying not to smile at how Hayden subtly needled his father.

Once the pudding had been served and consumed, Mrs. Atherton bade Evie withdraw with her to the sitting room while Sir Hector prepared to return to his office in the City. Evie hastily stuffed a final bite of vanilla mousse into her mouth and followed Mrs. Atherton out, still chewing.

A half hour of sipping tea while playing a silent game of cribbage followed. Mrs. Atherton, for all her dainty ways, played cards like a shark, and her points mounted up quickly on the board.

It was a relief to hear Sir Hector's rumbling voice approach, that gentlemen looking in to tell Evie and his wife good-bye. Mrs. Atherton dropped her last hand of cards and hurried to escort him to the door.

Hayden watched them go then strolled into the room and dropped to the sofa. "Whew," he said. "He went on a bit, didn't he?"

Evie left the card table and joined him. She sat on the other end of the sofa from Hayden, lest any servant peep in the open doorway and report the betrothed couple reposing too close to each other.

"I apologize for bringing it up," Evie said.

"You didn't. Mother did." Hayden slung his arm across the sofa's back and sent Evie his most winning smile. "What next, bride-to-be? Is the game afoot?"

CHAPTER 8

*J*amie leaned against a bookcase inside the British Museum, pretending to peruse an interesting tome he'd taken from one of the shelves. He supposed he'd look more convincing if it weren't a book on the insect *calosoma sycophanta* and its impact on the fruit trees of North America.

Around him, museum goers hurried through the courtyard on the way to gaze at the mummies in the Egyptian collection or the marbles from Ancient Greece. Fewer confidently entered the inner sanctum of the reading room, the space under the rotunda that only a privileged ticket holder could access.

Jamie glanced up from the charts of the six-legged pest's infiltration of New England and Canada, and scanned the visitors for Evie and whoever she'd come to meet.

His father's advice in his ears, Jamie had returned to the Langham the morning after he'd left Evie there, but he'd been too late. The family had departed the suite early, the concierge had told him, the mother and daughters journeying home to Bedfordshire.

Jamie had started to turn away from the concierge's desk,

disappointment blending with determination, when the concierge had mentioned that, by the way, the oldest daughter had not accompanied her mother and sisters. *She* had taken a cab to Upper Brook Street, to reside there with her fiancé's family.

"Did she mention doing anything else?" Jamie asked, trying not to sound too urgent. "Outings in the country? Visits to London's famous sights? Fittings for her wedding gear?"

"Nothing of that sort," the concierge, his black hair slick with pomade, said. "They seemed a modest family. Asked us to do very little for them—book tickets for the train, summon a cab to take them to the station. Very polite ladies." He nodded at Jamie as though congratulating him on his choice of friends. "And, oh yes, the young lady who remained in London did send a telegram."

The concierge closed his mouth after that information, hands behind his back, an innocent expression in place.

Jamie took his time asking the next question. He copied the concierge's stance, his joined hands resting on the tartan over his backside. "Do you remember at all the nature of this telegram?"

The concierge contrived to look scandalized. "You know I cannot possibly divulge the content of another person's messages, Mr. Mackenzie."

"No, of course not," Jamie agreed. "That would be most improper. A betrayal of confidence."

"Exactly." The concierge and Jamie stood in silence another moment, then the concierge inhaled sharply. "But I rather think if you enter the courtyard of the British Museum, placing your visit around eleven tomorrow morning, you might catch sight of the young lady."

Jamie barely suppressed his grin. "I see. You are a gem, Mr. Francis."

"So they tell me, sir." The concierge gave him a formal bow.

"Please convey my best to your mother and father and your dear sisters."

"That I will." Jamie fished a gold coin from his pocket and surreptitiously slipped it to the concierge under the guise of a handshake. "Good day to you."

"Good day, Mr. Mackenzie." The gold coin disappeared quickly, as though it never existed.

Jamie had spent the rest of the day discovering all he could about Hayden Atherton. Hayden was an only child who lived at home with his parents and assisted his stockbroker father at the company in which Sir Hector was a director. This information Jamie gleaned from various people he questioned, from doormen at clubs to friends in the City. Hayden was the apple of his father's eye, because he remained dutifully in London instead of gallivanting wherever young men gallivanted, and worked every day.

As I suspected, Jamie told himself. *A dull stick*.

He knew he was being unfair to a man he'd never met. Jamie's family was no stranger to business, and Ian had told Jamie that he could step into running the Mackenzie distillery any time he wished. Take over the reins so Ian could loll on the riverbank near his home north of Kilmorgan and fish all day. Ian had also told Jamie he didn't expect him to do this, leaving Jamie to make up his own mind.

Jamie supposed he'd meet Atherton soon enough, and judge his character then.

Or would he see him? The concierge had not mentioned Atherton at all, only implied Evie had sent a telegram to someone, setting up this meeting at the British Museum. Who? If she was staying in Atherton's house, she'd need not send him a telegram—she could simply discuss it with him there.

And who had she been looking for at the docks when she'd run into Jamie? She'd continued to hurry along after she'd departed from him, heading in the opposite direction from the ship, her mother and sisters nowhere in sight. She couldn't have been searching for Atherton, who hadn't bothered to take himself to Southampton to meet his own betrothed.

Jamie turned a page, pretending to be absorbed in a drawing of the insect, a rather pretty beetle with an iridescent green back. The painting of it was well done, showing how its colors changed with the light.

Laughter jerked his attention from the book. He raised his head to behold Evie rushing to embrace a young woman with sable hair and an excited smile.

Evie's dark hair straggled from its neat roll, and her simple frock skimmed her shapely body. Sunshine streaming from high windows made her hair gleam, her eyes sparkle.

The woman she greeted was about the same age as she, her frock cut to drape her body to its best advantage. She looked familiar, though Jamie could not place her at the moment.

Evie stepped from her friend, glanced around as though scanning for watchers, and caught sight of Jamie.

Her dismay could not be more obvious. The last person Evie wanted to see in that moment was Jamie Mackenzie. They stared at each other as time stretched, Evie disconcerted, Jamie's smile slow and triumphant.

When her friend asked a worried question, Evie hastily revised her countenance, pasting on a false expression of delighted surprise.

Jamie closed his book and dropped it to a table—his sister Belle would have been horrified if he'd shoved it back onto the shelf. *What if you put it in the wrong place, and no one could ever find it again?* he could hear her exclaiming. *Let the librarian take care of it.*

"Good morning, Miss McKnight," Jamie said as he moved forward to them. "What a lucky chance to meet you again."

"Indeed, it is a pleasure." Evie mouthed the words while behind her eyes the anguish at seeing him was vivid. "May I introduce my friend, Miss Iris Georgiou? She was on the rowing team with me at Girton."

So that was where Jamie had seen her. He recalled her collapsing in gales of laughter as Jamie tumbled into the river, courtesy of Evie.

"Charmed." Jamie extended a hand to Iris. "I remember you howling in mirth at my misfortune."

"Well, it *was* rather funny." Iris regarded him with a mischievous twinkle as she completed the handshake. She was quite lovely, the spindly girl in the rowing costume all but gone. Evie had introduced her as *Miss*. Not married, then.

"And my fiancé, Mr. Atherton."

A man Jamie had not noticed at all stepped forward. He now realized the fiancé had been there all along, but Evie had occupied Jamie's entire focus.

"Mackenzie." Atherton thrust out a hand.

No fatuous mustache, no silly flannels, and his smile was merry rather than inane. His handshake was firm as well.

The man stood a good six inches shorter than Jamie, but then Jamie had the uncommon height of the Mackenzie men. Atherton had blond hair and a trim beard, his brown eyes holding a modicum of intelligence.

"Atherton." Jamie couldn't help but harden his grip the slightest bit, liking the tiny flinch that pinched Atherton's lips.

They released the handshake but continued to assess each other. "The kindly Scotsman who rescued my dear fiancée and relocated her to an excellent hotel," Atherton said. "I am grateful you were on hand."

"I could hardly leave them stranded," Jamie said. "Alone at the station, with no one to come for them, no one to give them shelter. It was the least I could do."

If Atherton noticed Jamie's dig at his failure to look after his own fiancée, he made no indication. "The Scots are a hospitable people, I've heard." Atherton grinned. "At least when they aren't busy chasing the British army to Derby."

Jamie caught the flash of annoyance in Evie's eyes, but she said nothing.

"So close to London they came," Jamie said, voice hardening. "I lost family in the battles of that time. Great-great
uncles."

"That was long ago," Atherton said dismissively. "Now we
are all one country, and the Scots are the better for it."

"Are they now?" Jamie let his accent become more
pronounced.

"Of course. No more mad Highlanders tearing up the land.
Science, agriculture, and modernity are what makes up Scotland now."

"Ye've been there, have you?"

"No." Atherton did not bother to look embarrassed. "I
rarely travel farther than Oxfordshire. I go too far north, and
my skin begins to itch."

"Well, 'tis not for the faint of heart, the Highlands. You
claim it has all been tamed, but the wilderness there is vast.
Dangerous for the unwary."

"As I say." Atherton shuddered. "I'll stay in London, thank
you."

"*I'd* like to see the Highlands," Evie broke in.

Her eyes held the longing Jamie had sometimes caught in
his own, when he stayed too many months far from home. His
father sometimes abruptly raised his head to peer out to a
foggy London street, and Jamie would know he saw hills
rolling through the mist, land empty and wild stretching to the
knife-sharp mountains.

Jamie wanted to show the wilderness around his boyhood
home to Evie, wanted to watch her face light in delight when
she beheld its stark beauty. He wanted her family to be there
too, so he could watch Marjorie dance with the buoyancy of
youth, while Clara quietly appreciated the beauty, and Mrs.
McKnight breathed a relaxing sigh.

He'd do it, Jamie decided. He'd take Evie to the Highlands
and let her fall in love with them.

He abruptly changed the subject. "What have you come to

the museum to stare at? The gruesome mummies? The famous Rosetta Stone?"

"Miss Georgiou will show us pottery from her homeland," Atherton answered readily. "You know, Achilles and Spartans spearing each other on vases. She is Greek, though she grew up right here in England."

"The collection is indeed excellent," Jamie agreed, though it was clear Atherton knew nothing about it.

"Do join us, Mr. Mackenzie," Iris said.

"Yes, that would be just the ticket." Atherton clapped his gloved palms together. "Come with us, Mackenzie. Why not?"

Both Atherton and Miss Georgiou seemed eager to absorb Jamie into their company. Evie, on the other hand, was most reluctant.

"I'm certain Mr. Mackenzie has much to do." Evie sent Jamie a pointed look. "You came here to research, didn't you, Mr. Mackenzie?"

Jamie contrived a blank expression. "Passing the time. My sisters are agog for Egyptian antiquities and rather gave me the bug for them too."

"Surely it is your father who has the expertise in antiquities," Atherton said. "He is famous for his collections."

"Of Asian antiquities," Jamie corrected him. "Ming bowls in particular. My sisters, on the other hand, have Egypt mania. Anything dug out of the dirt and brought back to the museums holds their attention. I'm certain one or both of them will rush to Egypt any day and start rooting through tombs."

"Ladies do have funny whims." Atherton chuckled. "I'm sure you can persuade them to stay safely at home."

"You clearly have not met my sisters," Jamie said. "But let us be off to ancient Greece. Lead the way, Miss McKnight."

She did not wish to lead Jamie anywhere, he saw. Evie wanted him to rush to Egypt himself, fall back into his wadi, and leave her and her friends alone.

Her adamance made Jamie that much more determined to discover why.

———

EVIE MARCHED ACROSS THE COURTYARD AND UP THE STEPS to the wing that held the ancient Greek and Roman collections. Her stride was swift, her heels clicking on the polished floor.

Why Iris and Hayden had spontaneously invited Jamie along, she could not fathom. The three of them needed to discuss things, and they could not speak freely in front of him.

Besides, Jamie unnerved her. His tall, strong body made Hayden's appear thin and reedy. Not ten minutes ago, Evie had been congratulating herself on Hayden's good looks. When Hayden had handed her down from the hansom in front of the museum, passing ladies had regarded her with envy.

Jamie was handsome as well, but in a very different way. His red-brown hair was unruly as though wind-tossed—he eschewed the pomade that Hayden used to keep his mane tamed. Jamie's clean-shaven face was hard, his blue eyes dark.

His Scottish-style suit with kilt lay upon him casually, as though he could slip off the coat at any time, loosening his cravat and letting himself breathe. His chest would rise and fall, his loose shirt parting, and he'd send Evie a smile, his wicked eyes half closing.

That's better, he'd whisper.

Evie's heart constricted, and she nearly tripped on a step. A very strong grip steadied her.

"Easy, lass," Jamie said in her ear. "We want to see the vases, not carry you to a physician."

Evie gulped air. Jamie continued to hold her arm until they reached the top of the steps and turned into the gallery.

She glanced behind her to see if Hayden had noticed Jamie's assistance, but Hayden had Iris's arm tucked in his, and he listened as she spoke animatedly. By the time he and

Iris reached Jamie and Evie, Jamie was several feet from Evie, busily studying the bust of a long-dead Roman senator.

Hayden cheerfully offered his other arm to Evie, shutting out Jamie. Jamie said nothing, simply fell into step with the group as they made their way to the Greek collection. Jamie walked with his hands clasped behind him, his casualness both unnerving and intriguing.

Large vases in the Greek room reposed on plinths, with smaller ones set inside glass cases. Evie's interest was caught by the artistry of the black figures on red backgrounds, men and women frozen in acts of dancing, leaping, or fighting.

Iris examined each carefully, her agreeable mood vanishing as she looked over a case of small vessels that had red figures on black backgrounds. Evie wasn't certain whether to be relieved or worried when Iris signaled that the one they sought was not here.

Jamie studied the pottery in silence, head cocked as though taking in their beauty. Hayden was the only restless one, darting from case to case, impatiently sidestepping other visitors trying to view the collection.

"Huh." Jamie pointed at a slender jar in a case. "This one's mislabeled. Should be from Crete, not Attica."

Hayden moved quickly to him. "How do you know?"

"I've been to plenty of digs in Athens and other sites, and on Crete. Plus my uncle dragged me here and to all the galleries in London and Scotland when I was a lad, showing me the best art from around the world. Trying to improve my mind." Jamie tapped his head with his knuckles. "Not sure it had any effect."

"Are you an expert in Greek pottery?" Iris asked him eagerly, ignoring Evie's silencing glare.

"Not an expert as such." Jamie shook out his hand as though he'd hurt his fingers on his cranium. "But I know a bit. Enough to see that this is Minoan. But those in the basement typing the labels don't always know."

Iris gazed at him in hope. "Then perhaps you can—"

"Have you seen the Parthenon marbles, Mr. Mackenzie?" Evie abruptly gestured toward a sign that pointed the way to their display, needing to stop Iris before she blurted out too much.

Hayden caught on. "Beautiful things," he added with enthusiasm. "But maybe not a sight for the ladies, eh Mackenzie?" He winked.

Evie's irritation rose. She knew Hayden was trying to be amusing to distract Jamie from their purpose, but she found his method irksome. She could certainly gaze at nude men and women in marble relief and not be shocked.

"I have indeed seen them," Jamie answered, his tone deceptively mild. "But I'm certain the ladies would not need their smelling salts." His disparaging glance at Hayden told Evie he was as displeased with Hayden's attempt at repartee as she was.

"Excellent," Evie broke in. "Then you can indicate some of their finer points, Mr. Mackenzie. They're this way."

"A great lot of people are rushing to see the marbles at the moment." Jamie waved at a long queue of ladies and gentlemen outside the door to the next gallery, skirts and frock coats filling the space. "Quieter here."

"There are those who believe the marbles should go back to Greece," Hayden said, a glint in his eye she'd seen when he was goading his father. "Because Lord Elgin pretty much stole them, they claim. Rot, I say. They're much safer here."

Jamie faced him calmly. "Laws are being made now to ensure antiquities remain in the country where they're unearthed. Not that it stops thieves selling the things to tourists and collectors."

"Again, I say, much safer in this museum, or the Metropolitan in America, or in the Louvre." Hayden stuck out his chin. "If we hadn't hauled all these things here, they might have been lost forever. Would be a shame, eh?"

Jamie spread his hands. "Maybe true in the past, but times have changed. Shouldn't the people in those countries be able to see them in their museums?"

"Exactly as I say," Iris broke in. "Greek things belong in Greece." She trailed off as she caught Evie's warning gaze. Iris might give everything away if she entered another argument with Hayden.

Hayden ignored her. "Does that include your father's collection?" he asked Jamie, his look challenging. "By your argument, he should send all his Ming pieces back to China."

CHAPTER 9

*E*vie watched Jamie grow very still. She realized as she observed him that the affable, good-natured fellow he liked to show others was a facade. Behind it lay a formidable man, one who did not suffer fools gladly.

Jamie could easily pick up Hayden and crush him between his large hands. He chose not to, not because they were in a public museum, but because he *chose*.

The hard light in Jamie's eyes flickered in the shadowy gallery. Evie remembered when that gaze had focused on *her*, as the dripping, angry Jamie had climbed from the river and given her that fierce, demanding kiss.

"My father is well acquainted with scholars in China," Jamie said quietly to Hayden. "They know all about each bowl he has purchased, and its history. They exchange correspondence regularly. Those men know where the bowls are, and my father would be happy to return any to China if they ask."

"Scholars?" Hayden guffawed. "You mean he's not chums with the emperor?"

He was joking, but Jamie did not smile. "The emperor at the moment is a prisoner in his own palace. I have a feeling their dynasty won't last much longer."

Hayden opened his mouth to continue the debate, but Evie interposed herself between the two men. Her skin tingled when she intercepted Jamie's gaze.

"You do not have to answer his questions, Mr. Mackenzie," she said. "Mr. Atherton is being rude, though I cannot fathom why."

Jamie's dangerous expression softened. "Peacocks will strut when ladies are nearby, Miss McKnight."

Iris laughed, liking his answer, but Evie exhaled in exasperation. "Peacocks," she said. "That is a very apt comparison. *May* we get on with looking at the exhibitions?"

She swung away, striding purposefully onward.

Yesterday, Hayden had defended Jamie when Evie's father had disparaged Scotsmen in general and the Mackenzies in particular. But today Hayden had decided to poke fun at Jamie and his Scottishness, which for some reason Jamie was playing up.

Perhaps Hayden simply liked to take the opposing side in any argument he found himself in. He seemed to enjoy watching the other party scramble to justify themselves. Some of his conversations with Evie had followed that pattern. Why hadn't she noticed this before?

She caught Iris's arm and led her friend along the gallery, the gentlemen falling behind.

"It isn't here," Iris whispered.

"I see that," Evie whispered in return. "Or rather, I don't see." At least nothing that resembled the drawing Iris had sent her.

"It must be in the basement Mr. Mackenzie mentioned," Iris continued worriedly. "Trapped there."

Evie squeezed Iris's wrist. "No, that is a good thing. If it's tucked in a box in the cellar, it won't be missed. Maybe not for decades."

"Yes, but how are *we* to find it? If it is even in this building. The museum has other storage facilities, don't they?"

"Let us worry about one thing at a time. First, a way to get into the cellar."

"Could Mr. Mackenzie help?"

Evie paused in mid-step. "Jamie? I mean, Mr. Mackenzie? How could he?"

"He seems to know about ancient pottery—he'd be able to understand what is what. And he said he'd been coming to this museum all his life."

"Yes, but ..." Evie glanced behind them at Jamie and Hayden who were now conversing affably, blast them.

Iris had a point that Jamie could be a help, *if* they could trust him to keep his silence. He might have resources that they did not. Evie recalled how the employees of the Langham had fallen all over themselves to assist him and guessed he might have the same rapport with the staff here.

But if Jamie agreed to assist, that meant he'd spend much time with them, and Evie did not like how she was too aware of his nearness. With unnerving frequency, her mind flashed back to his tall body curving over hers, his wet but hot lips on her mouth ...

No, she should not be near him at all.

When she had spied Jamie today, lounging against a book-case, a tome in his large hands, the rest of the world had abruptly vanished. The museum, the echo of its visitors, Iris, her predicament. Hayden.

Nothing had existed in that moment but Jamie Mackenzie. And it had seemed quite natural.

Evie could not afford to let that happen again.

"I will ask him," Iris was saying.

Evie snapped her attention back to her. "Good heavens. No."

Iris, the beauty of the rowing team, could be quite stub-born, Evie remembered. Stubborn, headstrong, and fearless. All the reasons Evie had liked her.

"It is my father at risk," Iris said resolutely. "His reputation, his post—this could ruin his life. I will take any help I can find. I rather doubt Mr. Mackenzie will dash to the Greek government and tell them all that has happened."

"The less who know, the better," Evie tried.

"Please, Evie." Iris said *please*, but Evie knew she would talk to whomever she liked about this problem, which was, after all, hers. Evie had no reason to stand in the way of whatever Iris wished to do.

Except she needed to avoid Jamie and the strange feelings he was invoking in her. It had been so long since she'd had any feelings at all, and she wasn't certain she could manage this change in her heart.

Iris did not wait for her answer. "I will speak to him." She turned away in a swish of skirts.

Evie leapt after her. "Here? Now?"

"Of course not here," Iris hissed. "But yes, now. Let us adjourn to a teashop or some such. Sit in a corner where we won't be overheard."

Iris sped toward the gentlemen, and Evie could only follow.

"What do you think, Evie?" Hayden said as she neared. "Mackenzie is a member of one of my clubs. Isn't that jolly? We've agreed to dine and be friends."

"Oh, yes, very jolly," Evie snapped.

Gracious, would Jamie and Hayden decide to become best mates at this dinner? Would Hayden perhaps invite Jamie to the wedding?

She envisioned a future when Jamie would come around for supper once she and Hayden were settled. The two men would talk and joke as they drank whisky Jamie brought from his family's distillery, and Evie would sit mutely, trying to decide how to behave.

Hayden's smile widened. "Evie is a crosspatch today. Tired from her travels, no doubt."

Jamie's gaze went to Evie, understanding in his eyes. "No

doubt. But worry not about walking home or bouncing in a tedious hansom today. I brought the motorcar."

Damnation. That would put the final blow to Evie's equilibrium, riding beside Jamie in his motorcar or sitting behind him where she could observe the curve of his jaw, the thick wave of his red-brown hair.

"No need," Evie said sharply. "Iris wishes to retire to a teashop. There is one around the corner. Shall we go?"

She swept past both men before they could speak, her heart unsteady as she pattered toward the relative refuge of the museum's front doors.

———

JAMIE WATCHED EVIE STRIDE AHEAD OF HIM ALONG GREAT Russell Street, determinedly making for Bedford Square, home of the aforementioned teashop. Her skirts fluttered in the brisk wind, revealing her firm calves. She wore low Oxfords, practical shoes that encased her feet and trim ankles most enticingly.

She marched with head up, tendrils of dark hair escaping from under her plain hat, hands balled into fists. She had a straight back that curved into a nice waist, then a flare of hips that the skirt hugged. Strong legs carried her forward so purposefully that Atherton, escorting her, had to jog to catch up.

Jamie noted his quickened steps with satisfaction. The twit would never be able to keep up with Evie.

Atherton reminded him of any other upper-class idiot that proliferated London. They styled themselves as dashing men-about-town and pretended to be dangerous, but most were naive and harmless.

Atherton was arrogant, ignorant, and thought his opinion was the most important in the crowd, but at least he didn't ignore Evie or belittle her. He was rude to Jamie, but that was because he wanted to be the top rooster of the flock, a common enough response to a stranger in their midst.

Jamie was being generous to the man, he observed to himself. But he'd firmed his conviction that Atherton did not deserve a beautiful and vibrant woman like Evie.

"You don't like him." Iris Georgiou, who walked close to Jamie, said in a low voice. Iris was a lovely young woman, apparently unattached, and Jamie ought to turn his attentions to her. So why didn't he?

He politely offered his arm. "Atherton?" he asked as though he had no idea who she meant.

Iris slid her fingers to the crook of his elbow, but Jamie's heart didn't pump like mad as it did whenever Evie touched him. "You are polite, but you don't like him," she said.

Jamie shrugged. "I can see how he'd appeal to some." Gentlemen of like temperament, perhaps. He was a bit baffled by what Evie saw in him, though Atherton might have been a paragon of good manners while he courted her.

"I suppose," Iris answered doubtfully. "His father is a model of respectability and rather shoves this onto everyone. Mr. Atherton is a touch rebellious for that, and bandies his opinions about." Iris watched Atherton trot around the corner after Evie, her mouth turning down.

"You don't like him either," Jamie stated.

Iris shook her head. "I don't think he's right for our Evie."

"You've known her a long time?"

"Since university. Though I haven't seen her for a long while. She met Mr. Atherton, oh, a year ago now. She told me about him in her letters. He's at a loose end—he has a place in his father's business but he doesn't want to be tied to it for the rest of his life. Except he doesn't know how to do anything else. He won't try anything new, because he's afraid of being poor. Evie hasn't said this outright, but I can see that in him."

Jamie had some understanding about living in a father's shadow. He had not only a brilliant father but uncles who were all geniuses at something. Jamie was trying to be a genius, but whatever his particular talent was, it eluded him. *Except for getting myself smashed up, arrested, or in trouble,* he amended.

"Who do you think would be good enough for our Evie?" Jamie asked Iris as they turned up a narrow street that ended in Bedford Square.

Iris's eyes twinkled. "I'm not sure. Perhaps I haven't met him yet."

She laughed, and Jamie wondered if she'd seen right through him.

The teashop where Evie waited with Atherton was full of middle-aged, middle-class ladies, who looked up with interest at the four young people entering. Jamie saw them easily discern that Evie was with Atherton—Atherton bounded to the table and made a show of settling Evie. They also decided that Jamie was with Iris, which Iris found highly amusing. Jamie politely held her chair and made sure she was comfortable, deciding not to be a boor.

Iris grew quiet, though with an air of purpose, as the waitress brought tea and a large platter of scones and cakes. Evie became more agitated, splashing tea as she poured out. Atherton was the only one unbothered, shoving half a scone into his mouth before anyone else had reached for the food.

"Have you got a flask on you?" Atherton asked across the table to Jamie as he chewed. "Full of the best Scots whisky?"

Jamie did, in fact, but he saw no reason to upset the matrons in the tearoom by dolloping it into his and Atherton's cups.

Evie sank back into her chair, clenching her teacup, when Iris turned determinedly to Jamie. "The truth is, we want your help, Mr. Mackenzie," Iris said quietly.

Evie clearly did *not* want Jamie's help, but Iris launched into a tale that had Jamie forgetting about the whisky and his annoyance at Atherton. Atherton added to the narrative from time to time, though Evie sat like a stone.

Jamie leaned back when Iris and Atherton had finished. The teashop had begun to empty as the ladies finished their repasts, and soon the four were relatively alone.

"Have I got this right?" Jamie asked in amazement. "You want to nip down to the basement of the British Museum, nick an ancient jar, wrap it in paper, and decamp with it back to Athens?"

From the nods around the table, they did.

"It is very important, Mr. Mackenzie," Iris said. "My father stands to be shamed."

"Which is why you agreed so adamantly about antiquities staying in their own country," Jamie realized. "Your father gave this jar away when he shouldn't have? That is the gist of the matter?"

"He meant well." Iris sat in misery. "He was trying to bring about a treaty between Britain and Greece, and one of the ministers who had been sent to Athens admired the pottery. Father decided to gift him an alabastron."

"Without permission." Jamie chewed his lower lip. "Unwise."

"No one would have known," Iris said. "My father thought it an unimportant piece, sitting in dust on a basement shelf, but the British minister was impressed. So he should have been. An Athenian journalist traced a red-figure alabastron by Kontos, one of the few artisans who signed his pieces, to a storage room in the department of antiquities. When the journalist went to see the jar, it had gone. The department thinks it has only been misplaced, but when they realize they don't have it at all ..."

"There will be a hue and cry," Jamie finished. "Your poor dad."

"If anyone discovers my father simply handed it over to a British official, he is done for," Iris said unhappily. "He wanted to confess all, but I convinced him to come to London with me and try to get the jar back. The minister, unfortunately, was no help. He said he'd donated the jar to the British Museum, and that was the end of the matter. The museum hasn't even put it on display that we've seen, and so far have made no indication they know what it is. I fear to tell the museum curators outright what has happened and ask for the alabastron back, because the story will get out, and my father ruined all the same. They likely won't part with it anyway." She finished, dejected.

Jamie switched his gaze to Evie. "And what do you have to do with all this, McKnight?"

Atherton answered before Evie could. "Miss Georgiou thought Evie could help. So they arranged to meet once Evie returned from New York. Evie has the mad idea that we should steal it back." Atherton lifted his teacup, his eyes dancing. "What fun."

Jamie observed the three of them — Iris hopeful, Atherton entertained, and Evie distressed. Evie had not wanted them to tell him, Jamie recognized. Hence her irritation and long strides along the street.

"Why exactly did you confide in me?" Jamie asked. "What do you expect me to do?"

Atherton smirked. "Help us steal it, of course."

CHAPTER 10

*J*amie regarded the three of them in disbelief. "Why do you believe *I* can help?"

His resistance was a token one. As soon as he'd understood what they had in mind, he'd decided he'd be in it right next to Evie. It was a daft idea, but the hell he'd let her risk the attempt without him beside her.

Iris answered for the group. "Because you know people in the museum. And about antique pottery—you can help make sure we take back the correct item."

Jamie winced and rubbed his brow. "Please do not tell me you don't even know what this jar looks like."

"I have a drawing," Iris said. "And a photograph, though it's a bit blurry. I've never seen it myself, no."

"We are hoping it is labeled," Evie put in.

"Hoping it is ..." Jamie groaned. "Damnation." He took his hand from his face. "What is your plan?" he asked warily.

"Easy enough," Atherton leaned forward eagerly. "Wait until the museum is closed. Find a back window—it's an old building, and I'm certain we can force one open. Miss Georgiou did not see the jar on display today—we suspected it wouldn't be, but we thought we'd better check. It must be in storage, so we'll root around there until we find it. Should be quiet enough at night. The guards will only be patrolling the main part of the museum."

"Oh, aye?" Jamie said in amazement. "Root around in storerooms that contain tens of thousands of items and *hope* your pot is labeled? Meanwhile, someone calls the police when they see four people climbing through the back window. You won't have much time to search, trust me. And who knows who'll be in the basement rooms? Researchers and archeologists keep odd hours."

"Yes, I thought of all this," Evie stated, with an air of one who had argued her points and lost.

"How did you plan to carry off the alabastron? Put it under your coat and climb back out the window? And then what? Hail a hansom? Lug it to a Tube station?"

From the exchange of glances, this was exactly what they'd had in mind.

Jamie regarded them with pity. "Well, I'm glad ye decided to come to me. As thieves you are decidedly lacking in skills."

"Oh?" Atherton said, a bit huffily. "And you are good at it?"

"Let's say I've wriggled out of some tight places in my life. Let me think this over and come up with a better plan than your reckless one. At the very least, I'll provide the transportation. My cousin will lend me one of his motorcars."

Iris looked hopeful, but Atherton scoffed. "A noisy, chugging machine that draws every eye? Shall we pause in our getaway while you crank it to life?"

"Not necessarily." Jamie gave them a wise smile. "You leave the transport to me. Miss Georgiou, may I borrow your pictures of the jar? I will narrow down where it might be kept without everyone in London knowing there's an interest in it."

"Yes, of course." Iris began scrabbling through the loose bag she carried and pulled out a few thin papers. Evie took them from her, folded them, and passed them to Jamie, making sure their fingers did not touch as she handed them off.

Jamie tucked the pages into his pocket without looking at them. "Thank you. When will this event take place?"

Evie and Iris glanced at each other. "Soon," Evie said. "Iris does not know when her father will be called back to Athens — or when he'll flee there, riddled with guilt. We thought this Monday night."

It was Saturday. "No," Jamie said firmly. "If you rush things, they will go wrong. Give me time to research. I might even be able to fetch the jar myself without any window-breaking at all."

"That would be wonderful," Iris said in relief.

Atherton appeared disappointed in this scenario, but this was probably the most exciting event he'd been a part of in a long while. "I suppose you're right, Mackenzie. Very well — you find things out, and we'll wait for your report."

"Wiser to." Jamie traced the rim of his teacup. "One question. Why have you decided to trust me? I could run straight to the museum officials, or the minister in question, or anyone on the Cabinet who'd listen to me."

"You're a friend of Evie's," Iris said promptly.

"Besides, you're a Mackenzie," Atherton put in. "Everyone knows your duke uncle would stick it to our government anytime he was able. I've also heard you've run around the world a time or two, helping in hopeless causes."

So Atherton had looked into Jamie's background, had he? Jamie grinned at him. "You consider this a hopeless cause?"

Atherton laughed weakly. "I hope not."

"I haven't lost one yet." Jamie lifted his cup. "Let us drink to it, my friends."

They clicked cups and gulped tea, Evie relaxing at last. She alone had not put forth a reason why the group should trust Jamie.

"WILL YOU LET ME TALK YOU OUT OF THIS?" JAMIE ASKED Evie when they left the teashop. This time, Atherton escorted Iris, leaving Jamie to offer Evie his arm.

"No." Evie only lightly rested her fingers on Jamie's elbow, but the spark that leapt through him made him long to seize her and leap into the nearest carriage, wrest the reins from the driver, and not stop until he'd fled with her far from here.

Jamie drew a breath, calming his wild urge. "I wish I had friends who contemplated breaking into museums for me."

"Iris's father stands to lose everything. He could be made an example of by any of his rivals. The whole family might be disgraced, making things very difficult for Iris and her sisters." Evie sighed. "The safest course is to return the alabastron and be done with it."

"I do understand his predicament." Jamie rested his hand over hers and hid his regret when Evie quickly withdrew. "Shame he didn't find out what the devil this jar was before he went and gave it away."

"Yes, Iris is very irritated with her father." Evie walked stiffly, her arms now at her sides. "It seems he does things on whims. Even sending Iris to school in England was a whim, but it is one I'm happy he had."

"Good friends are a treasure," Jamie agreed.

"Where are yours?" Evie asked him abruptly.

Jamie blinked. "Pardon?"

"I have very dear friends, as well as my sisters. Each time I've encountered you, you've been alone."

Jamie hid a pang. "If you have to know, I have plenty of mates. I admit they're scattered around the world at the moment. A few deceased."

"Oh." Evie's voice changed. "I'm sorry."

"It happens." Jamie shut out thoughts of those killed in the hopeless causes he'd mentioned. "No one is immortal. But don't feel sorry for me. I come from a very large family, and my cousins and I are close. No matter how exasperating they are."

Evie's face softened with her smile. "Like Gavina. I met her."

"Did you?" Jamie's interest perked. "When? At Cambridge?"

"No. The night we stayed at the Langham. She dropped by looking for something and found us there."

Jamie's interest quickly turned to disquiet. "Did she now?"

Dropped by looking for something, had she? That smelled of a fat lie. Jamie thought of how quickly Alec had departed from him that night, after Jamie had been evasive about the Langham. Jamie wagered his wily coz had sent in Gavina to spy, the rat.

He wondered why she hadn't charged to him and demanded to know why he'd been evasive about Evie. Discretion? Not a word one associated with Gavina.

"I was glad to meet her," Evie was saying. "I found her quite agreeable."

Oh, Gavina could be agreeable. Or the most dangerous woman in London, depending on her mood.

"I will give her your regards," Jamie said. *When I see her and shake her.*

"Do. I'd be happy to meet her again."

Evie looked so pleased that Jamie didn't have the heart to explain what Gavina had truly been up to.

The others had halted to wait for them. "Where is this famous motorcar?" Atherton asked in eagerness.

"No need," Evie said quickly. "Here is a hansom." She waved at the driver. "Besides, your mother and father already admonished me for riding in the motorcar, Hayden, and I do not wish to displease them."

Atherton's regret was plain, but his eyes flickered when Evie mentioned his parents. He clearly did not want to sit through another lecture either.

"Well, I'll leave you to it," Jamie said as the cab halted. "I will report to you, McKnight, since you seem to be the general."

Atherton shot him an annoyed glance—he likely wanted to be the general, poor sod.

"Thank you, Mr. Mackenzie." Iris's words were sincere. "You are too kind."

"Yes, thank you." Evie echoed her friend. "I am staying with Mr. Atherton's family, so send word to both of us there."

Jamie wasn't certain he trusted a message handed to Atherton's servants, but he'd do what he could.

"You will hear from me soon," Jamie promised.

He handed Iris into the cab and made himself walk away before he leapt to assist Evie, using that as an excuse to stay near her warmth. Her faint smile of farewell as Atherton helped her in wrapped around his heart and tangled there.

———

MAC MACKENZIE LIVED WITH HIS WIFE ISABELLA AND family in a tall townhouse in North Audley Street. He'd once upon a time had a splendid home in Mount Street, but after problems in their marriage, followed by a fire, Mac had moved in with Isabella in North Audley Street. Theirs had been a complicated relationship, but all was sunshine now.

Jamie arrived at their home late in the afternoon and was admitted by a footman who told him Mac was in his studio.

That meant a climb to the very top of the house, which Jamie began, tramping heavily up the stairs.

On the second landing, Jamie met a young woman with red-blonde hair on her way down. She was in a white tennis dress with puffed sleeves, the skirt short enough to reveal her soft, low-heeled shoes.

"Where did you spring from, Jamie?" she asked breezily.

Aimee Mackenzie was three years older than Jamie, and

had hazel eyes that were almost golden. Though Aimee was not blood-related—she'd been adopted as a child away from cruel circumstances—she resembled the Mackenzies closely enough to make people whisper about her origins.

"The gray stones of London's streets," Jamie said. "Does Uncle Mac know you're going out showing your ankles?"

"Pish." Aimee laughed at him. "I'm meeting friends for a game, and I'm far too old for any man to be excited by my ankles."

Aimee wasn't old at all, and quite beautiful. Her unknown background, however, made the snobs of London warn their sons against proposing to her, which perturbed Jamie more than he could say.

Jamie shrugged as if unconcerned. "Well, smash a good lob, or whatever it is you do in tennis."

"You're hopeless. I will greet my friends for you. Half of them are in love with you, heaven knows why." Aimee sashayed past him in a swirl of white, bouncing on light feet.

It was his day for women to laugh at him, Jamie reflected, as he continued up the stairs to Mac's studio.

Jamie didn't bother knocking at the door that led off the small landing at the top of the staircase. Uncle Mac would never hear him. He stepped into a large room, well lit by skylights admitting whatever sunshine penetrated London's gloom.

Mac wore his usual painting gear, a plaid kerchief over his hair, a kilt slung casually about his hips, his feet bare and splattered with paint. Today he'd also donned a painting smock, loose at his neck. He must not yet have grown frenzied enough to tear the thing off and hurl it across the room.

He scowled at his canvas a moment before swiping bright red paint onto it. Jamie couldn't see the picture from this angle, but the palette, not to mention Mac's smock and kilt, held plenty of red, yellow, and orange.

Jamie knew better than to announce himself, or ask Uncle

Mac what he was painting, or speak to him in any way. He sauntered to the old sofa with sagging cushions and plopped himself onto it.

Mac went on slashing paint, all the while glaring at his creation. Jamie lifted a newspaper, likely one of Aunt Isabella's, and leafed through it while he waited.

He'd been in this room so often throughout his life, it was like a second home. As a child he'd played up here with his three cousins—Aimee, Eileen, and Robert—while Aunt Isabella lounged on this very sofa, reading, keeping an eye on the children, and humming under her breath.

When Jamie had become old enough to understand such things, he'd learned that sometimes Mac and Isabella shut themselves in here and locked the door, while Mac painted pictures of Isabella, nude ones. Eileen had informed him this in tones of hushed embarrassment, but Jamie, as they weren't *his* parents, found it amusing.

The newspaper he read was a recent one. Jamie found himself staring at a large photograph of the heiress Imogen Carmichael, taken as she'd stood on the docks after disembarking the *Baltic*.

The headlines were the usual rubbish: *American heiress crosses the seas in search of matrimonial bliss. Shall she have a duke? An earl? Perhaps even a prince?*

"Lovely girl." Uncle Mac now stood at the end of the sofa, minus palette and brush. "Poor thing. Excellent photograph of you, though."

Mac reached a beefy hand to turn the page, revealing an equally massive photograph of Jamie, turned toward the gangplank of the giant ship. Miss Carmichael couldn't be seen in this picture, but the manner in which the photos had been taken made it appear as though Jamie and Miss Carmichael gazed across the crowds at each other.

Mr. Jamie Mackenzie, most eligible nephew of the Duke of

Kilmorgan watches the arrival of the Baltic *and its very special passenger with great interest.*

Jamie recalled the photographer who'd set up his apparatus right next to him. He groaned and tossed the paper aside. "Damnation. If I see that photographer again, I'll turn him inside out."

Mac chuckled. "It's the curse of the Mackenzies. Any delicious tidbit about us that might turn to scandal is smacked into the newspapers."

"I am pleased I can amuse you, Uncle Mac."

"Don't let them cow you." Mac lost his smile, though his golden eyes danced. "Your aunt is more worried about the other party. She's afraid the young lady will have her heart crushed by you."

"I don't even know the bloody woman." Jamie tossed away the paper in exasperation. It crashed to the floor and lay still.

Mac dropped to the other end of the sofa, stretching out his long legs. "She's staying at the Langham, and you went there the other day."

"So did Gavina. Why isn't there a spread of photographs in a newspaper about that?"

"Hmm. In some very bohemian papers, there might be. So —you are not after the heiress?"

"No," Jamie said emphatically.

"Ah." Mac rubbed his head, staining the kerchief with a splotch of yellow paint. "I thought you'd come to ask my advice about how to court her."

"Ha. I know how *you* court women. Arrive uninvited to their debut ball and elope with them that very night."

A grin split Mac's face. "It worked, laddie. You know it did. I now have a beautiful wife and three adorable children. Don't tell Robbie I said that. He hates being called adorable."

"Your secret is safe with me," Jamie said without amusement.

Mac studied him with sudden shrewdness. He could shift

in an instant from careless barefoot artist to wise man with great insight who wouldn't let Jamie get away with anything.

"You're not usually bothered when you're plastered across the newspapers," Mac observed. "You laugh. Now you're growling and bad-tempered. Why?"

Because Evie might see those photos and draw the wrong conclusion. She was already half-convinced he was smitten with Miss Carmichael. He did not want Evie to believe it, or she might not trust his intentions toward *her*. Jamie wanted her to trust him without doubt.

The article was not fair to Miss Carmichael either. She must be wondering who the devil was this unkempt Highlander the newspapers insisted on pairing her with.

"The photographer on the dock annoyed me, that's all," Jamie said. "Cheek of him."

"I see." Mac didn't believe the explanation, but Jamie did not intend to elaborate. He didn't need to—Gavina would sooner or later spread the tale of Evie at the Langham.

Interesting that the photographer chappie, who'd had a perfect opportunity to snap a shot of Jamie with Evie, hadn't printed *that*. Because Evie was nobody, in the newspapers' eyes. Bloody fools.

"What I came to ask you about is Greek pots," Jamie said, returning to his purpose. "Or alabastrons. One in particular."

Mac blinked. "Greek …"

"Antiquities. The black ones with red figures on them. Valuable, are they?"

Mac rested elbows on knees as he peered at Jamie. "Why the devil are you asking me about Greek pottery? I'm not an expert."

"You dragged me to see them when I was younger," Jamie said impatiently. "Went on about how important it was that I became steeped in art."

"It *is* important. But I have cursory knowledge of Greek art. Let us say I wasn't attentive in school."

True, Mac had been a wild and carefree young man, running away as soon as he could to learn painting at the feet of Eduard Manet and Berthe Morisot.

"All right then, you will know *someone* who knows something."

Mac's eyes narrowed. "Are you going to tell me about your sudden fascination with Greek alabastrons?"

"I don't believe I am. Not now, anyway."

"Mmm."

Mac continued to study him, but what Jamie liked about Uncle Mac was that he didn't judge him. Uncle Cameron would growl and threaten until Jamie confessed, and Uncle Hart would pin him with a golden-eyed stare that would have Jamie either telling him everything or finding a sudden excuse to be elsewhere.

Mac assessed, but kept his thoughts to himself.

"I can probably dredge up an expert. I have a friend who works in the dusty bowels of the British Museum—"

"No. Not from there." A man alerted to what Jamie was searching for in the basement would notice its absence if Jamie's plan came off.

Mac's brows lowered. "All right, there's Clive Blackstone, but he's a stuffy git. Knows his urns from his bowls, though."

"I'm only seeking general knowledge," Jamie said. He considered what would make Mac back down from this quiet interrogation. "Want to impress a lady."

Mac's expression lightened, but Jamie could see in his eyes that the explanation didn't quite ring true.

"You're a Mackenzie, through and through. Never mind— I'll hunt up Blackstone and he'll bore you with a lecture. How soon do you need to impress this young woman?"

"Sooner the better." Jamie rose. "Tomorrow?"

Mac sprang lightly to his feet. "Tomorrow it is. Now, cease distracting me. I can't get my shadows right."

Mac was a brilliant painter, and Jamie had no doubt the

shadows would be the best ever done once he was finished. Jamie slid out past him, giving himself a glance at the painting —which was incredibly beautiful, even half-finished—and departed.

———

EVIE OPENED THE NOTE THAT LANDED AT HER PLACE AT THE Atherton breakfast table a few mornings later, her heart beating faster as she observed the scrawled *JM* at the bottom.

Amenhotep III, Thursday, six pm. Burn this.

Very melodramatic, Evie thought as she rose from her chair and made her way to the dining room fireplace. Sir Hector, buried in his newspaper, did not notice as Evie dropped the note to the flames and watched it crumple to ash.

The letters of Jamie's initials held fast until the end, when they vanished in a sudden spurt of flame.

CHAPTER 11

*A*t half past five in the evening on Thursday, Evie
skulked about the exhibits in the Egyptian wing of the
British Museum, trying not to check her watch too often.
Jamie's cryptic note meant she should meet him at the museum
at six, by the massive statue of Amenhotep III—or Amenhotep's head and arm, at least.

Evie nonchalantly gazed at the exhibits in the gallery,
working her way slowly toward the giant pillar that held the
pharaoh's colossal head. Jamie was nowhere in sight.

The museum would soon close to sightseers. A fine rain fell
outside, a mist rising. It would be a cold walk or hansom ride
back to Upper Brook Street if Mr. Mackenzie did not make an
appearance.

Evie moved to a stone sarcophagus, studying its hiero-
glyphs and pretending to read the card that told her all about
the piece.

A man called down the galleries that they would be closing.
*Please, ladies and gentlemen, make your way toward the doors, and
mind you retrieve your coats and umbrellas. Good evening.*

Evie hadn't relinquished her coat to the cloakroom, nor had
she brought an umbrella. She had no excuse to linger in the

gallery, as though waiting until the queue at the cloakroom grew smaller.

She reached Amenhotep's pedestal, feigning interest in the granite arm stretched beside it. It was rather spectacular, really, features perfectly chiseled in this very hard pink, black, and white speckled stone. The artisans had been quite skilled.

Good night, ladies and gentlemen.

People flowed through and out of the gallery, and soon the guard would come along to usher out the stragglers. Evie slid behind Amenhotep's pillar, casting about for an excuse as to why she wasn't pouring out with the rest of the guests.

She suppressed a yelp as a hand landed on her arm. Evie whirled to behold Jamie, garbed in a flowing black greatcoat over his suit and kilt.

"This way, lass," he said under his breath.

He towed her against the stream of people into a much emptier gallery, then around a corner to a shadowy corridor. A door here opened to his touch, and Jamie pulled Evie into a small room darkening with gathering dusk and the rain.

"What are we doing?" Evie whispered after Jamie had silently shut the door.

"Hiding." Jamie frowned at her. "Where are Miss Georgiou and Atherton? If you don't mind staying alone in here, I'll fetch them."

Evie shook her head. "Neither came with me."

Jamie's eyes glittered in the dim light. "What do you mean, neither came with you?"

"Hayden was ordered by his father to work with him tonight," Evie said, her mouth tight. "He could contrive no excuse to accompany me—not that his father would have accepted one. Sir Hector wouldn't have let him off even if Hayden had been in the last throes of consumption."

Evie could not suppress her irritation. She and Hayden had enjoyed speculating on Jamie's plans, coming up with wilder and wilder guesses about what he'd wished to do. Evie had felt closer to Hayden than she'd ever had as they'd shared this secret excitement.

Then Hayden had announced this morning that his father insisted on his help this evening. Evie, distressed, had told him to write to Jamie to postpone the scheme, but Hayden had bade her to go on, fetch the alabastron, and be done with it. Evie had taken a long time to talk herself into meeting Jamie alone, but she feared this would be their best, perhaps only, chance to fetch the alabastron. She'd decided to take the risk, and make certain she kept herself at arm's length from Jamie.

"I must be honest with you, lass." Jamie interrupted her thoughts. "I'm not sure Atherton would be of use to us anyway. But what about Miss Georgiou? This is her battle."

Evie shook her head. "I forbade her to come. If I am caught, or you are, it's a mad lark by young people trying to stave off their ennui. Or, if you'll not mind me saying, another wild scheme by one of the Mackenzies. If Iris was caught, everything would be so much worse—a diplomat's daughter trying to steal a Greek artifact from the British Museum? That would be all over the newspapers, her father ridiculed just the same."

"I take your point." Jamie nodded his approval, which for some reason pleased Evie inordinately. "Ah, well, lass, we will have to muddle through on our own."

"How? What is the wonderful plan you've come up with?"

"Something very simple." He turned a convenient key in the door, locking them in. "Now, we remain quiet until the guards have cleared the museum."

"Won't they check this room?" Evie whispered.

"No."

Jamie wouldn't explain why not. But the finality of his word made Evie believe him. She wondered if he'd slipped a guard a few coins to make sure this locked door was not bothered.

Rain fell steadily outside the high window, the gray patch

of sky growing darker as they waited. The small room was chilly, in spite of Evie's coat, but Jamie's nearby warmth kept her from shivering.

They didn't speak further. Evie feared any word or sound would carry in the emptying museum, and Jamie folded his arms and leaned against the wall, lips pressed together.

If a guard *did* open the door to find them here, what would he think? Not, *Aha, clever thieves have been discovered.* No, he'd believe Jamie and Evie were in here for amorous purposes. He might be shocked, or he might laugh.

It was a clever hiding place in that respect. Even if Hayden had come along, the guards would only have had the titillation of finding a young lady with *two* suitors. Evie's reputation would be in tatters—at least among the guards of the British Museum—but it was unlikely they would suspect an attempted a heist. Being tutted at by museum guards was better than spending a night in the nick.

In any event, no one approached the door, rattled the knob, or tried to unlock it. Either Jamie *had* paid the guards not to disturb them, or it did not occur to them that anyone would be daft enough to hide in this dank, dusty, cold, and cramped storage closet.

Jamie could have taken advantage of being alone with Evie, but he remained a few feet from her, the perfect gentleman. She'd heard that the Mackenzie men, including those of Jamie's generation, had the reputation for beguiling women into their beds whenever they wished. Ladies obliged by throwing themselves at their feet, sometimes literally.

Jamie made no move to enfold Evie in his arms, press her against the wall, take her mouth in a savage kiss. No giving into the excitement of their mission to slide his hands down her body, kissing her as he had that day by the sunny river.

A good thing, Evie reminded herself. She was an engaged young lady, he a from a family with a terrible reputation. A very good thing. No need to feel disappointed that he showed no interest.

Evie tried to make herself believe this as she hunkered against the cold wall. Jamie remained perfectly still, his bulk fading as the darkness took over in the streets outside.

She'd begun to imagine they'd been in this room for hours, when Jamie whispered, "Time, lass."

Evie suppressed a groan as she moved her stiff limbs. "You couldn't have brought a camp chair?" she asked softly. "Or a cot?"

Jamie chuckled, a quiet sound. "Couldn't smuggle them in under my coat. Now, silence."

The lock made the tiniest click, and then the door opened a slit. The dim night lights in the museum seemed bright to Evie's dark-accustomed eyes, and she closed them briefly.

"We'll take a moment to adjust." Jamie's warm breath brushed her ear. "Then down the stairs."

Evie nodded. After a long time, during which Evie tried to calm her breathing, Jamie stepped out into the corridor, nudging her to follow.

Evie lifted her skirt and went after him, immediately tripping over the door's threshold. Jamie grasped her elbow, steadying her. He gave her no admonishment or teasing criticism, as Hayden would, only guided her through the darkness.

She experienced a moment of watery panic when the floor seemed to vanish in front of her, and then realized they'd come to the top of a staircase. Evie clung shamelessly to Jamie's arm as he led her down the long flight, which emerged into the lower floor of the museum.

There were galleries here as well, filled with Assyrian relief sculptures. Fascinating pieces, but now they were so many black bulks in the deeper darkness.

Jamie seemed to know precisely where he was going. He towed her down the gallery, dodging pedestals and glass cases, the occasional window letting in very faint light.

He halted before a door at the end of the gallery. Unlike the door of the storage room upstairs, this one was tall, solid, and obviously meant to keep people out. The door handle was large, as was its lock. A formidable key would be needed.

Light flared, then Jamie pressed something hard into Evie's hand. "Hold that steady."

An electric torch, Evie marveled, studying the device. She had seen them but never used one. When Hayden had casually mentioned purchasing one at supper one night, his father had gone into a half-hour tirade about how newfangled toys were destroying Britain and the integrity of everyone in it.

The torch's light wasn't all that bright but it was enough to illuminate the lock. The torch was warm from the battery and its journey inside Jamie's coat.

Metal rattled as Jamie sorted through a ring of long, thin rods.

"Lockpicks?" Evie's whisper was nearly silent.

"Borrowed from m' cousin." Jamie's answer was equally soundless.

He chose one and inserted it into the lock, then inserted a second lockpick above it.

"Turn off the torch now," he whispered.

Evie had no idea how, but then her questing fingers found a switch that plunged them into darkness.

The scrape of the lockpicks sounded loud to Evie, who glanced nervously over her shoulder at the corridor behind them. Happily, no footsteps broke the quiet, no lights bobbed. The guards must be busy patrolling the upper floors, or perhaps having tea and a good natter.

Jamie continued to scrape, letting out a grunt in frustration.

Evie leaned to him. "Perhaps you ought to have brought your cousin."

"And have Uncle Cam thrash me until I can't walk for three years? No, thank you."

Evie knew Jamie exaggerated—at least she hoped so. "Is he that protective of his son?"

"Of his daughter. Yes, he is."

As the picks went on scratching Evie realized he must mean the beautiful Gavina. Gracious.

"Ah." The lock clicked and Jamie turned the handle, the door creaking open. He thrust the picks into his pocket, took the torch from Evie, and switched it on. "My lady." He gestured her inside.

Evie peered into the dank blackness that the torch barely illuminated. "No, no. You first."

Jamie chuckled and slipped inside. Evie followed closely, then Jamie shut the door firmly behind them.

Evie could not stop her gasp when Jamie flashed the torch around. The light revealed row upon row of shelves upon shelves, all of which were piled with boxes, bits of pottery, ledgers, and loose paper.

"Good heavens," she breathed.

Jamie walked slowly forward, Evie at his heels. She did not want to move beyond the circle of light.

"How the devil are we to find one jar in all of this?" Evie asked in shock.

"Because I now know exactly what we're looking for. An alabastron, not a jar."

"Yes, I know what it is, Mr. Scholar. It's for carrying oils or perfumes. This one is about eight inches high and four around, Iris says."

"With red-figure paintings. And …" Jamie passed Evie the torch again. She, not expecting it, almost dropped it, but managed to hang on to it. Jamie reached into a pocket inside his coat and pulled out some papers. Two were what Iris had given him, and a third held spidery writing. "Lady holding a necklace," he read. "A box of them at her feet. On the opposite side, a gent peddling more necklaces. Made in Attica some-where around 500 BC."

Evie shone the light on the paper, which contained a very detailed line drawing, much clearer than the vague sketch Iris had found. "Where did you get that?"

"From someone who knows much more about this alabastron than I do. Wizened old gent my Uncle Mac directed me to. I mentioned to him the piece that has the journalists in Greece all excited, and he knew all about it. He was happy for my interest, and didn't question why. Gave me all the details."

"I hope he won't peach about your many questions," Evie said darkly. "Especially when we're standing in the dock at the Old Bailey."

"Peach? Where did you learn words like that, young lady?" Jamie's voice held laughter. "Blackstone has no interest in governments or ministers or faux pas by diplomats. Mac says the man hasn't left his own house in ten years or more. He's interested in the things for their own sakes, and could care less where they are, who wants them, or why giving them away could wreck a person's life."

Evie gazed at the many shelves again. "Well, we can't be arrested for stealing if we can't locate it." She blew out a breath. "This could take all night."

Jamie turned the paper over. "Blackmore also knows a bloke who catalogs pieces for the museum. Logs them on a sheet, stashes the piece on a shelf. Many never to be seen again, even by the cataloger." He waved his hand toward their left. "Alabastrons from Attica, somewhere in this direction."

"That does not narrow it down much."

Jamie shrugged and tucked away the paper. "Better than nothing. Are you sure Atherton could not be here? Three searchers would make things quicker."

"Very sure. His father is a martinet. No excuses, least of all running about with his frivolous fiancée."

Jamie abruptly played the torch over her. "You? Frivolous?" He sounded incredulous.

Evie shielded her eyes. "I am not sure your tone is compli-
mentary, Mackenzie. You make me sound dull as ditchwater."

Jamie lowered the light. "The man will have the sweetest,
kindest, funniest young lady for a daughter-in-law, and he is
complaining? That is, as long as she'd not wielding an oar. Sir
Hector needs his head thumped."

He swung away, leaving Evie open-mouthed, her heart
speeding. The words, delivered in Jamie's offhand manner,
sank into her, a welcome fire in this chill dankness.

CHAPTER 12

She was right, Jamie reflected as they began to search the shelves. This would take all bloody night.

Not that Jamie minded groping about in the dark with Evie. They had to stick together, because he'd only brought one torch—he'd assumed Atherton would bring something of the sort along to help.

Sod Atherton. He should have told his father to go to the devil rather than let Evie venture to the museum to meet Jamie alone. Atherton would have known Iris wouldn't be here.

Jamie himself should have abandoned the plan as soon as Evie had told her Atherton wasn't coming, but he hadn't been able to bring himself to send her away.

Atherton's absence meant Jamie brushed against Evie time and again as they searched, breathed the scent of her, basked in her warmth. Upstairs in the tight storage closet, it had taken all his fortitude to stay as far from her as possible.

Evie's arm skimmed the length of his torso as she reached for a box. If her hand had gone any lower, she'd have found the beginning of a fine cockstand under his tartan.

"Not here," Evie said in disappointment as she peered inside the box. "This is impossible."

Jamie rubbed her shoulder. "Not impossible. Just tedious. There's a difference."

Her eyes flashed in the torch's light. "Is there, Mackenzie?"

She was annoyed, scared, and wanting to be elsewhere. He couldn't blame her.

Jamie softened his tone. "I've built flying machines—my life depends on whether I get everything right, down to the last tiny bolt. I've learned to go slowly and methodically. No action is trivial, and even an error can teach a very important lesson."

Evie regarded him in stillness. Bored with his bothersome lecture? "You *build* aeroplanes?

Not boredom. Excitement. Jamie felt something in him waken.

"Aye. And crash them. I have bones I feel on rainy nights. Building them has taught me to focus on one thing at a time."

Her scrutiny was flattering. Enticing. Hotly, hungrily so.

"Once we find Iris's alabastron, I'll take you up sometime," Jamie offered as though he didn't care one way or the other. Like a friend casually saying, *Let's have dinner one night*.

"Oh." Evie's smile blossomed. "I'd like that."

There were only two seats in an aeroplane. That meant Jamie and Evie alone. No Atherton.

Who must be a complete idiot. Why wouldn't the man move heaven and earth to be with Evie tonight? Why refuse to tell Jamie they had to postpone?

Jamie's curiosity stirred. If Atherton wasn't truly an ingenuous fool, then he was up to something.

Jamie motioned with the torch that they should get on with it ... before he took Evie into his arms and kissed her. And kissed her. They were quite alone in this room, and there were plenty of shelves, benches, chairs ...

The search took another two hours. Each shelf held boxes that were neatly labeled—a typed card on the shelf before them—but there were so many alabastrons in this basement that Jamie had already become thoroughly tired of them. Had the treasure hunters in Greece and Italy left *any* alabastrons unearthed?

"Wait." Evie's excited word dragged Jamie from his thoughts.

"Wait, what?" Jamie peered over her shoulder into the box she'd pulled down.

"I think this is it. Let me see the paper."

Jamie handed over Blackstone's description without much enthusiasm. They'd found several alabastrons with ladies trying on jewelry that almost, but didn't quite, match the one they searched for. None of them had been signed. A potter in ancient Attica must have made a job lot of these, pretending to be the famous bloke.

"Yes—look." Evie's fingers fluttered. "The necklaces are the same, the vessels hanging behind her are the same, the letters are the same."

"Kontos," Jamie read, his heart beating faster. The potter's name.

Evie's hands were steady on the alabastron though her body trembled with elation. "We did it, Mackenzie. We found it."

Jamie wanted to punch the air, then drag Evie into his arms and kiss her until they both gasped for breath.

He controlled himself with effort. Finding the blasted jar was only the first step. They were a long way from finished.

Jamie tugged a dark cloth from his coat pocket. He took the jar from Evie's grasp and wrapped it into a tight bundle. "Hold on to that."

"Certainly." Evie took the swaddled alabastron from him then watched, mystified, as he pulled a smaller but exquisitely made jar from another pocket. "What is *that*?"

"Something to keep the box from being empty." This jar was pretty, painted jet black with tiny red figures on it. It wasn't quite dry and smelled of shellac, but it would have to do.

"That looks nothing like Iris's alabastron," Evie pointed out.

"I know." Jamie placed it into the box, reflecting that it was a pity Robbie's work would be lost forever in this basement. He brought out a card and set it in front of the box, taking away the one that identified the vessel they'd just pilfered. *Pottery: Red-figure alabastron, 1908.*

The new one read *Pottery: Red-figure jar, 1908.*

"Where on earth did you obtain a piece of Greek pottery?" Evie asked in amazement. "I hope you didn't steal if from somewhere else."

Jamie tucked the old card into his coat. "My cousin made it."

"Gavina?"

"Robbie. Uncle Mac's son. He's becoming quite the artist, and is a very good copyist."

Evie gaped at him. "You asked if he could make an ancient-looking Greek jar for you? What on earth did he think?"

"He was happy to do it. Robbie likes a challenge."

"Do your cousins do everything you tell them to?" Evie asked in some exasperation. "Lend you lock picks, create a fake pot, ensure the concierge is bringing us food at the hotel?"

Jamie nodded. "Pretty much."

"You are an interesting man, Mackenzie."

"And you an interesting woman, McKnight. The lengths you'll go to, to help a friend."

Evie flushed. "Which we haven't done yet. What now? Do we wait until the museum opens in the morning and slide out among the visitors?"

"Not quite. The guards truly are diligent, and it's only a matter of time before they check down here. We are going to escape."

He flashed the torch at a dusty window high above them. He heard no response and brought the torch down to find Evie staring at him incredulously.

"Through that window? This is your marvelous idea?"

"There's a ladder." Jamie flashed the light on it. "That window emerges at ground level, on the north side of the building, where it's quietest. Nip around the corner, and you'll see my motorcar there."

"Motorcar?" Evie's eyes widened, blue and full of life. "You really did bring it. Hayden was right about the noise, you know."

"I thought of that—you'll understand when you reach it." Jamie handed Evie the torch and moved boxes he'd piled up by the window as he'd prepared the way this week, revealing the full extent of the ladder. "Off you go. Hide in the back of the motorcar and wait for me."

Evie started. "Wait for you? Are you not coming with me?"

"It's a bit of a tight fit for my frame. Don't worry, I scouted the way—why do you think it took me nearly a week to set things up?"

Evie lowered her voice, which had begun to rise. "Why didn't you nip in and find the alabastron while you were at it? Saved us much trouble?"

"Because I could only contrive a few minutes down here, and I didn't want to come too often. We needed a large stretch of time to properly search."

"Why don't we hide it down here and retrieve it tomorrow?" she demanded.

"Do you want to risk that? Some efficient charwoman discovering our bundle as she sweeps?"

"No." Evie clutched the cloth-bound jar to her chest. "Very well. Let us take the thing and be done."

"Exactly. I'll make sure you climb out without trouble. There's a berm right outside the window to give you some cover, but it won't be a soft landing. Up you go, and I'll hand you the jar."

Evie, resigned, relinquished the alabastron and put her foot on the first rung of the ladder. "Wait a minute. How will you get out? Sneak past the guards?"

"I'll ask them to let me out. I'm going to tell them I was caught in a room looking up something for my uncle when they locked the doors."

Evie's gaze turned impatient. "Why can't we both have been accidentally locked in? Instead of me climbing a ladder and running to your motorcar—in the rain?"

Jamie lost his amusement. "No, lass. What is the first thing they would assume if I emerged from a study room with you? I'm not having this adventure scar your reputation and cause your fiancée's family to turn you out. As far as the guards will be concerned, I was in here by myself, researching ancient art for Uncle Mac, and you will have nothing to do with any of it. Atherton was supposed to be here to help you, but as it is ..."

He watched Evie think it all through. "Oh, very well. Lucky I'm as fit as I am."

"I thought of that too." Jamie risked a grin. "Evie, the robust rower. Up you go."

"Not flattering, Mackenzie." Evie began to scramble up the ladder, not waiting for Jamie's assistance.

"That you are not a simpering, swooning chit who can't lift a teacup without having a rest afterward? A compliment, McKnight."

"I will consider whether to accept it."

Evie's voice faded as she climbed, then she ceased speaking altogether when she reached the window. Jamie had made certain it was unlatched.

Evie pushed it open, admitting a wave of cold, damp air into the stuffy basement. Jamie ascended the ladder, ready to assist her through and hand her the bundle once she made it outside.

Evie gathered her skirts. They were a bit shorter, he'd noted, like Aimee's tennis dress, but Evie wore stout, low-heeled boots instead of shoes for lawn tennis. Shapely legs appeared as she craned to see outside.

Jamie climbed up as far as he dared behind her, not wanting to overbalance the ladder and send them both crashing to the floor.

"Ready?" he whispered.

"Give me a moment."

Her beautiful calves flexed as she fixed the heavy window in place. Now to hope an enterprising constable wasn't strolling by outside.

Without warning, Evie swarmed upward, skirts swinging, and slithered out of the open window. Jamie had been ready to boost her, anticipating his hands on her soft backside, but she was gone before he could touch her.

Jamie quickly reached the window to see Evie, skirts hiked to her thighs, righting herself on the ground outside. White stockings hugged her legs, tied with satin garters. Jamie took a deep breath, sweat beading on his forehead.

There was almost no light on this corner of the building, Jamie's torch all the illumination they had. He pointed it downward to keep a betraying beam from shining across the road.

Evie crouched to look into the window. She was buttoned to her chin, but the curve of her breasts hovered at Jamie's eye level. He suppressed a growl of frustration—why had he thought this expedition a good idea?

Because the fiancé and friend were supposed to be here as a buffer between himself and Evie. Not Jamie and Evie working alone together.

Jamie could understand Evie's insistence that Iris stay behind—it was too much of a risk for her—but Atherton should have accompanied Evie, no matter what. The man was a cretin.

"Mackenzie." Evie startled him from his thoughts. "Stop woolgathering and hand me the pot."

Jamie passed the bundle to her without comment. "Go to the end of Montague Place and turn right. Mine is the only car on the street. Don't run. Walk casually, as though you have every business being there."

"It is raining, you know." The drops had started to patter down harder, the mist turning to full-on rain.

"Then walk quickly. I won't be long."

Evie stood up, shaking out skirts to hide her lovely limbs. She gave Jamie a glare but tucked the bundle under her coat and strode off.

He watched her with admiration. Evie moved just right, hurrying like a person annoyed by the rain but not one who'd just robbed a famous museum.

Jamie waited until she reached the corner, disappearing into the gloom, before he shut the window, descended the ladder, and made certain there was no trace of anyone having been in this room tonight.

———

Evie sped around the corner from Montague Place to Gower Street, relieved when she spied the bulk of a motorcar as promised. This was an entirely different motorcar, she saw as she neared it, from the one in which Jamie had squired them to the Langham.

This car was a marvel of luxury. Instead of having an open chassis like the red motorcar, a hard top enclosed it. A small seat for the driver was tucked in front, and larger, deeper seats for the passengers reposed behind it. Evie couldn't tell the color in the rainy murk, but something dark and gleaming.

Evie waited until the street was empty before she calmly opened a rear door and climbed inside.

Blankets had been piled on the cushioned seat. Evie pulled one around her and hunkered down into its welcome warmth.

It was cold outside, and wet, but Evie's heart beat hotly in triumph. They had the alabastron, thanks to Jamie. Iris could take it to Greece and slip it back into the collection from which it had come, and if their luck held, no one would be the wiser.

Evie laid herself on the seat, not wanting the silhouette of her head to show in the large windows. She dared peek out a time or two, but the pouring rain blotted out the bulk of the museum as well as much of the street. Very few were about— sensible people had retreated into their warm houses, and would be sitting down to a good supper about now. Evie's stomach growled.

She'd popped up a third time when she at last spied the large form of Jamie jogging leisurely toward the car.

He said nothing at all to her as he climbed inside, wiping rain from his face. Jamie glanced once into the back, Evie giving him a wan smile from her hiding place, then he turned resolutely forward.

Evie expected he'd have to crank-start the car, as he'd done at the station, but Jamie only pressed a button on the dash. No rumble of motor answered, not even a hum. Had the engine stalled? Would they have to hunt for transport in the rain after all?

Evie stifled a squeak when the car glided noiselessly forward. She noted then that there was no steering wheel, only a vertical lever that Jamie moved with his gloved hand.

The car rolled slowly along the street and around the corner of Bedford Square, continuing in its smooth but slow pace.

After a time, Jamie said to her over his shoulder, "You can sit up now."

Evie cautiously pressed aside the blanket and pushed herself to a sitting position. They were inching along the square, the rain slackening the slightest bit. Carriage lights, flameless ones, barely cut the gloom around them, but showed her that the car's color was deep green.

"An electric motorcar," Evie said in wonder. "I have to say, this was clever of you, Mackenzie."

"I did think a few things through, McKnight."

"You planned this entire thing, from how to find the alabastron to the getaway." Evie peered out the window. "A very slow getaway. Can we go any faster?"

"Speed draws attention," Jamie said easily. "We're just taking a stroll."

"A stroll, indeed. A man walking his dog just passed us."

Evie pointed to a tall gentleman in a greatcoat striding along with what looked like an Irish wolfhound, a huge creature.

"Are ye in a hurry to be somewhere?" Jamie asked her.

"Only to take this blasted pot to Iris." Evie pulled off her hat, her hair straggling. "And have a hot bath. And supper."

"Well, you can't walk into Miss Georgiou's hotel looking like a drowned rat. Her dad's there, isn't he?"

"You don't look much better," Evie returned. "I see a wet ferret, driving an electric motorcar. Do not worry, I had no intention of popping into her hotel in the middle of the night and secretly handing her a package in the shape of a Greek alabastron. We've set a meeting for tomorrow."

"It's not the middle of the night," Jamie said. "It's only gone nine. So, did ye plan to bounce back into Atherton's house, hiding that under your coat?"

"No." Evie glanced at the bulk of the wrapped alabastron in irritation. "Hayden was going to take care of that detail. Drat his father."

"No worries, love." Jamie navigated around another corner. "I have just the place for you to stash it. You go off, have your wash and supper, and fetch it in the morning."

"You mean you'll take it to your flat?" Evie asked worriedly. "I can hardly visit you to fetch it there." She'd be labeled fast if she entered a gentleman's establishment, even on an errand.

"Not my flat," Jamie reassured her. "It isn't far."

"That's a mercy." Evie watched another walker pass, a man hurrying home out of the rain. "Else we might not arrive until the sun rises."

"Very droll, McKnight. Enjoy the ride. This is one of the finest electric cars in the world."

The seat was indeed comfortable, in spite of the chill, the inside of the car paneled in polished marquetry. If Evie weren't so concerned about hiding the alabastron and sneaking herself back into Hayden's house, she might have found the going pleasant.

Jamie wound through smaller streets, bypassing Tottenham Court Road and Oxford Street, which were full of wagons and carriages. In a still narrower lane, he glided the car to a halt in front of a gate hung between high stone walls.

"What is this place?" Evie asked uneasily. She saw no one in the inky darkness except a few furtive shadows that flitted around a corner at the far end of the street.

"My cousin's lock-up." Jamie slid out of the car into rain that had started to pelt down again. "You drive it inside while I man the gate."

Evie popped out of the back door. "Drive? I can't drive a motorcar."

"There's nothing to it." Jamie held the door until Evie nervously slid into the driver's seat. "You push the tiller forward, like so, and it goes." His large, gloved hand covered hers and wrapped it around the vertical lever. "A nudge is all you need. Wait 'til I have the gate open."

Jamie shut the door and hastened to unlock a massive padlock and swing the gate wide. He'd halted the car so it was exactly out of range of the long gate, showing he'd done this many times.

He stepped inside the shelter of the cavernous interior and waved her in.

Evie gulped as she gingerly pressed the lever forward. It glided on its shaft, the handle still warm from Jamie's grip.

She jumped in excitement as the car moved forward. She was driving!

Jamie sprang back as she brushed past him, narrowly missing one of the gate posts, but then she was inside, the rain mercifully left behind. Jamie hadn't instructed Evie on how to stop the car, but when she pulled the lever back toward her, the car halted.

Jamie closed the gate, shutting them in, then lit a lantern to push away the darkness. He reached in through the car's window and touched a switch, and the motorcar's lights went black.

Evie sprang out when he withdrew, her heart racing. "That was glorious. How wonderful." What an exhilarating freedom to guide a vehicle with just a touch.

Jamie grinned at her. He was achingly handsome when he smiled. His hair was plastered to his face, his kilt clinging to a honed and muscular body.

Evie grinned back at him, excitement streaming through her. "We've done it." She gave a little hop, not caring how childish she looked.

Jamie caught her hands and swung her around, joining her dance of victory.

They'd found the alabastron and spirited it away, and here they were, triumphant, in a place far from home, where no one knew where Evie was.

It was like being tipsy from champagne, fizzing bubbles making her laugh. Jamie laughed with her, his rumbling voice merging with hers.

Evie spun until she was dizzy, then she found herself with her back to the cool fender of the bottle-green car, Jamie's warmth against her.

A well of happiness Evie had never experienced surged up to heat her body. Jamie's weight against her licked fire through her veins, which soared to blazing when his arms closed around her and his mouth came down on hers.

CHAPTER 13

*J*amie tasted Evie's gasp of surprise, then she was rising to him, seizing fistfuls of his coat, kissing him fully in return.

Her lips were hot, ripe, welcoming him. Jamie shoved his hand through her wet hair, tilting her to him, their mouths fusing, each seeking the other. Jamie's heart pumped rapidly, filling him with the wildness that only came with danger.

Evie *was* dangerous. With her dark blue eyes, her flyaway black hair, and her smile that made him breathless, she sparked something in him that had never flared before. Even the way she called him *Mackenzie*, as though they were still fellow students, filled him with joy. Teasing, familiar, comfortable.

His teeth scraped her lip, but she didn't pull away. Jamie firmed her against him with his arm around her waist, her body beneath the layers of clothing igniting desires that seared his blood.

She was desperate for loving, for affection, for passion. Jamie tasted it in her, felt it in her grasping hands.

Abruptly Evie wrenched her mouth from his, but she clung to him, eyes enormous, breath coming fast. They stared at each other a long moment, then Evie launched herself at Jamie again, kissing his face, his chin, the side of his neck.

Jamie let her feast, then he caught her, lifting her face to his once more. He kissed her lips then licked her cheek, teeth and tongue moving to her throat.

She tasted of salt and need and the distinctive fragrance of Evie. Jamie had never forgotten it, he realized now, in all the years he'd made light of his brief encounter with her.

Evie's breath scalded his face, her skin hot beneath his lips. It was cold in the lock-up, rain drumming on the high windows, but the air burned between the two of them.

Evie's fists thumped into Jamie's chest. Jamie felt the change in her, the awakening from her daze, reality rushing at them once more.

Jamie ended the kiss, and they held each other's gaze. Fires swam in Evie's eyes as well as sorrow, anger, regret, and vast confusion.

They still had hold of each other. Jamie couldn't relax his grip to step away, and neither, it seemed, could she.

"This ..." Evie's whisper was a croak. "This is wrong."

It wasn't wrong. It was right, the rightest Jamie had felt in his life. He'd roamed the world, seeking satisfaction and never quite finding it. Now he knew why.

Because it had been here, in the rainy and dank land of England, waiting for him. The world had shoved him and Evie together once before. Jamie had not understood, and walked away.

It was shoving them together again, and this time, he refused to ignore their fate.

Jamie touched her cheek. "*He* is wrong for you." His Mackenzie origins came through his voice, any Englishness pounded into him by an endless line of tutors vanishing. "Can you nae see that?"

Evie shook her head the slightest bit. "Does it matter?"

"Of course, it matters." Jamie's anger at Atherton surged.

"Ye want to be tied to a tedious fool the rest of your life, who abandons you when ye need him, who leaves ye to the mercy of a man like *me*?"

A swallow moved in Evie's throat. "I have my reasons, and I don't have much choice. I'm not clever or rich or talented, like ladies who become scholars or artists or ..."

She threw open her hands, which meant she let go of Jamie. It was cold without her touch.

Jamie understood what she meant—he'd heard his sisters, especially Belle, lamenting that if a lady wasn't attached to a man, she was considered nothing. Very few women found respect in their own right.

"But why *that* man?" he demanded. "Dear God, throw a brick, and you'll hit a dozen far better than the git."

"Because he'd have me." Evie's spirit was back, the sparkle in her eyes that proclaimed she was no wilting flower. "Do you believe I have my pick of eligible bachelors? I'm not your beautiful heiress who probably has received twenty-seven proposals since she landed in Southampton."

For a moment, Jamie had no idea who she was talking about, then he remembered Miss Carmichael. "She's not *my* heiress—"

"Oh no? I saw the newspaper. Your photo nice and large as you gazed longingly at the brilliant lady from over the sea."

"Hell and damnation." Jamie's frustrated heat blazed. "That was bloody journos, printing whatever will sell a paper. If I was longing for anything, it was t' see Danny's motorcar coming down the gangplank. I'd missed her." He swept his hand to the gleaming red car resting serenely at the lamplight's edge.

To his surprise, Evie burst out laughing. "You are ridiculous, Mackenzie."

Jamie relaxed, glad she hadn't taken the idiotic newspaper story seriously. But her laughter was shaky, nervous, and she kept herself against the side of the car, too far from him.

Jamie let out a long breath. "I'll keep arguing with you about marrying the stick as long as I know ye. But later, I think."

"Yes." Evie skimmed hands through her hair, though she'd not be able to right the mess. "I need to go home." She peered at him in worry. "What about the alabastron?"

"It will be safe here. But you can't go back to Atherton. Not like this."

"I know, I must look a fright." Evie groped at her hair again, several more hairpins clinking to the bricks. "I'll tell them I was caught in the rain—which is the truth." She swooped down and retrieved the pins, nearly banging into Jamie when she rose.

"Not because of that." Jamie put one hand on her shoulder to still her while he traced the dark love bite he'd left on her throat. "I marked ye. Didn't mean to, but ..." His need had made him lose every ounce of control he possessed.

Evie slapped her gloved hand to her neck in dismay. She turned to the lantern on the side of the electric car and used the polished chrome as a mirror.

"Blast." She glared up at Jamie, her eyes beautiful. "I suppose I can try to cover it with my coat ..."

"Not until you have a chance to clean yourself up," Jamie said firmly. "Atherton's house will be swarming with servants who'll report your state to the mistress. And they'll take your coat from you, I'll wager."

Evie briefly closed her eyes. "Yes, Mrs. Atherton has them all at her beck and call. What the devil am I to do? If this is your revenge on me for the river, Mackenzie—"

Jamie rested his hands on her shoulders once more, trying to quiet her agitation. "I'd think of a far more harrowing but less ruining way to avenge myself if I wanted to. Not that I will —your shove got me a little wet, is all, and your mates laughed at me. I've suffered far worse."

Evie did not appear to believe him. "Do tell, how am I to

sneak myself into the house without the nosy servants, who don't much like me anyway, noticing me?"

"You'll not go at all." Jamie caressed her, both to soothe her and to prevent himself from crushing his lips to hers again. "Send a note that you're staying with friends because it's too rainy to make your way back tonight."

"What friends? We've already agreed I can't go to Iris's hotel." Evie let out a near-hysterical laugh. "You aren't meaning to smuggle me into your lodgings, are you? I thought you didn't wish to ruin me."

Jamie shook his head. "The housekeeper there would roast me alive with her glare alone, and then tell me mum. I have a safer place in mind for you. Warm and comfortable, though you might have to put up with questions and chatter."

"The Langham?" Evie's agitation began to ease, but not quite. "Surely, the maids and concierge will wonder why you're tucking me there again. They might tell your mum too, or at least your uncle."

"No, no." Jamie circled his thumbs on her shoulders, resigning himself to letting her go. "Never worry, lass. I'll take good care of ye. Ye have my word on it."

———

EVIE WATCHED JAMIE LOCK THE POT INTO A SAFE THAT HAD been built into the wall. A false brick facade concealed the safe when it was closed again, as did a table loaded with tools and cans of oil.

When he was finished, Jamie handed her not only a key to the safe, but to the lock-up itself.

"That way you can come and fetch it any time," he said, pressing the keys into her hand. "You won't have to wait for me."

Jamie's fingers were warm against her palm, and Evie did her best to hide her trembling. Her mouth was raw from their unrestrained kisses, the ones that had made her want to throw Hayden's ring back at him and run off into the night with Jamie.

She had to be mad. She'd accepted Hayden's proposal for many reasons, and so far had been content with her choice. Hayden had his drawbacks, but he was stability, and her road to peace in her life. Jamie was peril, recklessness, *in*stability.

Why did Evie's little voice whisper, *freedom?*

Nonsense, Evie told herself as Jamie blew out the lantern and led her from the lock-up. He was tempting and exciting, but soon he'd be off flitting through the world, forgetting all about kissing Evie.

She was nothing to him, an acquaintance from the past he'd decided to help to entertain himself. A man from the great Mackenzie family had more important things in his life than Evie.

Her heart burning, she followed Jamie out into the darkness.

The wind and rain were colder than before when they emerged. Jamie locked the gate, testing the padlock to make sure all was secure, then tucked her arm through his to lead her onward. Evie didn't pull away, knowing she'd trip in the darkness if she didn't hang on to him.

Two toughs, possibly ones Evie had seen skulking nearby when they arrived, stepped in front of them.

Jamie halted without alarm, though he made sure his body was between Evie and the new arrivals. It was nice to have him there, tall like a tree and just as strong.

"All right, lads?" Jamie asked.

"Too bloody cold," one growled. He was solid with muscle, and his face bore scars from old fights.

"Aye, it's brass monkeys," Jamie agreed. "Do me a favor, gents. Make sure no one comes down this street that doesn't belong, all right?"

The second man laughed. "Just let 'em try."

"Keep them alive," Jamie told him sternly. "But send them off."

"Right you are, guv."

"Any hansoms about, have you seen?" Jamie asked.

"Aye, out on Baker Street is one or two," the first man said. "Visiting Sherlock Holmes." He chortled.

"Very amusing," Jamie said good-naturedly. "Good night, lads, and thank ye."

Jamie tossed them each a coin, metal ringing as the coins left his thumb. The two men caught them skillfully, and Jamie led Evie onward. The toughs actually touched their caps, one of them nodding and saying, "Ma'am."

Evie kept silent until they turned into Baker Street, finding streetlights once more.

"I thought we were going to be robbed," she said in relief. "How on earth did you do that?"

Jamie sent her a modest glance. "I didn't do anything. My cousin Alec thrashed the stuffing out of those blokes last week, and since then they've fallen all over themselves to do me favors."

"And what did you do while your cousin fought them?" Evie asked. "Stand by and collect wagers?"

"An excellent idea. I should have." Jamie shrugged. "I helped a little, but it was mostly Alec. He can channel our fighting ancestors when he wishes, and he wished to at the moment. Wagers." Jamie trailed off thoughtfully. "I'll keep that in mind."

Evie stopped herself from laughing hysterically as Jamie led her along the road. He was amassing favors from his cousins, it seemed. Lock picks, fake pots, handy motorcars and their lock-up with a safe, taming the neighborhood ruffians.

The toughs had been correct—two hansoms stood on the east side of the street, while another bearing passengers was just rolling away. Jamie sent up a loud whistle and raised his hand.

One of the hansoms obligingly peeled from its post and moved toward them through the rain and rising mist. Jamie handed Evie in, calling up to the cabbie as Evie settled a dusty lap robe over her skirts.

"Did you say Jubilee Place?" Evie asked as Jamie climbed in beside her. "Where on earth is that?"

"Chelsea," Jamie answered without worry.

He didn't explain, only looked out at the traffic as the cab started off at a fast pace.

The walls of the cab kept the rain off, mostly, but it was still bitterly cold. Evie huddled into Jamie's side, pushing away her qualms to gather up his warmth. Jamie didn't seem to mind, and obligingly slid his arm across the back of the seat so she could sit closer.

Dear heavens, she'd kissed this man, the thought knocked in Evie's brain. Not only kissed him, but tried to climb him like a wanton, nipping at his skin as much as he'd licked and bitten hers.

Jamie possibly had marks on him from *her* teeth, though his high-collared coat hid his throat from view. Evie's face was hot but, she realized, more from desire than shame.

The same desire had stirred years ago when Jamie had kissed her at the river. Tonight had been different, with still more heat, more desperation. If Evie had not broken from him, what might have happened?

Not long ago, Evie had been trying to imagine her wedding night with Hayden, her mind remaining a careful blank.

What she could picture vividly was Jamie over her in the darkness, his body a welcome weight, his strong hands roving her. His face would relax in passion, and he'd slide into her while Evie groaned, her body tasting a man for the first time. Jamie would be gentle, ensuring he didn't hurt her, easing her into this new desire.

The image warmed her even through tonight's cold. Jamie's bulk at her side inflamed her, until she could think of nothing but lying in his bed, *their* bed. Their kisses, their desires, the laughter they'd share.

Good heavens, what was the matter with her? Evie couldn't marry Hayden if she was having such thoughts about another man. Not just any man, *this* one, here by her side, while Hayden was stuck poring over tedious business details with his father.

Evie could not betray Hayden with fantasies of the exciting, fiery Jamie who would love whatever lady he chose with the intensity of a blazing sun.

But what choice did she have? Evie would be a fool to end a perfectly good betrothal because of her imagination. Jamie hadn't said, *He's wrong for you — marry me instead.* He hadn't even hinted he wanted to become Evie's lover. Jamie had kissed her, and she'd kissed him back, and that was the end of it.

And now she could not return to Hayden tonight, because she'd not pushed Jamie away soon enough. She should have immediately protested the kiss, but instead, she'd fallen into Jamie's arms and enjoyed every second.

The hansom took them south to Oxford Street then down Park Lane, past its elegant, well-lit mansions. The cab continued along the length of Hyde Park, around to Knightsbridge, then south again on Sloane Street.

Evie discerned the route only because she caught sight of street signs now and then. She knew little about this part of London. Whenever she and her mother and sisters traveled to Town to shop, they booked into the hotel on Regent Street they'd meant to stay in this time, ran their errands, and then stepped right back on the train to go home.

The rain streamed down as the cab halted in a tiny lane in front of a modest brick house. It looked respectable enough — quite nice, in fact.

Jamie leapt out and knocked on the door. A maid in a black frock and starched apron pulled it open, gazing out in bewilderment. When she saw Jamie, she smiled and swung the door wide.

Jamie stepped back to the hansom to help Evie descend then led her up the few steps and into the house.

Gavina Mackenzie hastened from a parlor as the agreeable heat of the house poured over Evie's cold body. Behind Gavina came another young woman with Jamie's eyes, and Evie glimpsed more ladies behind her.

"Miss McKnight?" Gavina asked in amazement, taking Evie's cold hands in hers. She bent a beautiful, gray-eyed glare on her cousin. "Jamie, what the devil have you done to her?"

CHAPTER 14

$\mathcal{E}$vie relinquished herself to Gavina's care without protest. Gavina towed her up a flight of stairs and into a well-lit room that was softly feminine. The bedchamber Evie used at the Athertons' home was stiff and informal, a severe contrast to this cozy space.

Gavina had called commands as they went, and now two maids appeared, hauling a tin bath between them. A third provided the steaming water to go with it. An older maid with red hair and a Scottish accent helped Evie out of her clothes, shooing everyone else away so Evie could bathe in private.

"I'm Agnes, love," the maid said as she helped Evie into the bath with competence. "Don't let the young ladies worry ye. High spirits, every one of them, but with hearts of gold. You soak a bit now, and you'll feel better when you emerge."

Agnes left a large cake of soap, thick towels, and a dressing gown on a nearby table and departed. Evie let out a long breath and leaned back, the hot water closing over her body.

She hadn't needed to ask whether Jamie had gone, because she'd heard him in the lane, giving a direction to the cabbie, and then the hansom had rumbled away. Evie shivered, though this was the warmest she'd been all night.

Difficult to believe that less than an hour ago, she'd been robbing a museum, then kissing Jamie, then squeezing next to him in the cab while she fantasized about being in bed with him.

Quite a night.

She'd always considered herself a good person, in spite of a few pranks she'd taken part in at university. Now she, engaged, had kissed another man. Not only that, she'd thoroughly enjoyed it. Was she fast, or had this been a single deviation in her character?

Evie knew, however, that if the opportunity presented itself, she'd kiss Jamie again.

The solution was simple. She would stay away from Jamie. He'd given her the key to the lock-up, and she could retrieve the alabastron by herself. Evie had no reason to contact him again.

Why did that thought make her heart sink?

Evie washed herself all over, taking the maid's advice to enjoy the soak. The Athertons had modern bathtubs, but Sir Hector begrudged every drop of hot water to anyone but himself, so Evie's baths at their home were quick and usually cool. It was nice to lie back and let her muscles loosen.

When the water became lukewarm, Evie hauled herself out of the tub, stepping onto the soft mat the maids had left, and luxuriated in the plush towels. The dressing gown was also warm and comfortable, Evie tying the tapes to hold it closed.

She moved to the dressing table and sat, wondering what to do with the tangle of her wet hair.

As though waiting for her cue, the door opened, and Gavina flowed in, followed by the other young woman Evie had seen downstairs.

"You look much happier," Gavina said cheerfully, as the second young lady shut the door. "This is Belle, Jamie's sister. The others agreed to not crowd you and will see you at breakfast."

Evie peered into the mirror at the two who hovered behind her. "Breakfast?" she asked in a daze.

"Of course," Belle answered. She had a low voice, pleasant, but with strength behind it. "We'd be churlish to send you out into this damp until after you've had a good sleep and a hearty breakfast. Our cook is splendid."

"Never mind about Mr. Atherton." Gavina waved him away. "I sent a note to his family explaining that you'd come to visit, and the weather was much too awful to send you home. It's raining buckets."

Gavina certainly knew much about Evie and her circumstances, but she was grateful Gavina had written the message for her. Evie would have fumbled for the words. "You are very kind," she said.

"Obnoxiously friendly, I think." Gavina grinned at her. "But when Jamie dumps a young lady on us, we must rise to the occasion."

"We've sent your clothes to be cleaned," Belle said. "I have a nightgown you can wear tonight, and a dress for tomorrow. You and I are about the same size, I think." Belle scanned Evie as though assessing her exact measurements.

"I can only thank …" Evie began to turn to them, but the dressing gown fell open at her throat, exposing the mark Jamie had left. It was dark and red, somewhat like a bruise, though not quite. Quickly she closed the gown, blushing hard.

Any hope the two ladies hadn't noticed were dashed. "I have some powder to cover that," Gavina said. "And Belle will lend you a shirtwaist with a high collar."

Evie gulped, fingers trembling as she held the placket closed. "Gracious, what you must think of me."

Belle answered. "We think you are a young woman bowled over by my brother. He's a maelstrom."

"He is," Evie agreed fervently.

"Jamie told us about the river incident before he went."

Gavina's lips twitched. "Good for you. A whack and a dunk. Exactly what he needed."

Evie opened her mouth to explain but ended up chuckling. "It *was* highly amusing."

"I imagine." Gavina let herself laugh, and Belle joined in. Belle's laughter was less loud, but her eyes sparkled with impish delight.

Evie began to feel better. She had imagined Jamie's cousin and sister being appalled at her behavior, and she'd known sisters who were quite protective of their brothers. But the two seemed to not blame her for her indiscretion tonight.

Gavina reached for a lacquered box on the dressing table, opening it to reveal a whitish powder. She opened another box that contained fat powder puffs, pristine and quite new.

"Give yourself a dousing of this in the morning," she advised. "Enough to cover but not enough to be obvious you're wearing powder. Aunt Izzy brought this to me from Paris, so you know it will be the best."

"This is far too generous," Evie began, entranced by the powder's lavender scent.

"Not at all," Gavina replied. "If you believe Jamie makes a habit of bringing us young women to look after, you are wrong. He's never done such a thing. Which tells us you are special."

"Hardly." Evie flushed and set down the box. "I barely know Jam— Mr. Mackenzie."

"And yet." Gavina gazed pointedly at Evie's throat. "Do not be embarrassed, my dear. The males of our family rather run over everyone and leave them not entirely certain what happened. Wear the powder and the frock, and say no more about it."

"I am supposed to marry Hayden." Evie closed the box of powder puffs, running her fingers along its smooth lid painted with roses. "I have been thinking perhaps I should not."

Gavina regarded Evie in the mirror, her eyes wise. "That is up to you, of course. But unless Jamie whisked you to Paris and thoroughly debauched you in a luxurious hotel, I would put it behind you. Tell me, did Jamie instigate the kissing, or did you?"

"He did." Evie cast her thoughts back to the cold lock-up and Jamie's hot mouth on hers. "I am fairly certain," she finished in a faint voice.

"There you are, then. Not your fault my cousin decided you needed kissing. You are blameless. He is not. Keep your fiancé if you love him, and kiss Jamie no more."

"I was arriving at the same conclusion," Evie said. Regret closed on her, and she studied the box to avoid Gavina's gaze.

"I believe she is sorry there was no luxurious Parisian hotel," Belle said with good humor.

Evie's face heated. Her imagination had very quickly put herself and Jamie in a soft bed with champagne. Neither of them had clothes on, of course.

"Ladies," Evie said, agonized. "Please."

Gavina laughed. "My dear, if you are going to be friends with Mackenzies, you must expect to be teased. And you *will* be friends with us." Gavina embraced her impulsively. "You're too adorable not to be."

Evie returned the embrace. She liked how easily the two accepted her—she felt as she did with her own sisters.

"We'll leave you to sleep." Belle patted Evie's shoulder. "Gavina is bunking in with me tonight." Her expression turned pained. "And please may we cease speaking of my brother's amorousness, both real and imagined? Bleh."

"We are comforting Evie." Gavina rose. "Though I rejoice we're not talking about *my* brother. That would be truly horrifying."

Evie rose with them, steadying herself on the back of the chair. "I envy you having brothers. I've only had sisters. I do love them, but I'd always hoped for a brother as well."

Gavina and Belle glanced at each other and laughed.

"Rejoice," Gavina said. "They are a world of trouble. We envy *you*."

"Good night, Evie," Belle said kindly. "Sleep well. Ring for whatever you need." She gestured to a button on the wall. "Agnes will do anything for you. She's a treasure. We'll see you at breakfast."

"Good night." Evie watched the two skim to the door, both ladies exuberant and graceful at the same time. "And thank you."

"Not at all. Come along, Belle. Let us go argue about how long you'll stay up reading with the lights on."

Belle rolled her eyes, and then with final good-nights, they were gone.

Evie blew out her breath. Belle had called Jamie a maelstrom, but his relations were as well. The whole family exuded energy.

Agnes returned as soon as the ladies had gone, her arms full of clothes. The nightgown she assisted Evie into did indeed fit well. Agnes bundled Evie into the bed, warmed by a hot brick, then called in the two sturdy maids to carry out the tub.

Evie lay back and watched Agnes flit about the room, hanging skirt, shirtwaist, and a jacket in the wardrobe, then tidying up before she turned out the gaslights and departed.

Evie dropped off quickly in her exhaustion, but her dreams were full of Jamie, the kisses he gave her palpable as he rolled over her in a warm, downy bed in a Parisian hotel.

———

JAMIE LEFT THE QUIET SUBURB OF CHELSEA ONCE HE'D SEEN Evie settled, and headed north again to Oxford Street and a building of serviced flats much like his own.

The men who lived here were professionals, with jobs in the City or in the halls of barristers, the building providing maid and butler service as well as meals, if the tenants desired.

Jamie knocked on the door of a flat on the third floor, and was admitted by a tall, very fair-haired man with flint-gray eyes. The hair was tousled as though he'd been tugging at it, and the eyes lit in relief at the sight of Jamie.

"Thank God it's you," Andrew McBride said, ushering Jamie inside. "I was afraid it was my clerk, demanding to know where my notes were—alphabetized and indexed to his satisfaction, and by the way, where are those fees I was supposed to have collected? A barrister's life is hell, Jamie. Hell. Especially a junior's."

Andrew waved for Jamie to find a chair among those piled with books and papers, while he produced a decanter from somewhere in the mess and poured them both a whisky.

After they'd sipped in companionable silence for a time, Jamie turned to the reason for his visit.

"I've come to you because you know everything there is to know about everyone. Or can find out, anyway."

Andrew's gray eyes stilled over his whisky glass. "Possibly," he said with caution.

"Chap called Hayden Atherton." Jamie rolled his crystal goblet between his fingers. "Son of Sir Hector Atherton."

Andrew's brows climbed. "Sir Hector I've heard of. Businessman. Stickler. No toleration for nonsense. Nonsense as defined by him, of course."

"Exactly. His son holds my interest. I need information on him."

Andrew set his whisky glass on his desk in the one space that held no papers. "I thought *you* knew everyone in Town."

"Only in certain circles. Smug sons of businessmen, not so much." Jamie let out a breath. "Actually the lad is friendly, chummy even. Maybe too much so."

Andrew's concern gave way to amusement. "Your face is all pinched up. He must be interesting for some reason. Is a lady involved?"

Jamie tried to ease his expression. "Why would you say that?"

Andrew laughed, a hearty sound. "Because I know you. Have known you since we were lads. It's the McKnight girl, isn't it?" His laughter grew louder. "Your face is all scrunched again. Is Jamie Mackenzie in love, at last?"

CHAPTER 15

"Calm yourself," Jamie growled. "She's not *the McKnight girl*. She's Miss Evie McKnight, and she's a friend."

"Not what Gavina thinks."

"Gavina is an imp." Jamie scowled at Andrew. "I should have known she'd spread tales." At least Gavina hadn't had time to inform Andrew that Jamie had brought Evie to her tonight, disheveled and thoroughly kissed.

"She won't blab outside the family." Andrew was Gavina's cousin on her mother's side. He was no blood relation to Jamie, but the Mackenzie and McBride offspring had grown up side by side.

"Evie's engaged to the blot," Jamie went on. "I want to make certain there's no sordid surprise he'll spring on her once he's got her to the altar."

"I see." Andrew pulled a sheet of paper to him and scribbled on it with a pencil. "Hayden Atherton. Address?"

"Upper Brook Street."

"Yes, Sir Hector is a *successful* businessman. Seems like your girl—excuse me, Miss McKnight—has done well for herself there. Son will inherit the lot?"

"Presumably." Jamie shifted in the chair, which was rickety and uncomfortable. "But something's wrong with the chap. Can't put my finger on it. Other than that he's an ass."

"Father or son?"

"Both. Never met the father, but if he's anything like the son ..."

Andrew's interest was piqued, Jamie could see, which boded well. Andrew, like his father, a famous KC, now retired, would stop at nothing to discover the truth once he'd decided to. Andrew had more vigor than anyone Jamie knew, including himself.

Andrew made a few more notes, then picked up his whisky. "I'll see what I can find out. When are you interested in having the information?"

"Anytime from right now."

"That soon? Well ..." Andrew made another note, swallowed the contents of his glass, and opened the decanter again. "Another?"

Jamie held his goblet out for Andrew to trickle more whisky into. Mackenzie single malt, of course.

"How are you, Andrew?" Jamie asked, relaxing a bit. "I haven't had much time to speak to you since I returned to the country."

"Not until you wanted a lady's betrothed investigated." Andrew chuckled. "It's no matter. I've been up to my ears in briefs. As the junior barrister, it's my job to do all the research and make sure my senior looks good." His expression became pained. "I'm usually sitting behind some of the densest men in Britain. We win cases only because I whisper into their ears what they should say. I used to be modest about that, but now I'm growing fed up." He broke off, mouth twisting wryly. "Your pardon, Jamie. You didn't come to listen to me whinge."

"I've missed it." Jamie shrugged. "You'll take silk soon, I'm sure. You're the son of Basher McBride."

"Don't I know it." Andrew drank deeply. "Whenever the court hears the name *McBride*, they perk up, then dissolve in disappointment when they see it's only me."

"It is hell being the son of a famous man," Jamie agreed.

They commiserated in silence a moment.

"How is my cousin Magdala?" Jamie asked.

Andrew's woeful expression told Jamie all he needed to know. "I imagine she's doing well. Enjoying learning how to be Scots at Kilmorgan Castle."

Magdala, who'd taken the surname Mackenzie, was a distant cousin, descended from Jamie's ancestors who'd fought at Culloden. She'd been raised in Newfoundland but decided to seek her relatives in Scotland to escape a bounder of a stepfather.

Andrew had instantly taken a fancy to her, but that had been ten years ago. Andrew had gone back to university then apprenticed in Middle Temple and now labored in a barristers' chambers, while Magdala had explored her new home and started working for the distillery.

Star-crossed, Jamie thought. But not really. Neither had married or even spoken about it. The two simply needed a push. He had some ideas on how to do that.

Jamie departed an hour later. He enjoyed spending time with Andrew, the man both intelligent and fun-loving.

He'd put wheels in motion, and Andrew, he knew, would leave no stone unturned. Jamie, however, was too impatient to wait. He could kick over a few stones himself.

He hailed another cab and bade it take him to St. James's and its cluster of exclusive clubs.

———

BREAKFAST IN CHELSEA WAS A LIVELY MEAL. EVIE COULDN'T remember when she'd laughed so much over the morning toast.

Gavina and Belle were already down when Evie entered the sunny morning room, its sideboard loaded with poached eggs, potatoes, and ham, with a large pot of tea to wash it all down. The ladies greeted her as though she were their dearest friend, and offered her the chair next to the head of the table, a seat of honor.

The other two ladies who shared this house, and Mrs. Barrow, their chaperone, arrived not long later. Mrs. Barrow was a thin, middle-aged woman with a warm smile and shrewd eyes. The ladies were sisters, Adeline and Gayle Hodgkinson, and were Mrs. Barrow's nieces.

The Hodgkinsons were a few years younger than the Mackenzies, the pair just down from Newnham at Cambridge, and had recently taken posts as assistants at the University College in Gower Street.

"We bring tea and make certain the ink pots are full," Adeline told Evie, making a face. "Ladies obviously know nothing about astronomy, never mind we both completed the full course."

"It is ever the way." Belle sighed and reached for cream for her tea. "Likewise women who wish to study medicine are turned away in derision. I have tried in vain to be accepted to a program."

"Cheer up, ladies," Mrs. Barrow said. "In my day it was considered disgraceful for women to have any sort of knowledge at all, unless they wanted to be pitied as bluestockings. Things are much better these days. Now, no more morose talk in front of our guest."

"I don't mind," Evie said sincerely. "I am interested."

The blouse and skirt Belle had lent Evie fit well, and the collar, a soft fold of lawn, closed at the throat with a horizontal row of pearl buttons. The collar well hid the embarrassing mark, and Evie had covered anything that might peek over it with dabs of powder.

She'd felt decadent wafting the silken powder over her

skin. Mrs. Atherton considered any woman who even thought about powder—or *paint*, as she termed it—a hussy.

The lively chatter went on, the talk turning to young men. Evie did not know those they spoke of, though they mentioned Mackenzie cousins and brothers. From the blushes on the Hodgkinson ladies' cheeks, they'd noticed and appreciated the handsomeness of the various Mackenzies.

Evie hadn't had a more enjoyable meal in a long time, but she knew she would have to depart soon. She must deliver the alabastron to Iris—she'd penned a note to her before breakfast telling her the mission had been a success—and then she'd return to Hayden's home.

Her heart sank at the thought of enduring another long day in the quiet, lugubrious house in Upper Brook Street, trying to keep busy with wedding plans. Hayden had promised that after they married, they'd take a pleasant flat in another part of town. Evie had been looking forward to starting a life with him, perhaps in sunny lodgings like these.

A life that Jamie Mackenzie would have nothing to do with.

After breakfast, Evie tried to take her leave, but the other ladies protested. She ought to wait until her clothes were cleaned. She must take luncheon with them at least, and possibly supper. Why not stay another night?

"We are starved for entertainment here, obviously," Gavina said as she escorted Evie upstairs. Agnes had left more clothes for Evie in the bedroom, and Gavina began to sort through them.

"You have all been so very kind," Evie said. "To me, a stranger."

"We know Jamie, is all." Gavina lifted a gray skirt and matching blouse, lovely garments, made of fine broadcloth, sturdy and yet elegant. "Belle's things are so very plain. She is determined to be a staid intellectual."

By contrast Gavina's frock, though not overly decorated,

was a light blue square-necked gown with a narrow but flowing skirt. A simple gold locket rested on her throat, and small, sedate gold earrings adorned her earlobes. Her thick golden-red hair was dressed in a soft roll that left a few wisps dangling.

Gavina was indeed beautiful, and Evie wondered why there was not a string of male suitors languishing on the pavement outside.

"Belle is quite clever," Evie said. Belle and the younger ladies had begun discussing the latest scientific questions after they'd finished dissecting the gentlemen of their acquaintance, leaving Evie bewildered.

"Immensely. Her father, my Uncle Ian, is brilliant at maths, and Belle inherited that. Megan inherited his musical ability."

"And Jamie?" Evie asked before she could stop herself. "Is he brilliant at maths or music as well?"

Gavina shook out another gray skirt that had a pretty braided trim at its hem. "Jamie is a lot like his mother—Aunt Beth. She is a warmhearted woman, who helps everyone who comes within her sphere. Jamie does that too. We all go to him when we're in trouble, or need advice, or just a listening ear. He's always available for us, except when he's off roaming the world, seeking ..." Gavina shrugged. "Whatever he's seeking. Jamie always seems to know how to fix everything."

Such as coming up with a plan to spirit away an alabastron from a museum. A plan that had worked.

"Gavina." Evie set down a skirt and rested her hip on the bed. "Would you be willing to accompany me to Jamie's lockup? Where he keeps the motorcars? I left something there, but I hesitate to go alone. The neighborhood was a bit frightening."

"Of course," Gavina responded without pausing. "But we'll need the key. Jamie has one, and Cousin Daniel and Violet. We—"

"I have a key," Evie said quickly. When Gavina's gaze snapped to her, Evie's face grew warm. "He lent it to me."

"Did he?" Gavina shoved the clothes aside and sat down on the bed next to Evie. "This is interesting."

"He wanted me to be able to fetch my item whenever I liked." Evie said the words rapidly, while Gavina's stare intensified. When Gavina continued to watch her without speaking, Evie grew impatient. "What is the matter? Jamie offered the key. I didn't demand it, or steal it."

"I know you didn't." Gavina's tone became apologetic. "I am just surprised, is all. Jamie has never given any one of us the key. If we want to go near the cars, we ask Daniel or Violet, or Jamie escorts us." A smile spread across Gavina's face. "I knew you were a special person, Evie."

"I rather think he does not want to bother with me," Evie returned. "I can go without interrupting him."

Gavina's mirth did not cease. "If you say so. I will indeed accompany you. I am now mad with curiosity as to what this item is."

"It isn't mine, actually. It belongs to a friend." Evie lowered her voice to a whisper. "And you must tell no one. Please."

Gavina pressed her hand to her heart. "I swear." She leapt to her feet. "Let me fetch my coat."

Evie was pleased Gavina so readily agreed to go with her, though she was not happy that she had to trust yet another person with this secret.

It occurred to her as Gavina bounded to the door that the logical person Evie should ask to take her to the lock-up was Hayden. But for some reason, Evie wasn't ready to face Hayden, not yet.

The sound of a horse and carriage halting in the lane outside made Gavina swerve to peer out the window.

"I may not have to take you, after all." Gavina sounded both disappointed and excited. "Here's Jamie himself."

Evie rushed to join her at the window. Jamie had indeed arrived, his presence filling the space below as he descended from a coach. Now he was advancing to the door, which opened before he could knock.

Gavina turned to Evie with a knowing look. "He certainly is adamant to squire you about. Though I'm hoping I can still go with you. I'm agog to learn what you've been up to."

"His coming here might have nothing to do with me," Evie argued. "He's likely here to visit his sister."

Gavina waved that away. "Jamie does not rush to this house so early to visit his sister. Or me, his annoying cousin." Her smile returned. "Let me see—he gives you a key to the hidden lock-up, he brings you here so your fiancé won't discover he gave you a love bite, *and* he gave you the love bite in the first place. This is delightful."

"Why?" Evie backed from the window, her heart pounding as she heard Jamie cheerily greeting Mrs. Barrow downstairs. "You know I am engaged. Why are you so pleased Jamie is doing all this?"

Gavina folded her hands, but she looked anything but prim. "Because I love Jamie, and I like you. I want him to be happy."

"But I am—"

"I know. Betrothed to another man. That is an obstacle, yes, but not an unsurmountable one. Jamie would never demand you break things off with Atherton if you don't want to—it isn't his way. However, if you find you are in love with Jamie, please do not let convention sway you into marrying Atherton because you feel it's your duty. The Mackenzies are an unconventional family, and everyone knows it."

"I don't *want* to fall in love." Evie's declaration was heartfelt. It revealed more than she intended, but first Jamie, then Gavina, were crashing through her carefully constructed world, ripping down the barriers she'd formed around her heart.

Gavina grew puzzled, but before she could question Evie, a

maid yanked open the door. "Mrs. Barrow is asking for yer," she said breathlessly. "Mr. Mackenzie's come to see Miss McKnight."

Gavina sent Evie a significant look, then led the way downstairs.

CHAPTER 16

*E*verything in Jamie gladdened at the site of Evie skimming down the stairs to him. But he shouldn't be surprised. Evie had appeared like a bolt from the blue, inflaming memories of a kiss he'd never forgotten.

He'd extended an invitation to meet with Atherton at a club today, and he looked forward to it. Andrew had already given Jamie some information—not on Atherton himself yet, but his father, which Jamie had digested with satisfaction.

The note, written in Andrew's unexpectedly neat hand, was folded in the pocket inside Jamie's coat. Jamie had sifted through plenty of gossip in the clubs last night, and he'd woken this morning much more optimistic.

"Jamie," Gavina sang out. She had a gleam in her eye, one that always worried him. "How lovely to see you again. And so soon."

"Gavina. Always a delight."

"Liar." Gavina dove into the parlor, leaving room in the tiny hall for Evie, while a maid tried to take Jamie's coat and hat.

"Mr. Mackenzie," Evie said formally. "Good morning."

"And to you, lass."

She looked well. Jamie recognized his sister's clothes, and

decided Evie brought out the style well. Understated but not subdued. Evie's dark hair gleamed, the high-collared blouse set off her slightly flushed face, and her eyes were pools of delicate blue. The clothes skimmed her figure, the skirt touching her legs and drawing Jamie's eyes there.

"Did you come to visit Belle?" Evie was asking.

"Eh?"

Jamie dragged his gaze to her face again, trying to cease imagining her legs bare and enticing. He'd had a nice glimpse of them last night when she'd gone out the window, but he'd not been in a position to do anything about it. That is, there'd been nothing wrong with the *position*, but they'd needed to get out of the museum as quickly as possible.

"I said, have you come to visit your sister?" Evie regarded him as though wondering whether he'd lost his wits.

The maid had faded away once Jamie gestured that he'd keep his coat and hat, and Mrs. Barrow and the others who lived here were strangely absent. Gavina had quietly shut the door to the parlor.

"No." Jamie groped for the words that came readily to his tongue when he complimented ladies, and found nothing. He stood like a gawping stick. "That is—do you want to retrieve our prize and deliver it to Miss Georgiou?" he asked awkwardly. "She's likely pacing a hole in the carpet."

"I did send her a note this morning, telling her all was well." Evie looked indignant he thought she hadn't. "But yes, I was about to go there myself. Gavina agreed to accompany me."

Of course, Gavina would have. Any hint of excitement, and she leapt to be first into the fray.

"I'm thinking you and I should go ourselves," Jamie said.

Evie nodded. "I agree. The fewer, the better. Shall I fetch my coat?"

She'd turned away, tendrils of hair wafting, before Jamie could answer. The servants of this house already liked her,

Jamie saw, as two maids burst from the door under the stairs carrying her coat and hat, thoroughly brushed and cleaned.

Gavina peeked out of the parlor, sending Jamie an inquiring glance, but Jamie gestured for her to stay behind. Gavina looked disappointed but nodded in understanding.

Jamie had hired a coach for the journey today, which waited on the doorstep. Evie liked the motorcars, but Jamie had decided they'd draw too much attention. Also the coach's cushioned seats and fireboxes would keep them snug in the ongoing rain and spring chill.

Jamie handed Evie in, climbing up beside her. To be civil, he took the seat facing her, though he'd much rather snuggle in beside her.

As Evie gazed across at him, a smile spread across her face, and Jamie's tension loosened. He'd feared he'd find her angry, embarrassed, upset, and refusing to look at him after their powerful kiss last night.

The smile told him she hadn't pushed the kiss from her mind. Evie had thought about it and had enjoyed reliving it.

Maybe they could discuss the kissing as they went. What they'd liked the most, what thoughts had streamed through their heads as their hearts pounded. Well, what had streamed through *Jamie's* head. Evie might be a lily-pure maiden and have no tawdry thoughts at all.

Perhaps Jamie could teach her how to form them. From Evie's smile, she might let him.

The coach jerked forward then abruptly ground to a halt, the coachman shouting a hasty, *Whoa!*

The top of a feminine hat appeared in the window and a gloved hand yanked at the door handle. The door was wrenched open to reveal Gavina, clad in a tailored coat and the matching dark blue hat.

Jamie politely sprang to assist her inside, hiding his irritation. He'd definitely indicated she should stay behind.

"Mrs. Barrow insisted," Gavina explained as she landed on

the seat next to Evie. "Can't let Miss McKnight ride around with the notorious Jamie Mackenzie without a chaperone. Since I am a relation, I was chosen." She settled her skirt as Jamie pulled the door closed and knocked on the roof to signal the coachman he should proceed. "You two carry on. Don't mind me."

Jamie thumped to his seat as the coach's momentum sent his backside to it. "Am I notorious?" he asked testily.

Evie's smile broadened. "Apparently females swoon at the sight of you."

"Bloody nonsense," Jamie grumbled.

"They swoon at your language too," Gavina said. "But truly, ignore me. I'd made up my mind to give you privacy, but Mrs. Barrow is right. Gadding about with you alone will get Evie gossiped about."

Evie's focus moved back to Jamie, the smile reappearing. Very dangerous of her to look at him like that.

Jamie forced his gaze from Evie, where it could linger all day, and returned it to Gavina. "Not a word about what you see and where we go," he ordered in his most commanding tone. "It is Evie's secret, not mine. So no gabbing to Alec or even to my sisters."

Gavina regarded him loftily. "I've already sworn my silence to Evie. Do not worry, Cousin. I can keep secrets when I want to."

The flicker in her eyes told Jamie she *had* kept some, deep down where no one would pry them out. He wondered about that, but let it go.

Jamie said little as they wound north toward Baker Street, but that did not mean they journeyed in silence. *He* said little, but the two ladies chattered about anything and everything.

Jamie leaned against the cushions, letting the feminine conversation flow over him like a soft breeze. He liked Evie's voice, low and seductive, though he wagered she had no idea how seductive it truly was.

He thought about the folded note in his pocket and experienced a moment of disquiet. He would cause Evie pain if his conclusions were correct. Jamie wanted to do everything on earth to keep her from hurt, but Evie deserved the truth.

The street that held the lock-up did not appear as sinister in daylight, merely seedy and rundown. Daniel preferred it like this, wanting no one to believe that very valuable motorcars were hidden in the dingy lock-up.

Jamie agreed with Daniel—if he kept the motorcars in a sleek garage with men in gloves wiping every speck of dust from them, they'd be a target. Danny had prototypes that would be worth millions to unscrupulous manufacturers. Daniel had patents, yes, but canny men could get around those. It happened all the time. Thus Daniel hid his cars away in this unlikely area of the metropolis.

Jamie saw no sign of the toughs. The lane was very quiet, which was either lucky, or else the toughs were keeping anyone from taking a shortcut through it.

He descended, then reached for Evie's hand, knowing better than to tell her to wait in the carriage.

Gavina, however, remained seated. "You go on," she said serenely. "I'll keep a lookout."

Evie's hand in Jamie's was warm, and he did not want to release it once she was steady on the ground. She lightly withdrew, holding her skirt from the damp street.

Jamie unlocked the gate and opened it enough for him and Evie to slip through. Cold and darkness greeted them, along with the familiar scents of exhaust, oil, and metal polish.

Evie went directly to the false wall as Jamie lit a lantern. "You'd never know anything was here." She ran her hand over the bricks in wonder.

"Violet designed this." Jamie gently pried the panel open to reveal the small safe. "She learned to conceal apparatus for the fortune-telling shows she used to do with her mother."

Evie's eyes widened. "You mean they were frauds?"

"Oh, yes." Jamie answered. "They traveled around the Continent, holding seances, foretelling the future. Violet believes her mother truly had the gift but contends she never did herself. She's just good at understanding much about people at first glance."

"On the voyage from New York, the young ladies were wild for her to tell their fortunes," Evie said. "Clara wanted to have her palm read, but our mother said it was all bunk."

Jamie chuckled. "Violet would agree with you." He studied her, a sensible-looking young woman in her practical coat and hat with no frills, nothing taking away from her beautiful eyes. "You never wanted your fortune told?"

"No, indeed." Evie's answer was too quick, and she glanced away. "I know all there is to know about myself."

An interesting statement. Jamie didn't press her, but turned away and unlocked the safe.

The bundle containing the alabastron sat inside, unharmed, just as they'd left it.

Jamie lifted it out gingerly. Evie peeled back a corner of the cloth, breathing out in relief when she revealed the jar's painted figures.

"I saw nothing in the newspapers this morning about a sensational theft at the British Museum," she said, covering it up again.

"Aye, they might notice in fifty years that something is gone, and by then it will be a curious mystery, nothing more."

"Unless the British minister who donated it demands to see it displayed," Evie said glumly.

"He won't." Jamie carefully set the bundle on the nearest table and closed and locked the safe. "Sir Geoffrey Hammond. He has no idea what he was given. *Some old Greek vase*, he said. *Not even a proper big one. I accepted it to be polite, then handed the damned thing to the museum. If I kept it in my house, my housekeeper would smash it, the clumsy cow.*"

Evie gaped at him in shock. "You know him?"

"Uncle David does—he's not really my uncle, but a very close friend of Uncle Hart's. Uncle David knows everyone in government. He gave me the name of Sir Geoffrey's usual club. I decided to darken its door, happened to run into the minister, and mentioned I'd heard he'd received a gift when he went off to Greece, wasn't that splendid?"

Evie fixed Jamie with a hard stare. "Happened to run into him?"

"I wanted to make certain he had no interest in the alabastron, and he does not. Sir Geoffrey turned the conversation quite readily to a lady he'd seen on the music hall stage and also to the health of his cows in Hertfordshire."

"As long as he doesn't confuse the two," Evie said, her face straight.

Jamie's tension dissolved into laughter. "Dear Lord, McKnight I—" He jerked as he realized that his next words would have been, *I love you.* "You're a fine woman," he amended.

If Evie noticed the slip, she made no sign. "And you're a clever man, Mackenzie. I'm very glad Iris brought you into our little conspiracy."

"As am I, or I'd be wondering today why you were in the nick."

"Do you think Hayden and I couldn't have pulled it off?" Evie glanced into the shadows when she said this, as though worried someone was there to overhear. The lock-up was empty, though. Jamie would have known if anyone else had been here.

"I didn't notice darling Hayden in attendance last night," Jamie said, trying to sound offhand.

"No, he wasn't."

Jamie waited for Evie to defend Atherton, explain again how he'd had to work for his father, with no choice in the matter. Evie only gazed at the motorcars lined up side by side, gleaming in the dim light.

"I for one, am glad." Jamie cupped Evie's face with one hand. He couldn't stop himself.

"I'm not sure whether to be glad or sorry." Evie's response was a near whisper.

"I'm also happy you didn't punch me in the nose."

Evie's laughter rippled. "It's a nice nose. I didn't want to mar it."

"Already marred," Jamie touched the dent where a large bloke had gotten in a good blow in a boxing match eight years ago. He should have paid more attention to the lessons from Uncle Mac's pugilist valet. He didn't move his other hand from Evie's face, letting his thumb trace her cheek. "Lass, promise me …"

Evie stilled, her breath touching his gloved hand. "Promise you what?"

"Not to confess to Atherton to ease your conscience. No good will come of that."

Evie went pink under his touch. "I agree. His mother and father would grind me to dust. I'm not sure Hayden could save me, or would be willing to."

"If I were Atherton, I'd shoot me."

Evie blinked. "Shoot you? As in a duel? A hundred years ago, perhaps. In any case, Hayden would never do such a thing."

True, Atherton likely wouldn't resort to violence. He was the sort who'd find a way to destroy a man without coming near him.

Jamie caressed her cheek once more. "If you were mine, and another man dared touch you, I'd tear him apart." He leaned to her, as though she were a magnet that drew his iron soul. "I can barely stand the thought of you marrying the twit, of you smiling across the table at him every night." He brushed a finger across her forehead. "I know you want to go through with it, even if Atherton's wrong for you."

"It doesn't matter."

Jamie stilled. Evie's declaration was low-voiced, with pain behind it.

"Doesn't matter? It matters, Evie. It matters more than anything. Don't give yourself to the wrong person. That way lies misery."

She flicked her gaze to him, her eyes a mystery. "Are you telling me *you* are the right person?"

"I don't know." Jamie knew damned well he was, but he doubted Evie would believe him at the moment. "But don't go to Atherton if you aren't absolutely certain of him. Don't bind yourself like that. And don't bleat to me that a woman must marry or be nothing. That doesn't have to be true."

Evie remained silent, telling him she hadn't revealed all her reasoning for marrying Atherton. There was something more to it.

If Atherton had some hold over her, something she was willing to marry him to protect, Jamie would kill him. Never mind that duels were a hundred years out of date. Jamie would hand the man a pistol and then pot him. He was a crack shot.

"Do you speak from experience?" Evie asked him abruptly.

Jamie's brows rose. "Experience? What are you on about, lass?"

"You said it was misery giving yourself to the wrong person. Have you done that?"

"Not I." Jamie had never given himself completely to anyone, which accounted for the empty feeling drilling into his heart now. "But I've seen it happen and heard the tales, especially in my own family. My dad and uncles went through so much hurting before they found love. I don't want to watch that happen to you."

"You will not have to watch anything." Evie stepped briskly from him, breaking their contact. "I will marry Hayden, and you will go off somewhere in the world and live your own life. I know you've become chummy with Hayden, but I think after our marriage, you should not visit us."

Chummy. Part of Jamie wanted to laugh. He was civil to the man to serve his own ends, but he'd not say that to Evie.

The other half of him wanted to touch her again, pull her into his arms, kiss her until she promised to show Atherton the door. If she didn't want Jamie in her life, so be it, but he would not let her promise herself to a man she loathed.

"And that's the end of it, then?" Jamie let the question hold the hint of a growl.

"Yes. It must be."

Evie now should give him a decided nod, turn with a swirl of skirts, and march out the door, back to the carriage. Their time together finished.

Instead she stood still, her body moving slightly toward him as though the magnet now felt the pull of Jamie.

Jamie laced an arm around her, and Evie sagged against him, as though relieved he'd broken the tension.

"Look at me and tell me you love him." Jamie's voice was low, insistent. "Tell me that, and I'll leave you be. I'll never speak to you again, find another country to live my life in."

"It is none of your business who I love." The response was haughty but delivered in faint, cracked words.

"It is my business. It is because I want your happiness. More than anything, I want that."

Evie started at his fervor. "Why?"

To hell with it. "Because I'm in love with you, lass."

CHAPTER 17

*E*vie's heartbeat slowed to a crawl, then abruptly accelerated until she was breathless.

Jamie Mackenzie had just said he loved her.

His blue eyes were quiet, all teasing absent. A lock of his red-brown hair curved over his face, shadowing his cheek in the lantern light.

This beautiful, funny, gallant, amazing man had said that he loved her, but this couldn't be real. Evie had pushed away love, the pain of it too much for her. Hayden was safe. A friend. That was all she needed.

"I don't quite believe you," she heard herself say. She didn't dare.

Jamie's brows slammed down. "No?" He released her, and Evie took a step back, off-balance. "Why the devil would I spend a week planning to steal a blasted piece of pottery out of a museum so you could help a woman I barely know? Why would I have rushed around in the pouring rain last night when I could have been snug at my father's house sampling his best whisky and cigars? Or getting very drunk with my friends at a hell somewhere? Why should I do all that, if not for you?"

"I don't know," Evie stammered. "I thought you were

trying to rub Hayden's nose in it—show him you could do everything better than he."

"I don't give a damn about what Hayden Atherton thinks of me," Jamie growled. "I give a damn about what *you* think of me. I always have."

"Always?" Evie's voice shook. "Always is a long time."

"It's hell." Jamie's harsh words pierced her heart. "It's forever." He slammed his arms around her and pulled her up to him, bringing their faces an inch apart. "Damn you, lass."

His lips brushed hers with the last word. Evie waited for the kiss, but it didn't come. Jamie seemed frozen, as though longing to kiss her but not being able to make the final connection.

Evie rose on her tiptoes and made the connection for him.

Jamie stilled for a long moment, then he kissed her back with a fierceness that weakened her.

Evie clung to him shamelessly, wanting this kiss, coaxing him against her. Her vows to herself, promises sworn last night as well as years ago, shattered and fell to the oil-spattered floor.

She shouldn't do this, yet everything in her craved it. This man shook her and fulfilled her in a way Hayden never would, and she knew it.

Jamie cupped her breast with his hard hand. His touch seared, awakening need.

The kiss bruised her lips then moved to her cheek, teeth scraping her jaw. Jamie's tongue traced a scalding trail to her ear, and Evie emitted a raw noise when he nipped her earlobe.

His broad, strong back was firm beneath her fingers. Evie wanted to feel his skin bare as she pulled him down to her in the night, Jamie warming her with his mouth, his hands, his body.

She wanted it with vehemence. The shock of this awareness jolted her, but she could not let him go. Evie touched Jamie's face and kissed him once more.

A cold burst of air made her jump, but Jamie didn't cease kissing her, and Evie didn't push him away. His eyes were closed, dark red lashes stark against his skin, his hard face softened with desire.

Gavina's soft cough drifted to them.

Jamie carefully finished the kiss, taking his time. He brushed moisture from Evie's lips, softly tapping the lower one, before he turned to Gavina.

"Aye, all right." His rumbling voice was leisurely, Jamie not at all ashamed of being caught kissing Evie. "Give us a moment."

"You might not have a moment." Gavina spoke without urgency and no surprise she'd found Evie in Jamie's arms. "There's a nice constable walking up the street, wondering why a carriage has been sitting here so long."

Evie's gaze darted nervously to the bundle of the alabastron. Logic told her the constable could know nothing of it—he was probably more worried about someone breaking into the lock-up.

"If it's Constable Taylor, he knows me." Jamie gathered up the bundle without haste, took Evie's hand, and led her out.

They stepped into the breeze, but the chill couldn't cut the heat in Evie's body. Jamie's kisses burned on her lips, and she thought she'd never be cold again.

"Morning, Taylor," Jamie called to the constable. He assisted Evie into the carriage, handed up the package, closed the gate, and fastened the padlock.

The constable's scowl turned to a grin of recognition. "Morning, sir." He touched his helmet. "Ladies."

Jamie helped Gavina into the coach and sprang up behind her. "Carry on, Constable. Best to your missus."

"Thank you, sir. Good day to you." The constable stood solidly near the lock-up, watching as the carriage rolled away down the lane.

Evie closed her eyes against Gavina's stare and hugged the bundle to her chest over her rapidly beating heart.

———

EVIE'S MEETING WITH IRIS WAS TO OCCUR AT BROWN'S Hotel, which lay between Dover and Albemarle Streets in Mayfair. Less than half an hour after they left the lock-up, Jamie's coach halted in the narrow street in front of the hotel's long facade, a uniformed man springing forward to open the carriage door.

"I'll be leaving you ladies here," Jamie announced.

Evie didn't like the knife of disappointment his statement caused. "Iris's father is out," she said, hoping this would change his mind. "We arranged it."

Jamie jumped to the pavement, thanking the doorman and turning to assist Evie out. "Exactly why a down-at-heels Scot shouldn't be escorting you in. Iris's papa would hear of it and object." He steadied Evie before reaching for Gavina. "The carriage can stay—the driver will take you wherever you wish."

"Kind of you," Gavina said, and she nodded graciously at the doorman. "Thank you, sir. We are here to visit our friend Miss Georgiou."

Gavina swept inside as though she were royalty, the doorman and several pageboys rushing after her.

Attendants swarmed Evie as well, one trying to relieve her of the wrapped alabastron. "No, no, I will carry this," she said, clutching it tightly. "It is a gift, and very fragile."

"I assure you, madam—" a porter began.

"Better let her keep it," Jamie advised him. "She'll never let me hear the end of it, if you don't." The porter backed off at his statement, and Evie breathed out in relief.

The porter snapped his fingers at boys who raced to hold open the doors for Evie. Jamie waited until Evie was safely inside, then he turned and sauntered away down the quiet street.

Evie watched him go through the glass of the hotel's front door. Did Jamie deliberately move so his kilt outlined his backside, so a gust of wind revealed his strong thighs beneath it?

She watched until a hurrying pageboy brushed past her, jerking her attention back to the lobby. Gavina was already waiting at the lift, a gleaming brass affair fitted into a bend of a staircase. Evie composed her expression and hurried to join her.

Gavina was mercifully silent as they rode up three floors, the uniformed man operating the lift guiding it in equal silence. He bade them a good morning as they exited, Gavina returning the farewell.

Gavina thrust her arm through Evie's as they hastened along the hall toward Iris's suite. "You and I will have a talk, later," she promised.

Someone definitely needed to speak to Evie and set her straight. Her whirlwind mind and confusion were doing her no good.

Evie pressed the bell beside the door at the end of the corridor, and a maid admitted them into a foyer that held a polished table under a small chandelier. When Evie scurried into the suite's sitting room, Iris rushed from the window to embrace her.

"I thought you'd never come." Iris's black hair was awry, as though she'd been running her hands through it. "You did bring it?"

Gavina emerged from the foyer after handing the maid her coat and hat, and Iris slammed her lips closed.

"This is Gavina Mackenzie," Evie assured her. "Jamie's cousin."

"Oh." Iris relaxed a fraction then extended a hand with the pretty manners she could assume. "Very pleased to meet you."

"Miss Georgiou." Gavina shook her hand heartily. "Never worry. I will not betray you, whatever it is you're up to."

Iris shot a glance at Evie as the two ladies' hands slid apart.

Evie set down the bundle and relinquished her coat and hat to the maid, who discreetly vanished into the next room, shutting the door with a firm click.

"Jamie dropped me on Gavina's doorstep last night," Evie said. "I couldn't go to Hayden's home in the state I was in."

Iris's brows climbed until they met the hair that curled on her forehead. "State?"

"Because of the rain. We were caught in it." Evie tried to ignore Gavina's knowing look.

"I think you had better tell me all about it," Iris said. "But first …"

She lifted the bundle and carried it to the dining table on the far side of the sitting area. Evie and Gavina followed, the three of them taking seats around the table while Iris peeled the cloths from the alabastron.

Iris let out a long breath as the red and black painted curves of the jar came into view. "Thank God," Iris said in a rush.

"My word." Gavina brushed her finger over the swell of the vessel, outlining the lady with the necklaces. "This is beautiful. I'm guessing it's priceless?"

"Yes." Iris gave a decided nod. "Which is why it must go back to Greece."

Gavina's eyes sparkled, as though she was catching on to the nature of their crime. "Can you get it there? Don't people search luggage, and so forth? Both in this country and Greece?"

Iris folded the cloths tightly over the jar as though she feared to look at it any longer. The beauty faded, the black covering fabric drab.

The cloths reminded her of Jamie, Evie thought suddenly. His kilt was ragged at the hem, his coat a casual one that anyone might wear, never mind Jamie was the nephew of a duke and son of a very wealthy lord. Inside the understated clothing was a man who shone brightly—largehearted, intelligent, and giving.

"I have made arrangements," Iris said, sending them a mysterious glance.

Iris had always enjoyed intrigue and subterfuge, Evie remembered. The young ladies of Girton, who weren't supposed to drink brandy or smoke cigars, enjoyed them in secret thanks to Iris.

"Perhaps we should go to Greece with you," Gavina offered. "Make sure the jar gets into the right hands."

Her eagerness made Evie believe she'd pack her things and set off tonight. Iris's eyes glinted with the same eagerness, and Evie flinched. The two of them were much alike.

"Or you can calmly carry out your plan," Evie said sternly. "Your father would wonder at the additions to your party and why you were so anxious to go home."

Iris sighed. "You are right, but this has been quite nerve-wracking. Father is terribly morose, and I can't explain to him what we're doing. He'd try to stop me." Iris brushed her hand over the wrapped jar. "I knew I was right to contact you, Evie. I can't ever express my gratitude. Anything you need, you tell me, and it's yours."

Evie had the feeling Iris would hand over a live cheetah if Evie requested it. "I'm perfectly happy as I am. But thank you."

"The offer stands," Iris said generously. "Now, tell me how you managed to retrieve it. Was Hayden any help at all? Or did he blunder about, as I feared?"

"He wasn't there," Evie said before she could stop herself.

Iris's brows went up again. "It was you and Mr. Mackenzie? And Miss Mackenzie?" She glanced at Gavina for confirmation.

Gavina shrugged. "No, I had no knowledge of any of this. Unhappily so."

"Oh?" Iris's focus moved to Evie and stayed there. "Do tell, Evie."

"You make it sound rather sordid." Evie tried to assume a disapproving tone.

"You and my cousin, alone, carrying out a nefarious theft." Gavina shook her head in mock sorrow. "Not sordid at all."

"We spent almost the entire time searching the blasted basement," Evie said defensively. "It was dark and cold and dank. Then I had to hide in the back seat of a motorcar while it poured rain. Adventures are mostly uncomfortable and distressing."

"No, no." Gavina wagged her finger. "Entire story. From the beginning."

Two pairs of eyes, one midnight dark, the other sea-gray, pinned her. Evie heaved a sigh, knowing she'd never leave here until she told them, and began.

As she spoke, she relived the darkness of the shadowy cellar, and then Jamie and his torch turning the spooky place into an ordinary, almost cheerful one. Jamie's warm presence behind her on the ladder, the gladness Evie had felt when she'd seen him making his way toward the motorcar where she'd hidden.

The elation when they'd realized they'd successfully rescued the alabastron, and then the searing kiss that had changed Evie forever.

Evie said nothing of the kiss, of course, giving her listeners a truncated version of what happened at the lock-up. She ended the tale with Jamie leaving her at Gavina's.

"Gavina and the other ladies of the house kindly took me in," Evie concluded. "Which is where I wrote the note to you, Iris." She spread her hands. "And here I am."

Gavina knew quite well Evie had left out bits, but thankfully she said nothing.

Evie should depart now, as the mission had been accomplished, Iris in possession of the alabastron. She should ask the carriage driver Jamie had hired to take her to Upper Brook Street, or she might walk there—it wasn't far—and leave the carriage for Gavina.

Time to put aside the adventure, laughter, and her friends, and resume her role as the devoted fiancée of Hayden Atherton, heir to Sir Hector and his fortune.

A few days ago, she'd have been content to do so. Would have thought nothing of it. But Jamie had dived back into Evie's life and ruined everything.

The contentment Evie had sought, had thought she'd found on the return from New York, had splintered. Jamie's presence had shoved a wrench into her plans, twisting this way and that.

She knew she could not stay away from the Athertons' much longer. A night spent with friends was one thing. Avoiding the house entirely was something else. Hayden would start to wonder why she didn't want to come home.

Which she did not.

"Let's have a splendid tea," Evie exclaimed abruptly. "With lots of cake."

The other two, who had launched into a discussion of their time at Cambridge, broke off and stared at her.

"It's early for tea," Iris said dubiously.

"But not for luncheon," Gavina said, catching Evie's enthusiasm. "Evie needs to be rewarded for a job well done."

Iris nodded agreement. "Shall I ring for a tray? They have splendid food here."

"No, indeed." Gavina sprang to her feet, her energy compelling. "We shall go to a restaurant, a perfectly decadent one. We're old enough to gad about by ourselves, young ladies together. And anyway, everyone expects me to be shocking."

"Yes, let's," Evie said in relief. "Unless you don't want to leave this, Iris." She touched the wrapped alabastron.

Iris lifted the bundle as she rose, tucking it under her arm.

"Won't be a tick." She dashed into an adjoining room, slamming the door. Before Gavina or Evie could exchange speculations about what she would do with the thing, Iris emerged.

Evie hoped she'd put the alabastron someplace safe, where a maid wouldn't find it. But Iris seemed serene, so Evie said nothing. Evie's part in obtaining the alabastron was over. It was up to Iris now to return it to Greece.

She somehow knew that wouldn't be the end of it, but Evie followed the excited Gavina and Iris out, tamping down on her misgivings.

———

JAMIE ENTERED THE PORTLAND CLUB IN ST. JAMES'S AND left his greatcoat with the doorman. Though it was only just after noon, the card rooms Jamie bypassed on the way to the library were full.

"Mackenzie, there you are." Hayden Atherton waved him over to two leather chairs pulled up to a small table. A waiter appeared from nowhere to deposit two glasses of whisky and a decanter and then vanish. "I was about to give up."

"Errands to run." Jamie shook Atherton's offered hand and seated himself, crossing his stretched-out legs. He took up the whisky. "To the ladies," he said, raising his glass.

"Always a worthy toast." Atherton sat down and clicked his glass to Jamie's.

The whisky was better than average, Jamie found as he sipped, but his nose detected a too-smoky scent, the burn from a whisky barrel that hadn't been prepared well. Any other man would think this whisky fine, but Jamie's palate had been trained by Ian Mackenzie, the best distiller in Scotland.

Jamie set his glass aside. "Thank you for seeing me. My apologies for being late."

"Not at all. The Portland is a jolly place to spend time, though my father will expect me before long. Philanthropic clubs are all right, in his book, but ones meant for card playing and a chin-wag, like this, are not."

"Yes, your father can be a stickler." Jamie removed a cigar from the humidor next to him, sniffed it, then bit off its end and lit it. He gestured to the humidor, but Atherton shook his head. Probably his father disapproved of cigars as well.

"He can be indeed," Atherton answered without offense. "Which was why I had to beg off last night. Evie understood, bless the girl."

"She did. I am pleased to tell you that the expedition was a success."

Atherton raised his glass. "Hear, hear."

Jamie returned the toast out of politeness and took another sip. Definitely should have rejected that barrel.

"I've been making inquiries about your father." Jamie puffed the cigar, which erased the slightly acrid aftertaste of the whisky. "Hope you don't mind. I was curious."

Atherton raised his brows but shrugged. "Not at all. I can tell you anything you wish to know. Can't understand why the devil you would want such knowledge, but I allow gentlemen their hobbies."

Jamie set aside the cigar and drew out the paper he'd received from Andrew. "What I learned is that your father keeps a rigid timetable." He opened the page as though refreshing his memory, but he knew every word by heart. "He leaves for his office at nine in the morning, dines at home at one, then returns to the office again to work until six. Has his supper at seven, on the dot."

"Yes." Atherton laughed again, but looked pained. "Can set your watch by the old fellow. It was always a relief to go off to school after a holiday home."

Jamie tucked the paper back into his pocket and rested his hands on the arms of the chair.

"After supper, your father takes a few sips of brandy, for medicinal purposes, and then retires, at nine o'clock, every night, without fail. Never brings work home, always does it at the office. He divides his day into exact categories, and none of those categories ever mix."

"True. True."

Atherton was slow. Jamie would have to spell it out for him.

"So, lad, when you said you couldn't attend last night because your father kept you at the office working with him, you were a liar." Jamie turned what his mother called the Mackenzie stare onto Atherton. "Where the devil were ye?"

CHAPTER 18

For a moment, Atherton gaped at him. Then, instead
of spluttering a denial, flustered and embarrassed,
Atherton sank back in his seat with his annoying chortle.

"Very well, Mackenzie. You caught me. Wasn't worried
that Evie would—she avoids conversation with my father at all
costs. But it was your fault, you know. You switched the day to
Thursday."

Jamie kept his face straight, though he hadn't expected this
answer. "And Thursdays are important to you?"

"Of course. If you'd chosen Wednesday, or Friday, or
Monday or any other day, I'd have been there with bells on.
Or perhaps not, as we needed to be silent." More inane
laughter.

Jamie fought down the urge to punch Atherton in the face.
"Why didn't ye send word that another day would be better?
Instead of Evie going out alone with me?"

"Because she was so adamant that she get her hands on the
blasted jar and give it to Miss Georgiou. If Evie stayed home
with me, she'd have tumbled to my ruse, so I sent her off. Miss
Georgiou is a stunner, by the way, and unmarried. You ought

to try your luck there, Mackenzie. She'd make a splendid wife for a chap, even if she's foreign."

Jamie wasn't certain Iris would be flattered by his description. "Want to tell me about her?"

"Miss Georgiou?" Atherton feigned puzzlement, then he grinned. "No, I know who you mean. Better still, would you like to meet her?"

"Is that allowed?" Jamie pressed down the rage building inside him. "It's Friday."

Atherton burst out laughing. "You are a wag, Mackenzie. But she won't mind." He lifted his glass and drained it. "Drink up, and off we'll go."

———

ATHERTON TOOK JAMIE IN A HANSOM TO A SMALL HOUSE north of St. Pancras Station. The station itself was a wonder of the age, a huge cathedral-like building on the outside, with massive, modern iron arches over the trains' platforms on the inside. In one of the tiny lanes behind this gothic edifice, Atherton descended the hackney and knocked peremptorily on a white-painted door.

This was opened by a startled charwoman who scuttled aside, holding her broom, as Atherton greeted her merrily. The char watched him enter the house, then shook her head and began sweeping the step.

Jamie tipped his cap to her as the hansom clopped away. "Afternoon, love."

The char straightened up, back stiff. "Sir."

"Lovely day after all the rain, eh?" Jamie gestured into the house with a tilt of his head. "He come here often?"

"Every Thursday." The charwoman sniffed. She had a red-blotched face that had once been pretty and a scarf over her graying hair. "Like clockwork."

"No awkwardness if he comes today?" Some women took a different lover each day of the week.

"Nah. She's smitten with him, the silly chit. Lord knows why."

"He's generous?"

"He's all right. Better than some, I suppose." The woman looked Jamie up and down. "You hoping to slide in?"

"No, indeed. My heart is taken."

The woman gave him an approving nod. "Good."

Jamie took her work-worn hand, palming her a coin. "For your family," he said in a quiet voice, then entered the house.

"Where are you, Mackenzie?" Atherton's voice rang from a small parlor. Jamie entered it to find Atherton with his arm slung around a small woman with glossy brown hair, a wide smile, and large blue eyes. "This is Brigitte."

"Mrs. Mason," the woman corrected Atherton with an impish smile. "He always forgets that part. I'm a widow, love. Don't worry. No husband's going to leap out and shout *Aha!*"

Jamie smiled his appreciation of her humor. "How do you do? Jamie Mackenzie, at your service."

"Well, ain't you the posh one?" Brigitte's smile lit up the room—Jamie could understand what Atherton saw in her.

"His uncle is a duke," Atherton informed her.

"Oh, is he?" Brigitte made an exaggerated curtsy. "Charmed, I'm sure."

Jamie laughed—Atherton did not deserve this woman. He did not deserve Evie either.

Jamie had planned to confront and threaten Atherton here, but he swiftly changed his mind. Brigitte was no practiced seductress, and she did not need drama and rage in her front parlor.

He read years of penury in Brigitte's eyes, and fear that they would come again. A widow, she'd said, though that did not necessarily mean a legal marriage. Whatever husband she'd had likely had not left her much.

Atherton must lease this house and pay Brigitte's expenses. Probably had for years.

"Do have a seat Mr. Mackenzie." Brigitte waved him to one of the parlor's soft chairs. "I'll scare up some tea. Though I warn you, Cook don't like to be bothered between meals."

"Let me go down." Atherton nearly danced to the door. "I can charm her. She likes me. Heaven knows why."

"Because she thinks you need fattening up," Brigitte called after him, then Atherton was gone, the door banging behind him.

Jamie settled himself in an armchair large enough to take his limbs, and gave the room an approving once-over. "Very cozy."

"Ain't it? Can't complain." Brigitte seated herself on a chair facing him, hands on her lap.

"How long have you known Atherton?" Jamie asked her.

Brigitte considered. "Oh, five years? About that."

Jamie gentled his tone. "You know he's going to be married."

Brigitte shrugged, but Jamie read pain in the gesture. "A bloke has to marry someone, don't he? And he can't marry me —his pa would die of apoplexy. Hayden's got to carry on the family line. Makes no difference to us."

No doubt Atherton had already worked out a strategy. Thursdays with Brigitte would be sacrosanct. Jamie imagined he'd claim a standing meeting at his club every Thursday— possibly he was already doing so. He'd explain that the meetings always ran late, and he might as well stay the night there. Very tidy.

But how long would it be before Evie, no fool, discovered his ruse? She'd then be stuck in a marriage with the idiot, because a divorce would ruin her, even if Atherton was at fault.

A judge might also decide that if Atherton wasn't neglecting or harming Evie, then no divorce would be granted.

Atherton might sheepishly vow to never go back to Brigitte, but Jamie guessed the promise wouldn't last long.

Also, if Atherton *did* break off his adultery, then Brigitte would more than likely be turned out of this charming house and have nowhere to go.

Bloody man, Jamie growled to himself. Two women wretched, and Atherton would waltz on through his life with an idiotic grin on his face.

"You can do better, lass," Jamie said, unable to remain silent.

Brigitte's gaze became coy. "Are you offering yourself? In your friend's own house? Cheeky."

"No," Jamie answered in seriousness. "I'm spoken for. But you're a fine young woman, and worth ten of him."

Brigitte lost her amusement. "Maybe. Maybe not. But there's not much wrong with him, is there? He's rich, he's friendly, and he's very punctual." Her smile flashed briefly. "I always know he'll arrive here on Thursday at exactly eight in the evening, then go at eight in the morning, on the dot."

"Like his father." The words slipped out.

Brigitte shuddered. "That ogre. Drives poor Hayden spare sometimes. But Hayden's much softer than the old bugger. He's not cruel, not like some I've known. I'm very comfortable here." Her gaze turned skewering, as though warning Jamie not to take away what she'd found.

Jamie lifted his hand in a placating gesture. "I'm observing that he doesn't deserve you, is all. If you're happy, and he's happy, who am I to interfere?" Jamie let hardness enter his tone. "But if he ever *is* cruel, you tell me, and I will deal with him."

"Oh, yes?" Brigitte's light mood returned, but Jamie saw she understood his offer. "You'll be my guardian angel, will you?"

"Why not?" Jamie settled back, hearing Atherton's

laughter and light footsteps returning. "I enjoy it. Just remember."

Brigitte nodded. "I will. Don't you worry." She rose and opened the door, reaching for the tray Atherton balanced on his arms. "Give me that before you drop it, daft lad."

Atherton relinquished the tray and beamed at Jamie. He was a happy man, everything right in his world.

———

Gavina bade the carriage driver take them to a restaurant called Argyle's on Regent Street, named so because it stood near the corner of Argyle Street. It was highly fashionable, an opulent eatery in one of the original buildings that made up Regent Street's crescent.

All of London seemed to be here today, but Gavina had a word with the manager, and the three ladies were shown to a fine table in the center of the room.

"Aunt Eleanor brings me here all the time," Gavina explained as waiters thronged around them to offer napkins and a light white wine fit for young ladies. "Mama is often busy helping Papa during racing season, so Aunt Eleanor takes it upon herself to whisk me around to all the modish places. Listening to her dissect them all in her lovely voice is hilarious."

"Are we being very scandalous?" Evie asked as she sipped the wine the sommelier had served them. It was light and crisp, quite refreshing. "Three ladies out without gentlemen or older female relatives?"

"Very, but times are changing," Gavina answered. "Everyone would have fainted in Mama's day, though she and Aunt Eleanor, not to mention Aunt Izzy, would have come out like this anyway, if Argyle's had existed then."

Evie noticed she hadn't mentioned Jamie's mother. "What about your Aunt Beth?"

"Ah, she'd have talked them out of it. Scandal for scandal's sake is not worth the trouble, in Aunt Beth's opinion. My mum and aunts like her so much, they'd stay home to please her."

"Jamie has a kindhearted family," Evie said, thinking of Belle.

"He does indeed," Gavina agreed. "Sometimes it frustrates him to live up to their happiness, if that makes any sense. Uncle Ian is brilliant and compassionate, and Aunt Beth is loving and sweet. Everyone expects Jamie to be a genius philanthropist or something, instead of simply … himself."

"I think he's fine the way he is," Evie said before she could stop the words.

Both ladies turned interested gazes her way. Evie floundered, trying to cover her embarrassment, and was saved only by a haughty waiter halting to inquire what they would like from the offerings today.

"Let me order," Gavina said, and then asked for a string of things, half of which Evie didn't recognize the names of. She exchanged a glance with Iris, who shrugged, and they let Gavina carry on.

To Evie's relief, they had no chance to resume the conversation before the soups came out—velvet, creamy bisque—followed by a cool aspic.

"The restaurant is crowded," Iris remarked as they ate. "Our hotel is very full as well."

"The Olympics," Gavina said. "People have flocked from all over the world."

Indeed, which was why Evie's mother hadn't been able to beg a room at their usual London hotel. Which had led to Jamie offering his uncle's suite, which had led to so much more. The Olympics committee didn't know what they'd done to Evie's life.

"Not that it is a terrible thing to see all the athletes." Iris indicated a group of young men who sauntered to a table, led by the maître d'hôtel. Heads turned to watch the gentlemen's lithe grace.

"It is not," Gavina said as one young man nodded in their direction. "How polite they are. And forward at the same time."

"Are they runners, do you think?" Evie asked. "They're slender rather than muscular."

"Perhaps we could tell if they showed us their legs," Iris suggested. "They'll run with them bare, why not give us a glimpse now?"

The same young man regarded them quizzically as they stared at him, and the three ladies fell into laughter, interrupted only by the waiters bringing them further dishes.

Evie noted the young men continued to cast glances in their direction, especially at Gavina, who was a radiant light, and Iris, a shining beauty. Any lad would be lucky to catch the eye of either of them, Evie thought without resentment.

"I'd love to have been on a rowing team," Gavina was saying when Evie returned her attention to the meal. "But I can't row a stroke. I'm much better at tennis—singles, that is. Probably because I play alone and don't have to worry about keeping pace with others."

"Rowers do have to learn to work together," Iris said. "Evie was our fearless leader. We won many matches with her shouting at us."

Gavina's brows rose. "I can't imagine Evie as the heavy-handed captain of the ship."

"Oh, believe it," Iris said with mirth. "Captain Bly, we called her. Only on the river, of course. Off the river, she's a sweetie."

"She is indeed," Gavina said warmly, making Evie flush. "Did you continue rowing after university?" When both Evie and Iris answered in the negative, Gavina continued, "Pity. Then maybe you could have been Olympians too."

Iris wrinkled her nose. "The only rowing teams competing are men. Ladies are too delicate, did you not know?"

"Rot that," Gavina scoffed. "I wager you could beat the male teams, hands down."

Gavina was being a generous friend, but Iris's eyes lighted in a way Evie knew could spell disaster.

"We ought to try," Iris said excitedly. "Gather the rest of the team and show the men how it's done."

"Sarah and Alice are married now." Evie put a note of caution in her reply. "And Alice has little ones. They've put their rowing days behind them."

"I'll ask them," Iris proclaimed happily.

Evie did not bother arguing with her. Alice and Sarah would probably laugh and decide Iris was being Iris, and let the matter drop.

But she understood Iris's enthusiasm. Evie recalled their camaraderie on the river, the soaring joy of skimming through the water, oars moving in unison, their triumph when they were first across the finish line. The closeness of the four, who knew each other's deepest secrets.

But those days were gone, when Evie had been young, silly, and happy. Alice and Sarah had found their true loves and started new lives. Iris had returned to Greece, and the foursome now communicated by letters when they could. And Evie …

She groped for a change in topic. "Look," she said in relief that she'd found one. "Isn't that Miss Carmichael?"

Evie pointed with her fork at the fair-haired young woman who was being seated at a table not far from them, directly under the light of a large chandelier. An older woman with a pinched face spoke sternly to her.

Miss Carmichael, instead of listening, had turned her gaze to where Evie, Gavina, and Iris giggled together. The loneliness on the young woman's face tugged at Evie's heart.

"The heiress," Iris said. "Everyone at our hotel is talking about her, though she and her family are at the Langham."

Evie hadn't seen her there, but her family probably locked her tightly away when they weren't parading her about.

"Her parents want her to land a titled husband," Gavina said. "So they can strand her in England and boast to their friends that their daughter is a duchess or a countess or some such."

Miss Carmichael was alone, as usual. No sisters, brothers, or friends to keep her company, only her parents or chaperones, like the one who scowled at her now. Whatever friendships she'd had in New York must have been severed when her family had transported her thousands of miles to London.

As only a handful of titled gentlemen at any time were young, handsome, and single, Miss Carmichael might well find herself shackled to an elderly aristocrat who'd plop her in the middle of the country somewhere and expect her to run his large estate and raise his children, without a thought to her personal happiness.

The stern woman unexpectedly left the table and disappeared somewhere, probably to the kitchen to lecture the chefs on what to prepare for her charge.

Evie dabbed her mouth with her napkin and surged to her feet. "I'm going to speak to her."

Iris brightened. "Aren't there rigid rules of introduction in this country?" she asked, even as she rose.

"I saw Miss Carmichael on the ship," Evie said. "She'll remember me from there."

"And my cousin Violet told her fortune," Gavina said, joining them. "You see? We're practically acquainted already. Shall we ladies? Before the prune-faced biddy returns."

Evie led them to Miss Carmichael's table, the athletic gentlemen turning in their seats to watch them pass.

"Miss Carmichael," Evie said when they halted at her table. "Good afternoon. I'm Evie McKnight. I longed to speak to you on the *Baltic*, but Mama forbade me from approaching you. Impolite, she said."

A hopeful smile appeared on Miss Carmichael's face. "I saw you too, with your sisters. You seemed to be having a marvelous time." Her voice was gentle and smooth, different from the harsh accent Evie had expected. "I am Imogen. How do you do?"

Evie shook Miss Carmichael's hand, noting that her grip was firm, though her palm was soft. "Miss Gavina Mackenzie and Miss Iris Georgiou," she said, waving at the others. "We're mates from university, having an outrageously loud natter together. I hope we didn't disturb you."

"Not at all." Miss Carmichael shook the other two ladies' hands in turn. "You shouldn't apologize for being lively. I have —I *had* lively school friends too."

Her family had indeed ripped her from all she loved. Evie felt ashamed of how she'd teased Jamie about his interest in Miss Carmichael. Jealousy, Evie realized. Jamie, regardless of his lack of title, could be the perfect match for this young woman.

Evie had already run out of things to say, so she fell back on the small talk drilled into her since childhood. "Did you enjoy the voyage?"

"I was ill for a good part of it." Miss Carmichael laughed ruefully. "My mother told me not to mention that."

No, she must be the perfect racehorse. Highly strung but always elegant. Nothing unpleasant, like seasickness, was allowed to mar her.

"My sister Clara was green much of the time too," Evie confided. "Marjorie was not. Her health is appallingly good. It was my task to keep her from climbing all over the ship."

Miss Carmichael laughed again, the strain about her eyes relaxing.

Not for long. The prune-faced biddy strode back in a

hurry, her expression thunderous. Miss Carmichael's smile faded like sunshine behind threatening clouds.

"So pleased to have met you," Miss Carmichael jabbered. "I am afraid you must go."

Gavina stood her ground, giving the approaching biddy a frosty look. "We hope to see you again," she said sincerely.

"We're at the Langham," Miss Carmichael answered in a near-whisper.

"Ladies." The biddy glared at the three, mouth puckered. "I am certain you mean well, but Miss Carmichael is not to become acquainted with anyone her parents have not introduced her to."

"Pity," Gavina said. She scrabbled in her handbag and thrust a cardboard rectangle at the woman. "Please give my card to her mother and father, in case they decide they'd like to introduce us."

Miss Carmichael's eyes widened at the same time her mouth twitched. Iris turned away to hide her laughter. Evie stood by Gavina, sending Miss Carmichael a reassuring smile.

The woman snatched the card from Gavina and frowned at the name but tucked it into her pocket. "Now, Miss Carmichael shall eat her dinner. Good day, ladies."

"Good day, Miss Carmichael," Evie said in the friendliest tone she could muster.

Iris and Gavina chimed in, and Miss Carmichael, looking happier than Evie had yet seen her, returned the farewell.

"Good heavens, what a farce," Gavina muttered as they glided away. "They probably lock her in her bedroom at night and rub all kinds of concoctions on her skin to keep her complexion pure. We ought to kidnap her and take her out for a fine time."

Iris agreed, appearing keen to snatch the girl away here and now, but Evie shook her head.

"Her parents might lock her in more tightly if we did," she warned, "or even take her back to America."

"Where she'd be much happier," Gavina said. "It's cruel to render someone miserable to satisfy your own ambitions. I propose we—" She broke off. "Oh, there are Alec and Mal. I'm surprised the doorman let them in." She waved, and the younger of the two men who'd entered the foyer waved back.

"Gavina," the younger one said, when the three reached them. "I'm surprised they admitted you."

"I've just said that about you. What are you scoundrels doing here?"

"Taking lunch," the younger man said. "We're hungry. They have food here."

"But you can't put your elbows on the table and quaff your whisky at the Argyle," Gavina said. "Better find a pub. These are my friends, Miss McKnight and Miss Georgiou. Ladies, these reprobates are Alec and Malcolm Mackenzie. Uncle Hart's miscreant offspring."

"Charmed." The younger man, Malcolm, had dark red hair and eyes like Jamie's, though the blue of them was lighter. "What beautiful friends you have, Gavina. Where have you been hiding them?"

"Away from you," Gavina answered good-naturedly.

Malcolm gazed into the dining room. "And what delectable young woman were you speaking with? I could feast on the sight of *her*, instead of the fine beefsteak this place is supposed to serve."

"Spare her, please," Gavina said. "You wouldn't be able to get close anyway. She has a dragon guarding her."

Malcolm rubbed his hands and shot Evie a wink. "I love a challenge."

Gavina's expression became exasperated, but she didn't pursue it. Evie had the feeling that Malcolm—he'd be Lord Malcolm Mackenzie—spouted these sorts of things all the time.

The older one, Lord Alec, had said not a word. He was

staring at Iris, golden eyes fixed, hard face still, looking for all the world like he'd been poleaxed.

————

"ATHERTON." JAMIE GREETED HIM IN THE PORTLAND CLUB much later that evening.

After leaving Brigitte's home and parting ways with Atherton this afternoon, Jamie had sent a note to Evie advising her to spend another night with Gavina. He'd made a few more inquiries then arranged to meet with Atherton again.

Atherton took his seat and signaled the waiter to bring them another decanter of whisky. "I do enjoy your company, Mackenzie, but my father will start lecturing me about gadding about in clubs all the day long."

"You won't see much more of me after this." Jamie waved away the glass of whisky the waiter poured for them and paused until the man had retreated.

"Oh? Are you traveling somewhere?"

"No," Jamie answered, leaning back in his chair. "But you probably won't want to speak to me again once we are done." He sent Atherton a beatific smile. "I'm here to blackmail you."

CHAPTER 19

*A*therton started, his color rising, then he appeared to relax. "Very amusing, Mackenzie."

"I am serious." Jamie touched his fingertips together. "A wise man told me I should learn all I could about a problem before deciding how to approach it. That things aren't always what they seem. Today, you handed me the last piece of the puzzle."

Atherton blinked. "You mean introducing you to Brigitte? What the devil, Mackenzie." His smile returned, becoming a smirk. "If you are threatening to blackmail me over Brigitte, I must say, do your worst. She is not a secret to my friends. Many men take mistresses. I wager you have?"

"I've had love affairs, yes," Jamie conceded. "But no, I've never taken what you call a mistress. Whenever I have a lover, that lady is the focus of my attention. I don't keep her dangling on a string while I pursue another. That's not fair to either of them."

"Fair?" Atherton scoffed. "It has nothing to do with being fair. It is the way of the world."

"And if Miss McKnight discovers your mistress?" Jamie

said, holding in his anger with effort. "Do you think *she'd* believe it was fair?"

"A wife never knows," Atherton said with a superior air. "And even if she does find out, she says nothing and looks the other way. Husbands have mistresses, and a good wife doesn't needle him about it."

Jamie let out an exaggerated sigh. "You dig your grave so very deep. You say all men take mistresses. Does your father?"

Atherton's expression turned incredulous. "Good Lord, no. Now you're delving into the realm of fairy tales. My father, I believe, has lain with a woman exactly once, and here is the result." He spread his arms.

"It is always difficult to believe our parents were ever young and lusty," Jamie said. "Mine, however, still kiss passionately in the halls of the ancestral home. One has to slide around them." He shook his head in feigned despair. "My father, actually, saved my mother from an unfortunate betrothal. I have decided to do the same for Evie."

Atherton lost his amusement. "You mean Miss McKnight," he said coldly. "Her betrothal isn't unfortunate. Evie is marrying into an old family—I will inherit my father's business when he retires and a pile of cash at his death. Evie will drip jewels and be the envy of every lady in London. I'm not a bounder who'll keep his wife in rags while he frolics the night away at music halls." He glowered, vastly indignant.

"I am certain you'd give her many gifts," Jamie agreed. "Ensuring she was so dependent on you that she could never leave you or have any sort of life of her own."

Atherton regarded Jamie as though he were a simpleton. "Why would she need her own life? She'll keep house and tend the children, as wives do."

Jamie clenched his hands on the arms of the chair. Losing his temper and striking the man would be satisfying but wouldn't help Evie.

"Shut it, Atherton." Jamie dropped his geniality. "You're going to do something for me."

"Am I? And what is that?" Atherton took a weary sip of whisky, but his hand trembled.

"You will write a letter to Evie. In this letter, you will confess all. Your false excuse for not joining us at the museum, Brigitte, your cozy house where you spend every Thursday. You will tell Evie that you intended to keep said cozy house and charming young lady—who does not deserve the likes of you, by the way—throughout your marriage, and your expectation was that Evie would understand."

Atherton gaped, astounded. "I will, will I?"

"You will end the letter by offering to release Evie from the engagement with no shame to her. No recriminations, no begging her to keep you on, no suits for breach of agreement. She will be free of you without stain." Jamie gave the room a glance. "I don't see a desk in here. Let's find a writing room, and you can begin."

Atherton didn't move. "And if I don't pen this letter, then what? You thrash me?"

Jamie considered. "Oh, I might thrash you for the enjoyment of it. Or I might let my cousin Alec do it. He enjoys beating on full-of-themselves Englishmen. He's never quite forgiven them for killing his ancestors back in the '45. Not to mention the '15, and all the other battles in between."

Atherton's face had lost color. "Assault is a crime."

"That is true. Not that Alec—or I—would let you report said crime. I doubt you'd even be able to speak after Alec was finished. Anyway, no, my idea was not to thrash you."

"Then what?" Atherton's hand was definitely shaking as he took another defiant sip of the too-sharp whisky. "You did say you'd come to blackmail me. I suppose the letter is my payment to you?"

"Perhaps *blackmail* is the wrong word. Threaten you, is more what I mean. You write that letter or—"

"Or what?" Atherton snapped. "You'll tell Evie yourself? Where? In your bed?"

"Careful." Jamie's voice went icy. "Be very, very careful what you say about Evie. In fact, do not even speak her name anymore. She is Miss McKnight to you, and I don't want you even saying that."

"How dare—"

"If you do not write the letter, no, I will not tell Evie." Jamie pinned Atherton with his very-Mackenzie stare. "I will tell your father."

Atherton made a sound that was not a word. His eyes took on terror. "You wouldn't."

"I would. I will tell your morally exacting, austere, and uncompromising father about your infidelity and your lies. Your family is an uncomplicated one. You don't have a tangle of titles, entails, and land eternally snarled to ensure you'll have an income for life, or at least an estate to live on and servants to look after you, even if you're skint. Your father can either leave you all his lovely wealth or turn you out to starve. Entirely his decision."

From Atherton's rigidity, he understood the situation. "My father said Scots were filth," he snarled. "I was fool enough to argue with him. But he is right."

"My mother is English," Jamie said easily. "So, I am only half filth. Perhaps this half." He gestured along the right side of his body. "You will also not tell your father of any of this or blame Evie's departure on her. *You* take the blame. Tell him she grew tired of your fatuousness. He'll believe that."

"You bloody—"

Jamie rose. "Let us adjourn to that writing room. I will dictate the letter for you, so you won't put in any pathetic sniveling. You own up to what you've done, you release her, and that is the end of it."

Atherton sprang to his feet. "I'll kill you for this, Mackenzie."

"Many men have said such to me. And yet, here I stand."

"I'll ruin you." Spittle flecked the corners of Atherton's mouth. "I'll have you blackballed from every club in Britain, including this one. You won't be accepted anywhere."

"Such a tragedy for me." Jamie gestured him to the door. "Write the letter first, and then the committee can boot me out all they like."

Atherton's body inclined slightly toward Jamie, as though ready to launch into him on the moment. Jamie, a tall Scot in a kilt and informal shirt and coat, his hair awry, his boots muddy, only gazed back at him, unruffled. Any doorman of any club could turn Jamie away until he dressed better, but they never did.

Atherton made one more snarl of rage, then he tore out the door, Jamie following more slowly.

Jamie hoped Atherton would try to run, so he could have the fun of tackling him and dragging him bodily to the writing room, but Atherton turned the correct direction and marched to the room of his own accord.

———

EVIE HAD RECEIVED THE NOTE FROM JAMIE THAT afternoon when they'd returned from their meal out, Iris now back at her hotel, which advised her to remain with Gavina and Belle another night.

Very important you do, Jamie had written. *You do not want to be at the Atherton house this evening.*

Evie had expressed skepticism when showing the message to her friends, but Gavina and Belle had been delighted. They were convinced Jamie would not tell Evie to stay with them if it wasn't important.

They trusted him, Evie realized. Evie had already learned that Gavina was not a frail, timorous woman who obeyed orders without question, and neither was Belle. They'd not believe in Jamie if they had no reason to.

Evie admitted that dining with the ladies and Mrs. Barrow was a much pleasanter way to spend the evening than listening to Sir Hector growl, his wife agree with every word, and his son jab at Sir Hector when he could, pretending he was clever.

Evie's blue gown had been cleaned and pressed, feeling crisp and new when she'd donned it before dining. However, she'd liked Belle's unfussy attire and decided to emulate it when next she shopped with her mother for clothing.

They gathered in the parlor after supper for reading, or card games, or puzzles—everyone did as they liked—reminding Evie of nights at her house at Girton. She'd missed such things more than she'd realized.

Agnes, the maid, entered unannounced just as Evie was winning at a hand of rummy, and handed her a thick envelope.

"A love letter," Gayle Hodgkinson speculated. "A nice, long juicy one." Her sister nudged her, but both giggled.

The letter was indeed from Hayden, though he'd never sent Evie passionate missives before.

During her New York sojourn, Evie had received a letter from Hayden exactly once a week, in which he noted in general what he'd been doing at the office with his father, some interesting thing he'd seen on the streets between there and home, and giving her a comment on the current weather. He'd end with well wishes from his mother and himself, to her and her mother. The letter had been the same each week, punctual and predictable.

Hayden had never sat down and penned a long, heartfelt letter expressing his love. Doubtless he hadn't now, either. This was probably some document having to do with their upcoming nuptials that she had to sign.

"Read it in my sitting room," Mrs. Barrow offered. "Away from prying eyes."

"No need." Evie crossed the room to a relatively private corner by the fire. "This will do."

She slid her thumb under the envelope's seal and slit it open, pulling out the folded papers without sitting down. It usually took about thirty seconds to digest Hayden's correspondence.

The first words of perfunctory greeting slid by, followed by a long page full of Hayden's scrawl. Evie continued to read, becoming very still as her eyes moved down the paper.

The letter couldn't possibly say what it did. The words flowed into her mind but meant nothing, had nothing to do with her — did they?

You have my deepest apologies for causing you pain …

… reason for not helping you Thursday evening was a falsehood.

… house in Camden Town, which holds my mistress of five years.

… Thursday is my day for her … Loyalty to her is my first concern.

… releasing you from our betrothal without a stain on you. I will confess to dissolution and walk away for your own good.

Be well,

Hayden Atherton

Evie's legs gave way, and she found herself falling onto the chair behind her, the room speeding past.

Gavina was at her side in an instant, followed by Mrs. Barrow and Belle, Agnes appearing like an angel who knew when evil had entered.

"Darling, what is it?" Gavina's voice was gentle and quiet, all brashness gone.

Evie could not speak, could not move. She made no resistance when Gavina slid the pages from her numb fingers.

Thoughts tumbled through Evie's head as Gavina read the letter, exclaiming out loud before she handed it to Mrs. Barrow.

Hayden excusing himself every Thursday evening, claiming a meeting at his club to discuss stocks and bonds or some such.

Evie had not paid much attention, and even his father had approved of this activity.

She hadn't questioned when Hayden had said his father demanded his presence the night of the museum heist, though she'd never seen Sir Hector work at home. She assumed it was an important project that needed their attention. She'd had no urge to ask Sir Hector if this were true, didn't much like speaking to the man at all.

Thursday is my day for her ...

Evie should be outraged, gutted, devastated, but she could only sit in the chair while the too-warm fire played over her and ice flowed through her veins.

She contrasted the courteous and respectful phrases in this letter to Hayden's cheerful, brief style in the missives to New York, which he'd written dutifully. She saw with stark clarity now that only duty had prompted him.

Jamie had sent her instructions to remain at Gavina's. *You do not want to be at the Atherton house this evening.* Because he'd known Hayden would send her this letter. Knew every word of it. Had told Hayden exactly what to write.

Evie rose abruptly, her stomach roiling. "I must speak to Jamie."

Gavina slid her arm around her as Belle read the letter over Mrs. Barrow's shoulder. Belle's expression held distress and anger, the things Evie should feel.

"Perhaps you'd better have a cup of tea instead," Gavina said in a kind voice. "With a splash of brandy." Agnes nodded at once and hurried away.

"No." Evie balled her fists. "This is *his* doing. I want to know why."

"Jamie's ...?" Gavina wrinkled her brow. "Yes, I see what you mean. But, I'm sorry, my dear, I don't think Mr. Atherton's letter is a ruse."

"Oh, I know it is the truth. It is just like Hayden to believe he can have all he wants, and everyone will be happy to give it to him." Evie broke off, throat tight. "But Jamie had a hand in this confession. I want to speak to him."

Mrs. Barrow took over. "In the morning. Gavina is right, what's best is a cup of tea with a bit of spirits, and a sound sleep."

"No." Evie jerked from Gavina's grasp. "You are kind, but no. I won't sleep. I must see him." She started across the parlor. "Where are his lodgings?"

Belle was next to her, stopping Evie from flying out the door with a surprisingly strong grip. "Do not run to his flat and get yourself talked about. Let me find out where Jamie is tonight and bring him here."

"He'll never come," Gavina predicted. "To a houseful of women who will browbeat him?"

"He'll come," Belle said in a hard voice. "I'll make certain of it." She released Evie and stalked into the hall and out the front door, determination in every step.

As it happened, Jamie did not return with Belle to the house. Instead, a half hour after she'd gone, Belle arrived in a large landau pulled by fine gray horses. A groom who'd hung on the back of the coach spoke to the maid at the door, as the inhabitants of the house watched from the parlor window. The maid in turn babbled something to Agnes, who hurried into the room.

"You are to go, Miss McKnight," Agnes said urgently. "Come. I have your coat ready."

"Go where?" Evie asked in bewilderment.

"Belgrave Square," Agnes announced.

CHAPTER 20

The landau was the most sumptuous Evie had ever ridden in. The seats were upholstered in gray velvet, the walls paneled in a marquetry of sinuously curved leaves and vines. A fire box warmed her feet, and gleaming lamps lit the space. Belle had pulled the curtains closed, shutting them into a plush box.

Belle said nothing as the coach rolled northward to Belgrave Square. The journey did not take long, and soon a footman was opening the carriage door before a brick mansion with tall, arched windows and a porticoed front door. Light shone in every window, the entire house glowing with it.

"Are they having a soiree?" Evie asked nervously once she was on the pavement. She had no intention of walking into a houseful of guests from the cream of society.

"No, it's just the family," Belle answered beside her. "Mum likes everything lit up at night. When she was companion to the lady who lived here before, the house was always gloomy."

Despite Belle's offhand reference to her mother's humbler origins, Evie well knew the Mackenzies could afford the gas and oil that made so much light possible. They were one of the wealthiest families in Britain.

Evie's nervousness didn't dim. Meeting Jamie's family might be just as harrowing as the scrutiny of the *haut ton*.

The enormous front hall was empty when they entered, a blazing chandelier hanging silently above them. A large staircase, equally empty and silent, bent out of sight at the far end of the hall.

Another footman calmly took Evie's and Belle's coats, hats, and gloves, then Belle gestured Evie to follow her. They went up the stairs, a thick runner muffling their steps.

Evie might consider the house lovely at any other time. There was cozy seating on the landing, and tables with knick-knacks ranging from costly trinkets to obvious souvenirs from family outings.

The first floor was as still as the ground floor below. If anyone was in the house, they kept out of sight and very quiet.

Belle opened a door along the hall and ushered Evie into a small sitting room furnished for comfort rather than grandeur. Overstuffed chairs had been drawn to the fireplace, books adorned every shelf, and a small piano graced one corner. A chamber to take leisure in, to enjoy.

Except for Belle and Evie, the sitting room was empty. "He'll be down directly," Belle said, and before Evie could protest, she slipped out and was gone, closing the door behind her.

Evie gazed at the door for one frozen moment, poised to flee. Had she been summoned to speak to Jamie? Or the formidable Ian Mackenzie and his beautiful but steely wife, Beth?

Evie had never met them, but she'd heard plenty of stories about the soft-spoken woman who'd inherited a fortune and then married the mad Ian Mackenzie. Beth Mackenzie was not to be trifled with, people said, then in the same breath proclaimed what a dear she was.

Evie should not have come here. She should have remained

home and wrestled with her pain of Hayden's confession, but her agitation had not let her sit still.

It did not let her be still now. She began to pace restlessly, wandering the comfortable chamber but unable to leave it. Belle hadn't locked the door, but Evie knew the family wanted her to stay. Besides, she had no way of returning to Gavina's except for a walk through the dark streets alone.

Would Gavina and Mrs. Barrow even let her stay if she went back? Perhaps for a day or two out of kindness, but she could not stop there forever.

Evie's family was in Bedfordshire, believing her happily ensconced in the Atherton household, where she'd remain until the wedding. She'd have to tell them what had happened, beg them to fetch her home.

Evie pressed her hands to her face, her eyes dry, then she ran her fingers along the piano's keyboard.

She knew how to play—she and her sisters had taken lessons—but she hadn't played in some time. The Athertons had a piano, but it was only for show. No one actually made music with it.

Evie plunked herself down on the piano stool, calling to mind an easy piece she'd practiced long ago. Simple chords for the left hand, a running melody on the right. No Mozart or Chopin, but exercises from a student's music book.

"My sister loves that piano," Jamie rumbled from across the room. "She says it has a better voice than many concert grands she's played."

Evie snatched her fingers from the keys and spun around. Jamie stood by the door, as easy as he pleased, same kilt and coat he'd worn earlier today hanging from hips and shoulders.

She rose, all the words she'd wanted to throw at him vanishing. Was this why Jamie had commanded her here? So he could wipe her mind of the furious shouts she'd prepared, and melt her as usual?

Evie strengthened her resolve, standing her ground as she faced him. "You knew I'd receive that letter tonight."

Jamie closed the door but halted halfway across the carpet, not approaching her too closely. "You see why I thought it best you were at Belle's when you did."

"Because you told Hayden to write it," she said rigidly. "And exactly what to say. He'd never think of phrases like that on his own."

"True, I suggested to him how to break it to you."

Evie's throat constricted. "Why did you at all? What has it to do with you?"

Jamie's frown only made him more handsome. "You deserved to know the truth, lass."

"Was it the truth?"

"Aye." Jamie nodded, his face somber. "I met Atherton's lady."

"You *met* her? Did you follow him? Spy on — "

"Atherton took me to see her." Jamie cut across her words. "He insisted. Thought it would impress me." His frown grew more formidable. "He's a blackguard of the worst kind, Evie. He was ready to deceive you all your life and thought nothing about it."

"Blackguard? Do people still use that word?" Evie's laugh was mirthless. "How do I know any of this is fact?"

Jamie took a step closer. "I think you know it is."

Yes, she did. Hayden would never have admitted such a thing otherwise. He'd have refused in outrage and sent Jamie off, and possibly now be telling Evie what a blackguard *Jamie* was.

Hayden would not have broken the engagement without a compelling reason — he'd been perfectly happy to marry Evie, pleased he'd found a woman who met his parents' exacting standards. And even if Hayden had wanted to extract himself from the betrothal, he'd have found a way that put him in a better light.

"But why is it your business?" Evie persisted. "Why have you decided to interfere in my life? For your entertainment? To laugh about it with your so very large and very close family? Is that why I am here—so they can listen and laugh?" She scanned the room as though searching for peepholes through which his sisters, parents, and many cousins could watch them.

"Entertainment?" Jamie's voice rose. "I am trying to save you from a life of heartbreak. Do you think I'm laughing about that? I care about you, Evie. I want you to be happy. You wouldn't have been with that ineffectual toad, and I couldn't let you throw yourself away on him."

"But isn't that *my* choice?" Evie struck her chest with an open hand. "I should decide whom I marry, not *you*. *I* decide if my fiancé is a loathsome blackguard, not you."

"Fair point." Jamie nodded. "It *is* your decision. But if I hadn't made Atherton confess, you'd not have found out until too late. Hate me all you want, love, banish me to the wilderness, but you needed to know what kind of man he is."

"Which I would have discovered on my own. Hayden is not good at subterfuge." His first ideas for stealing back the alabastron had bordered on the ludicrous.

"And as I said, by then it would be too late. You'd have been married to the idiot."

Evie found herself closer to Jamie, though she didn't remember moving her feet. "It is still my business. My choice to marry him or not, no matter what he does."

Jamie sent her an incredulous look. "You'd be happy married to an adulterous prig? I'm sorry, Evie, I mistook you for a lady with some pride."

"No, I wouldn't have been happy." The sting of Hayden's betrayal smarted. *But,* Evie's little voice asked, *was it because of her pride or a broken heart?* "What I am trying to point out, Mr. Mackenzie, is that it was none of your concern."

"Tell me this, lass. If any of your sisters, or your friends—

Iris, say—had been about to marry a dolt with a steady mistress, would you have informed them? Or quietly stepped aside and let them make up their own minds? Because it was none of your business?"

The argument was sound, but Evie was too enraged to care. "Of course, I would tell them," she shouted. "But I would *tell* them, not conduct a farce and arrange it all for everyone. You gave us stage directions and decided the outcome beforehand, blast you."

"Because if I hadn't, Atherton wouldn't have admitted it." Jamie's shout matched hers. "Even if I'd told you, showed you the evidence, you might not have believed me. Atherton could have convinced you I was duping you for some reason of my own, and you'd have believed *him*."

"I wonder why that would be?" Evie widened her eyes. "Oh, yes, because you keep kissing me, and telling me things you can't possibly feel. I'd have agreed with him that you'd have done anything to break us up."

"Things I can't possibly feel?" Jamie was right in front of her now, his strong body obstructing her senses. "You mean me telling you I loved you? I can't feel that, can I?"

"You flit around the world without a care," Evie argued, trying to keep her thoughts coherent. "Rescuing people and flying in machines, having perfectly good adventures on your own. Why should you suddenly run into me again and decide you're in love? We hadn't spoken in years."

"You ran into *me*." Jamie poked a finger to his chest. "No, I didn't suddenly decide when you banged into me on the dock. I thought you were the nuisance you always were, only this time without an oar. But watching you, talking with you, stealing a bloody jar with you, I learned about you, understood you, wanted to know you even better." Jamie's volume increased as the words tumbled out. "And I don't want you marrying a man who will hurt you, and hurt you. Don't want to watch you fade through the years as he drains your happiness, your spirit, your life."

Evie swallowed, not liking how much his voice wrapped around her heart. "Hayden wouldn't have hurt me. Not like that. He never could have hurt me."

Jamie's brows drew down, his voice quieting abruptly. "What do you mean by that?"

She'd said too much. "Nothing. I'm just … flustered."

"No, you said that with conviction. Atherton could never have hurt you, why? Because you're not in love with him?"

Evie took a step back. "Again, we are straying into territory that is none of your business."

"You give me hope." Jamie's mouth curved into a feral smile. "You don't love the bastard. That is excellent news. But why would you marry the sod if you didn't love him? For his money? Oh, please, don't tell me you're that mercenary, lass."

"No, of course not," Evie returned angrily. "Women *must* marry, do you not know? Or be pitied as a poor relation."

"Which you would not be. Your family is very fond of you. What is the real reason?" Jamie cupped her chin. "Tell me, or I will kiss you silly."

Not much of a threat. Evie drew close to him again as his hand warmed her, the need for his mouth on hers intense.

She could stop this right now, with the truth.

"Very well." Evie forced herself to step away, trying not to feel empty when his touch was gone. "I will tell you. Not many know this—my mother, but even she didn't understand fully." She drew a breath. "I was engaged before. Or, nearly. I met a man after I finished university. We had agreed to marry, were very happy. Then he died." She broke off. The immediate anguish had faded but the ache was still there. "I only had three months with him."

"Evie." Jamie's voice softened, compassion filling it. "Love. I'm so sorry."

"He had a defect in his heart, apparently." Evie was

surprised she could speak of it so steadily. "No one knew, not even he. The doctors didn't realize until ... after."

"Love." The word overflowed with sympathy.

Jamie's strong hand rested on her arm and he towed Evie to a sofa, pulling her down to it with him. He gathered her to him, no longer arguing or making declarations, simply holding her.

Evie couldn't cry. She'd long ago used up the tears that had torn at her young heart. Ethan had been twenty-one, and she had been nearly that.

"We were walking." Evie had never confessed exactly what had happened to anyone, except a cursory explanation to their parents and the doctor. Now she found herself resting her head on Jamie's strong shoulder, telling him everything. "He just fell, folded up on himself. It was so quick. I tried to stand him up, but he could barely move. I ran for help, and by the time I got back, he was breathing his last. I held him as he died."

"Lass." Jamie kissed her hair, then rested his cheek on her head, his warmth a comfort.

"He'd never actually asked me to marry him. We just decided between ourselves that we wanted that. We were going to tell everyone at the end of that summer, make it official." Tears should have spilled then, but Evie's eyes were dry and tight.

"What was his name?" The question was gentle, not prying.

"Ethan Stanfield. His family was from the Cotswolds. I met him in London when my parents and I journeyed from Cambridge at the end of my last year. A shopping trip. It was a chance encounter, at a bookshop. We both reached for the same copy of an adventure novel."

They'd discovered shared taste in reading, in music, in almost everything. It had been a magical time, three short months, that had ended while their love was blooming.

Evie fell silent, wondering when the acute pain had turned

to dullness, and how Jamie had made the words flow from her when they never had before.

He asked no questions. Evie heard his heart beating beneath his coat, felt the solidness of him beside her.

They sat thus for a long time, while the immense house remained quiet, as though giving her this time to work through the unsettled tangle of her emotions.

"That is why you wanted to marry Atherton," Jamie said. "Because you never wanted to feel like that again."

Evie nodded into his chest. She should be surprised he understood, but she somehow was not. "Hayden was friendly, never mean or callous. It would be easy to marry him, and try to forget."

"I wish I'd known." Jamie's voice had gone soft, just above a whisper. "I'm so sorry, love. You were right to want to punch me in the nose."

"It doesn't mean I'm happy Hayden kept a secret mistress." Evie raised her head. "The fool. Do you think he loves her?"

Jamie's blue eyes were in shadow as he gazed down at her. "I met the lady only briefly, but yes, I think so. They rub along very well."

"Why doesn't he marry *her*, then?" Evie pounded one fist into the giving sofa. "I know why—his father. If Hayden had any backbone, he'd marry her anyway and defy the man. But he never will." She sighed. "I will not punch you. I should thank you for saving me from a horrible father-in-law."

"I'm not sorry I told you," Jamie said. "You deserved to know. But I should have found a better way. You are right to be angry at me. I'm so used to solving everyone's problems that I thought you'd want me to solve yours."

Evie's emotions, after the upheaval, were heading downward into quiet unhappiness. "I suppose you did what you thought best. Hayden needed to tell me himself, and if you hadn't dictated what to say, he'd have prevaricated and pretended, and made our parting my fault."

A woman breaking an engagement could be as scandalous as her obtaining a divorce, depending on the reason. The woman could be labeled a jilt as well and criticized for walking away from a perfectly good match.

Jamie gathered Evie closer. "I've bricked myself into a corner, haven't I? I've let myself fall in love with you, and you never want to love anyone again."

"I never said I didn't want to love again," Evie objected, then subsided. "It's simply easier if I don't."

"I won't presume to speak for this good man, Mr. Stanfield. But would he like it if you refused to love? If it were me, I'd be a bit put out that you used my memory to keep yourself from feeling. As if it were my fault."

Evie frowned uncomfortably and laid her head back on Jamie's shoulder. It was so easy to rest against him.

"No, you should not presume, but I admit I hadn't thought of it that way. Still, I doubt Ethan would want me to forget all about him and fly to someone else."

"If it has been, what, four years since you left Cambridge? Then you haven't exactly flown anywhere."

"That is true." Evie sighed. "He was the kindest man I knew."

Jamie brushed a kiss to her forehead. "I really am so sorry, lass. Thank you for telling me."

"I've never told anyone before." It had felt good to speak about it, as though she'd finally found someone she could unburden herself to, someone who'd understand.

"I am honored, then." His voice vibrated beneath her ear.

"Perhaps I told you because I know you've lost friends," Evie went on.

"I have." Jamie cleared his throat. "Never a lover, but very close friends. One in a battle he shouldn't have been fighting."

"I'm sorry." Evie touched his chest. "It's a hard thing."

"Aye, it is."

They descended into silence once more. In that room, with

its quiet tranquility, against the unshakable Jamie, Evie at last found solace.

She had hoped that by marrying Hayden, she might gain a sort of peace, but Evie now realized she'd deluded herself. She'd liked Hayden because he was different from Ethan. No danger of losing her heart and betraying her first love.

Jamie was nothing like Ethan either. Jamie walked through life with the confidence that everyone would either get out of his way or become his devoted friend. Evie had watched such things happen already.

Ethan had been quietly good, self-effacing even. No one much noticed him, and no one had a bad word to say about him.

Losing him had been the hardest thing Evie had experienced. Hayden's betrayal was a tiny bite compared to that.

Evie realized, as she leaned into Jamie's strength, that losing *this* man would hurt her as well. A hurt that would take an age to heal.

"We're both very sad at the moment," Jamie said. "But what I've learned, love, is that it's fine to be sad. Those we lost deserve to be remembered, and mourned. But it is fine to be happy as well. One doesn't cancel out the other."

"Very philosophical."

"But true." Evie felt his Jamie's in her hair again. "Do you want to go back with Belle? Or stay and meet the family? At least my mother and dad? I must tell you that when Belle arrived looking for me, Mum rather insisted she bring you here."

CHAPTER 21

*J*amie waited while Evie went silent. Of course, she wouldn't want to stay. She'd prefer retreating to Gavina's and Belle's lodgings, or might even ask to be conveyed to her parents' home in Bedfordshire.

She hadn't wept about Hayden, or Ethan, whom she'd loved and lost, though Jamie had heard the deep sorrow in her words. Evie's eyes were dry, but not because she felt nothing. She'd been cried out.

His fury at Atherton rose anew. How could the man not have realized what Evie carried inside her? Jamie hadn't either, or he wouldn't have blundered about like an ox, but Atherton had known her a year. He hadn't seen what was behind Evie's facade, because he hadn't bothered to look.

"Very well," Evie startled Jamie by saying. "I don't mind meeting your mother and father."

Jamie leapt to his feet, extending his hand to help her rise. "Shall we put on a brave face?" he asked her as she stood. "Don't worry, they aren't as frightening as everyone says. They'll be angry at *me*, not you."

Evie moved to a mirror and tried to smooth her hair. She

looked perfectly beautiful with it awry, but Jamie had grown up with sisters and knew the futility of telling her that.

"No one should be angry at you," she said, turning to him. "Except me, of course."

Jamie conceded this. "Aye, well. I will hope that maybe in time you'll forgive me."

"I have much to think about," she said softly.

"You do." Jamie wouldn't push her, as much as he wanted to. Atherton was an ass, and she was well rid of him, but Jamie knew he could not simply leap in and win her. The situation was more complex than that.

He wasn't certain that meeting Mackenzies would help, but his mother had been adamant.

Jamie led Evie from the sitting room and along the hall to the larger drawing room at the front of the house, where the few soirees Beth held, with Aunt Izzy's help, took place. Most nights in this house were quiet, which suited Jamie. He found it restful. When life grew too arduous, his home was a refuge.

Jamie's entire family had gathered in the drawing room, each pretending to be engrossed in reading or embroidery or the piano—a larger version of the Pleyel piano in the small sitting room. Only Jamie's father was truly absorbed, turning his mind to whatever mathematics equations he was writing at lightning speed at the desk.

Even Ian's valet, Curry, had contrived to be there. He held a tray of tea things, which one of the maids could have brought in, but Curry, loyal to Ian for decades, was as nosy as any Mackenzie.

Beth rose as Jamie and Evie entered, putting aside her embroidery. Mum hated embroidery, another indication that each person had quickly feigned an activity when they heard him and Evie approach.

"May I present Miss McKnight." Jamie led Evie forward, lifting her hand like a swain at an old-fashioned ball. "You may all bow or curtsy as you see fit."

"Don't be rude, Jamie." Beth came to them, a true smile on her face. "Welcome, my dear. My son might be flippant, but we are so very glad to meet you. And so sorry it had to be in this fashion."

Beth's glance at Jamie bore the barest hint of recrimination, but Jamie knew he'd be in for a lecture later. For now, Beth locked her arm through Evie's and guided her into the room.

Megan had leapt up from the piano stool, her face wreathed in smiles. No recrimination from his sweet little sister, at least.

"How do you do, Miss McKnight?" Megan extended her hand. "I'm Megan, the youngest. Belle has told me about you, and good thing, because I have heard nothing at all from Jamie."

Well, maybe not as sweet as she looked. Evie began to relax as she took Megan's hand.

"You arrived at the perfect time," Belle said, setting aside her book. "Curry has brought tea. Perhaps you ought to set it down, Curry."

Curry made a show of depositing the tray carefully on a table. "Earl Gray, Oolong, and Darjeeling," he announced. "Whatever your preference, miss. And Cook has put on her famous cakes."

"Excellent," Beth said. "Thank her for me, Curry. Ian." Beth led Evie past Jamie's sisters and the tempting tea tray, to where his father sat, still writing his equations. "Come and meet Miss McKnight."

For a moment, Ian did not respond. The pencil continued to scratch, Ian writing numbers with neat precision. At the end of an equation, his hand finally stilled.

Ian deliberately lifted the pencil, turned it perpendicular to the writing, and laid it down in the exact center of the paper. He straightened his back and unfolded to his feet, turning in silence toward Beth and Evie.

Jamie moved to Evie's side as Evie gazed up at Ian, blinking a little when Ian did not greet her.

Jamie touched Evie's arm. "This is her, Dad."

Ian flicked his gaze to Jamie, his golden eyes meeting his son's. "I know," he said, as though Jamie was a simpleton.

Evie extended her hand. "How do you do, Lord Ian?"

Ian moved his gaze from Jamie to Evie's slim hand, suntanned and sturdy.

Without a word, Ian reached for her, but instead of shaking the offered hand, he tucked it into the crook of his arm. Turning, he led her across the large room to a set of chairs near one of the windows. The nook provided a nice vista to the park across the road on a sunny day, a cozy corner with the drapes closed at night.

Jamie started after them in some worry, but Beth pulled him back, a pleased smile on her face.

"Let him get to know her," Beth said. "Megan, will you give us some music?"

————

EVIE FELT HER TENSION AND HURT FADE A BIT AS LORD IAN Mackenzie assisted her to a chair and took the one facing her.

Behind them a sweet melody sprang up from the piano, one neither too loud and dramatic, nor too soft and cloying. The music spoke of joy, serene and untroubled. Evie had no idea what the song was, but she found it soothing.

Ian's eyes were like pieces of dark gold. He closely resembled Jamie, or what Jamie would become in twenty-five years. Lord Ian was a solid man, large hands resting on his knees, his face hard but handsome. No softness about him. His physique spoke of long walks across the Highlands through sun, wind, and rain.

Like Jamie's, Ian's kilt was well-worn but obviously comfortable. Thick socks encased firm calves, and Ian wore his coat loosely closed over a shirt with no waistcoat, as Jamie did.

Jamie tried to emulate him, Evie saw with sudden insight. Jamie admired this man and wanted to be everything he was.

Perhaps that was Jamie's pain. He feared he'd be compared to the famous Lord Ian and always be found wanting. Maybe many had already done such a thing.

Evie had suffered loss, but Jamie's heartache was loving this father and knowing he could never be exactly like him.

Ian said nothing at all. He didn't meet Evie's eyes but still managed to gaze at her with the intensity of an alert lion. He gave her no hard, unscrupulous once-over, as Sir Hector Atherton had done when Hayden had presented Evie to him. Ian simply took her in as though waiting to decide what he thought of her.

Evie could have broken the silence with an awkward and inane statement about the weather or his lovely house, or glanced across at Jamie for reassurance. But as the moments stretched, she found she had no wish to do so. Ian didn't sit mutely because of any distressing reason, but because he knew there was no need for words.

The lovely music drew to a close, but Megan began another piece immediately. The fire, which was low on this spring night, relaxed Evie further with its warmth.

"He believes he has to live up to me." Ian's voice held the low rumbling note of Jamie's, but with a subtle difference. He spoke with the experience of years, in the manner of one who had suffered greatly but found peace, and who'd learned the value of stillness. "To be what they expect him to be as my son."

Ian didn't elaborate on who "they" were, but Evie understood. *They* were the world, those who judged Jamie because he was Scottish, wealthy, and the son of a supposed madman.

Evie did not answer, somehow knowing Ian did not expect her to.

"He is the most wonderful boy in the world," Ian continued. "The perfect gift." His eyes softened, crinkles appearing at the corners. "Because his mother gave him to me."

Evie couldn't curtail her reaction to that. She reached forward before she could stop herself and laid her hand on his strong arm.

Lord Ian didn't like to be touched, people whispered. *Very odd about it, but then, that entire family is mad.*

Evie quickly withdrew, but Ian captured her hand before she could return it to her lap. He deliberately enclosed it in both his big ones and gently squeezed.

"*You* are a gift," he informed Evie. Lord Ian briefly met her eyes, like a flash of sunbeam escaping a cloud. "A gift for him."

"Oh." Evie now understood why Beth Mackenzie had fallen in love with this man, and why Beth was so serene. She sensed that their long marriage was full of deep awareness, a love that needed no reassurance. "You are very kind, sir."

Ian's brows drew together the slightest bit. He carefully settled Evie's hand back on her lap and released her. "It is not kindness."

He hadn't been giving her platitudes, she realized, but speaking the truth as he saw it.

"I understand." Evie gave him a nod.

Ian waited a long moment, then he returned the nod, but as one who'd been told it was the polite thing to do.

His instincts were different, Evie perceived. Not wrong, not worse, only different. Right for him.

Megan began another piece, again with a sweet complexity that was more powerful than dramatic, banging chords. "What is this music?" she asked Ian.

"Beethoven. One of his Bagatelles."

Evie's brows went up. "I never knew he wrote such lyrical music."

"He did." Ian's eyes softened again, and the hint of a smile became a real one. "Megan plays it perfectly, and with all her heart."

"She is very talented," Evie agreed.

"She is also a gift."

The proud parent shone through. Evie saw that Ian loved his children with more intensity than anyone would comprehend. She hoped the three of *them* comprehended it—sometimes it was difficult to discern a parent's love.

This had never been a difficulty in Evie's own family, where her father and mother had showered their daughters with love and affection since their birth. They'd managed to without coddling or overindulging them, which, Evie reflected now, had been quite a feat. She must ask her mother for advice when she had her own children.

Her heart plummeted. She was no longer an engaged young lady, looking forward to her marriage and to filling her nursery.

And yet, there was relief. The idea that she would not have to marry Hayden made her limbs slack with gladness.

In addition, when she pictured the father of her mist-shrouded future children, it was not Hayden Atherton who stood at the cradle, gazing fondly into it.

The man was Jamie Mackenzie, who at present was resting against the piano while he watched his sister play. Jamie would lift his son or daughter, holding the babe carefully, the love in his eyes the same that Evie saw now in Ian's.

Jamie's pose at the piano was casual, but Evie read his tension. She saw similar tension in Beth and Belle, the two now residing on a sofa, quietly talking together. The only one untroubled was Megan, who swayed a little with her playing, her face taking on the glow of one lost in beauty.

"We should ease their worry," Evie whispered to Ian.

For a moment, Evie thought he did not know what she meant, then the smile flashed again, the Mackenzie roguishness shining through.

Lord Ian rose, assisted Evie from her chair, tucked her hand through his arm again, and led her back to the center of the room.

———

JAMIE BREATHED EASIER WHEN EVIE RETURNED WITH HIS father, the agitation in Evie's eyes nearly gone. Jamie's acquaintances, men and women alike, had frozen in fear of Ian Mackenzie, leaving his presence as fast as they could, using any excuse to go.

By contrast, Evie rested her hand on the crook of Ian's elbow, a smile pulling at her lips. She and Ian might have been old friends stepping aside for a chat to catch up on things.

Ian's gaze went straight to Beth, as usual. He took Evie's hand and placed it on Jamie's arm, then stepped to Beth and gathered her to his side.

"Supper," he said. "Miss McKnight will be staying."

Evie started, but she didn't protest. She also did not remove her hand from Jamie's arm.

"Indeed, you must," Beth said to Evie. "I've told Curry to have a bedchamber prepared for you as well. It is late, and there is no need for you to squeeze into the little house in Chelsea."

"Gavina will be disappointed," Belle said. "But I'm happy to have my bed to myself again. I'll go assure her that all is well."

"After supper, miss," Beth said sternly. "It's not often I have all my ducks at home for a meal. We promise not to overwhelm you, Evie, dear."

Beth gave her one of her warmest smiles then waltzed away, Ian's arm around her. Ian leaned to Beth as they went out the door, pulling her closer as they walked.

"One of Mrs. Grafton's suppers is not to be missed," Belle

informed Evie. "I promise, you will not regret it." She hastened after her parents, gray skirt swinging.

Behind them, Megan continued to play. She became absorbed in the music, as usual, forgetting that anyone else was in the room.

Jamie rested his hand on Evie's, her fingers warm. "My father can complete an interrogation without saying a word."

Evie glanced up at him in surprise. "There was no interrogation. He is lovely."

She hadn't realized what had happened in that corner, then. Jamie also knew from Evie's answer that Ian had been gentle because he'd wanted to be.

A glow spread in his heart. Ian was an excellent judge of character—Jamie had known his father would like Evie, as would his mother.

And why wouldn't they? With her snapping blue eyes and ready laughter, anyone would be glad to have Evie in their home.

As Jamie was.

Megan's voice floated across the room above the melody. "If you wish to kiss each other, do not mind me."

Evie jumped. "Indeed, no—"

Jamie stopped her denial with his lips.

Under him, Evie went still. Jamie slid his hand behind her neck, coaxing her up to him, and brushed kisses to her lips, tender ones, demanding nothing.

Just when he thought she'd push him away, Evie responded, opening to him, making that delicious little sound in her throat.

Jamie tasted her sorrow, but also her passion, a need she'd kept buried for a long time. Perhaps she had done so because of her grief, but Jamie also sensed she'd locked it away where Atherton wouldn't find it.

Now Atherton was gone, expunged from her life. Her passion flared, and Jamie touched it.

He knew Megan wasn't watching them. She'd either be gazing at her fingers flying over the keys or staring off into space, going wherever the music took her, mere mortals unable to follow.

Jamie cupped Evie's waist, his thumb sliding to skim her breast. Evie tugged him closer, which put his growing cock-stand against her. She'd feel that through her thin skirt and his kilt, and Jamie wasn't one bit ashamed.

Evie McKnight was beautiful, Jamie wanted her, and he'd do whatever it took to have her.

He was tempted to rush her upstairs to his bedchamber, high in the house and away from those of his sisters and parents. But Ian, Beth, and Belle would be waiting in the dining room, and Curry would find them, in that uncanny way of his. The man knew where everyone in the family was at all times.

Jamie eased from their kiss, though he kept Evie pressed to him. He touched her cheek, fingers in her silken hair.

"You are beautiful, lass."

"Always ready with a compliment, Mackenzie." Her voice was faint, cracked.

Jamie couldn't stop his grin. "I'll be making many of them, McKnight."

He forced himself to release her, took her arm, and guided her from the room in search of supper.

———

MEGAN MACKENZIE GAZED BLATANTLY AFTER THEM. SHE hadn't missed the kiss and how much desire it had contained, though she'd pretended to concentrate on the music.

Lovely to see Jamie captivated by a woman, and a sweet one at that. Belle had told Megan the tale in her cursory way — Belle thought the fewer words used about anything the better

—but Megan had read that Evie was vivacious, kindhearted, and very interested in Jamie.

Megan hadn't failed to note the way Evie's gaze had rested on Jamie the entire time she'd been in this room, except for the brief interval with their father. When Ian had led Evie back to Jamie, Evie had smiled the moment her eyes met his.

Evie would do Jamie good, and Megan could cease worrying about him.

Whether anyone would ever show the same sort of devotion to the eccentric Mackenzie sisters was another matter. Megan sighed and went back to deciphering Alkin's *Les Quartre Ages*.

She had her music. Belle had her studies of science and medicine. That should be enough, should it not?

Megan scowled at the piece, notes dancing before her eyes, quit the piano, and hurried to rejoin the warmth of her family.

CHAPTER 22

The supper was full of laughter, chatter, and wonderful food, all of which calmed Evie's turmoil, or at least pushed it aside.

She did not argue that she'd already dined at Gavina's— that meal seemed long ago and far away, and her hunger had returned with a vengeance. Likewise, Belle had no qualms about tucking into another supper.

The footmen served Evie first, at Beth's direction, and seemed eager to offer her the best of everything. Evie sipped blissful soup, ate tender beef in a savory gravy, vegetables roasted to perfection, and buttery sauces that slid across the tongue.

She could eat as slowly or quickly as she pleased, as Beth did not adhere to the rigid rule that no one consumed a bite after the lady of the household laid down her eating utensils.

Evie was seated next to Megan and across from Jamie. Unlike Belle, who spoke with serious authority on many topics, including the theory of special relativity, which Evie had only a vague notion about, Megan asked Evie about New York and the crossing on the *Baltic*, sighing over her descriptions of the society ladies and their beautiful gowns.

Both sisters did everything to draw Evie into the conversation, to which Beth contributed plenty of opinions. Ian did not say much, only ate in silence, but when he did speak, it was to interject a nugget of wisdom or a calm addition to Belle's scientific explanations, then to go quiet again.

Very different from Sir Hector's diatribes, which Evie was expected to agree with without question.

The butler carried in a sweet pudding, which Curry liberally poured brandy over and lit, while Evie and the Mackenzie ladies oohed in delight. Evie had never seen such a display apart from plum puddings at Christmas. A special treat, Beth said, for their special guest.

This pudding was custardy and full of cinnamon and cloves, filling Evie's mouth with splendid tastes.

Jamie spoke very little, though whenever Evie glanced up from her plate, she'd find Jamie's eyes on her. Once when he caught her gaze, he curled his tongue around a strawberry that had graced the top of his slice of pudding. Evie went very hot and quickly looked away.

After they'd consumed the dessert, and Evie was more stuffed than she'd been in an age, Beth announced that Evie must be tired, and she'd see her to her chamber.

Evie was surprised the ladies weren't ushered to the parlor to sip tea, gossip, and fall into boredom while the gentlemen smoked cigars and drank brandy until they'd had their fill. But the entire family filed out of the dining room, Jamie with them. He bade Evie a civil goodnight, though she caught a flicker of dark promise in the back of his eyes, and disappeared into the recesses of the house.

Beth led Evie upstairs alone. "I thought you might have had enough of Mackenzies for one day," Beth told her as they entered a well-lit chamber with a crackling fire and a high bedstead with light yellow hangings.

"Supper was wonderful," Evie said sincerely. "You have all been so kind."

"Kind, but overwhelming." Beth sent Evie a knowing look. "They can leave you breathless, the Mackenzie men. Be thankful you had only Ian and Jamie to put up with tonight."

"My life changed today," Evie said, pressing her hands together as she sank to the bed. "That has overwhelmed me enough."

Beth sat down beside her. "I too once thought my life's path well-paved, with very few twists and bends. Then I met Ian." She smiled. "I ran all the way to France to deal with my feelings for him." She patted Evie's knee. "I hope you will not flee so far. I do like having Jamie home."

Evie let out a nervous laugh. "Do you mean Jamie would chase me to France?"

"I have seen the way he looks at you. I believe he'd be on the very train you caught, and the boat as well."

"I like Jamie, I truly do." Evie couldn't lie about that. She liked kissing him too, even if it made her confusion dance and spin. "I hope he will give me a little time. I need to think."

Beth shook her head. "If I know my son, he won't. But that might not be a bad thing. We can wallow in indecision a long while, counseling ourselves to bide our time, when in reality, we are only hiding from the choice. I have learned to act on things instead of brooding over them." Beth's expression became stern. "However, if you decide to break Jamie's heart, please do it cleanly, and leave him be. No asking him for time, or claiming uncertainty. Either you love him or you do not. Do not leave him dancing on a string. I grow weary of ladies who do such things."

At the moment, Evie was barely certain about her own name. "I have no intention of breaking Jamie's heart, I assure you."

"Just be careful, is all I ask. Tonight, you can rest safely here. Curry has arranged for your clothes and things to be brought from the Athertons, so you will never have to return there. And I will write to your mother tonight to explain what

happened. Better the news comes from a disinterested party—
though I rather do have an interest." Beth's smile deepened.

"I feel very decadent for you to do all this for me," Evie
said. "And rather helpless."

Beth patted her again, more firmly. "We all need to be
fussed over from time to time. Let me indulge myself
pampering you tonight. Tomorrow, you can hold up your head
and be an independent woman once again."

"My mother might have a few things to say about that,"
Evie said shakily.

"I believe your mother will understand better than you
realize." Beth rose. She smoothed Evie's hair and then pressed
a kiss to her forehead, as though Evie were one of her own
daughters. "Sleep well. My maid will come to help you to bed.
She's warmed a nightgown for you."

Evie bade Beth a calm goodnight, and the lady glided from
the room. Evie unclenched her clasped hands when the door
closed. It had been all she could do not to throw her arms
around Beth and weep without restraint.

————

JAMIE PACED IAN'S STUDY, A GLASS OF MACKENZIE MALT IN
one hand. He felt his father watching him, though whenever he
turned, Ian seemed to have his attention on a thick book.

"This is one my craving for adventure won't solve," Jamie
announced after he'd ruminated a good half hour.

Ian placed a bookmark in the book, closed it, and set it on
the desk. "Why would you want to solve it with adventure?" he
asked.

"Easier," Jamie said. "A man in need of rescue. An enemy
to thwart, a village to save. A corrupt mine overseer to replace.
Easily dealt with."

"Speaking to Evie is safer than any of those," Ian pointed
out.

THE SINFUL WAYS OF JAMIE MACKENZIE

Jamie scrunched up his face. "Is it? I think I'd rather dangle upside-down from a moving train again."

Ian's gaze roved to the Ming bowl that rested in its glass case. He switched around the bowls from time to time, moving each to this lone case for a spell, so he had the chance to examine each one. Some collectors hoarded things and forgot what they had, but Ian appreciated each and every item.

"You did not ruin her life," Ian declared. "You saved it. Sir Hector Atherton has been embezzling from his company. Small amounts that he has returned. But one day, he will take too much and not be able to put it back. His son will be ruined. Evie would have been ruined too, had she married him."

Jamie's mouth hung open. "Embezzling? The snake." Andrew had noted that Sir Hector abhorred gambling— perhaps the man had lost a bit of money and thought he'd dip into his company's funds to compensate. Jamie shot his father a sharp gaze. "Wait a moment, how the devil do you know this?"

"I made inquiries about him."

Jamie ran an unsteady hand through his thick hair. "So, when you told me to find out all I could about Atherton, you did too?" Of course, Ian had. When Jamie's father was interested in a thing, he was very thorough. "I asked Andrew McBride to dig a little. Why didn't he find out about the embezzlement?"

"He did. But you had already acted. I received Andrew's note just before you arrived tonight."

Jamie huffed a laugh. "Good old Andrew. All right then, thank heavens I uncovered Hayden's peccadillo with his mistress. Poor fellow—I should probably warn him about his father. Though he wouldn't believe me."

"No." Ian watched Jamie closely.

"I will warn Brigitte instead. She might be able to convince Hayden to put a stop to it." Jamie drew a long breath. "Very well, I am a saint for rescuing Evie from that family. That does not mean she'll embrace this one."

Ian observed him a while longer, his golden eyes meeting Jamie's. "I was very afraid the night you were born."

"So you've told me." Jamie spread his arms. "But I am well and robust, and so is Mother."

"That night, I knew for certain I'd been right to make Beth mine."

Jamie had not heard this particular detail before. "You hadn't been certain prior to that? I thought the moment you saw Mother in that theatre box, you knew she was true and pure and the one for you."

Ian didn't smile. "I did. But I was afraid I'd made her unhappy by pursuing her. I nearly got her killed." His eyes darkened, the remembered terror of that still tapping at him. "The night you were born, when Beth looked at me as I held you, I knew. She regretted nothing."

"Mother is besotted with you," Jamie said, nodding. "Embarrassingly so, sometimes."

Ian pinned him with his gaze, as though willing Jamie to understand his point. "I knew that my instincts had been right. I'd done what I needed to for both of us to find happiness."

Jamie sobered. "You mean that is what I must do with Evie."

"You must give her what she needs."

A bratty son? Jamie wanted to joke, but he held his tongue.

Ian was telling Jamie he must decide his path and then forge it. If Jamie loved Evie, then he couldn't simply give up. He had set things in motion, and he must continue.

"Atherton would have given her much wealth," Jamie said slowly. "That is, if his stupid father didn't land himself in prison and his family in the workhouse. She'd have had a mansion in Mayfair, invitations to all the society dos in Atherton's world, and be dressed in beautiful gowns and jewels to prove how successful the Athertons are. I don't think Evie will be impressed by that sort of thing."

Jamie imagined that handing Evie a glittering necklace would only earn him a puzzled look. She wouldn't turn gooey-eyed and throw herself into his arms because of a few baubles. Jewels were not what would win her.

He thought he understood what would.

"I do know what she needs." Jamie's confidence resurged. "Something Atherton would never have been able to give her, because the idiot wouldn't have thought of it."

Jamie flashed his father a triumphant smile. Ian nodded, as though he understood exactly what Jamie had in mind, and maybe he did. He'd probably been waiting for his slow-thinking son to catch up.

"I will tell Hart." Ian picked up his book and opened it, finished with the discussion.

Jamie had been interpreting his father's words for years, and he knew exactly what Ian meant. Ian would instruct Hart to prepare Jamie a suite for himself and a wife and family in the massive Kilmorgan Castle that was the Mackenzie family seat. Aunt Eleanor would do the actual preparing, which meant she would bombard Jamie and Evie with questions once she knew.

Ian also meant, Jamie peeling back the man's words even more, that he believed Jamie would succeed.

Which made Jamie know he would. His heart light, he drained his whisky and left the room, whistling a merry tune.

———

THREE DAYS LATER, EVIE BOARDED A TRAIN WITH A SWARM of Mackenzies to head to Newmarket and the racing meet there.

For the last three days, she'd barely been able to sit down. Her trunk had arrived from the Athertons' the morning after her first night at the Belgrave Square house, her gowns, hats, and shoes packed neatly. Evie had half expected her clothes to be cut to ribbons, but everything was present, and looked as though they had been freshly washed and pressed.

"What did you say to them?" Evie asked Curry when she found the man in an upstairs chamber, where he sat mending one of Lord Ian's coats.

Curry had been a pickpocket once, Megan had told her, before becoming their father's devoted servant. He'd married Katie Sullivan, who had once been Beth's companion, Katie now ruling below stairs as head housekeeper.

"Say to them, Miss?" Curry rose, his form lithe, hair black with only a bit of gray at the temples. Evie could well imagine his nimble fingers lifting pocketbooks from unwary pedestrians.

"To the servants at Sir Hector's house. My clothes are pristine. More so than when I packed them in the first place."

"Don't know what yer mean, Miss." Curry blinked in bewilderment, though Evie caught an impish twinkle in his eyes. "Maybe they're conscientious, like."

"Well, whatever you did, I thank you."

"Pleased to be of service, Miss." Curry winked as he sat down, pretending to scowl at a rent in Ian's coat.

Evie imagined he'd gone below stairs at the house in Upper Brook Street and told the Atherton servants in no uncertain terms that Miss McKnight's clothing was to be packed precisely or they'd answer to him. Hayden's mother would no doubt have preferred the maids to dump Evie's things into the trunk and set it out on the side of the road.

She imagined Mrs. Atherton was not happy with Evie for the broken engagement. Though Hayden's letter had promised he'd take the blame, his mother would blame Evie, no matter what.

Not that Evie had heard one word from Hayden, Mrs.

Atherton, or Sir Hector. Jamie and his family, she suspected, were protecting her from that.

She'd not had any time to be alone with Jamie since their kiss in the drawing room, which she also suspected was by design. Megan and Beth took Evie shopping. Ostensibly, *they* went shopping and brought Evie with them, but Evie somehow ended up with new hats and gloves and an order for new gowns, which Evie had asked for in Belle's neat style.

After supper each night, the entire family adjourned to the smaller sitting room where Evie had first been ushered. While Megan played the piano and Ian read, Beth, Jamie, and Evie would turn to card or board games. They couldn't let Ian play, Jamie explained, because he always won. Ian pretended not to hear him.

Then Megan would link arms with Evie and walk with her up to bed. Evie began to feel close to the gentle Megan, who was a year younger than she was. Megan's dream was to compose and perform music, though she had difficulty convincing others to take her seriously. She'd start a position teaching a young lady in the autumn, which she was looking forward to, though it meant leaving home.

To be certain, Jamie flirted outrageously with Evie, sending her long and intense looks, as well as smiles across the supper table that warmed her bones. But he kept his distance. No more stolen kisses, not even a brush of hands.

She was grateful for the Mackenzies' hospitality—no one could have been better hosts. But soon, her mother and father would arrive, and Evie would go home with them. She'd see nothing of Jamie after that, which was as it should be. But Evie didn't like the hollow feeling the thought gave her.

Evie's mother had written her a long letter, telling her she'd received Beth's news of the ended engagement. To Evie's surprise, her mother had gone on a bit about her relief—she and her father hadn't wanted to stand in the way of Evie's

happiness, and the Athertons had seemed a decent family, but
...

Even they had seen that Hayden was wrong for Evie. *He is
wrong for you,* Jamie had told her, rumbling words that still
seared in her heart. *Can you nae see that?*

In the meantime, the Mackenzies readied themselves for
the start of the racing season, where they'd cheer on Uncle
Cameron's horses. As the McKnights would not reach London
for another week, Evie's mother's letter said, Beth saw no
reason why Evie shouldn't accompany them to Newmarket.

Ian had commandeered an entire train car for the journey
—the families of both Ian and Mac, as well as Hart's offspring,
would travel together. Hart and Eleanor would join them at
Newmarket, Hart finishing up business in London. Gavina
also journeyed with the group, her brother and parents already
at Newmarket with the horses.

In the jumble in the train corridor, as the mob divided itself
into the first-class compartments, somehow Evie, when she sat
down, found herself alone with Jamie.

Jamie slid the door of the compartment closed and pulled
down the shade, shutting out Gavina's glance inside and her
big smile, and dropped to the seat opposite Evie.

"Well now," Jamie said, his gaze holding heat. "It's a bit of
a journey to Cambridgeshire. What shall we do to fill the
time?"

CHAPTER 23

*J*amie's heart moved in slow, thick beats as he met Evie's stunned gaze across the compartment.

He'd not mistaken the longing glances she'd sent him earlier in the week, while the family had conspired to keep them apart, as Jamie had requested.

He agreed with his father that he needed to continue what he'd started without a break, but he'd also wanted Evie to have a chance to rest. To recover from her shock of Hayden's duplicity, to arrange her life into new lines.

Evie was free. Free of the dispassionate marriage she'd contemplated, free to either continue her past grief or walk through new avenues.

The heat in Evie's eyes now told him she felt the stirrings of need, the yearning for her arms around another person, to forget her confusion for a while.

"I am certain one of your cousins will bound in any moment with a sudden need for a chat." Evie's nose wrinkled with her smile. "I like your cousins."

"I usually do too, but they won't." Jamie leisurely reached over and turned the lock on the door. "I've already taken care of the tickets. No one will disturb us unless you want them to."

Evie glanced at the door latch, within easy reach of her. She could rise and walk out if she liked. Jamie wouldn't stop her.

"Will we have our heart-to-heart talk?" she asked him, her voice quieting. "I am not certain what's in my heart."

"We may talk if you like." Jamie rose slowly and sat down beside her. He put himself between her and the outer window, not the door, still offering her escape. "I had other things in mind."

Pink spread across her cheeks. "Such as?"

Jamie shrugged. "Kissing without interruption? Maybe we'll like it better—maybe we won't."

"You mean, find out whether we are truly attracted to each other?" Evie cocked her head. "Or if we simply found the danger of it exciting? Interesting experiment, Mackenzie."

"Glad you approve, McKnight."

"I did not say I approved." Evie's smile belied her words. "Did you plan to ravish me, and then ask me if I minded?"

No wonder he was falling in love with this woman. Her salty tongue, her combined innocence and worldliness, the way her eyes shone when she teased him, had Jamie's mind alight with possibilities.

"Not with my entire family down the corridor who would thrash me if I did." Jamie leaned back and rested his hands at his sides. "Why don't you do whatever you like?" He turned his head and met her gaze. "With me."

Evie lost her smile. "What exactly do you mean?"

Jamie spread his arms. "I am here, for your delectation. You do as you please, or nothing at all." In truth, if she pulled out a novel and started reading it, he'd die on the spot. But he wanted this first venture to be up to her.

For a long time, Evie quietly studied him. Not in trepidation or distaste, but with flattering interest. Jamie saw her understand that they were truly alone, that this train compartment with the shades pulled down provided them a private world of their own.

Slowly Evie unpinned and set aside her hat then unbuttoned and slid off her coat.

The simple movements, she making herself comfortable in the warm compartment, was one of the most sensuous things Jamie had ever seen. The coat was a barrier, representing the outside world. Evie put it from her so she could be with him, so nothing would stand between them.

Or else she was just overheated. Jamie told his imagination to cease, but he was growing hard, his blood hot with anticipation.

Evie left the coat in the seat and rose. She braced herself on the rack above him as the train swerved, taking them through the streets of London and eastward.

Today she'd donned a gown of light blue that brought out her eyes, with an easy swinging skirt. The collar of her buttoned-up bodice skimmed her throat, covering the place Jamie had given her a love bite. He longed to undo the buttons, peel down the collar, lick the place he'd bitten her, perhaps put another mark there.

Jamie made himself rest his hands on the seat and not touch her. This was her adventure, not his.

He held his breath as Evie swayed with the movement of the train, contemplating him with an intensity that had his entire body throbbing.

He let out that breath in a rush when Evie slid one knee beside his left thigh, then steadied herself with her hands on his chest. She slid her other knee next to his right thigh and lowered herself to his lap.

Jamie caught her around the waist, balancing her as she straddled him, unable to keep from touching her any longer.

She cupped his face in her hands, continuing to study him, thumbs brushing his shaven cheeks. Evie regarded him for a long while, then she leaned down and slowly kissed him.

Her lips held warmth. Jamie met the kiss with his own, unable to simply sit and let her have her way with him. She tasted of tea and cream, sweetened with a hint of honey. Jamie's hands roved her back, the thin fabric of her gown letting him feel every curve of her.

The kiss went on, taking its time, savoring. Evie brushed her fingertips over his face, as though enjoying the faint buzz of whiskers that were already growing back.

Their kisses at the lock-up and at the house had been truncated, even frantic. Now Evie kissed him thoroughly, deliberately, releasing him only to trail kisses along his jaw to his ear. Jamie groaned softly as her teeth brushed his earlobe.

"Love," he whispered. "Where did you learn that?"

"From you." Her breath tickled inside him.

"Oh, aye?" Jamie closed his eyes as her kisses moved across his jaw once more, back to his chin. "What else have ye learned?"

Evie sat up, still on his lap, Jamie's hands supporting her. She ran one finger under the low collar of his shirt and unbuttoned the top button.

"Why don't you wear waistcoats and cravats like other gentlemen?" she asked, her voice whisper-soft.

"Because I'm a mad Scotsman." Jamie sucked in a breath as she touched the hollow of his throat. "I need to be ready to tramp across the moors and fight off our enemies."

"In London?"

"Ye never know where a savage Highlander might appear."

Evie's laughter shook her delightfully. "You *want* to be eccentric. It keeps people from finding out too much about you."

Jamie shrugged. "Ye might be right. Or else it's too much of a bother to put on all those clothes, tying myself up like a package."

Evie undid another button. Jamie wore an undershirt beneath, but Evie's questing fingers unbuttoned that too. She spread the lapels of both garments and rested her hand flat on his chest.

"Your heart is beating so rapidly," she said with a touch of wonder.

"How can it help it?" Jamie's voice was choked. "A beautiful woman is undressing me."

Her skirts warmed his legs, her firm backside on his knees making it hard to breathe.

Evie ran her hands down his torso, the fabric parting for her. She traced each muscle of his abdomen, her fascination returning, fingers tickling.

Evie grew bolder as she skimmed her hands over his chest, segueing from hesitant touch to stronger questing. She let the dark red hair on his chest curl over her fingertips, then brushed her hand more firmly through them, her nails scratching the slightest bit.

That eroticism, coupled with her innocence, had Jamie's hips lifting, his cock very hard. He'd vowed he wouldn't ravish her, but his control was near to snapping.

A river of fire washed him when she slid fingertips beneath the waistband of his kilt.

"Lass," Jamie growled. "I don't know if I have that much control."

Evie regarded him cheekily. "I must ask if it's true what they say about Scotsmen and kilts."

"Depends." Jamie tried to shrug. "On a warm summer's day, yes. A cool winter, no. I like to keep my balls attached."

Evie's laughter returned. "We are being very naughty."

"I don't mind." Jamie grasped her wrist. "But careful, love. I don't know how long I can contain myself."

Evie leaned to him. "Is the rumor true, Mackenzie? On this day?"

"No." Jamie had to admit this, regretfully. "If I'm at the racetrack, and there's a wind ..."

Evie's smile lit more fires inside him. "That would indeed be unfortunate."

She withdrew her hand and kissed him again. Jamie wasn't certain whether to be disappointed or glad as he gathered her to him. Kissing was safer, though not when she nibbled on his lip. Jamie caught her tongue, suckling it and drawing a gasp from her.

What was left of his composure evaporated when she broke the kiss and tugged at his waistband. "I want to see."

"Ah, love, you're killing me."

Evie ran her hand along the smooth front of the kilt. "How does it fasten? It's not like a skirt, though some people mock it as such."

"In the old days, ye rolled yourself up in it." Jamie had to gently disengage her and push her to her feet. "In modern times, it's buckles and things."

He rose and showed her the buckles that held the kilt closed on either side. On the right side, near the hem, was a pin that bore the Mackenzie crest.

"It fastens there too?" Evie asked with interest.

"No." Jamie peeled back the top layer, showing her it was the only one that held the pin. "It weights it a bit, so it doesn't fly up."

It was a strange thing, modeling the garment he'd run around in since he was a lad to the lady he wished to win. He wanted her ripping it from him, not standing back and admiring the plaid.

"The fabric is lovely." Evie brushed fingertips along his right thigh.

He swallowed. "Woven by ladies in remote cottages on our clan lands. They're very proud of their work."

"They should be. It's beautiful."

"I'll have them make you one, if you like. Ladies wear kilts too."

Evie continued to rub the green and blue plaid, her fingers warming his hip. "I couldn't ask you to do that."

"I'll do it anyway. They'll be chuffed."

"Such intricate pleats." Evie had moved behind him, her touch finding the curve of his backside.

"Their specialty. Back in Old Malcolm's day, ye pleated your kilt by hand—but those were great kilts, worn over the whole body. I'm happy to have most of the work done for me—faster to dress in the morning."

Jamie heard himself babbling nonsense, but his brain had gone to sleep with Evie rubbing his backside through the wool.

His body, on the other hand, was very much awake and alive. More alive than it had been in a long time. Forget soaring over the Persian desert—he'd rather be here in this train with Evie lightly touching him and making him wild.

Evie began working the buckles that held the kilt in place. Before Jamie could stop her, she had one open and then the next, and the next. The unbelted kilt quickly sagged down his thighs.

She lightly put her hand on Jamie's chest and pushed him backward. He obediently sat down in the seat, his heart racing.

Once again, she rested her knees on either side of him, not quite embracing him but wonderfully intimate. Her hand slid beneath the loosened kilt and then inside his drawers, coming to rest on the very hard cock beneath.

Evie stilled, her eyes widening. Her hand twitched once, and Jamie thought she would jerk away, stand up, and flee the compartment. Maybe move to America and never speak to him again.

She'd never touched a man, that was certain. Jamie felt a flash of hot triumph. He was her first. Atherton hadn't earned this beautiful thing Evie was doing to him now.

Evie's fingers relaxed, and she gave his cock a tentative swipe with her thumb. Jamie couldn't stop his groan, his barely coherent thoughts scattering.

He groaned again as she roved her hand over him, her eyes on his. Jamie tried to muffle the sound—he did not want a concerned Mackenzie forcing open the door to rescue him.

He wanted only to be rescued by *this* lass, time and again.

Evie's palm enclosed his tip, her cheeks flushed with both shyness and excitement. She had no idea what to do with him, knew no courtesans' tricks of prolonging the pleasure before expertly bringing him off.

Jamie could teach her, though ...

The thought bunched exhilaration deep inside him, threatening to burst out all over her hands. She'd definitely flee him if he did that.

Jamie took deep breaths, using techniques he'd learned to calm his body and still his mind. Evie was new to this, and had been working her way through many emotions. He didn't want to frighten her.

Then again, she might simply be enjoying herself with the fool who'd thrown himself at her feet.

Ah, well. Let her enjoy.

Jamie slid his hand between them and rested it over hers, gently guiding her closed fingers on his shaft.

"I've never ..." Evie broke off, teeth working her lip.

"It's no matter." Jamie could barely speak. Her lip reddened, the moisture beckoning. Jamie dragged her to him and kissed her once more.

Her mouth was a place of splendor, where he wanted to linger for a long time. As the kiss went on, Evie moved her hand on his cock, up and down, up and down. Her kiss turned deeper, and Jamie pulled her closer, drawing her lip between his teeth.

As Evie's hand worked its magic, Jamie's hips left the seat, wanting to thrust. He wrapped his arms around her, his head going back on the cushions while she brought him nearer and nearer the brink.

"No. Love." Jamie jerked her from him as he came, no

longer able to control himself. His body was on fire, amazing sensations pounding at him, stealing his breath.

Evie slid to her feet while Jamie caught hold of his cock, he trying to swallow his groans of pure pleasure. He shook all over, the release powerful.

Good thing he'd brought a change of clothes, Jamie thought dimly. Tucked nicely into his valise on the rack above them.

Jamie forced himself to settle, his heart still racing. He wanted to be in a bed with her, where he could thrust inside her and finish this properly, wanted it with deep yearning.

He turned his head and gazed at beautiful Evie, who had returned to the seat beside him, watching him with uncertainty. His eyes were half-closed, his face flushed with warmth.

"Sorry, lass."

Evie swallowed. "Was that supposed to happen?"

"Aye, it was." Jamie pulled his kilt up over his bare lap. "A beautiful thing. I'm trying not to frighten you."

A smile touched her lips. "I'm not frightened."

No, she was fearless. "Thank you for giving me that gift, love. I'll return the favor, in due time."

"Return it?" Evie's eyes went starry with her blush.

Did she have no idea a woman could feel the hot rush he'd just experienced? Possibly not. The thought of teaching her this truth made Jamie begin to harden again.

"I will, indeed. Not here. When we have time. I want to do it properly."

Evie's joy faded a bit. "I can't … I might not marry. I don't want to have a child. That is … I mean, I *do* want …"

Jamie laid his fingers over her lips, hating the pain he read in her. She did long for a child, but he knew what she meant. She did not want a baby borne in shame, shunned by the world.

"You don't have to worry about that with me, love. I can give you much pleasure, and let your virtue remain intact."

Now she frowned. "How on earth are you going to do that? My virtue is stained already just by being in here with you." The frown softened. "Not that I regret it."

"I'm glad you don't. I don't regret it either." Jamie touched the tip of her nose. "Trust me, love. I will show you worlds of pleasure."

To his pure delight, Evie's smile deepened. "All right then."

———

EVIE TRIED TO ACT NORMALLY WHEN THEY DISEMBARKED the train, she leaving the compartment well before Jamie did to mingle with the Mackenzie cousins. As she'd closed the door behind her, Jamie had been reaching for his valise, sending her a wink as he told her goodbye.

Her hands in her resumed gloves tingled. She'd never touched a man like that before. Hayden had been adamant about saving everything until after the wedding, and Ethan and she had been too innocent to truly know how to explore each other.

Jamie had showed her a different world that existed between men and women. A brief glimpse, to be sure, but what visions that small glimpse promised!

The boisterous Mac Mackenzie led the family out of the train car at Newmarket, his beautiful wife, Isabella, never far from his side. Ian and Beth emerged from a private compartment at the end of the car, Ian more relaxed than Evie had seen him, Beth surreptitiously straightening her bodice.

Evie blinked a moment when she realized what that meant. *Good heavens.*

Several landaus waited to convey them to a nearby hotel. Evie piled into one with Gavina, Belle, Megan, and Mac's two daughters, the carriage soon filled with feminine laughter. Evie searched for Jamie, who dashed from the train, valise in hand, to leap into an open landau with the dangerous-looking Alec, his brother Malcolm, and the sunny-faced Robbie Mackenzie, maker of the fake Greek pot.

Evie barely had time to refresh herself at the hotel—she would room with Gavina—before they were back in the carriages, heading for the racetracks.

There Evie met Lord Cameron and his wife, Ainsley, as they entered the box reserved for the Mackenzie family. Lord Cameron was a huge man, a few inches taller than his brothers, with a granite-like face, his expression harsh.

That expression smoothed as Gavina danced to embrace him. Lord Cameron looked much more human as he returned his daughter's hug, his pride in her evident. Stuart Mackenzie, Gavina's younger brother, who had been helping his father with the horses, greeted Evie with an amiable welcome.

"Where is my other good-for-nothing son?" Cameron asked the crowd at large.

Jamie answered from where he stood with Alec and Mal. "Daniel will be here tomorrow. He and Violet and family are motoring down."

"Daniel and his motorcars." Cameron pretended exasperation. "Bloody infernal machines."

"Which you love to be driven in." His wife teased him. Ainsley Mackenzie had very fair hair and gray eyes—Gavina resembled her greatly. Cameron was never far from Ainsley, who grasped his arm comfortably, the love between the two evident.

Later, after the first race—Evie joining in the mad cheering as Cameron's filly sprinted to the finish—Hart, Duke of Kilmorgan, and his duchess arrived.

Evie had seen Hart Mackenzie's photograph in newspapers and spied him at London theatres the rare times she had attended with her mother and sisters. Gossipers had been happy to point out the famous duke, tall and forbidding, stonily leading his wife to her seat in their box.

When Beth presented Evie to him, she saw that the hard

face, like Lord Cameron's, disguised deep feeling, which shone out through his eagle-like eyes.

The duke did not question Evie's presence. Beth said, "And *this* is Miss McKnight," as though the duke knew all about her and had only been waiting to meet her in person.

Evie remembered how to curtsy, though she wasn't quite certain what one did when meeting a duke. Her parents' circle contained one baronet that everyone fussed over, but no one actually curtsied to him.

The duchess, cheerfully addressed as Aunt El by her nieces and nephews, wrapped a firm hand around Evie's arm and led her away from the duke once polite greetings had been exchanged, no curtsies needed.

"Now then, Miss McKnight," Eleanor said once they were on the other side of the box. "Tell me plainly. What are your intentions toward our Jamie?"

CHAPTER 24

$\mathscr{E}$leanor Mackenzie pinned her brilliant blue eyes on Evie and waited for an answer.

"Intentions?" Evie floundered. "We are friends. Old friends. I pushed him in a river once. Not on purpose."

Eleanor's smile flashed like sunshine. "Yes, I have heard the story, which is quite delightful. But I am asking whether you are in love with him."

Evie started. "I don't really know," she managed.

"Of course you know," the duchess said. "If you search inside yourself, you'll know. I am not trying to push you, dear. But I speak from experience—it is much better to get these things cleared up right away, so you can commence being happy without struggle and strain. Jamie adores you. I can tell."

Evie did not believe her face had ever been hotter.

The one image that took hold of her brain was how Jamie's eyes had darkened to deep blue, like a bottomless lake, as he'd released while she'd stroked him. She still felt the shape and firmness of his cock in her hand, his smooth, warm skin, the hot excitement that tightened in her belly.

Eleanor's skewering gaze made Evie warmer still, and she

groped for an answer. "I have not had much time to consider," she stammered.

Eleanor's tone held sympathy. "No, I imagine you haven't. When the Mackenzie men fix on you, you don't know where you are, and you realize there is no escape. But it doesn't really matter, because you don't truly want to escape. And even when you do run, you realize they have become a part of you that you can never lose again. Then there you are at the altar, with a bishop pronouncing you man and wife. It is quite unnerving, but worth every moment, I assure you."

"Auntie El." Jamie's voice cut over her last words. "Please cease terrifying my guest."

Eleanor turned to Jamie without worry. "I? Terrifying? No, my nephew, what is terrifying is being surrounded by this family and not understanding what you've got yourself into. But surrender, dear." Eleanor gently touched Evie's cheek. "Enjoy every second."

She beamed at them both and floated back to the crowd, the sun glowing on her golden red hair.

"My apologies for not rescuing you sooner." Jamie stood a breath from her, as though it was most natural to do so. "Aunt Eleanor can be daunting."

"She is only looking out for you." Evie watched Eleanor slide her arm around Ainsley's waist and give her sister-in-law a kiss on the cheek.

"I can look after myself, thank you." Jamie surveyed the full box with a pained expression. "Maybe it was a mistake to bring you here with the entire family. They're intimidating, en masse." He grimaced. "Huh, they're intimidating one at a time. Why do you think I spend so much time rushing about the world?"

"I like them." Evie tried not to think of how close she'd snuggled to Jamie in the train, how she'd enjoyed smoothing her hand over the back of his kilt. Jamie Mackenzie, all to herself, hers to touch, to kiss ... "They remind me of my family, only there is much more of them, of course."

"You are very brave." Jamie's expression was solemn. "Admirably so."

"And you are teasing. Your family is perfectly fine. Very close. Loving."

"Too close. They knew every detail about you before you arrived at the train, including how we met and how much time we've spent together. And I have told them very, very little."

"You are Lord Ian's oldest son. Naturally, they are worried about whatever young lady latches on to you." Evie surveyed the chattering, laughing, red- and golden-haired family, with dark Beth and her daughters contrasting them. "Perhaps they think I am after the family silver."

Jamie broke into his rumbling laugh. "You keep reminding me why I'm in love with you. But we'll never have a second to ourselves in Newmarket. Tomorrow, you and I are sliding away for a bit of peace, alone. I know just the place to take you."

"Do you?" Evie asked, trying to keep her heart quiet at his easy declarations of love. "I lived at Cambridge for three years, but I admit, I know little about this part of the county. I never went far from my college, except for rowing meets."

"I've been coming to Newmarket since I was born. Uncle Cam trains here when he's not in Berkshire. I'll show you wonders. Tomorrow." Jamie sent her a pointed look as Alec, Mal, and Mac's daughter, Eileen, descended upon them.

Evie nodded at him and then turned to be encompassed in another group of Mackenzies.

———

AFTER THE NEXT MORNING'S RACES, JAMIE MADE GOOD ON his word and walked Evie from the track and out to a hired coach.

Evie had let herself be talked into a small flutter, and following Jamie's advice, had actually won five pounds. She felt quite rich. Lord Cameron never wagered on his own horses, Jamie said, knowing he had an unfair advantage, but Evie was welcome to.

It was a lovely May morning, the countryside green and inviting, few clouds marring the very blue sky. When England had fair weather, the days could indeed be delicious.

The driver stopped the coach in a country lane far to the north and west of Newmarket, empty fields stretching in all directions.

"Where are we?" Evie asked in puzzlement when Jamie handed her down.

Jamie waved at the driver, who touched his hat and clattered the carriage away, leaving Evie with Jamie in the middle of nowhere.

"Cambridgeshire," Jamie said. "Come along."

"Yes, I realize it is Cambridgeshire, Mackenzie." Evie tramped after Jamie, who'd started along a narrow path that led through a meadow. She was thankful she'd worn good, stout shoes. "Perhaps you could be more specific?"

"Careful, it's a little marshy here," Jamie called back to her. "What is Cambridgeshire named for? The bridge across the River Cam. The town that sprang up around it has been known since the very olden days as Cambridge. That ancient river is our destination."

So narrating, Jamie led her onward. Evie smelled the damp of the river before it suddenly spread before them, meandering lazily between its green banks.

They must be downriver from Cambridge itself—the river flowed north. In this lonely stretch was a small pier, and at the end of this pier a flat, narrow boat bobbed in the current.

"Is that a scull?" Evie gathered her skirts and hastened onto the pier, her heart beating faster in excitement. Long and gleaming, the scull beckoned, two pairs of oars lashed and stowed inside it. "There's no one in sight. Who would leave it here?"

"I would." Jamie was grinning when he turned to her. "It's yours, McKnight. Just be careful when you're flinging the oars about."

Evie stared at him, dumbfounded. "You are giving me a racing scull?"

Jamie shrugged, turning away so she could not see what was in his eyes. "Why not?"

At one time Evie's greatest joy had been flying across the water, rowing like mad with her best friends, wind in her hair, spray on her skin. She'd sorrowfully given up the sport when she'd finished at Girton, knowing she'd have to settle down and be a grownup lady. No more time for exciting things like rowing.

She clasped her hands, her smile growing so wide it hurt. "Good heavens, Jamie. I'll never remember how to row it. I'll be in the drink."

"I wager you won't." Jamie joined her at the end of the pier. "Go on. Get in."

"It's a double scull," she pointed out. "It needs two rowers."

Jamie gave her a casual nod as though wondering why she mentioned it. "I thought maybe you could teach me."

Evie started to laugh. "You are astonishing, Mackenzie."

"Just don't drown me, McKnight."

Evie, unable to stop smiling, freed the oars and laid them on the pier. She set the near oar in its lock and balanced the second across the scull before she climbed down into the seat, surprised how easily she did it. She fit the second oar as she sat, then the far oar of the other pair.

"Easy," she said as Jamie began to descend gingerly toward her. "Don't capsize us."

Jamie stepped in, sitting down hard as the boat moved under his weight. Evie had taken the seat in the rear, and he now crouched in front of her, the length of his strong back within reach.

"I go out in boats on Scottish lochs," Jamie said. "Not an easy task, I tell you. I row myself and whatever cousin wants to come along—or my dad—and fish."

"A rowboat is not the same as a racing scull," Evie instructed him calmly. She slid his second oar into its slot then untied the scull and pushed them from the pier, angling so they drifted backward into the current instead of straight sideways.

Astonishing how the technique returned to her. The oars felt right in Evie's hands, and she took an experimental stroke. The scull skimmed along obediently, in a smart line.

"We'll have to pull exactly together," she informed Jamie. "Or we'll be all over the place. Ready?"

"Indeed, I am, ma'am."

"Very well then—stroke!"

Their first attempt had Evie laughing as the scull wavered and spun. Jamie cursed but after a little practice, he caught on how to glide the oars across the water instead of digging them in too far. The two eventually found a rhythm that began to propel them upstream.

Jamie's arms worked, his back coming at her as they leaned into each stroke and reached for the next one. Evie could tell he'd never rowed anything like a light scull before, but he learned quickly. He did blunder when Evie tried to turn them, lifting and splashing his oars down at the wrong moment.

Evie gave him some pointers, then called instructions to him, the commands easily rolling from her tongue. She'd guided her team in her heady salad days, commanding with her shouts as they'd rowed their way to victory.

She and Jamie zigzagged along the river, Evie yelping when Jamie deliberately splashed her. His laughter rang out over the water as she retaliated.

It was a beautiful day, the sky arching its rich blue above

them, the river quiet except for their voices, laughter, and the soft tap of the oars.

The scull moved well, Jamie and Evie learning to pull in exact cadence. Evie recalled how the world had gone away when she and her friends had flown along the river, its banks a green blur.

The experience was even better with Jamie, the pair of them stretching and bending, arms moving in unison. His strength lent speed to the craft, while her skill steered them with precision.

At last Jamie shipped his oars, holding them a few inches above the water. "Whew. That's enough for me." He turned and peered past her. "How far are we from the pier?"

"Probably half a mile. And it's downstream." She pointed the other direction.

"'Struth. More rowing then."

"It's heaven."

Evie could not calm her elation. How had Jamie known that this was exactly what she needed? To propel herself across the water, to laugh in the freedom?

"Why would you give me such a gift?" she asked him.

"Eh?" Jamie swiveled to peer at her, which tilted the scull too far. Evie quickly righted them. "Why not? Men shower the women they love with jewels, but I thought you'd like this better."

Evie abruptly shoved herself forward in her seat and kissed the cheek that turned to her. "Thank you, Jamie. I can't accept it, of course."

"Rubbish." Jamie scowled. "I'll carry it on my back and drop it on your doorstep, if I have to. You won't be able to refuse it then."

Evie rested her chin on his shoulder. It was so natural to touch him, to lean on him. "My mother will say it is not appropriate."

"We'll think of a story to placate her." Jamie turned his

head and kissed the bridge of her nose. "You are taking this thing home, love. I have no use for it. That is, I'll have it shipped to you. I doubt my dad would be happy if we tried to shove a rowboat into the train car."

Evie straightened, her heart singing. Her mother's objections were an obstacle she would overcome. "You show a talent for rowing—once you caught on, anyway."

"Because this is a calm, placid river. It's easy to pretend I have the knack. If we took this on a choppy loch in the freezing wind, I'd be overboard."

Evie laughed, because today, everything was worth laughing at.

They resumed their journey to the pier, Evie easing the scull to the end of the dock. Jamie threw a line around a ring and tied them up, then tried to gallantly leap to the pier and hand Evie out.

He nearly fell in, windmilling his arms until he regained his balance and leapt quickly onto the dock. He turned around, scowling down at Evie as she burst out laughing.

"Amused, are ye?"

She nodded, holding her sides.

Jamie made growling noises but took up the oars that Evie handed him once she ceased laughing, she easily keeping the boat still.

Evie accepted the hand he extended to help her from the scull. She stepped lightly to the pier, trying not to be awed at his strength, before they lashed the oars to the boat and headed for the path. Somehow, her fingers were entwined with Jamie's.

"Well, Mackenzie," Evie said to hide her sudden agitation. "Did you enjoy your sail with Captain Bly?"

Jamie peered at her quizzically. "You were nowhere near Captain Bly, love. You're competent, and you know how to command."

"Aw." Evie bumped him with her shoulder. "I don't think I've ever had a better compliment."

"Then your life has been hollow, my love. Now, let's see if I can make you even happier. Ah, here it is."

It was a large basket tucked beside a warm boulder. Jamie had arranged a picnic too, it seemed. Evie imagined the devoted Curry slipping out here when they were on the river, and leaving the basket for them, along with a thick blanket.

Jamie carried basket and blanket over a stile separating fields, and into a meadow that sloped to the river. Under the gentle sunshine, he spread out the blanket and opened the basket, revealing a stack of wrapped sandwiches, scones, cakes, a bottle of wine and glasses, and a flask of tea with cups.

"I love ingenuity," Jamie said as they seated themselves, and he poured steaming tea. "A genius learns to make a vacuum flask, and mere mortals can enjoy a hot cup of tea in the middle of a field without building a fire."

Evie accepted her cup and clicked it against his. "Very thoughtful of you."

Jamie liked gadgets, she realized—the battery torch, a vacuum flask, the motorcars. He dressed and spoke like an old-fashioned and romanticized Scot, but he embraced the modern world with all his heart.

They ate a very good lunch, washed down with more tea and a strong, bold wine. After packing up the remains, they lay together on the blanket, Evie's head on Jamie's shoulder, and watched the clouds slide by.

Evie breathed out, something like peace stealing over her. She'd been half in turmoil, half numb since she'd read Hayden's letter, drifting and afraid. What she would do now, she had no idea.

That didn't matter at the moment. Here in this field, with Jamie, she was free. No ties to anyone, no worries about her future. This point of *now* was much more important. The earth was at her back, a quiet breeze on her face, the man who'd rescued her from a life she'd have regretted by her side.

Jamie had saved her from an empty, lonely fate. Evie rolled onto her side, leaned over Jamie, and kissed him.

He slid his arms around her and pulled her to him, rendering the kiss long and satisfying. When they parted, Jamie's eyes sparkled with sin.

"Time for me to return the favor, love."

CHAPTER 25

"*F*avor?" Evie blurted, but she knew what Jamie meant.

"Ye gave me great pleasure on our train journey." Jamie's smile was wicked. "Time for me to give *you* that pleasure now."

Evie gulped. "How?"

The only thing Evie knew a man liked to do with a woman was lie with her—that euphemism meant sliding his hard organ inside her.

Mrs. McKnight had told Evie and Clara all about it after Evie had accepted Hayden's proposal last year, declaring them both ready for such knowledge. Her mother had blushed but stated that having a man you loved share your bed wasn't a bad thing at all.

Evie wouldn't mind with Jamie, she realized with a suddenness that left her breathless. She'd dreamed of him often since Southampton, of Jamie's weight on her in the darkness, he loving her all night in decadence.

Jamie's laughter vibrated under her. "Don't look so worried."

Evie's face heated. "I meant that we are in the middle of a field. Where anyone might walk past or float by on the river."

Jamie raised his head and scanned the empty countryside. "Not many about today. I'll risk it."

"But …" Evie pictured herself embarrassingly nude while a farmer wandered along, perhaps to check his field or fetch a recalcitrant cow.

Then again, why did the prospect of being caught while Jamie loved her send tingling excitement through every nerve?

"But what?" The gleam in Jamie's eyes made the excitement grow.

"It's a little cold for us not to be wearing clothes." Evie said the words hurriedly, her face growing hotter still.

Jamie stared at her incredulously a moment, then he collapsed onto his back and went off into gales of laughter. He wrapped his arms around himself and laughed to the sky. It was a beautiful sound, twining Evie's heart.

"Why are you laughing at me?" she demanded. "Perhaps you are used to baring your backside in country meadows all over the world, but I am not."

This made Jamie roar even more. His whole body shook, his eyes streaming.

Abruptly, he heaved himself up, wiping his eyes with the backs of his hands. "Love, I am so glad you slammed into me on the Southampton dock. I'd have missed this wonderful time with you."

He stopped the argument she'd drawn breath to continue with another kiss. Evie forgot what she meant to say, letting the gentleness of the kiss return her to the place of tranquility, where her life halted so she could be only with Jamie.

She found herself on her back on the blanket, Jamie coming to rest at her side. He propped himself on his elbow, gazing at her as though she was the most beautiful thing he'd ever seen.

"I want you to worry about nothing." Jamie's low voice spread hot prickles along her spine. "I won't distress you, and I won't ask you to strip." The heat in his eyes increased. "A pity, but there it is. Maybe later."

Evie realized then what he meant to do. She'd eased his clothes open and touched him on the train. Jamie would do the same to her.

Her body moved closer to his of its own accord. Evie began to tremble, wanting his hands on her so much it unnerved her.

Jamie brushed her hair from her forehead. He kissed her there, then the tip of her nose, then her lips again. His mouth was warm, spreading heat.

He slid his hand to her chest, slowing to cup each breast. Evie wore a corset, but the fabric was thin enough for her to feel a hot tingle as he teased each nipple with his thumb.

When he removed his touch, Evie swallowed her disappointment, though his large hand resting on her belly wasn't bad either. She sucked in a breath when he moved that hand to her thigh, and then to the join of her legs, the skirt only a thin barrier.

Crazed sensations sprang up where he touched. Evie gazed at him with wide eyes, emotions tumbling through her.

"Lie back, love," Jamie whispered. "I'll take good care of you."

Evie, trembling, tried to relax. But sharp need seized her, keeping her limbs stiff.

Jamie skimmed his hand down her skirt, all the way to her ankle boots. She felt a breeze there, followed by his fingers under her skirt and petticoat, his firm touch on her stockinged calf.

His hand swept up her leg to her garter then the slice of skin between it and the hem of her knickers. She stifled a gasp, hands balling.

"A nice fine cotton," Jamie announced as he brushed her drawers. Evie felt cool air on her legs as he neatly folded back the skirts. "Satin ribbon to hold them closed, beautiful on you."

His fingers worked, and the drawers loosened and moved

downward. Evie jumped when the warmth of his hand brushed her bare abdomen.

"Easy, love." Jamie's touch was light though it grew bolder as she calmed.

Evie closed her eyes, letting herself still under his caress and the sunshine. He ran his thumb across her belly, resting his hand there to let her get used to him against her bare skin.

Then his fingers, broad and strong, slid between her legs. Evie stiffened again, but Jamie stroked her forehead to soothe her. He lay close beside her, leaning to brush kisses to her mouth then closing her eyes with his lips.

Evie gasped when he moved his hand among the curls between her thighs. She'd never had anyone touch her there before, only herself when she washed. She'd never experienced anything special when she swiped a washcloth over herself, not realizing there was anything to feel.

Jamie showed her how wrong she'd been. He parted her most intimate place with one finger, engulfing her in fire.

Evie held her breath, her entire body tightening. The sensation was powerful, exciting, and at the same time, terrifying.

Jamie kissed her again, his lips tender. "Shh," he whispered. "Let yourself enjoy it."

Evie released her breath and drew another long one. While Jamie waited, she forced her muscles, one by one, to loosen.

"That's my Evie." Jamie brushed a kiss to the corner of her mouth. "I'll give you joy, I promise."

Evie nodded and reached up to touch his cheek.

The next moment, she arched against his hand as he stroked a place that scalded. Then his finger slid into her, penetrating what nothing ever had. Evie's hips lifted of their own accord, her body wanting the feeling, more and more of it. Never wanted it to stop.

Jamie kissed her as his finger penetrated her liquid heat.

Evie rocked under him, gasping out loud when he added a second finger.

"I can't," she whispered.

"Why not?" Jamie licked the seam of her lips. "This is what I felt when you brought me off, little devil."

"Was it?" Evie had loved playing with him, watching his face relax in pleasure.

"Oh, yes, my lass."

Evie sucked in a breath as he slid yet another finger inside her. She was so wet that there was no resistance, just intensity as Jamie slid his fingers in and out, mimicking what a man did with a woman when they made love fully.

If *that* was anything like this ... Evie groaned, the sound surprising her. Jamie's thumb brushed the fiery place again. That coupled with his fingers inside her rocked her body, her hips moving in time with Jamie's strokes.

Dark heat erased the world. Evie half rose, a wail tearing from her mouth. She needed what he was doing, yearned for it, dragging herself against Jamie's hand in search of it. She'd gone mad, the passion that flooded her unlike anything she'd experienced in her life.

"Please," she heard herself beg. *"Please."*

"Love." Jamie kissed her, but she wrenched her mouth from his.

Evie heard her cries fill the still spring air, rising into the vast sky. She couldn't stifle them, had no idea she should.

She rocked into Jamie, he holding her safely while her world shattered into a million jagged pieces that fell away, leaving nothing but joy behind.

———

JAMIE CRADLED EVIE AS SHE CAME DOWN FROM THE climax, easing his fingers from her as she quieted. She was shaking, clinging to him, her breath little sobs.

Jamie eased a handkerchief from his pocket and dabbed his hand dry. She'd been so very wet, coming quickly after he'd started to pleasure her. Her first time, he realized. She'd never experienced this sweet release, not even at her own hand. She wouldn't have been so surprised by it otherwise.

Evie wound herself around him, covering his face with kisses, her response so unhindered that Jamie was rock hard.

He'd love to lay her down on this blanket, rid them both of intervening clothes and take her fully. He'd drive into her, she'd rise to him, and they'd both be shouting their ecstasy.

But this was not the time, and he'd promised to leave her virtue intact. Jamie had a place in mind for her ultimate seduction—though he had a few details to work out. He'd wait until then. Well, he'd try anyway.

Evie gradually settled and Jamie stretched out beside her, holding her while she rested her head on his shoulder, her skirts bunched to her knees.

They lay quietly for a long time, the breeze softly touching them. Jamie nuzzled her hair, and she touched kisses to his chin, then they simply lay together, Jamie loving this uncomplicated time alone with her.

A train's whistle sounded in the distance, mournful and low.

Jamie supposed he should suggest they start back. He had a carriage waiting in the nearest village to take them to Newmarket, part of his arrangements for the day. If he kept Evie away too long, it wouldn't matter that she remained technically virtuous. She'd be ruined by speculation of what they'd been doing out here, and speculation wouldn't be far from wrong.

Evie sat up, adjusting her skirts, and studied him. Jamie rose on his elbows, crossing his feet at the ankles while he regarded her in return.

"Jamie," Evie said in a low voice. "Would you marry me?"

CHAPTER 26

*J*amie went very still, his heart slowing to painful thuds. Had Evie just asked …

She had to be joking. Jamie peered up at her, finding her blue eyes watchful.

"Would I?" Jamie repeated slowly. "Is that a rhetorical question? As in, would I ever eat beetroot?"

"No, I mean, should we get married?"

"Ah." Jamie sat up carefully, the lump in his throat nearly choking him. She offered on a plate what he wanted. He also knew she offered it for the wrong reasons.

"No," he said, his voice so quiet he almost didn't hear himself.

Evie blinked, then drew back. "No?"

Jamie reached for her hand. She didn't resist, but her fingers lay stiffly in his palm. "No, love. Because you are think-ing, *He's not so bad. I like his family. He gave me a fine gift* — the scull, I mean. *I need to marry someone, so why not?*"

Evie's face bloomed bright red. "Why do you presume to know the thoughts in my head?"

"I'm right, aren't I? Or close to it. Very similar to what you told yourself before accepting Atherton's offer."

Evie's flush deepened. As Jamie had observed before, her blushes always betrayed her.

"Well, why not?" she asked tightly. "All of what you say is true, and we do get on." Her lips parted as hurt entered her eyes. "Unless you truly don't want to. Unless this is all a brief diversion before you rush off to Africa, or someplace, to drive cars or fly aeroplanes or whatever you do there."

Anger bubbled up through Jamie's disappointment. "Diversion, is it? I told you I was in love with you, woman."

"Then it makes no sense why you are refusing. Perhaps you fall in love with ladies left and right, wherever you go."

"No, this is the first time for me." Jamie touched his heart. "Making it wonderful, and terrifying. And that is why I am saying no."

Evie regarded him in confusion then growing mortification. She sprang to her feet and snatched up the basket.

"Very well. Never mind." She turned away and bent her head as though adjusting the basket's fastenings. "When we return to Newmarket, please instruct the coachman to let me off at the train station. I will return to Bedfordshire at once."

Jamie was up beside her in a heartbeat, prying the basket from her grip. "No, indeed, you won't. I have more things to show you, McKnight."

"Why not? Or have I given you a new and hilarious tale to relate to your cousins?"

Evie swung away, beginning a march down the path as though she'd storm all the way to Newmarket. Jamie snatched up the blanket and strode after her.

"The carriage is this way." He pointed in the opposite direction.

Evie growled in her throat, turned around, and pushed past him. "You do not need to walk with me. I will meet you there."

"There is only one path." Jamie fell into step beside her. "As we go, I can explain why I refused your so very tempting offer."

"Oh?" she asked in a chill voice. "Do tell."

"Damnation," Jamie said with feeling. "Because I don't want to be only the man you turn to when you find your heart broken. You are trying to forget your humiliation at Atherton's hands and your grief when your first love was taken from you. I don't want to be your consolation." He pulled her to a stop, dropping the basket and blanket to cup her shoulders. "I want you to marry me, because you look at me and love me. Love *me*. And see no one else."

Evie's eyes were too bright. "I understand."

"I don't think you do." Jamie let out a breath, lowering his hands. "I love you, Evie McKnight. I want to win you over. I want your heart to yearn for me, and your head to stay out of its way."

"Win me over?" Evie asked shakily. "Is that what this is? The scull, the picnic, the ..." She swallowed, unable to name the pleasuring.

"Aye. And I have a long way to go. If at the end, you still don't love me, well then." Jamie made himself shrug. "I'll rush off to Africa and climb mountains or beat my way through jungles."

"But you won't simply agree to marry me now and save yourself all the bother?"

Jamie's temper splintered. "Courting you is not a bloody bother. You've convinced yourself you're not worth the trouble. I damn Atherton for making you believe you had to settle for him. I want you to *love* me — I'm not after a convenient wife. If that's all the marriage you want, then to hell with you."

He jerked up the basket and blanket, which chose that moment to try to tangle itself around his legs, and strode off down the path, wrestling the blanket into submission as he went.

He expected Evie to call him back, beg his pardon, or at least shout at him in return. She said nothing.

Jamie continued to walk, rage boiling through him. He

knew Evie had suffered deep hurt, first by the death of her tender, young love, and then by Atherton who hadn't valued what he'd been damned lucky to find. That hurt colored how she looked at Jamie, and he'd do everything in his power to rip away her pain and make her see *him*.

Very few people did see him. Jamie stood in his father's shadow, and always had—said the rest of the world who wasn't actually Ian or Beth Mackenzie.

Evie had gazed at him with sparkling eyes the first time he'd met her at the Cam and again when she'd barreled into him on Southampton's pier, unaware he was anyone but himself.

Now her vision had gone hazy, clouded by Atherton's idiocy.

Bloody Sassenach bastard.

Presently Jamie heard Evie's boots crunching on rocks on the path behind him, but she said nothing at all.

It was a silent ride back to Newmarket, whereupon Evie shut herself in her bedchamber and rarely spoke to Jamie for the remainder of their stay there.

———

"SCOTLAND?" EVIE REGARDED BETH BLANKLY AFTER THE fourth day at Newmarket. Beth had just announced that the entire family would remove to Kilmorgan in Scotland the very next morning, and Evie should accompany them. "But my mother is to travel to London to escort me home," she protested.

Evie was surprised how empty she felt when saying the words, perhaps because she was reluctant to face her family and their sympathy. Though she'd vowed to Jamie she'd return home immediately after their wonderful and dismaying outing, she'd realized she was in no hurry to retreat in defeat.

"That is no trouble," Beth said brightly. "I have written to your mother, and she agrees that a sojourn in Scotland would do you good."

"Did she?" Evie asked in surprise.

"Indeed, she did. Now, do not worry about your clothes. What we ordered for you in London will be sent on to Kilmorgan, and Eleanor employs a wonderful dressmaker if you need more."

Beth bustled off, leaving Evie bewildered.

Good heavens. They all wanted her paired with Jamie — even her own mother. Mrs. McKnight would have summoned Evie home if she truly thought Evie should be there.

Evie should be upset by Beth's insistence, and demand to go home, but she could not bring herself to argue. She wanted to stay, and she knew why.

She wished to remain near Jamie, even if he was furious with her. Evie cursed her tongue for blurting out the proposal, but she'd been in a daze of afterglow, hardly knowing what she was saying. He'd accused her of wanting to use him to soften her hurt, to assuage her fear of being unwanted, and he'd been right.

I don't want to be your consolation.

Evie couldn't blame him. She didn't want that either.

But though Jamie had refused her, Evie didn't want to be parted from him. How fickle were her emotions?

Evie's jumbled thoughts were mercifully distracted by the scramble to journey to Scotland. The duke's private railway carriage was ordered and would be coupled to the train on which Lord Ian once more had booked an entire car. There would be plenty of room for the entire family.

Jamie's cousin Daniel had arrived with his wife and two children, and so had a tall man who looked very much like Hart. Chief Superintendent Fellows, Beth had introduced him, with his wife, who was Isabella's sister. With him were two sons, who were in their last years at university, and a daughter who much resembled her mother.

Evie was introduced to so many that she privately began a chart to keep track of them all.

In the confusion of boarding the train and sorting themselves out, Evie found herself in Hart's private car with Beth and Ian, the duke and duchess, Megan and Belle. What had happened to Jamie, she didn't know. Before she could excuse herself and move back to the other car, the train started.

"Of course, you are riding with us," Eleanor said when Evie expressed concern. "It is a long way, and the beds in our little rooms are so much more comfortable than the converted ones in a regular compartment. Such a nice thing for an overnight journey. I always thought Hart terribly decadent to keep his own train car—he does love to show off—but I have adapted quite nicely. It is cozy, so I forgive it its decadence."

The duchess proved to be correct—Evie's tiny bedroom was quite comfortable, and she slept soundly, soothed by the movement of the train. It had been the first night since her unforgettable day with Jamie that she'd found solace in sleep.

True to his word, Jamie had shipped the scull to Evie's home, so she could use it upon her return. He'd done it even though he'd made it clear he was not happy with her.

Another man might have returned the scull from whence it had come to spite her. But Jamie was not mean, Evie had seen, which had become especially apparent since their arrival in Newmarket.

He'd kept Daniel's nine-year-old son, Dougal, from being duped by a bookmaker, who'd rubbed his hands when he'd seen the grandson of the famous Lord Cameron trying to place his first bet.

Jamie had patiently searched the town for a piano so Megan, who was worried about not playing for too long a stretch, could practice, and made certain that Lord Alec, who always looked fierce about something, kept his fiery temper under control.

Lord Alec himself told Evie an anecdote about Jamie when

she'd found herself next to him at one of the family's chaotic suppers in the Newmarket hotel.

"He got himself kidnapped once," Alec said, dangling a glass of whisky from his fingers. "In my place. Always has to be the center of attention."

CHAPTER 27

"Kidnapped?" Evie asked, eyes widening. She glanced at Jamie, who was engrossed in something Malcolm related with much waving of arms. Jamie seemed perfectly unscarred from such a traumatic event.

Alec leaned toward her, warming to his tale. "Jamie was ten, and I was seven. Men broke into Kilmorgan Castle, hoping to capture the duke's heir and hold him for ransom, or ... who knows?" Alec shrugged. "Jamie jumps up and declares *he's* Alec Mackenzie, and they snatched him instead. He did it because he was afraid I was too small to survive them. I was affronted at the time, but he was likely right."

"Kind of him," Evie said in admiration.

"Aye, Jamie has pluck. And he never once lorded that over me."

Jamie wouldn't, Evie realized. He was the sort of man who helped because he cared, not because he wanted glory.

When they arrived at the station of the remote village called Kilmorgan Halt, the entire population of the tiny place descended upon them. They called greetings, snatched up bags, and organized them all into carriages and carts to help them reach the duke's home.

Kilmorgan Castle, Evie saw as they approached, was not a castle at all. A gigantic manor house sprawled in a hollow, with craggy mountains receding into a haze beyond it. Northern Scotland was cold and gray at the moment, but a beam of sunlight touched the house, turning the brick blazing gold.

"It's beautiful," Evie breathed as she descended from the carriage. "And large." The massive building dominated its grounds.

"Good thing it is." Gavina grinned at her. "There are so many of us."

Gavina threaded her arm through Evie's and swept her into a vaulted front hall. A gigantic vase of flowers reposed on a table in the middle of this hall, a staircase wrapping around it. Paintings of Mackenzie men and ladies adorned the walls that rose three stories, including a large portrait of Hart Mackenzie on the first landing.

The house had been divided into five wings, one for each of the brothers and their families, the fifth for guests. The Mackenzies quickly dispersed into their disparate halls, their shouts and calls making the silent place come alive. Dogs had appeared from the back, barking greetings and swarming around the families, adding to the noise.

Gavina led Evie not to the guest wing, but to Ian's. "Aunt Beth insists you stay with them." She squeezed Evie's arm. "We'll have such fun, with all the cousins together. I've already organized the poker game. Don't worry, we play for farthings." With that, Gavina scurried away, leaving Evie alone in a huge bedchamber with the most sumptuous bed she'd ever seen.

Beth was her first visitor, arriving after Evie's trunk was delivered. Evie had sent away the maid who wanted to unpack it, wishing to sort through her things herself.

Beth immediately began to help. "Now, I know you feel we are pushing you at Jamie," she said without preliminary. "But please, do not worry about that. You are a guest, and I want you to be at your ease. Jamie is a good lad, and naturally as his mother, I want him to be happy." Beth sank to Evie's bed, a cluster of ribbons in her hand. "I love him to bits, if I'm honest. When I hear stories of him falling out of the sky, or nearly toppling from a train far from home, I want to clutch him to me, and never let him go." She held the ribbons to her chest, as though the gesture would keep him safe.

Evie joined her on the bed. "You'd like it if he settled down."

"I would. And he has promised to." Beth gazed at Evie, compassion in her eyes. "Truth to tell, I'd love to see him marry you. You have an adventurous spirit, like his own—the fact that you have weathered this family with good cheer tells me that. But I would never coerce you into a marriage you did not want. I once tried to make a practical match myself, and I bless the day my Ian destroyed it for me. I'd have been terribly unhappy, and I would not have quite known why. My advice to you, dear, is to marry with your heart, or not at all."

"I am beginning to realize that this is wise." Evie sighed. "Though it is difficult to fly in the face of convention. Everyone wants a woman to marry, no matter what."

"Ian taught me how to ignore convention. And ladies nowadays have a few more choices than they did in my time. Belle is trying very hard to pursue a career in medicine, and though it is difficult for her, I have no doubt she will succeed, one way or another. Megan too, with her music. Marriage would be nice for them, but right now their hearts guide them in another direction. Gavina is trying to find her niche as well, but chasing down a man to marry is not what she has in mind. If my girls *do* find kind gentlemen to love them, I will be glad, but if not, they are still worthy of all the love Ian and I can give them. I'm certain, from your mother's letters, that she and your father feel the same way about you."

Evie nodded, tears welling. "You are a wonderful, wonderful woman." She flung her arms around Beth, sobbing into her shoulder.

"There now." Beth held her close, her embrace comforting. "You poor lamb. We've worn you out."

"No," Evie said brokenly. "You've taken care of me."

"Ah, well," Beth said, patting her tenderly. "That is what Mackenzies do."

———

THE MACKENZIE COUSINS SENSED THE TENSION BETWEEN Jamie and Evie and ceased making certain the two ended up next to each other, to Evie's relief. Evie wondered if Beth had given them a pointed hint.

There was so much to do at Kilmorgan Castle that Evie barely had time to brood. Meals were lively, and then there were tramps to the ruins of the original castle, or horseback rides up into the crags, a tour of the distillery, and visits to the village and to other homes in the area.

Jamie spent much time at the distillery with Ian, who ran the business. Jamie would inherit the position, Gavina told Evie, when Ian finally decided to retire. Jamie also helped Cameron train horses or fished with Ian and his male cousins, though Megan often accompanied them.

Gavina's poker game took place a week after their arrival. Evie was seated opposite Jamie at the large oval table in a sitting room in Cameron's wing—which was for the best, she declared silently, no matter how much her mutinous self wanted to be next to him.

Most of the younger Mackenzies were present, except for Daniel's brood—Violet had declared they were not yet old enough to face the family card sharps. Jamie studied his cards without a glance at Evie.

They stuck to a simple game of five-card draw, trying to gain pairs, straights, flushes, and so forth. Evie knew the rudiments of poker, having played forbidden games at Girton. Not long into the evening, she'd already gathered a large pile of farthings.

"Evie, you're a ringer," Alec declared as he threw down his cards after another loss. "You're obviously an expert."

"I wouldn't say that." Evie gathered up cards and passed them to Gavina, who was acting as the dealer. "It's easy to tell when you're bluffing, Alec. You rub the top of your ear."

Alec froze, golden eyes flicking to her. "What are you talking about, lass?"

Jamie chuckled as he picked up cards Gavina tossed to him. "In game parlance, it's called a *tell*," he said. "Thank you, Evie." He turned to Alec. "She wins because she's smarter than you."

"All right, don't rub my nose in it," Alec growled.

"Don't you mean your ear?" Jamie returned. He shot Evie a glance, eyes twinkling, as the others laughed. He didn't smile, but it was the friendliest look he'd sent her all week.

"He does that when he likes a woman too," Eileen, Mac's daughter, put in. "Brushes his ear like that. We saw the American girl, Miss Carmichael, at the theatre in London, and Alec was there, just rubbing, rubbing."

Alec's face grew mottled, his eyes dangerous. "She's a lovely lass, is all. I have no interest in her, so keep your observations to yourself."

Eileen stuck her tongue out at him and sorted her cards in her hand.

Evie recalled how Alec had gone still when he'd beheld *Iris* at the restaurant, not Miss Carmichael. Evie believed him when he said he had no designs on the heiress. Well, well, this could be interesting.

Jamie was watching her again. While the others babbled about Miss Carmichael, he gave her a slow wink.

Why did her blood begin to heat? Evie should remain cool and then depart as planned after her sojourn here. She could not allow her confusion to keep churning.

"Never mind Miss Carmichael," Alec's brother, Mal, was saying. "Miss Letitia O'Keefe is more who I have in mind. Dark-haired beauty."

"Mmm," Gavina said warningly. "I'd be careful there, Mal. She's out for a title. A courtesy title won't do, I think. She'd want the heir, not the spare."

"Och." Mal scowled at his cards. "Ye know too many ladies, Gavina. You always spoil it."

He protested a bit too much, Evie observed. While Alec had been floored by Iris, Mal had been watching Miss Carmichael quite avidly.

"I know which are predatory and which are sweet, is all," Gavina said. "Miss O'Keefe will set her cap for Alec, not you."

"No, she will not," Alec rumbled. "I've met her, Malcolm. She's got that hunter's gleam in her eye. I'll stay far from her, thank you."

"Don't disparage a lady, Alec," Jamie admonished. "It's likely her mama who is pushing her at a dukedom. Not her fault."

"Yes, be kind to her, Alec," Gavina said, reversing her warning.

Alec threw down his cards. "I'm not going to rush to the altar with a lady to avoid being rude to her." He shook his head. "You all are mad."

In the general laughter, Jamie shot Evie another look, this one with the hint of a smile. *My family,* he seemed to be saying. *I love the whole exasperating lot of them.*

Evie returned the glance, her heart warming from its shaky coldness.

As the night wore on, the cousins one by one departed to turn in. Evie was surprised it had gone two in the morning when Gavina declared the game officially over. Evie couldn't remember when she'd had such an enjoyable night.

She helped Gavina tidy the card table then scooped her

farthings into a bag Gavina lent her and departed for the long walk to her chamber.

Jamie leaned on a pillar in the wide hall outside the sitting room, pushing from it to fall into step with her as she passed.

"I can buy quite a lot of penny candy with this." Evie nervously jingled the bag. She had no idea what to say to Jamie that didn't sound inane.

"I might help ye," Jamie said, the hint of smile returning. "But I'm off home tomorrow."

Evie halted, the coins clinking. "Home? You mean your flat in London?" She did not like how the floor seemed to drop from beneath her feet at this news.

Jamie shook his head. "To my family's home, not far north of here. Where I grew up. I have a few things to take care of." He stepped in front of her, his strong body barring her way. "Will you come with me?"

CHAPTER 28

*J*amie met Evie in the cool of the following morning in a coach he'd convinced Uncle Hart to lend him. He'd been surprised when Evie agreed to travel with him to the home where he'd spent happy days, but he didn't argue.

"We can ride most of the way, though it's rough," Jamie explained. "The last half mile we'll walk. Much easier on the horses and carriage, not to mention our backsides."

Evie consented serenely, and off they went.

Even the weather cooperated. The mists and rains that had dogged them since they'd arrived lifted, revealing Scotland at its most beautiful. The high mountains around Ian Mackenzie's home glowed in the sunlight, blue sky softened by wisps of cloud.

Ian's house was not as grand as Kilmorgan, being about one quarter the size, but Jamie found it just right for him. Here he'd learned to walk and ride—one following closely upon the other—run wild in the woods and on the hills, fish, and dream.

A lawn had been put in behind the garden, though it was difficult to maintain with the rest of Scotland trying to grow in.

The garden itself was a riot of plants that Beth and Megan tended, with a path leading from it to the stables.

Evie walked sturdily next to Jamie as they tramped the last bit of road to the house. She'd said little on the journey, and Jamie had not prodded her. They'd been polite and neutral, like strangers who happened to be traveling the same direction.

Evie halted outside the back garden, taking in the house's golden bricks, many gables, and deep eaves. Flowers had begun to bloom, his mother's daffodils and tulips springing up in a mass of colors.

Jamie clasped her elbow as the back door opened. "I forgot to warn you. Do you like dogs?"

"Indeed, I do." Evie sent him a puzzled glance. "Why are you asking? There are plenty of dogs at Kilmorgan."

"Aye, and they dozed in the garden or by the fire. These were kept home for a reason."

The house's caretaker, Murray, would have seen Jamie coming and known that Molly and Fergus would howl like banshees if they weren't let out to greet him.

They came at him now, two streaks of black, barking a joyous welcome. They were bird dogs, large and friendly, slobbery, and strong. Fergus leapt with vigor, landing against Jamie with all four paws.

Jamie caught him, trying to lower the dog before they both fell to the ground. Fergus wriggled his hundred-pound body in great excitement, bathing Jamie's face in doggy kisses.

Evie laughed in pure delight. Then she squeaked as Molly, no less enthusiastic than Fergus, reared up to plant her large and muddy paws on Evie's chest.

Instead of screaming with horror and batting her away, Evie dropped her handbag and patted Molly with both hands, declaring she'd never seen a prettier girl.

Jamie at last shoved Fergus from him, then caught him before he could jump on Evie.

"Fergus, and Molly." Jamie seized Molly's collar. The dogs

quieted the slightest bit in his grip but wagged tails so hard they swayed from side to side with the momentum. "This is Evie. Ye be good to her, now."

"They're adorable." Evie leaned to stroke both, one hand on each. "We have dogs at home, not quite so large or eager, I'll grant. I miss them."

Her melancholy caught at Jamie's heart. Well, there was something he could do about that.

He finally managed to calm Fergus and Molly long enough to lead them and Evie into the house.

"You'll have to take them for a good run," Jamie instructed Murray, the large, silent man with a wide smile who waited for Jamie and Evie with obvious pleasure. "This is Miss McKnight. Will you show her to a room where she can freshen up?"

Evie's gown had become a mess of mud, and black dog hairs clung to her fawn-colored gloves. She was flushed with pleasure, however, and greeted Murray with her warm-hearted friendliness.

Murray, without saying a word, led Evie inside and down a hall toward the guest suite that was always ready for visiting family or friends.

Jamie patted the dogs until Murray returned, then relinquished them to the man, who whistled at them to follow him out.

Murray was a man of few words. He would be considered a dour Scot except for the smile he beamed out on everyone. He had more friends down the pub than any man in the Highlands, though he rarely spoke to anyone.

Jamie raced upstairs and washed hands and face in his old bedroom that welcomed him with its familiarity. He heard Evie's step once he'd finished and went out to find her studying the portraits that lined the lower hall, many of them painted by Uncle Mac.

She gazed up at the family portrait Mac had done when

Megan had been about three. Beth sat serenely on a chair, Megan with her red-brown curls, chubby on her mother's lap. Belle, a few years older, leaned on the chair near Beth's hand. She was a little more serious than sunny Megan, but her intelligence showed on her face. Mac had caught her well.

Ian Mackenzie stood behind this group, his large hand resting on Beth's shoulder. He gazed straight out of the painting, his golden eyes holding strength and quietness. Mac had painted his younger brother with much affection.

Jamie was on the opposite side of the chair from Belle. Six years old, he stood on sturdy legs, arms folded, grinning out of the picture. He wore a Mackenzie great kilt that sagged about his knees, a black jacket, and a bonnet holding the crest of the Mackenzies.

"I considered myself very grown up," Jamie informed Evie as he halted behind her. "Ready to take up a claymore and conquer the world."

Evie didn't pull away from his closeness. "I see a hardy young fellow very sure of himself."

"I was robust. Sure of myself ... not always."

Evie turned to face him, her eyes soft. "Is that why you went around the world, seeking adventure?"

"Seeking something." Jamie daringly rested his hands on her waist. "I had to come home to find it."

Evie's lips parted as though she wanted to ask him what. Jamie stilled the question by kissing her.

He'd made himself stay away from her for days, and it had nearly wrecked him. He'd had nothing but erotic dreams about Evie since the day he'd touched her by the river.

Now her mouth was once more beneath his, her tongue slipping between his parted lips.

Jamie's self-control snapped. He hungrily took her mouth, hands supporting her head, her hair silken against his fingers. One day he'd strip out every hairpin and pull the glossy dark mass over his naked body.

Evie made that exciting noise in her throat, meaning her surrender was near. Jamie stepped against her, thighs to her hips, wanting to take her down to the stairs and drive himself into her.

She'd open to him, as wet and needy as she'd been when he'd pleasured her. He'd go slowly at first, carefully, so she wouldn't be hurt.

Then he'd teach her. Every position, every technique he'd learned in his life around the world—he would show her. He'd watch her yield to passion, dissolving under his hands.

Evie's lips were hot, her mouth seeking. She clung to the lapels of his coat, all anger in her gone. Sorrow had gone too. Frenzy and need remained.

Murray's heavy tread was the only thing that brought Jamie back to the present. With him came the clicking steps of the dogs, less exuberant now, but panting and happy.

Jamie eased from Evie, lowering her hands from his coat just as both dogs careened around a corner and scrambled toward them.

Evie eagerly bent down to pat them again.

"Let's venture outside," he said. "It's too rare a day to stay in here, and the dogs will have farther to roam."

Evie gave him a nod and Jamie led her out, past Murray, whose smile had turned to a knowing grin. Cheeky sod.

The garden, Beth's pride and joy, encircled three sides of the house. In the weeks of Scotland's short summer, Beth would be here on her hands and knees, planting, weeding, tilling. The gardeners had learned to let her do as she pleased but were ready to lend help when she asked for it.

As a result, this patch of land was lush and thriving, with not only flowers but vegetables and greens that found their way to the supper table.

Evie loved it, he could see. Her face glowed with delight as she took it all in, the mountains a perfect backdrop. Jamie led her to the sunniest side of the house, where benches and tables had been set.

He handed her to a white-painted iron bench and sank down beside her. Neither spoke as the breeze played, bringing with it the scent of fresh flowers and newly turned earth.

Evie tilted her head back, letting the sun warm her face. Her mouth was relaxed, lips quirked in a little smile.

"What are you thinking?" Jamie asked quietly.

"Mmm?" Evie lifted her head and opened her eyes, the blue of them like mountain columbines. "I was thinking I was happy. That I haven't been in so very long."

"Ah." Jamie forced his gaze from her, pretending to take in the woods that opened from the base of the lawn.

Evie's tone changed to concern. "What is it? You sound sad."

"Sad because I have to leave you."

"Leave?" Evie asked, perplexed. "To go where?"

Dare he believe she was distressed? "I have many things to do. Things that will take me out of Scotland, maybe to the Continent. I don't know when I'll be back."

"Oh." There was no mistaking Evie's alarmed hurt. She tried to remain collected, but her voice shook. "I see."

"I *will* be back, though." Jamie turned to her fully. "How could I stay away from you, love? But I think you ought to go home. I brought you here—to Scotland and Kilmorgan—so you could find peace." He tucked a lock of her hair behind her ear. "Which you have."

Evie pulled from him. "So, you're sending me away?"

"Not *sending* you. You go where you please. But yes, I think it's time. Go back to your family. Live your own life. Learn to be Evie."

The hurt increased. "You think I'm hiding here." A swallow moved her throat. "Perhaps I am. Here I can breathe, I can laugh. I've finally woken." Her eyes were moist, but they narrowed. "I don't have to obey you, Mackenzie."

"No," Jamie said impatiently. "You can do whatever you bloody well please."

Evie rose to her feet. "Oh, certainly, if what I bloody well please is exactly what you want me to do. You believe I should go home, so off I must flit?"

Jamie rose, her fiery temper coupled with his anger making him randy. "All right then, go back to Kilmorgan and drift around its many halls. Do what the devil you like. I thought you'd like to see your mum and sisters again, and the dogs you said you missed. But I'll dismiss the carriage I arranged, and send word to the maids at Kilmorgan to unpack your things."

"You packed my things?" Evie's words rang through the colorful garden.

"Not myself." Damn it all, she was the most maddening woman. "I was trying to do something nice for you. Pardon the hell out of me."

"Nice? You ordering me about, deciding what I will and won't do? Humiliating me by letting me declare myself, and then patting me on the head and telling me what I feel and don't feel?"

"You are still angry at me for refusing you?" Jamie demanded. "When you know you only asked me as a salve for your past? I was right, wasn't I? *He'll do. Why not?*"

"Well, I've changed my mind," Evie said with fire. "I don't need to be married. Look at Gavina, and your sisters. Intelligent ladies who have plenty to occupy them, none needing a man to make them complete. I've decided to take a page from their book."

She was so beautiful as she glared at him, declaring her independence. As Jamie had wanted that for her all along, he rejoiced.

You must give her what she needs, Ian had advised. Jamie had revised this to *What she needs, that only I can give her.*

Joy. Freedom. Happiness. She'd stated moments ago that she'd been happy for the first time in a very long while.

Time to let her go, at least for now. Let her live with that happiness, with herself, with that peace.

Only, he'd made her angry at him. She always would be, Jamie realized. Angry, then laughing, then exasperated.

He loved her.

"Exactly," Jamie answered. "Go home. Be free. Away from the pestering Jamie."

"I don't want to be away from you," Evie shouted. "I want to be with you, blast you."

She wasn't supposed to. She was supposed to waft merrily away while Jamie started the next part of his plans to woo her.

He scrubbed his hands through his hair. "Well, I *have* to go. I thought you'd be glad."

"Glad?" Her glare intensified. "After you kicked your way into my life whether I liked it or not, and made me love you? Why should I be glad? But now you are finished, and I ought to be too?"

"*Love.*" Jamie heard only the one word. "Oh, lass, don't joke with me about that."

"I am not joking." Evie's eyes blazed. "I love you, Jamie Mackenzie. Damn you."

What was left of Jamie's composure snapped.

He seized Evie and dragged her to him, his mouth on hers. The kiss was hard, brief, bruising. When he pulled away, Evie gasped for breath.

Jamie didn't let her catch that breath. He closed his hand around her wrist and pulled her with him into the house, past the startled Murray, up the stairs, and down the hall into his bedroom.

As he slammed the door, he heard Murray snap his fingers at the dogs, and lead them outside in a discreet retreat.

CHAPTER 29

$\mathcal{E}$vie's fury at Jamie clawed excitement through her as Jamie kicked the door shut and turned her with hard hands into his embrace.

His strength heightened her already giddy need. She knew she'd have to struggle to get away, but she no longer wanted to.

Jamie lifted her around the waist and set her on the edge of the sturdy bedstead, then stepped between her legs to kiss her. His mouth opened hers, and Evie kissed him back without restraint.

She started when he began tugging her skirts upward, but Evie did not break the kiss. If he hadn't touched her as he had on the riverbank, she'd have been filled with agitation, but now she eagerly craved the sensations she remembered.

She was supposed to be angry with him. And she was, but Evie's anger fled on a hot wave of desire.

Jamie slid his hands to her drawers, which he loosened. Instead of dipping inside them as he had before, he quickly pulled them from her and tossed them onto the bed.

Evie drew a sharp breath, their mouths parting. She felt

very odd with nothing between her bare skin and her skirts, but the feeling brought elation.

Evie had never done naughty things before, especially those naughty things one experienced with a man. Now she embraced them. Jamie could teach her so much, she realized, heart thudding.

Jamie's eyes darkened as he pushed her skirts out of his way. He ran the edge of his hand between her parted legs, and Evie made a quick sound of delight.

"Love." Jamie's gaze went to the dark hair at her most private place, which was hot and damp. "Your beauty never stops."

Evie melted under his flattery and his touch, unable to speak. She lay back on her elbows, trying not to squirm, while Jamie caressed her, sounds like whimpers dragging from her. She lifted her hips, wanting more, and Jamie chuckled.

"In a moment, greedy lass." He leaned and pressed a kiss right over the hottest place, and Evie let out a cry.

Jamie shed his jacket and shirt, kicked out of his shoes and socks, and fumbled with the buckles of his kilt. Evie lounged back and watched her delectable Highlander come into view.

The kilt at last loosened, and Jamie dropped it on top of his shirt and coat. He wore closely fitting underdrawers that outlined his thighs and the ridge of his cock. His undershirt came off, revealing a hard, sculpted chest dusted with dark red hair.

Evie held her breath as he slid the underdrawers down his legs and stepped out of them.

The body she gazed at had nothing wrong with it. Jamie was a beautiful man, possessing the wild strength of this place.

Scars crossed his chest from whatever wrecks and fights he'd gotten himself into. One scar brushed his hip, drawing Evie's eyes, before his hardness, which lifted toward her, distracted her from all else.

She'd touched that and played with it, bringing Jamie to

his peak without realizing what she did. Evie wanted to touch him again, to savor his smooth, hot skin, the hardness like steel beneath. She balled her hands, willing them to keep still.

"It's all right, love." Jamie drifted closer. "Do as you please."

Evie sat all the way up, her skirts hiding her bareness. She reached for him, his eyes closing when she folded her hand around him.

Stroking him on the train, when they'd barely been able to move, had been enjoyable. This was even better, her tall, marvelous man bared for her delectation.

She drew her hand down his cock, and Jamie groaned, his head going back. Encouraged, Evie stroked more firmly, liking the way he thrust into her palm.

His shaft fascinated her, large and rigid, curls of dark red hair at its base. The hair was wiry, wrapping her fingers.

Jamie flexed his hands at his sides, his thighs tightening. He raised his head and gazed down at Evie, eyes half closed and warm with desire.

Evie continued to stroke, Jamie's breath coming faster. When Evie trickled her fingers over the intriguing tip, Jamie growled and forced her hand away.

"I can't," he said, voice ragged. "I need ..."

He trailed off, shaking his head. He dragged Evie's skirts up again, this time lifting her hips with one hand and baring her fully. She shivered at the sensation of the coverlet against her skin.

"Are ye cold?" Jamie asked with sudden concern. "Let me warm ye, love."

He stepped between her knees, scooping her legs over his arms. The mattress was high enough that Jamie's tip just touched her opening. His fingers had singed her, but the gentle press of his cock was searing.

Instead of pushing himself inside, Jamie stilled, waiting. Evie knew she could say no, tell him to go, or leave this house

herself. Jamie wouldn't hinder her—she knew him well
enough now to understand that.

Evie closed her hands around his broad wrists and tugged
her to him, giving him a quick nod. *Yes, please.*

Jamie stifled a groan and slid partway inside her.

The light in the room became suddenly more golden. Heat
opened Evie, softened her at the unfamiliar feeling of Jamie
thick inside her.

"I'll try not to hurt you, love." His voice was quiet, reassuring her even through his own need.

Jamie must realize Evie had never lain with a man. Of
course, he knew it—her naivety had screamed itself at him at
every turn.

Evie gave him another nod, telling him she was ready.
Jamie caressed her, touch quiet, then he slowly, slowly eased
himself farther inside.

One tight, searing moment gripped Evie's body, and then it
was gone, replaced with the fullness of Jamie.

Again, he waited, letting her grow used to him, his hands
on her strong, caring. Then, when Evie relaxed, he began to
thrust.

His hard length inside her was maddeningly glorious. Evie
squeezed down on him without understanding what she did.
Jamie's gasping moan told her he felt it, and she squeezed
again, her eyes widening as he thrust all the way inside.

He rocked into her, his face taut, eyes open to let her
drown in the beautiful blue of them. Evie wanted him on top of
her, to feel his weight, but this position let him penetrate her
fully, allowed him to pinch just above where his cock went in.

The sight of him there, buried in her, coupled with his
fingers on her, wrenched a wail from her throat. The dark joy
that had crashed into her by the river came at her again, this
time twice as hard.

Evie cried out again, both in excitement and in sorrow that
this would end soon. Then the fleeting sorrow vanished, and

she knew nothing but fire, and the rightness of this man inside her.

Jamie's thrusts sped, Evie rocking beneath him, clutching handfuls of the bedcovers as a deluge of white-hot sensation crashed over her.

Jamie suddenly pulled out, his touch vanishing too. Evie blinked in bewilderment, choking back a sob at his absence.

Before she could blurt questions, Jamie lifted her, shifting her to lie fully on the bed, her head on his pillows. Then he climbed over her, as she'd longed for him to do.

Jamie loosened her shirtwaist, opening it to reveal her short corset. He competently unlaced the strings that held it closed in the back, slipping the tiny sleeves from her shoulders, sliding the corset off and then the small shirt that lay under it.

Evie still wore her skirts, shoes, and stockings, while he was bare, but Jamie didn't pause to relieve her of the rest of her clothes. He leaned to kiss her breast, teeth catching on one nipple, before he slid back inside her.

Evie arched to meet him, her body now warm and loose. Jamie pressed into her leisurely, smiling at her, close enough for slow kisses. Evie touched his face, loving the sandpaper feel of his whiskers, the thick warmth of his hair.

A sinful light entered Jamie's eyes. He lifted Evie under her hips and sat back on his heels, she straddling him while he went straight up into her.

The potent fire returned, bursting over Evie before she could draw breath. The wildness made her scream, and then words poured forth, Evie crying Jamie's name, shouting that she loved him, begging him for more and more.

Jamie steadied her while he loved her, his body slick with sweat, her breasts tight against his chest. Evie clung to him, her hair coming down to pool around them, her voice hoarse with her cries.

Just when Evie thought she could take no more—she

shook her head and moaned—Jamie gave a shout that ended in a long groan.

He shoved her from him, Evie landing against the mattress, her voice catching on a cry.

Jamie sprang from the bed and reached for his discarded underdrawers. He wrapped them around his hardness before he let out another growling groan and sank against the side of the bed, shuddering. Then he dropped his head forward and went still.

"Jamie?" Evie asked into the silence, her voice a croak. "Are you well?"

Jamie's back worked as he rubbed himself dry, but when he turned to her, his smile was broad, joy lighting his eyes. "I'm very, very well, thank you."

Evie's entire body tingled under his heated gaze. "What happened?"

Jamie's grin didn't waver. "Which part? I think many things happened in the last half hour or so."

"The last thing. When you suddenly stopped."

Jamie tossed his drawers to a bare patch of carpet. "That was so I wouldn't drop a babe in you, love. Ye don't need that."

Evie's belly squeezed, the joy of their lovemaking lingering. She did want a child, very much so, one who looked like Jamie, one she would care for and raise in the loving way she had been.

But he was right that having a babe without a husband would spell her doom, and the child's too.

It also meant Jamie didn't intend to rush them out to a chapel and marry her today.

Evie cursed herself anew for blurting the foolish proposal that day by the river. He was right—she had suggested it in her frustration with her failed betrothal with Hayden, her worry that she'd have to face her empty life alone.

Jamie had been offended rather than charmed, and Evie

did not blame him. He'd argued that he wanted to be loved for himself, not used as a crutch. Evie wanted the same.

But she loved him. She had no doubt of that now. Perhaps they could begin again, using this day of bliss as a start.

Jamie climbed onto the bed beside her. Evie thrust away her doubts, determined to enjoy what she had in this moment.

Jamie, with tenderness, rid Evie of the rest of her garments. Then he curled against her, pulling a quilt over them both. He kissed her in slow afterglow, contentment settling over them, while the golden light of the Highlands bathed the room in softness.

———

JAMIE MADE LOVE TO HER AGAIN AFTER THEY'D RESTED, AND then a third time. He pulled out at the last minute each time, crashing back down beside her, breathing hard.

After the third loving, Evie fell into a profound sleep, waking when Jamie gently shook her. The sun was setting, the light fading, and Evie knew they had to depart.

They dressed each other, Jamie fetching clean things from his wardrobe, the process prolonged by their kissing and touching. But at long last, Jamie led Evie from his bedchamber and back down the stairs.

It was difficult for Evie to say goodbye to the house, to the dogs, to Murray. She'd only met them this day, but they'd already nestled into her heart.

The Kilmorgan coach awaited them at the road, which they walked to, the coachman having fished with a crony who lived nearby while he waited. He proudly held up two gleaming fish he'd take back to the Kilmorgan kitchens.

Evie and Jamie did not speak during the ten-mile, slightly fishy smelling ride back to Kilmorgan. Evie rested her head on Jamie's shoulder, and he held her close.

Once at Kilmorgan, Evie stopped outside the front door of the well-lit and welcoming mansion.

"Do you still plan to leave?" she asked Jamie.

He regarded her somberly. "I must. I will tell you about it when the business is done."

Evie's throat tightened, but she nodded. "Then I will go home. You are right. It is time."

———

"YOU HAVE A TELEGRAM, EVIE." MARJORIE DANCED IN WITH it. "The telegraph boy from the village is *so* handsome, is he not? He moved here with his mum while we were in New York."

Marjorie spun in place, holding the telegram to her chest. Evie, in the conservatory on the south end of the house, where warm sunshine poured through the greenery, watched her in exasperation.

She did not like the way her heart fluttered, hoping against hope that the telegram was from Jamie. Three weeks had passed since their beautiful lovemaking in his bedroom in Scotland, and she'd not heard one word from him.

He might not be coming back, Evie told herself. And what of it? Jamie had given her a taste of happiness, showed her that she could be content by and with herself. Now she could move on with her life. Evie tried to make herself believe that was enough.

Beth had been understanding about Evie's request to return home, though she'd barely concealed her disappointment.

Ian had said little when Evie had bade him goodbye, but he'd looked deep into her eyes for a time, as though memorizing her. He'd not seemed disappointed at all, but confident.

The Mackenzie cousins had embraced her—at least the ladies had—and the young men had expressed sorrow at this parting. She was a brick, Mal had told her, and welcome to stay with them anytime.

Megan had teared up as she'd hugged Evie goodbye, and Evie's eyes too had been moist. Gavina's hug was exuberant, and she'd vowed that Evie could come and stay with them in London whenever she liked. Her eyes had also been suspiciously bright when she turned away.

Quiet Belle had held Evie hard. "Never worry about Jamie," she'd whispered. "He loves you. I see that. He'll come around." She'd nodded at Evie when she'd released her, her confidence matching Ian's. "I'll miss you," Belle had concluded.

"I'll miss you too," Evie returned, her heart aching. "I'll miss you all."

They'd gone en masse to the station and put her on the three-car train that would take her to Inverness, where she would change for the long ride back to Bedfordshire. Evie had waved to the mob of Mackenzies as long as she could, then said a silent farewell to the Highlands, the crisp air and misty sky already imprinted on her heart.

Coming home had been bittersweet. Evie had been happier to see her sisters and parents than she'd thought she could be, all of them weeping in gladness, even her father, when they'd met her at the station. She hadn't taken one step from the train before she'd been smothered by hugs, tears, and kisses.

After the first few days of rejoicing, all of them babbling to each other everything that had happened since they'd parted in London, Evie had grown restless. The scull Jamie had bought her had been delivered during her time in Scotland, and she spent warm afternoons in the narrow river down the hill from the house, either on her own or with Marjorie, who wasn't a bad rower herself.

The scull could be rowed by one, though it was a little awkward. Evie took to practicing between the river's musty banks, her muscles hardening again as she grew used to the exercise.

But she could only remember Jamie's strong back before her as they'd zigzagged over the Cam, laughing and getting too wet, and then the wild pleasure he'd taught her after their sumptuous picnic.

Evie told herself she needed to wrest her thoughts from their fixation on Jamie. To put other plans in motion. To that end, she'd written letters to old friends, and this telegram could be the answer to one of them.

"Marjorie, please cease dancing and hand it to me," Evie said, returning to the present. "Telegrams are sent because someone wants to convey urgent information. That means they should be read without delay."

"That is so." Marjorie held out the envelope. "It isn't from Mr. Mackenzie."

"How do you know that?" Evie demanded, her heart beating too swiftly.

"The lad told me—he'd asked the postmistress. It's from Miss Georgiou, although he couldn't pronounce the name."

"Iris?" Evie snatched the envelope from Marjorie's fingers and tore it open.

The few lines on the paper had Evie stiffening.

Father found jar. Wants to return it. At wits' end. Please help.

CHAPTER 30

$\mathcal{J}$ amie had hoped to conclude his business with the agents and bank clerks in a few weeks, but the transactions took him into the first part of June to complete.

He'd thought the remote area would be idyllic, and it was, but country offices moved slowly. Money had to go through London, and a deed changing hands in the area Jamie had in mind was not of the utmost importance to those in the City. At least he hadn't had to journey to France, his man of business able to complete everything via letter.

It was with relief that Jamie signed the last papers at the London office and pocketed a ring of heavy keys.

Now to Bedfordshire.

The morning of his departure from London a footman in his building of service flats dropped a newspaper on his doorstep. Jamie fetched it to read while he finished his last cup of coffee.

Standing at the table in his small dining room, he turned to the second page, and stopped, a dollop of coffee splashing, unheeded, to the story.

British Minister and Greek Nobleman Deliver Priceless Alabastron to Athens.

Jamie sat down, mouth agape, coffee forgotten.

The gist of the story, embellished with flowery phrases about cooperation between two nations and the grandeur of ancient Greece and Athenian democracy, was that Stefanos Georgiou, thinking to gift a British cabinet minister a small alabastron, discovered that it was indeed a rare example of red-figure pottery from ancient Athens, made by the potter Kontos. Georgiou declared he could not possibly keep such a piece from of his native land, and the British minister, Sir Geoffrey Hammond, generously offered to decline it, both men deciding that it would be best displayed in a museum in Athens.

The story included a photograph of Iris's father, beaming proudly, and the dumpy, white-haired and pompous-looking minister, the pair of them touching the lip of the alabastron that reposed on a table between them.

The background of the photo was shadowy, as always in newspapers, but Jamie could just make out the figures of two young ladies. One of them he'd know anywhere.

Jamie set down the paper, absently brushing off the droplets of spilled coffee. Then he began to laugh.

He hadn't laughed so hard in a long time — except when he was with Evie. Jamie wiped his eyes and thrust the coffee cup and paper aside.

"What a lady," he proclaimed to no one. "I knew she was the love of my life."

———

EVIE FINISHED WRITING HER LAST LETTER, MAKING FINAL arrangements for the meeting on the Thames, when a peculiar sound made her look up and out the sitting room's front window.

She dropped her pen, the ink on its nib splattering her clean page.

Chugging up the drive of her family home was a bright red motorcar, one she recognized. Its top was down, the driver with gloved hands competent on the wheel, sun burnishing his red-brown hair. Jamie never liked to wear a hat in a car.

Evie ought to sit sedately and wait for Jamie to reach the house, knock on the front door, and inquire to see her. And then longer while the footman took Jamie's coat and wended his way to the sitting room to ask if Evie would receive Mr. Mackenzie. Still longer while Evie waited for her mother to come in from the garden to chaperone them.

She abandoned propriety at once and raced outside through the French doors, hurrying around the house to reach the front portico at the same time the motorcar did. She barely beat Marjorie and Clara, who both emerged excitedly from the front door.

Jamie pulled the motorcar to a halt and set the gears before gracefully unfolding himself from the driver's seat.

"Good morning, ladies."

Evie's mother and father were the next to emerge, their breathlessness showing they'd come from their corners of the house with as much haste. Mrs. McKnight still held a garden trowel in her mud-covered gloves.

"Sir, Ma'am." Jamie continued his greeting without pause. "I have come to invite Miss McKnight for a drive, if she is free." His blue eyes sparkled with humor as he took in Evie.

"*I* am Miss McKnight," Marjorie said at once, bounding forward. "And I happen to be free this morning."

"He means, Evie, goose," Clara said, aghast.

"I know." Marjorie wrinkled her nose at Jamie. "I was teasing. You know I was teasing, don't you, Mr. Mackenzie?"

"You are a true wit." Jamie winked at her. "I should be more precise. I have come to invite Miss *Evie* McKnight for a drive, if she is free."

All eyes turned to Evie.

"Well." Evie could barely form words. "I will have to check my diary."

A chorus of *Evie!* and *Go on!* burst around her, Jamie's grin flashing as Evie's sisters and parents chorused.

Jamie jogged around the motorcar and opened the passenger door. Evie, heart banging, slid into the seat, pretending to coolly smooth her hair while Jamie returned to the driver's side. He waved an arm to Evie's family and glided the motorcar forward.

"Where are we going?" Evie asked as they rumbled down the drive. This car moved much faster than the electric one had but lacked its smoothness.

Jamie sent her a wry glance. He pulled onto the main road, the tires bumping over wagon ruts. "In my father's day, when a young man called for a lady in his two-seater buggy, was this the first question from her lips? Or was she flattered by his attention?"

"A motorcar is different," Evie said. "The vehicle is always more exciting than its driver."

"Crush a man, will you? Where we are going remains to be seen. By you, that is. *I* know where it is."

"Rowing again?" Evie asked. "I've left my scull."

She couldn't halt the flip words rolling from her tongue. She wanted to demand to know what the devil Jamie had been up to in the last five weeks. *Five weeks, three days, four hours.*

She wanted to tell him how she'd feared she'd never see him again, blurt out all the words she'd wanted to shout at him, both angry and loving.

Instead, only silly banter emerged, nothing at all what she meant.

"Not this time. Though—" Jamie broke off. "Never mind. I have difficulty keeping a secret."

"I've watched you play poker. You hold your cards very close to your chest, I'd say."

"Very droll, my lady." Jamie reached across Evie to a compartment in the dashboard, his arm just brushing her chest. A drop of perspiration rolled down the back of her neck.

Jamie retrieved what looked like a newspaper cutting, one with dried dark blotches in the margins. "This is your doing, I take it?"

Evie studied the paper he handed her. It was the story from the *Illustrated London News* about the alabastron making its way back to Greece.

"Oh, yes." Evie put a hint of surprise in her tone, as though she'd forgotten this trivial event. "I thought it best. Iris was very upset when her father caught her trying to hide the alabastron in her luggage—they were packing up to return to Athens."

"You thought it best, did you?" Jamie slowed at a fork in the road, peering down each turning as though trying to remember directions. He jerked the car along the left-hand route. "And you persuaded Sir Geoffrey Hammond to allow Iris's dad to return it and pretend they'd decided this together?"

"Yes."

Jamie slammed the car to a halt, the tires skidding, and swung to her.

"I love you madly, Evie, but will you please cease tormenting me? How did you do it? You have a honeyed tongue—I well know—but persuading the arrogant and dim Sir Geoffrey to go along with your ruse? How the devil did ye manage it?"

Evie wanted to laugh. Jamie was itching to know, wild to hear about an adventure he'd had no part of. When Evie had received Iris's telegram, she'd immediately longed to seek him out but had stopped herself. It was something she'd had to do on her own.

Or at least, somewhat on her own.

"Perhaps we should continue on our way," she said.

"Before a farm wagon comes along and runs us down. I'll explain everything. I promise."

Jamie changed the gear and moved the car forward once more. "It will be about twenty more minutes to our destination. Plenty of time for a story."

Evie could have pointed out that he was keeping their destination a secret from *her*, but she relented.

"I consulted with your Uncle Hart," she said. "Or rather, with Gavina, who took me to your Aunt Eleanor, and thence to Uncle Hart."

"Uncle Hart?" Jamie repeated in amazement. "A good choice, I grant you, but you rather rushed into the lion's den."

"He's not so terrible." Evie had taken to calling him *Uncle Hart*, and the formidable man had not minded. "He knew the minister in question and introduced me to him. Uncle Hart also brought your father with us to help persuade the minister to do as I suggested."

Jamie put one gloved hand to his mouth as though pained. "Oh, love, I'm imagining it."

The minister had been very flattered at the attention of the lofty duke, Evie told Jamie, though he'd made a few digs at him. Apparently the two did not see eye to eye politically.

Sir Geoffrey, at Hart's request, had been prepared to humor Evie and listen to her, but with an air of one utterly patronizing a young lady. When Ian had entered the room, however, everything changed.

Ian had done nothing, only regarded the man while Evie explained what she needed Sir Geoffrey to do. When Evie had finished, she had seen in Sir Geoffrey's eyes that he would refuse, simply because he could.

Then Ian had moved to stand behind him. He'd leaned from his tall height to speak words into Sir Geoffrey's ear that Evie hadn't heard. Sir Geoffrey had jumped.

Hart had moved to his other side, laying a hand on his

shoulder, and Sir Geoffrey had abruptly started babbling that he'd help Evie all he could.

Hart had added the incentive that Sir Geoffrey would have his name put before the public, who would admire him for his generosity. Sir Geoffrey had agreed to do exactly as they'd outlined.

After that, they'd brought in Mr. Georgiou, who had been waiting with the alabastron, and a journalist Hart had alerted. The journalist eagerly lapped up the story, and the photographer with him had snapped pictures.

"The photographer was the one from the docks in Southampton," Evie said. "Remember?"

"Aye, I remember him." Jamie's scowl was dark. "The one who made me look like a mooning fool over one young lady, when I was entirely absorbed in another."

The way Jamie's eyes went straight to her made Evie's heart tremble. "I set him straight, by the way," she said quickly. "Miss Carmichael is reprieved from your advances. I feel this photographer has redeemed himself by catching such a nice image of Iris's father becoming a national hero."

"I won't thrash the man then." Jamie shrugged grudgingly, then he flashed his smile at her, the one she'd missed all these weeks. "You're a treasure, Evie, lass. I'm sorry I missed the excitement, but you turned the tables more neatly than I could have. I'd have blustered and coerced, but you simply marched in with all guns blazing. My perfect lady." His admiration warmed her through as he swerved the car down a narrow lane that ran through a stand of trees. "Ah, here we are."

The car emerged from the copse and Jamie halted in front of a lovely little cottage. Ivy covered bright red brick to the slightly crooked chimney, and the shutters and front door gleamed with fresh black paint. A garden behind a low wall surrounded the house, the tableau thoroughly charming.

"Oh, how beautiful." Evie stepped from the car, not waiting for him to open her door. "Who lives here?"

Jamie's gaze held warmth along with a bit of tension. "You do," he said.

CHAPTER 31

*E*vie stared at Jamie in disbelief. "I don't live here, I—"
She broke off, her mouth too dry to continue.

Jamie removed a ring of keys from his pocket. "It's not far
from your mum and dad's, it's on the same little river as their
house, but it's wider here, better for rowing. There's a scull in
the shed yonder, a single one, so you can row to your heart's
content." He spoke quickly, as though needing to get through
the speech. "A maid and a cook will come in each day, so you
don't have to worry about the meals and cleaning. You can do
as you like here—send antiquities back to Greece, become a
champion rower, or whatever you please. It's a place to be
yourself."

"Jamie—"

"I know you'll say you can't accept it," he cut in. "But it's
too late. Your name is on the deed, and the cottage is paid for.
It took some machinations to finish the business, which is why
I waited so long to seek you. The man who owned it is now an
expatriate in France but wasn't certain he wanted to sell, and
the correspondence, not to mention the banks, took longer
than I anticipated. I wanted to hand it to you, fait accompli."

"But ..." It was adorable, this house. Evie opened the gate

and wandered dreamily through the garden, wondering if the cottage would be as delightful on the inside.

Jamie leapt ahead of her to unlock the door, then he handed her the keys and gestured her in.

It *was* as enchanting on the inside Evie saw as she stepped over the threshold. A small foyer led to a flagstone hall, its whitewashed walls endearingly crooked but solid. A sitting room, flooded with sunshine, looked out over the garden. A dining room opened from the opposite side of the hall, and a narrow stair at the end of the corridor led above.

Evie skimmed up the staircase. Three bedrooms awaited her on the upper floor, one with a cozy bed and a big wardrobe to hold plenty of clothes, plus a cushioned seat in a recessed window.

Across the hall from this was a study with a desk and a shelf full of books, its window showing a view to the river. The third bedroom was equally cozy, if smaller. For her visiting sisters, perhaps, or Gavina, or Iris.

"Did you put in the furniture too?" Evie asked Jamie, who stood at the top of the stairs.

"I did. I had a bit of advice from Megan and Belle, who have excellent taste." Jamie contrived to look modest, as though he'd had little to do with the decorating, but Evie believed differently. He'd added all the things he'd known she'd love.

"It is the most beautiful cottage I've ever seen." Evie inhaled in excitement, then let out the breath, trying to stem her hopes. "But a young lady can't live alone without shocking the world."

Jamie shrugged. "Use it as a retreat then, for days you're bothered. Or ..."

He lost all casualness, his tension returning. Jamie removed a small box from his pocket, and to Evie's utter astonishment, dropped to one knee, right there on the bare hall floor.

"We could share it together," he finished.

Jamie opened the box. Inside lay a ring studded with sapphires surrounding the largest diamond Evie had ever seen.

She opened her mouth to answer, but nothing emerged.

"I was given instruction on how to do this." Jamie's playfulness had deserted him, everything about him rigid. "I am not sure how long I'm supposed to remain in the pose—possibly until this knee starts hurting like holy hell."

Again, Evie tried to answer, but all that came out was a dry huff.

Jamie cleared his throat. "Maybe I'm doing it wrong." He shifted his stance, kilt falling to give Evie a fine look at his strong thigh.

"Will ye marry me, McKnight?" he rumbled.

He spoke from his heart, she could see in his eyes. Jamie asked because he wanted to be with *her*, Evie.

Evie wanted *him*. Not to save her from the humiliation of her betrothal to Hayden, not as a salve for her earlier, tragic love. When she'd burst forth with her proposal at the river, she'd been hurt and wanting to cling to the happiness he'd showed her a glimpse of that day.

She no longer had any hesitation. Jamie filled her thoughts, her dreams, her heart. During their time apart, she'd been able to think of little *but* him. Not only the taste of eroticism he'd given her, but his laughter, his voice, the way she'd find him watching her with a sinful glimmer in his eyes.

When she'd needed help, she'd immediately turned to his family. Without hesitation. They'd aided her without question and without demanding anything in return.

The Mackenzies had made her a part of them because they loved Jamie, and they extended that love to her.

Evie at last found her voice. Happiness poured through her loosening her tongue and filling her with light.

"Of course, I will marry you, Mackenzie," she answered in a near shout.

"Whew." Jamie's eyes lost their apprehension. "Does that mean I can get up?"

Evie flew at him. She seized his wrists and dragged him to his feet, then she went straight into his arms, burying her face against his chest.

His heart pounded beneath her lips, and she kissed him, right over his racing heart.

Jamie pulled her up to him, their mouths meeting in a frenzied kiss. The ring, cool and heavy, slid onto Evie's finger as the kiss went on, she tasting his relief and his longing. His hands roved her back, her waist, her breasts, as though he wanted to learn her in this wonderful moment.

At last Jamie eased away, running his thumb across her lower lip. "I love you so much, Evie." The declaration was low, gruff.

Evie answered with all her heart. "I love *you*, Jamie."

"Good." Jamie's shoulders sagged, and then the wicked light returned to his eyes. "Shall we try out the bed?"

Evie growled in her throat. She grabbed the lapels of Jamie's coat and began yanking it from his shoulders. The coat became a dark pool on the floor, then Jamie guided her with firm hands into the bedroom.

He lifted her from her feet and laid her on the bed before he came down on her, kissing, touching.

"I'd wanted our first time to be here," he murmured. "Not that I mind it was in my chamber at home, in a place full of happy memories."

"I didn't mind either." Evie brushed his face with her fingertips. "*This* house will now have happy memories too."

"McKnight, lass, you are a beautiful thing. And I love you so."

Evie laughed, joy letting her do no less. "You won't be able to call me that much longer, you know."

Jamie's slow smile spread across his face as her words sank

in. His laughter was low, rumbling, sending dark currents through her.

In a few moments, their clothes were gone, and Jamie, bare, hard, and delicious, slid inside her, letting out a heartfelt groan as Evie welcomed him in.

Jamie brushed his hand through her hair as he began to thrust, rapid, deep thrusts that had her begging for more.

"That's my lass." Jamie's whisper wound around her heart. "I love you ... Mrs. Mackenzie."

"I love *you*." Evie found it easy to say the words, and knew she was complete. "My Jamie."

EPILOGUE

Late June 1908

*T*he crowd that gathered on the bank of the Thames near Richmond were mostly Mackenzies, along with Evie's family, but also tourists and those who'd come to see if the ladies could indeed win this friendly match.

Friendly, Jamie thought, hiding a grin. The wagering in the pubs last night had been savage.

The ladies couldn't compete in the Olympics, of course, so said the committee and the head of the men's rowing team, no matter that Jamie had pointed out the unfairness of this. But the British team had agreed to an informal race with Evie and her lady rowers.

While Evie had sojourned in Bedfordshire, she'd written to the former members of her team to support Iris's excited idea that they race the men. The other two young women had readily agreed, likely eager to return to an enjoyment of their youth.

When the two ladies had arrived at the house in Chelsea to

meet Evie, the greetings had been deafening. Jamie had been introduced as the new fiancé.

Of course, Alice and Sarah had remembered him from the oar incident, and Jamie had taken his fair share of ribbing. He'd escaped, pursued by girlish laughter, to meet Alec in a tavern and down much whisky.

Evie and her team had taken lodgings in a house in Richmond for a few weeks to practice rowing and to relearn working together. Evie had decided that if they could not find their old magic, she would withdraw the challenge. She saw no reason to humiliate her friends for her pride.

But the team had fallen back into familiar patterns, and Evie had become happily confident.

The morning dawned, the banks filling with spectators. Jamie escorted Evie to the river, helping the team lower their boat and prepare it. He stayed well away from the oars.

"Wish us luck," Evie said breathlessly as she prepared to board.

Jamie caught her around the waist and pressed a hard kiss to her mouth. "Ye won't need luck."

Evie sent him a smile that warmed him to his toes. He'd had to stay away from her too much since they'd celebrated their engagement in the cottage, but it wouldn't be for much longer. Their wedding was planned for September, and every Mackenzie was throwing him- or herself into making it the grandest wedding in the history of Mackenzie weddings.

Jamie did not confess his worries about that. He had his own ideas but let his family fuss around them. He was the first of the younger cousins to wed, and his aunts and mother were ecstatic.

Evie scrambled nimbly into her place in the four-seat scull Jamie had procured for them. The other members were already aboard, itching to begin. Eight oars rose in perfect formation then dipped into the water, skimming the craft toward the starting line.

The race would be a straight mile, no turning. The men's team had stipulated this, afraid, Evie had told Jamie wryly, that the fragile ladies might shatter if they had to navigate around a post. So kind of them to worry for them.

The men's team rowed confidently into place. Jamie studied the lads as their scull passed, the four young men smugly believing they'd leave the ladies well behind. *Silly things,* Jamie imagined them thinking. *They'll learn not to play with the natural order of things.*

The fools had no idea.

Jamie rejoined his family for the start. Belle, next to him, bounced with excitement.

"Show no mercy, ladies!" she shouted through her cupped hands.

Megan yelled beside her. "Trounce them good!"

"The pair of *you* would have been handy at Culloden," Jamie observed.

"Of course we would have been," Belle informed him. "Those redcoats would have run."

"In terror, aye, I agree." Jamie let out a whoop as the starter fired his pistol and dropped a flag into the water.

The men's boat leapt forward, the four lads rowing strongly. The ladies started more slowly but smoothly. Not long later, the two boats were keeping pace with each other.

The crowd hurried along the footpath, moving toward the finish mark. The boats glided through the water, oars rising and falling in perfect rhythm. It looked effortless, but Jamie knew the knotting and tightening of arms, the ache of legs as each rower strove to keep the pace.

At least *his* muscles had ached the few times Evie had taken him rowing in the past weeks. *She'd* climbed out of the blasted scull without any stiffness at all.

Beth lifted her skirts and raced down the path with her daughters and Evie's sisters, followed by many more Mackenzies. Ian came alongside Jamie and laid a heavy hand on his shoulder.

Jamie halted, and Ian did as well, the others rushing past while Jamie and Ian stood like islands in the stream.

"If you intend to ask who I wagered on, Dad—the ladies, of course," Jamie told Ian when the man said nothing. "Not only because I'm madly in love with one of them. I've watched them train. They're good."

"Jamie." Ian interrupted Jamie's rambling. "I love you, son."

Jamie burned with gladness at the words from his father's lips, the father who rarely spoke of his emotions. Not that Ian never said it—he had, and often, over the years—but Jamie always thrilled at his father's affection.

"I love you too, Dad." Jamie didn't comment on Ian's choice to tell him this in the middle of a scurrying crowd. Ian would see nothing wrong with it, or care if anyone else did. The love was more important than what other people thought of them.

"Evie loves you," Ian went on. "I can see that."

"Well." Jamie shrugged. "She puts up with me. A good thing in a wife."

"It was well done, Jamie. You gave her yourself."

Jamie warmed with the praise. "You told me I ought to give her what she needed. I decided that what she needed was joy. And a big, loving, wonderful family that loves so intensely we drive each other spare. I didn't want to erase her past love but show her she can have something like it again. Deep happiness."

Jamie heard himself babbling again, but Ian's smile broadened.

"You are a wise lad." A pause. "You always have been. My pride."

Jamie felt himself melting under his father's touch, the

small child he had been desperate to win the respect of the man he'd admired, loved, almost worshipped.

Ian at this moment was acknowledging those early efforts, telling Jamie he'd understood and had loved Jamie no matter what he did.

Ian loved, unconditionally. It was his strength, Jamie realized, the one Beth had seen all those years ago, and what she'd revealed to Ian himself.

"Dad." Jamie's throat tightened. "You're going to make me weep."

Ian's grip strengthened, and Jamie saw moisture in his father's eyes. Then Ian flashed his rare grin and removed his touch.

They turned together and walked along the riverbank to catch up with their excited family, perfect understanding between them.

———

"PUT YOUR BACKS INTO IT, LADIES!" EVIE SHOUTED ABOVE the wind and the swish and splash of oars. "Don't drop at the last!"

The hardest point of a race was the end, when they were nearing exhaustion but still had a fair bit to go. All their training, stamina, strength, and skill had to come together to give them the final push.

Evie's heart sped, elation spurring her on. The men's team was neck and neck with them, the captain shouting at his team as Evie did to hers.

"Come on, boys. Don't let ladies in ruffled skirts have us!"

"Make them taste our wake!" Evie yelled.

The ladies shouted their agreement, the team energetic and determined. Evie now saved her breath for rowing. The end was near.

The four of them pulled in exact momentum, their oars

moving as one. Rowers won as a team—if one of them tried for personal glory, they'd destroy the unity and very probably lose the race.

The banks flashed past, packed with a cheering crowd. Evie knew some of the spectators hoped the ladies would best the gents, and others had come to see the gents teach women their place.

Evie simply wanted to row. The scull flew across the water, the speed galvanizing her. The only thing more exhilarating was being with Jamie, the pair of them loving each other in the sunshine of their sleepy cottage.

They'd keep that house, Jamie said, after their marriage, as their retreat from the world, a quiet place all their own. He also promised to build her a larger home near Ian and Beth's in Scotland. Thus, they'd have a home close to each of their families, a touch that made Evie love him all the more.

The finishing post was coming up.

"Now!" Evie screamed.

The team obeyed, the ladies unleashing their secret weapon —the last burst of energy they'd saved for the end. It was how Evie's team had won all those heats at Girton, and how they'd win now.

The men tried to follow suit, but they'd wasted much of their strength making certain the women didn't get ahead of them earlier. Evie and her ladies had contented themselves with simply keeping pace, and now they sprinted.

Their scull pulled ahead. The men shouted at each other, cursing the air blue. Evie and the ladies rowed in silence, putting every ounce of endurance into their last push.

Evie and team shot past the finishing post, their scull an entire length ahead of the men's.

Screaming and yelling erupted on the bank. Evie barked a command, and the eight oars lifted, the ladies breathing hard but letting the scull drift on, the four of them pretending serenity.

Evie scanned the bank as they glided past. Every Mackenzie was there on the shore, shouting for them, the younger ones leaping and dancing as Evie and her ladies took their victory.

Jamie spread his arms, his grin telling Evie he'd had no doubts. His father next to him, silently smiled, his arm around Beth, who clapped excitedly. Belle and Megan held each other's hands and danced in a circle together. Marjorie and Clara joined them, Clara forgetting her poise in her excitement.

Beautiful Aimee blew kisses at them, her sister and brother shouting their glee. Mac, their father, roared his appreciation, Isabella quietly smiling her approval. Cameron shouted some choice disparaging words at the men's team.

Hart stood without speaking, but his proud look told Evie how pleased he was with her. Eleanor, next to him, threw away dignity to stamp her feet and yell, punching the air with her fists. Ainsley, between her and Cameron, did the same.

The rest of the cousins waved, yelled, or danced. Malcolm did a complicated jig, his kilt flying as he kicked up his feet.

The McBride families were there as well, tall Andrew losing his barrister composure to join Malcolm in his dance. The dark-haired Priti, Elliot McBride's daughter, linked arms with Caitriona, Andrew's sister, both cheering hard.

Gavina stood next to, unbelievably, Miss Carmichael, the American heiress, her bewildered parents behind her. Gavina pointed both forefingers at Miss Carmichael and mouthed, *I kidnapped her.*

Jamie was the first to reach the pier where the team landed the scull. The rest of the family followed, but Jamie was there for Evie. He hauled her onto the pier, spinning her in his arms while he kissed and kissed her.

Evie laughed, holding on to her Highlander, her Jamie, the man who'd rescued her.

Behind him others were handing out her teammates, including two robust men pleased and happy with Sarah and

Alice. Alice's small children reached for their mother, declaring how proud they were of her.

Lord Alec reached to help Iris from the scull. As Iris's feet touched the pier, Alec suddenly snaked an arm around her and kissed her hard on the lips.

The kiss didn't last long, and was lost among the tumult of the revelers, but Evie saw it, as did Jamie. Iris stood, stunned, losing her usual merriment as Alec spun from her and strode away.

"Now, that will be something," Jamie murmured to Evie. He kissed her, mouth warm. "Ye did it, lass. I knew you would."

"Quite satisfying." Evie grinned at the gentlemen's team, who were trying to be gracious in conceding the race. "But I admit, exhausting. I think I will not do that again for a long while."

"You'll have plenty of time to rest. We can laze about our house, get it ready for our cozy married life."

"Plenty of time?" Evie stared at him. "What are you talking about, Mackenzie? There's a wedding to plan. Our time won't be our own."

Jamie groaned in agreement, then his wicked smile returned. "I might have to abduct you now and then. Just to make sure you still love me, McKnight."

"Please do." Evie nuzzled his cheek, pressing a tiny kiss to his earlobe. "I'll be counting on you, Mackenzie."

Jamie's next kiss held dark promise, the glint in his eyes when he released her heating her through. He flicked his tongue at her, causing the heat to become incandescent.

Jamie then took her hand and led her onto the bank where her family and his were waiting.

The Mackenzies surrounded Evie and Jamie, absorbing Evie into them and chasing away all gloom with the sunshine of their understanding and love.

AUTHOR'S NOTE

Thank you for reading! The Mackenzie family has expanded quite a bit since I wrote Book 1, *The Madness of Lord Ian Mackenzie*.

As the series progressed, I revisited the main characters in several shorter works: two Christmas stories and *A Mackenzie Clan Gathering*, where I could show glimpses of how the sons and daughters of the Mackenzie brothers were growing up. (See the "Also by" page to find titles and links of these books.)

I debated a long time about writing books on the next generation, but I had so many reader requests, and I so enjoyed getting to know Jamie, his sisters, and cousins in the novellas, that I decided to let their stories be told.

Jamie was a natural place to start, as he is the oldest of the younger generation (Daniel, technically is, but his tale has already been done in *The Wicked Deeds of Daniel Mackenzie*). Next, Belle meets her hero, as does Megan. Sparks have begun between Hart's son Alec and Evie's friend Iris, and between Mal and Miss Carmichael. (I admit I have created a problem for myself in having the Mackenzies name children after ancestors, because I will have to make sure the Edwardian Alec and

Mal are not confused with the 18th-century ones, whose tales have already been told).

I also have special stories in mind for Gavina, Aimee, Priti, Andrew McBride, and many more of the cousins. To keep them all straight, see the Mackenzie Family Tree at the end of this book!

While the series will run into the years of WWI, I have already made the decision not to turn the saga into a tragedy. All of the Mackenzies will make it through just fine. These will always be tales of happily ever after.

I hope you enjoy them! To stay informed of the books as they are released, please join my email newsletter at

http://eepurl.com/47kLL

and check my website:

http://www.jenniferashley.com

All my best,

Jennifer Ashley

ALSO BY JENNIFER ASHLEY

Historical Romances

The Mackenzies Series

(Victorian Era)

The Madness of Lord Ian Mackenzie

Lady Isabella's Scandalous Marriage

The Many Sins of Lord Cameron

The Duke's Perfect Wife

A Mackenzie Family Christmas: The Perfect Gift

The Seduction of Elliot McBride

The Untamed Mackenzie

The Wicked Deeds of Daniel Mackenzie

Scandal and the Duchess

Rules for a Proper Governess

A Mackenzie Clan Gathering

A Rogue Meets a Scandalous Lady

A Mackenzie Yuletide

(in print in A Mackenzie Clan Christmas)

(18th-Century Mackenzies, Jacobite Uprising)

The Stolen Mackenzie Bride

Alec Mackenzie's Art of Seduction

The Devilish Lord Will

Fiona and the Three Wise Highlanders

Mackenzies II (Edwardian Era)

The Sinful Ways of Jamie Mackenzie

Regency Bon Bons

(short, sweet Regencies)

A First-Footer for Lady Jane

Duke in Search of a Duchess

A Kiss for Luck

Historical Mysteries

Kat Holloway "Below Stairs" Victorian Mysteries

(writing as Jennifer Ashley)

A Soupçon of Poison

Death Below Stairs

Scandal Above Stairs

Death in Kew Gardens

Murder in the East End

Death at the Crystal Palace

The Secret of Bow Lane

Leonidas the Gladiator Mysteries

(writing as Ashley Gardner)

Blood of a Gladiator

Blood Debts

A Gladiator's Tale

The Ring that Caesar Wore

MACKENZIE FAMILY TREE

Ferdinand Daniel Mackenzie (Old Dan) 1330-1395
First Duke of Kilmorgan
= m. Lady Margaret Duncannon
|
Fourteen generations
|
Daniel William Mackenzie 1685-1746(?)
(9th Duke of Kilmorgan)
= m. Allison MacNab
|
6 sons
Daniel Duncannon Mackenzie (Duncan) (1710-1746)

William Ferdinand Mackenzie (1714-1746?)
=m. **Josette Oswald**
|
Glenna Oswald (stepdaughter)
Duncan Ian Mackenzie (1748-1836)
Abby Anne Mackenzie (1750-1838)
(Ancestors of Magdala Mackenzie)

Magnus Ian Mackenzie (1715-1734)
Angus William Mackenzie (1716-1746)

Alec William Ian Mackenzie (1716-1746?)
=m. Genevieve Millar (d. 1746)
|
Jenny (Genevieve Allison Mary) Mackenzie (1746-1837)

=m2. **Lady Celia Fotheringhay**
|
Magnus Edward Mackenzie (1747-1835)
Catherine Mary Mackenzie (1750-1836)

Malcolm Daniel Mackenzie (1720-1802)
(10th Duke of Kilmorgan from 1746)

= m. **Lady Mary Lennox**
|
Angus Roland Mackenzie 1747-1822
(11th Duke of Kilmorgan)
= m. Donnag Fleming
(ancestor of **David Fleming**)
|
William Ian Mackenzie (The Rake) 1780-1850
(12th Duke of Kilmorgan)
= m. Lady Elizabeth Ross
|
Daniel Mackenzie, 13th Duke of Kilmorgan (1824-1874)
(1st Duke of Kilmorgan, English from 1855)
= m. Elspeth Cameron (d. 1864)
|

Hart Mackenzie (b. 1844)
14th Duke of Kilmorgan from 1874
(2nd Duke of Kilmorgan, English)

= m1. Lady Sarah Graham (d. 1876)

|

(Hart Graham Mackenzie, d. 1876)

= m2. **Lady Eleanor Ramsay**

|

Hart Alec Graham Mackenzie (b. 1885)
Malcolm Ian Mackenzie (b. 1887)

Cameron Mackenzie
= m1. Lady Elizabeth Cavendish (d. 1866)

|

Daniel Mackenzie = m. **Violet Devereaux**

|

Fluer Mackenzie (b. 1891)
Dougal Mackenzie (b. 1899)

Cameron Mackenzie = m2. **Ainsley Douglas**

|

Gavina Mackenzie (b. 1883)
Stuart Mackenzie (b. 1885)

"Mac" (Roland Ferdinand) Mackenzie
= m. **Lady Isabella Scranton**

|

Aimee Mackenzie (b. 1879, adopted 1881)
Eileen Mackenzie (b. 1882)
Robert Mackenzie (b. 1883)

Ian Mackenzie = m. **Beth Ackerley**

|

Jamie Mackenzie (b. 1882)
Isabella Elizabeth Mackenzie (Belle) (b. 1883)
Megan Mackenzie (b. 1885)

Lloyd Fellows = m. **Lady Louisa Scranton**
|
Elizabeth Fellows (b. 1886)
William Fellows (b. 1888)
Matthew Fellows (b. 1889)

David Fleming = m. **Sophie Tierney**
|
Lucas Fleming (b. 1894)

McBride Family

Patrick McBride = m. Rona McDougal

Sinclair McBride = m.1 Margaret Davies (d. 1878)
|
Caitriona (b. 1875)
Andrew (b. 1877)

m.2 **Roberta "Bertie" Frasier**
|
Marcus (b. 1886)
Elena (b. 1888)

Elliot McBride = m. **Juliana St. John**
|
Priti McBride (b. 1881)
Gemma (b. 1885)
Patrick (b. 1886)

Ainsley McBride = m.1 John Douglas (d. 1879)
|
Gavina Douglas (d.)

= m.2 **Lord Cameron Mackenzie**

|

Gavina Mackenzie (b. 1883)
Stuart Mackenzie (b. 1885)

Steven McBride (Captain, Army)
= m. **Rose Barclay**
(Dowager Duchess of Southdown)
|
Helen Rona (b. 1887)

Note: Names in **bold** indicate main characters in the
Mackenzie series

ABOUT THE AUTHOR

New York Times bestselling and award-winning author Jennifer Ashley has more than 100 published novels and novellas in mystery, romance, historical fiction, and urban fantasy under the names Jennifer Ashley, Allyson James, and Ashley Gardner. Jennifer's books have been translated into more than a dozen languages and have earned starred reviews in *Publisher's Weekly* and *Booklist*. When she isn't writing, Jennifer enjoys playing music (guitar, piano, flute), reading, hiking, cooking, and building dollhouse miniatures.

More about Jennifer's books can be found at
http://www.jenniferashley.com

To keep up to date on her new releases, join her newsletter here:

http://eepurl.com/47kLL

Made in United States
North Haven, CT
22 November 2021

11387651R00195